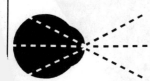

This Large Print Book carries the
Seal of Approval of N.A.V.H.

THINGS HALF IN SHADOW

THINGS HALF IN SHADOW

ALAN FINN

THORNDIKE PRESS

A part of Gale, Cengage Learning

GALE
CENGAGE Learning·

Farmington Hills, Mich • San Francisco • New York • Waterville, Maine
Meriden, Conn • Mason, Ohio • Chicago

GALE
CENGAGE Learning®

Thorndike Press® Large Print Crime Scene.
The text of this Large Print edition is unabridged.
Other aspects of the book may vary from the original edition.
Set in 16 pt. Plantin.

LIBRARY OF CONGRESS CATALOGING-IN-PUBLICATION DATA

Finn, Alan.
  Things half in shadow / by Alan Finn. — Large print edition.
    pages cm. — (Thorndike Press large print crime scene)
    ISBN 978-1-4104-7898-6 (hardcover) — ISBN 1-4104-7898-X (hardcover)
    1. Magicians—Fiction. 2. Murder—Investigation—Fiction. 3. Large type books. I. Title.
  PS3606.I555T55 2015b
  813'.6—dc23   2015004819

Published in 2015 by arrangement with Gallery Books, a division of Simon & Schuster, Inc.

Printed in Mexico
1 2 3 4 5 6 7 19 18 17 16 15

In loving memory of Shane Edwards and Ruth Trapane. I am deeply proud to have called you family.

FOREWORD

When people mention Lenora Grimes Pastor, if they still speak of her at all, many insist that she was killed by a ghost. While a sensational claim, it makes a certain amount of sense. Philadelphia, as it would happen, is filled with spirits. All of that history colliding with the new and the now. Wherever the past piles up, layer after dusty layer, ghosts are sure to linger.

Ah, but already I'm getting ahead of myself. I assumed that was going to happen. I just didn't expect it to be in the second paragraph of this folly I'm about to undertake. So, lest I make more of a fool of myself than I already have, I will start with the basics.

The first bit of information you should know is that my name is generally acknowledged to be Edward Clark. The second is that I was born in Philadelphia, Pennsylvania, and reside here still. The third is that this chronicle, or memoir, or whatever you care to call it is being written at the behest of my granddaughter, Isabel, who currently sits across from me, nose buried in a volume of ghost stories. She's a macabre one, that girl, and when I told her I also knew a ghost story or two, she demanded that I write them down. I offered to simply tell her these strange-but-true tales, but she wanted none of that. She said I needed to preserve them for posterity's sake. So that is what I'm doing.

The former reporter in me wants to simply be straightforward with the whole thing. Who, what, where, when, and, that odd man out, how. It would certainly save me a lot of writing and to whoever may see this a lot of reading. But there's no fun in that, is there? No detail or nuance. Certainly no suspense. So I will try my best to provide all of those things and more. After all, everyone enjoys a juicy tale.

As for those good yarns I promised Isabel, I happen to have several. My life, humble as it may be, has been filled with experiences of a most unusual kind. This particular tale, as I mentioned earlier, concerns Lenora Grimes Pastor and the ghost that people claim to have killed her. I suppose it's easy to see how such a theory persists. As the years pass — fifty, in this instance — rumor solidifies into fact, which is all too often mistaken for truth.

Now, at the risk of disappointing those who believe the stories of Mrs. Pastor's demise, I must state that, no, she was not actually killed by a ghost. Or a spirit. Or a ghoulish creature that dragged her screaming into the under-world. I can say with authority that no such outlandishness occurred.

I know this because I was there when she died. I was, in fact, the last person she spoke to, although there is some debate over whether she was actually the one doing the speaking. Remember, I said that no spirits killed her, not that there weren't any present.

In truth, the moment of Mrs. Pastor's death was so unremarkable compared with every-thing else going on that it took those of us at the scene several minutes to realize she had even passed on at all.

The real remarkable moments, the ones no one mentions because they were never known to begin with, happened just before Mrs. Pastor's death and in the days that followed. Although five decades have passed and the ratio of events I have forgotten compared with the ones I have not continues to tip ever closer toward senility, I remember everything about that time. I recall those days so vividly that, if I close my eyes, I can see them unfold-ing before me, much like those moving pictures they now show over on Eighth Street.

But there's more to this story than the supernatural. So, before I talk about Mrs. Pastor, I must mention everything else going on in my life at the time, because it's all connected. All those strange encounters. The loves lost and found. The laughter and the tragedy and the quiet moments in between.

And ghosts, of course.

I must talk at length about ghosts. For while they didn't kill Mrs. Pastor, without them I never would have been able to learn the truth about who really did.

Edward Clark
Winter, 1919

■ ■ ■ ■

Book One:
In Which I Make
the Acquaintance
of the Remorseless
Charlatan Known
as Lucy Collins

■ ■ ■ ■

I

For lack of a better starting point, I shall begin this particular tale on a foggy morning in April of 1869. The mist rose off the water in thick, brownish puffs that reminded me of cannon smoke. It moved in the same skittish manner — an ever-shifting curtain of haze that offered fleeting glimpses of Petty's Island as the fog approached the dock. I felt a familiar, unwelcome shudder of dread when the fog crashed over us. Tucked in its rolling tendrils was a heady stew of familiar odors. Damp earth. Dirty water. Decay.

With the fog in my eyes and its smell in my nostrils, I couldn't help but think of Antietam. So much was the same. The early morning chill. The silhouettes of men shimmering within the mist. The stench, getting stronger. As another wall of haze moved in, I cast my eyes to the ground, expecting to see it strewn with the shredded corpses of my fallen brothers.

But I was not at Antietam. I was right here

in Philadelphia. On the waterfront of the Delaware River, to be precise, the city sprawling westward behind me. The smell that rode with the fog was merely the remains of yesterday's catch, sitting a few yards away in a rotting pile of fish guts and lopped heads. The ground, instead of bearing dozens of broken bodies, contained only one. A woman. Fully intact, but dead nonetheless.

Dressed in a gray shift that clung to her body, she looked more girl than woman. Her blond hair, darkened by the water from which she had been pulled, spread across the dock like dredged-up kelp. Sand, pebbles, and streaks of mud stuck to her pale flesh. With her eyes closed and body still, she looked at peace, although I was certain she hadn't died that way.

It was not, incidentally, the first corpse I had seen that week. I'd seen two the day before — an unlucky pair that had been stabbed in an alleyway on the city's southern tip. Sailors, caught on the wrong end of a drunkard's Bowie knife. After witnessing a sight such as that, a dead girl wasn't so shocking.

Not that I was easily shocked to begin with. In my line of work, death came with the territory. As a reporter for the *Philadelphia Evening Bulletin,* I was called on to write about a wide assortment of subjects, but the one I covered the most was crime. Murders, mainly. And for a place nicknamed the City of Brotherly Love, there were an alarming number of them.

But the girl on the ground, it seemed, wasn't a murder victim. At least that's what Inspector William Barclay, standing on the other side of her body, thought.

"She drowned," he told me. "The crew of the Cooper's Point ferry spotted her floating in the river."

The ferry was docked at Pier 49, ready to make the morning's first crossing to Camden. Just beyond it, an impatient crowd grew along the end of Shackamaxon Street, waiting to board, with those in the front trying to peer past the line of policemen blocking their way. The rest of the waterfront rattled with activity, even at that early hour. The lumber mills and steelworks to the south were clanging and buzzing beasts. To the north of us, Kentucky boats filled with coal pushed out onto the river. But on the edge of the pier, it was just me, Barclay, and the dead girl.

"So there's nothing suspicious about her death?" I asked.

Barclay shook his head. "Not particularly. Of course, that's ultimately for the coroner to decide."

"I assume he'll rule it an accidental drowning," I said. "But what do *you* think?"

Barclay, who had seen even more death than myself, tried to avoid looking at the

15

corpse again. Instead, he stared at the pile of fish scraps nearby. A fair number of birds — gulls, mostly, but also a handful of crows — circled it, swooping down at regular intervals to scoop up pieces of the stinking bounty. Barclay watched two gulls battle for a bit of tail before saying, "If she was found in the water, then logic dictates that she also died there. So, to answer your question, yes. I believe that this poor girl drowned in the river."

He looked to me, hoping his answer was satisfactory. He could tell from my expression that it was not.

"You don't agree?"

"Not precisely," I said, pausing to let Barclay issue the sigh that I knew was coming. When you spend lengthy periods of time with someone, as I had with William Barclay, you quickly learn their particular habits. For Barclay, that included shifting his weight to his left leg and putting his hands on his hips when he was impatient or sighing when he was annoyed. Since his hands had already fixed themselves on his hips as soon as I arrived, I knew what was next.

"I know your readers are a bloodthirsty lot," Barclay said, "but try not to turn what's simply a tragic accident into sensationalistic fodder for your newspaper."

I intended to do no such thing, although I couldn't hold the accusation against Barclay.

16

The *Bulletin*'s readers were rather ghoulish. No crime was too foul, bloody, or unthinkable for them. There was a reason the motto among the city's crime reporters was "The morbider, the merrier."

"I'm not wishing that this girl had been brutally butchered," I said. "All I'm asking is that you not be so quick to conclude what killed her."

Because Philadelphia is flanked by two rivers, I had seen a fair number of drowning deaths. The lack of oxygen colors the faces of most victims a pale purple. Their bodies are often bloated. Quite a few of them have pieces of flesh missing from the hungry fish that found them before any human got the chance.

The pitiful creature at my feet possessed none of these telltale signs. Granted, she could have thrown herself into the chilly Delaware only minutes before she had been found, yet it looked to me that something else was at work. If it wasn't for the soaked clothing and the dirt on her skin, someone waiting for the ferry couldn't have been blamed for thinking she was still alive and merely napping on the bleached wood of the pier.

"She looks at peace," I said. "As if she had passed in her sleep."

Barclay sighed again. "So you're a trained coroner now, I see."

"I'm simply saying that she doesn't look like a drowning victim. Surely, you can see that."

"All I see," Barclay said, "is that it was a bad idea to grant you access to the police department that your competitors in the press do without. I'm sure the gentlemen at the *Times* or the *Public Ledger* wouldn't ask me to second-guess myself."

"They also didn't save your life on the battlefield," I replied. "Or have you forgotten about that?"

"How could I when you're always around to remind me? Now, do you have any more questions or can I proceed without further interruption?"

I had no doubt that Barclay was speaking in jest. He and I had been friends for close to seven years now, having met as members of the Union Army. While it was true that, during a surprise skirmish in a Virginia forest, I threw him to the ground before a minié ball to the skull could do the honors, I think he rather enjoyed having me around. Whenever a ghastly crime occurred, Barclay sent a policeman to my house to whisk me to the scene. That's exactly what had happened earlier that morning. Much earlier than I would have preferred or was prepared for. The bell at the front door clanging at five o'clock had not only jerked me from a deep sleep, but sent Lionel, my butler, practically tumbling down the stairs to answer it.

But now, forty-five minutes later, I was starting to wonder why Barclay had felt it necessary to disturb my slumber and almost cause physical harm to a member of my household staff.

"If this is a simple case of drowning," I said, "then why am I here? Why are you, for that matter? Certainly a few policemen could handle this. It doesn't seem important enough to take an inspector away from his home so early in the morning."

"It's about the girl's identity, Edward."

"Do you know who she is?"

Barclay turned to face the river, where another wave of fog was threatening to crash upon the shore. "We do not. That's the reason I summoned you."

"Ah. You want my bloodthirsty readers to try to identify her."

"Exactly. No matter how she died — and I fully believe it was accidental drowning, by the way — we've found nothing to indicate who she is or where she came from. From what I can tell, she looks like she was relatively healthy."

What he meant was that the girl didn't resemble those desperate or ill women who sometimes threw themselves into the drink, their pockets stuffed with bricks. Nor did she look like one of the prostitutes who prowled the waterfront. Occasionally, those same

19

wretched women would be found floating down the river, done in by either their employers or one of their customers.

"You think she has family somewhere in the city?" I asked.

"I do."

"Has no one reported a girl of her description missing?"

Barclay shook his head. "Not yet, anyway. But a vivid description of her in today's *Evening Bulletin* might help us find out who this poor thing is."

The fog bank he had been watching rolled onto shore and enveloped the pier. A policeman burst out of it, leaving tendrils of haze in his wake as he ran toward us.

"Inspector," he called, "someone is demanding to be allowed onto the pier."

"Tell them to wait for the ferry like everyone else," Barclay snapped.

"They don't want the ferry, sir. They want to see the girl. They think they know her."

We both turned to the crowd at the cusp of the pier, which materialized into view as the fog bank drifted farther inland. At the front were two women, one young and the other much older. Their arms were linked as they tried to bypass the wall of policemen. The younger one spotted me and Barclay standing next to the dead girl. The wail of grief that followed told us both that she did indeed know the victim.

"Well then, Barclay," I said quietly, "it appears you don't need the help of the *Bulletin* readers after all."

Barclay took a few steps toward the street and ordered his men to let them pass. As the women, arms now linked more tightly, continued onward in halting steps, I got a better look at them. The younger one appeared to be thirteen or so, although her face was so contorted by anguish that it was difficult to tell. The older woman appeared to be approaching forty. Unlike the girl, her features were as blank and unreadable as a recently erased blackboard.

When they reached us, the girl fell to her knees, keening and crying next to the corpse. The other woman — her mother, very likely, for the resemblance was undeniable — remained standing. She kept hold of her daughter's hand while staring not at the body but at the river from where it had come.

She said something to the girl in German, words too quick and rough for me to comprehend. Her daughter eventually stood and, still weeping, wrapped her arms around her mother's waist. Barclay gave her a moment to compose herself before saying, "I take it that you know this girl?"

The girl looked first to her mother, who nodded faintly, then to Barclay. When she spoke, every word was punctuated with grief.

"Yes, sir. She is my sister, Sophie."

Barclay gave me a brief, knowing look. This turn of events wasn't a surprise to either of us.

"I'm sorry for your loss," he said.

The woman nudged the girl. A brief exchange in German followed, their conversation both hurried and hushed.

"My mother thanks you for your condolences," the girl eventually told Barclay.

"I'm going to need to ask a few questions," he replied. "Giving me your names would be a good start."

"I am Louisa Kruger." The girl gestured to the other woman. "This is my mother, Margarethe."

I stepped away from them, listening at a discreet distance while Barclay and Margarethe Kruger conversed, using young Louisa as an interpreter. During this complex back-and-forth, I learned that the family lived in Fishtown, just a few blocks from the waterfront. Sophie had last been seen at nine o'clock the previous night, when she climbed into the bed she shared with her sister. Sometime during the night, Louisa awoke to find her sister gone. When she hadn't returned by dawn, Margarethe knew something was wrong, and they went looking for her.

"And you don't know when or why she left?" Barclay asked Louisa.

"No, sir. When I fell asleep, she was there. When I awoke, she wasn't."

"Does your mother have any idea?"

"She doesn't, sir."

"Did your sister disappear like this often?"

I watched Mrs. Kruger's face as Louisa repeated the question in German. The woman's stoic expression didn't change, even as she shook her head. Her daughter, however, revealed her emotions freely, making it clear she didn't agree with her mother.

"Wir mussen ihm sagen," she said.

Margarethe Kruger shook her head again. *"Nein."*

Barclay moved his gaze back and forth between them. "Is there something wrong?"

"My mother does not want me to tell you that Sophie often left our home during the night," Louisa said, eyeing her mother with caution. "I am grateful she does not understand English, so I can tell you without her disapproval."

"Why did your sister leave so frequently?"

"I do not know, sir. I was usually asleep when it happened. But sometimes I heard people at the door, whispering if Sophie was awake. Sometimes she wouldn't be, and my mother would wake her and send her off with the people who had called."

"You never asked why?"

"I did once," Louisa said. "But Mother slapped me and said, *'Die neugier ist ein gift.'* "

"What does that mean?"

Louisa lowered her eyes. "Curiosity is a

23

poison."

Barclay stroked his chin before tugging slightly on the ends of his mustache. It was another one of his gestures that I knew well, indicating he was confused by something and trying to make sense of it all. I often said it made him look like a villain in a penny dreadful.

"How long have you been looking for your sister today?" he asked.

"An hour, sir."

I glanced at my pocket watch, seeing that Louisa and her mother had been walking the streets since well before five o'clock. They must have searched every square inch of Fishtown before reaching the waterfront and seeing the crowd gathered there.

"When Sophie left during the night, was it uncommon for her to return after sunrise?" asked Barclay.

"Sometimes," Louisa said, "she would arrive as late as seven or eight."

"If that's the case, why did you and your mother go looking for her so early?"

The girl turned to her mother again and presented the question. This time, a flicker of emotion passed over Mrs. Kruger's face, as quick and unwieldy as the tufts of fog sliding off the river. But it was enough for me to tell she was feeling an enormous amount of pain. The hurt filled her voice as she uttered her response in German.

"My mother says we needed to go looking for Sophie because she knew she wasn't going to return," Louisa said on her behalf.

"She suspected your sister had run away?"

Louisa shook her head. "No, sir. My mother says she knew my sister was already dead."

Barclay's eyes widened. I suspect mine did the same. For a moment, I thought a mistake was made and that something had been lost in translation. Then Barclay said, "How could she possibly know that?"

"Because," Louisa said, "Sophie told her so."

II

The *Philadelphia Evening Bulletin* was headquartered in a rather dim and drafty building on Chestnut Street. Four floors high, it sat in the middle of the block like a weathered mausoleum. Surely that's what the building's architects intended, because the interior had a distinctly cryptlike feel. Its interior was gray and lifeless, with walls stained by the smoke of gaslights and rooms that echoed every footstep, cough, and chuckle. It was, I must truthfully report, a depressing place of business.

The room in which the reporters toiled took up an entire floor. Most of the space was filled with paper-strewn desks arranged in a rigid grid that provided little room to walk between them. The arrangement made the office feel like a sweatshop for which the main product was words.

Directly below us was the printing press, a massive contraption that, when at full steam, rumbled with enough ferocity to shake the floor we trod upon. The smell of grease and ink wafted upward through cracks in the floorboards, often making those of us in its path dizzy. Faintings were so common that I kept a small vial of smelling salts in the top drawer of my desk.

The telegraph station occupied the floor above us, where news from across the nation arrived with an incessant *tick, tick, tick*ing that could drive a man mad if he let it. Above that, on the top floor, was space reserved for editors and other important decision makers. They each got their own office, with access to windows — a subject of much envy. Here, sunlight was a luxury.

That morning, though, I was one of the lucky few able to bask in the sun's rays. It was five hours after my experience on Pier 49 and my editor, Mr. Hamilton Gray, was perusing my account of those events. The fog, which dissipated not long after I left the waterfront, had been replaced by a sun as yellow and pleasing as a daffodil. As Mr. Gray read over my work, I leaned back in the chair in front of his desk, stretching slightly so that the sunlight could warm my face.

"I don't understand, Clark," Mr. Gray suddenly said, frowning.

In keeping with his name, Hamilton Gray was the most colorless man I've ever met. His faded clothes, his uninflected voice, even his personality all rendered him about as exciting as a patch of mud on a scorching day. His skin retained an ashen shade, making it difficult to pinpoint his age. Some said he was only forty. My own guess was that he was a few years shy of seventy.

"What's so difficult to understand?" I asked.

"You expect me to believe that this drowned girl *informed* her mother of her death?"

"So the mother says," I replied. "According to her, it happened at quarter to five this morning."

"But that's not even possible. The girl — this Sophie Kruger — was most likely floating in the water at that hour."

It was preposterous, there's no denying it. Yet Margarethe Kruger seemed convinced of it as she told the story to her daughter, who in turn told Barclay and myself what had occurred. Mrs. Kruger insisted that she had been awakened before daybreak by the sound of someone in the bedroom she shared with her two daughters. When she opened her eyes, she saw Sophie standing in the center of the room, wearing the same gray dress in which she had drowned. Her daughter stayed motionless a moment before opening her mouth to speak.

"She said, *'Mutter, ich bin verloren,'* " I told Mr. Gray. "It means, 'Mother, I am lost.' "

After that, according to her mother, Sophie Kruger's words ended, although her mouth remained open. That's when a single bee crawled from between her lips and flew into the room.

"A bee?" asked Mr. Gray, positively flummoxed by that part of my article.

"Yes. A honeybee. Margarethe Kruger swore by it. Then she said that when she blinked, her daughter was gone."

According to Louisa Kruger, the family lived in a narrow, two-story home deep in the heart of Fishtown. The downstairs contained a kitchen and not much else. The entirety of the upstairs was the bedroom. There were no footfalls following Sophie out of the room, no creaking of the stairs. Louisa said she and her mother thoroughly searched both floors moments later, finding no indication that Sophie had been there. The front door was still locked, as were the windows.

"But how in heaven's name is all of this possible?" Mr. Gray asked. "How was this Sophie girl able to quickly enter and exit the house if she was dead in the water at that time?"

I provided him with the same answer that had been given to me. "Margarethe Kruger claims it was Sophie's ghost."

At last, Mr. Gray showed an emotion other than abject confusion. Lifting his brow in surprise, he said, "Her *ghost*?"

"Or her spirit. Or some unexplained manifestation. All I know is that Mrs. Kruger claims to have seen her daughter in that room. She heard her daughter speak. Then she was gone in an instant. Even more odd is what allegedly occurred after that. After searching both upstairs and down, Margarethe and Louisa returned to the bedroom. In the middle of the floor — right where Mrs. Kruger claimed to have seen poor, doomed Sophie — was a honeybee."

"Come now, Clark, you don't believe any of this, do you?"

The rectangle of sunlight coming through the window had shifted slightly, forcing me to tilt farther in my chair. I stretched to meet it while saying, "Of course not. Ghosts don't exist. It may have been a figment of her imagination, perhaps. Or maybe a mother's intuition that something was wrong. But as for spirits or omens or whatnot, that's just pure rubbish."

"I quite agree," Mr. Gray said. "And as your editor, I insist we leave all of that out of this article. We'll present the facts, Clark. A girl drowned and was found by some fishermen. It's news, not fiction. There's no need for you to try to be Edgar Allan Poe."

He set the article on his desk, removed his wire-framed spectacles, and wiped them with a silk handkerchief plucked from his jacket pocket. He was pondering something, which caused me no small amount of unease. As a reporter, I didn't like it when my editor thought too much.

"However, I do think it's serendipitous that this whole odd incident has come about," he said, resting the spectacles once again on the bridge of his nose. "I was speaking to Mr. Peacock the other afternoon."

Mr. Gray was referring to Gibson Peacock, the *Bulletin*'s owner and publisher, a position that made him feared and revered in equal measure.

"He was telling me about an unfortunate experience he and his wife had to endure a fortnight ago," Mr. Gray continued. "As you well know, they lost their youngest son at Gettysburg and haven't been quite the same since. They sought out the services of a medium to try to contact him from the Great Beyond."

That was, sadly, not an uncommon occurrence. The war had taken a devastating toll on both sides of the conflict, and it was difficult to find a family that wasn't somehow affected. Such widespread loss left a collective wound that was still being felt four years later. Many had turned to religion to soothe their pain. Others, such as the Peacocks, went

30

down the path of Spiritualism, which was becoming ever more popular in the city.

"Say no more," I replied. "The medium was a charlatan."

"Unfortunately, she was."

The revelation didn't surprise me in the least. Mediums of dubious morals had been roaming from town to town for years, no better than a band of gypsies. They brought with them all sorts of illusions that the gullible and the grieving took to be real. Spirit cabinets and apparitions and mesmerized tables floating in midair. None of it, I was certain, amounted to anything more than parlor tricks.

"I assume that during the séance, she claimed to have contacted their son," I said. "But it soon became apparent that she was merely an impostor."

Mr. Gray confirmed my suspicions with a nod. "The entire ordeal left Mrs. Peacock heartbroken and Mr. Peacock considering contacting the authorities. He refrained only because he didn't want his good name to be smeared in the pages of our rival newspapers. Instead, he advised this horrible woman that it would be in her best interest to leave the city immediately, which she did."

"It's a sad story indeed," I said, not quite knowing how else to respond. "But what does this have to do with me?"

"Mr. Peacock understands that what happened to him and his wife is now a common occurrence. He also knows that this city is teeming with these dubious mediums. So, as a service to our readers, he is determined to rid Philadelphia of this greedy scourge once and for all."

"How does he plan to do this?"

"By using the pages of the *Evening Bulletin* to expose them for the fraudulent creatures they are," Mr. Gray said triumphantly.

It was the most animated I had ever seen him, and it made me suspicious that Mr. Peacock was somehow in the next room, eavesdropping on our conversation. I stood, loath to move from the sunlight but eager to leave before he said anything more.

"That will make an interesting assignment for whoever is fortunate enough to receive it."

"That lucky reporter," Mr. Gray said before I could make my escape, "is you, Clark."

I returned to the chair, suddenly weary. I knew I was about to be pulled into something I did not want to be a part of. In fact, I felt the cold and clammy hands of this plan wrapping around me, and not even the direct beam of the sun could chase away its chilly fingers.

"I'm flattered, sir," I managed to say, when in truth I felt no such emotion. "But I write about crime."

"Which makes you the ideal man for the

job. These are, after all, crimes of one sort or another. False advertising. Deception. Preying on innocent victims in the pursuit of wealth."

Even though he was right, I found myself protesting nonetheless. I was by nature an independent man. I did not like being told what to do, especially when those orders involved stating the obvious to anyone with a lick of common sense.

"Just how do you propose I do this?" I inquired. "Write an article for the front page saying, 'Mediums, please leave the city'? I'll be the laughingstock of Philadelphia."

I could already picture the looks, jabs, and crude asides from my fellow reporters. Lord only knew what my fiancée and her family would think.

"You'll do no such thing," Mr. Gray said. "What Mr. Peacock suggested, and what I wholeheartedly endorsed, is that this endeavor be undertaken with the utmost secrecy."

I sank deeper into my chair as Mr. Gray prattled on about this covert mission of retribution. The plan, if I understood it correctly, was for me to visit each of the city's mediums — or at least those with the most prominence — and take part in their séances. For these visits, I was to concoct a new identity. A fabricated name, along with a fictional loved one I was trying to reach.

Perhaps even a tearful story about how my beloved wife or son was snatched from this earth far too soon. During each séance, I was to closely observe the goings-on in the room, being mindful of signs of trickery or deceit. Each week, my latest exploit would be published in the Sunday edition of the *Bulletin,* much to the delight of readers and to the embarrassment of myself.

"That won't work for very long," I said, still trying to wriggle my way out of the assignment. "After one or two such articles, every medium in the city will be on the lookout for me. Many, especially the most experienced ones, likely won't let me get near one of their séances."

"Even the exposure of a few will do the city a world of good," Mr. Gray said. "I'm certain you'll have the gratitude of Mr. Peacock. This could be the beginning of a new and illustrious career for you."

I wanted to tell him that I rather preferred my current career. As for fame and fortune, I didn't want or need them. Thanks to my father, I already had enough money — and infamy — to last me a lifetime. Instead, I said, "It still confuses me why you think I'm the right man for this particular assignment. Certainly there's someone else here who would be more eager to take on the responsibility. Mr. Portlock, perhaps. He's just as good as I am."

34

Mr. Gray could not be swayed. "But you're perfect for this medium hokum. You have the exact rational — and, dare I say, doubting — attitude we're looking for. These types of criminals are known to engage in chicanery and simple illusions that many assume to be real. I know of no better person to reveal these tricks than you, Clark. I'm certain you'll be able to see through every single deception, especially considering how adept you are at illusions."

These "illusions" that Mr. Gray was referring to didn't deserve such a description. I occasionally performed them on days when the news was slow or during holiday parties. Things like pulling coins from someone's ear or making a handkerchief disappear in my balled-up hands. They were the simplest tricks — something anyone could learn during the course of an afternoon. Yet they never failed to impress people. And when they invariably asked how I acquired such skill, I was at a loss about what to tell them. Certainly not the truth.

"That hardly qualifies me to be a spy for the newspaper."

"Not a spy," Mr. Gray said. "Think of it as being an investigator. Honestly, Clark, I thought you'd jump at the chance to do this. Considering the subjects you write about, I assumed you had a sense of adventure."

"There's not an adventurous bone in my

body." I glanced at my pocket watch. It was nearing noon, and I didn't wish to be late for my lunch date with Violet and her family. "Now, will that be all?"

He removed his spectacles and, once again, began to wipe them in a rough, circular motion. "I know I can't force you to take on this assignment, Clark. If you pass it up, a good dozen other men will gladly do it. I only ask that you consider it."

"I'll do so. Good day, sir."

"And a good day to you, Clark. I look forward to hearing your response."

I considered the assignment only for as long as it took me to leave his office. By the time I reached the first floor, I had already made up my mind to have no part in Mr. Peacock's or Mr. Gray's machinations. Although I agreed that Philadelphia possessed far too many mediums of dubious ability, I was not the man who could stop them. Quite frankly, no man could.

My mood brightened somewhat as I departed the *Bulletin* building. Outside, the sky was a shade of blue I hadn't seen since September. It was rich and shimmering, like a crystalline pool that, if you dove into it, you might never want to resurface. The leaves were beginning to sprout on the trees — ripe, green buds ready to unfurl in the sunlight.

All around me, the streets and sidewalks were quickly filling as lunchtime approached.

Buggies, coaches, and wagonettes rumbled down the street, accompanied by the steady hoofbeats of the horses pulling them forward. On the sidewalks, women strolled in giggling, gossiping pairs or arm in arm with gentlemen. The springtime fashions had reached the city, in colors that rivaled the blooms in Franklin Park. Dresses of pink and lavender and cerulean blue were paraded down the boulevard. Many were elaborate concoctions, the skirts bustled in the back and festooned with bows, silk ribbons, and fabric that rippled downward in tiers. A majority of the men were equally well dressed, walking proudly in frock coats, vests, white shirts, and thin silk ties knotted tightly against the throat. I saw dozens of top hats like my own, although there were quite a few men out and about in bowlers. The younger fellows in the crowd, seeking to differentiate themselves from their elders, wore sack suits, which required no tailor. I owned no such garment myself, but Violet told me it was only a matter of time before every man in town would be wearing one.

Lining the sidewalk was a veritable army of food vendors selling their wares out of wooden crates, wheelbarrows, and small wagons decked out with flags, banners, and ribbons. They shouted what was on offer, their voices combining to form an aural menu that echoed up and down the street.

"Shad for sale! Fresh shad! Plucked straight from the Delaware!"

"Pepperpot! All hot! All hot!"

"Oysters on ice for an agreeable price! Oysteeeeeeeeeeerrrrrrrrs."

At the corner of Chestnut and Eighth Street, I saw a boy — ten, if a day — waving leaflets at passersby. A good deal of those on the sidewalk shuffled away just beyond his reach. I was not as fortunate. When I attempted to pass, the boy shoved the handout against my stomach, refusing to move until I accepted it.

I gave it a cursory glance, seeing a well-rendered illustration of a young woman in a white dress. She was exceedingly attractive, with alabaster skin and delicate features framed by a curtain of hair twisted into ringlets. Her head was tilted slightly to offer a better view of her swanlike neck. Although the intent of her pose was to convey seriousness, I noticed details that suggested otherwise. Her rosebud lips seemed ready to break into a knowing smile, and her eyes glistened with amusement.

Some text placed above the image told me the woman's identity. "Mrs. Lucy Collins," it read, "preferred medium of presidents and kings." Below the illustration was a list of services Mrs. Collins apparently offered. "Séances! Spirit rappings! Private sittings!"

My pleasant mood soured in an instant.

Clearly she was an impostor, just the type of person Mr. Gray and Mr. Peacock wanted me to expose. It seemed I couldn't escape talk of mediums no matter where I went.

"Trying to contact a loved one now in the hereafter?" the boy asked. "Mrs. Collins can do it. Satisfaction guaranteed. She's the preferred medium of presidents and kings."

"So I've read," I replied. "But tell me, boy, if this Mrs. Collins is so world renowned, why does she need someone like you hawking her services on a street corner like a snake-oil salesman?"

While the boy, clad in brown trousers and a surprisingly clean white shirt, was better dressed than most street urchins, he nonetheless behaved like one. Sweeping a lock of brown hair away from his eyes, he stared up at me, nostrils flaring.

"You, sir, are a skeptic," he announced in the booming voice of a carnival barker.

I shook my head. "No. I'm a realist."

"Mrs. Collins warned me about folks like you. She says you'll need more convincing than others."

"And my friend the police inspector warned me about folks like you and your employer," I replied with a smile. "He tells me you'll have my wallet within minutes."

I resumed walking, the boy shouting after me, "You're only afraid of what you might discover, sir! Pay a visit to Mrs. Collins and you'll be a believer!"

I didn't turn around to answer. There was no use arguing with a child, especially one as precociously devious as this one seemed to be. Besides, I didn't want to have another minute of my time wasted on mediums and séances and Spiritualists. I took the leaflet and folded it in half, purposefully forming the crease across Mrs. Collins's face. I then shoved it deep into my coat pocket, intent on throwing it into the fire as soon as I reached home.

III

Philadelphia in 1869 was surely a golden age for facial hair. Being a man of modesty, I boasted only a mustache the same black shade as my pomaded hair and kept neatly trimmed to gentlemanly proportions. Walking the city's streets, however, one could see beards, mustaches, and sideburns of every shape, size, and style. It was commonplace to spot impressively slicked mustaches with curlicues at the ends and narrow beards of a foot or more that flowed off chins like waterfalls. One reporter at the *Bulletin* possessed a pair of sideburns so wildly overgrown it looked as if two woodland creatures had been affixed to his cheeks.

Yet none of them could hold a candle to the facial hair displayed by Mr. Thornton

Willoughby.

It began with the hair, which swept upward in a silver wave that crested at the top of his head before trickling down the back of his neck to his collar. Jutting out of it like jetties were the sideburns, which started at the ears and traveled in a wide strip of whiskers down to his chin. The facial foliage was so thick that it was difficult to discern where the sideburns ended and his beard began. That beard, by the way, dripped to Mr. Willoughby's chest and rose and fell with his breathing.

Yet the highlight of this display, the pièce de résistance, was his mustache, which defied logic and gravity in equal measure. Bushier than a squirrel's tail, it stretched a good three inches past his cheeks in both directions. When he spoke, the edges quivered up and down, a movement that invariably managed to hypnotize whomever he was addressing. That afternoon, that person happened to be yours truly, and Mr. Willoughby's mustache was particularly animated as he talked about where I should live once I married his daughter.

"It's not a decision to be entered into lightly," he was saying. "I'm hoping the two of you have given it plenty of thought."

We hadn't, actually. My assumption was that once Violet and I became man and wife, we would move into my place on Locust

Street. It was certainly large enough, with plenty of space to start a family of our own, if that was in the cards.

"I was thinking we could take the house on Broad Street, Father. No one has lived there for years. It's just sitting there completely empty."

This was spoken by Violet Willoughby, my beloved. She sat to my right, as pretty and delicate as her name implied. To my left was her mother, Marjorie, a handsome woman who, like any true Philadelphia matron at the time, never left the house without a hat. The one she had on that day was gray, with white silk roses spilling onto the floppy brim.

"Why, that's a wonderful idea!" Mrs. Willoughby exclaimed. "It would be so nice to see some life in that old place."

Thus began a good five minutes of talk about the house on Broad Street, a structure I had never seen or heard anything about until that afternoon. Yet from what Violet and her parents said, it was a glorious place. It apparently rested on a green patch of land in a desirable neighborhood. Not too large, or too small. Built, as Mr. Willoughby claimed, to the highest specifications. The only reason they left it, Mrs. Willoughby said, was because they outgrew it when the twin boys came along, settling instead in their current home, a mansion west of the Schuylkill River. Yet, Violet added, they never sold it, just in case they one day wanted to return.

It all sounded lovely as the three of them pelted me with details, but at that moment I could only think about my rumbling stomach. We were in the dining room of the Continental Hotel, menus at the ready, although it was expected of us to defer to Mr. Willoughby, who would ultimately order for the entire party. Because there had been no time that morning to eat a proper breakfast, I was certifiably starving. Yet before we could begin, one more member of our group needed to arrive.

That would be Violet's younger brother, Jasper. His chair, situated between Violet and Mrs. Willoughby, sat empty. And his delayed arrival gave Mr. Willoughby the opportunity to ask me another mustache-quivering question.

"Tell me, Edward, do you always envision yourself mucking around at that newspaper of yours?"

Before I could answer, I caught sight of the maître d' rushing Jasper toward our table. Violet's brother, nineteen at the time, was as thin as a rail and, unlike his father, clean of facial hair. The lack of whiskers brought attention to his pale skin, drawn cheeks, and swollen, sleepless eyes.

"Please forgive my lateness," he muttered in lieu of a greeting. "I overslept."

His father, ignoring the apology, turned to

me and said, "The road to ruin can be measured in tardiness. It's a lesson I wish my son here would understand."

"I didn't feel well," Jasper replied with exasperation. "If I had any sense, I'd still be in bed."

"You seemed well enough last night," Violet said. "There was so much noise and stumbling about in your room that it woke me up. What were you doing awake at such an odd hour?"

"I didn't get in until then."

At that moment, a waiter at the table next to ours dropped a fork, which rang off the marble floor. Jasper placed a hand to his temples and winced.

"What kept you out so late, dear?" Mrs. Willoughby asked him. "You left right after dinner."

"Friends," Jasper mumbled. "I ran into some old friends."

"Anyone we might know?"

He offered a quick shake of his head. "I shouldn't think so."

Before anyone could pose another query to the poor boy, our waiter at last came round. Mr. Willoughby ordered for the table a light lunch of oysters, carrot soup, broiled salmon, and spring lamb. During the meal, I gorged myself as discreetly as possible while weighing in briefly on topics such as the weather ("Perfect"), the impending connection of the

Union Pacific and Central Pacific railroads ("Quite an achievement, to be sure"), and what time of year Violet and I wanted to have our wedding ("I defer to my lovely fiancée"). During coffee and dessert, however, the conversation again inevitably returned to what I did for a living.

"How well does being a newspaper man pay, Edward?" Mr. Willoughby asked before taking a sip of coffee.

"Well enough," I said. "Although I doubt it will make anyone a fortune. Aside from the owners, of course."

"I imagine not. If it's wealth you want to acquire, then I suggest you enter into a different profession. My door is always open, Edward, if that day should come."

Thornton Willoughby, I must add, was the owner of the Willoughby Hat Company, maker of fine head wear for both men and women. He began his career as a milliner on Market Street, known for his reasonable prices and solid workmanship. His modest shop became so popular that he stayed awake for days on end, sewing until his fingers bled in order to meet demand. He soon opened a factory, which kept on growing until he eventually found himself overseeing one of the largest hat manufacturers on the East Coast. According to Violet, he hadn't touched a needle and thread in at least twenty years.

"I appreciate that kind offer," I said, as I

45

did whenever he frequently made it. "But I'm utterly satisfied with my current career and income level."

"Father, Edward doesn't need the money," Violet added. "He has plenty of it."

In my interactions with the entire Willoughby family, I noticed a pattern. First, Mr. Willoughby spoke, followed by Violet's opinion. After that, it was Mrs. Willoughby's turn to weigh in. Jasper mostly remained mute.

On cue, Mrs. Willoughby said, "That's right, your parents left you well off, didn't they, Mr. Clark?"

"Very well off."

With Jasper staying silent, it was again Mr. Willoughby's turn. "I recall Violet mentioning that your father was in shipping."

"Exports," I said, sticking to the lie I had concocted many years earlier. "He and my mother perished when one of his ships sank in the Atlantic. I was just a boy when it happened."

Violet, the first member of the family to whom I revealed this untruth, gave her parents a reprimanding look, as if all their questions had caused me undue emotional distress. "Because he was so young, the company was sold and Edward inherited everything. So there's no need to worry about money."

"I think what concerns my husband are the subjects you write about," Mrs. Willoughby told me. "Criminals and hoodlums and killers. It's all so ghastly."

There was no easy answer that could make the Willoughbys understand why I wrote about such things. I couldn't tell them what had really happened to my parents and how that incident fifteen years ago had shaped me ever since. I couldn't explain that, by studying man's inhumanity toward his fellow man, I hoped to understand the events that tore my family apart. If the Willoughbys ever discovered the truth about that, I knew without a doubt that Violet would want nothing to do with me. Her parents would surely see to that.

"Whatever I do, your daughter will be well provided for," I assured them. "I admit that I don't need to hold down a job. I could live well enough without one. But I want to be a contributing member of society. A working man such as yourself, Mr. Willoughby."

That seemed to please him well enough, which in turn pleased his wife, which in turn made Violet place her hand upon mine, lean against me, and whisper in my ear, "You're doing beautifully."

Buoyed by her comment, I added, "If it's any consolation, I do turn down some assignments. Just this morning, I refused to undertake a rather dubious request from my editor. It seems he wanted me to play spy and catch some of the city's mediums deceiving their customers."

Surprisingly, this set off a minor debate at the table, with half of the Willoughby family in support of mediums and the other half firmly against. Somehow I ended up playing moderator, eliciting comments from both sides.

"It's quackery!" Mr. Willoughby thundered. "Just a bunch of thieves trying to separate hard-working citizens from their money!"

"Certainly not all of them are criminals," Violet countered. "There are so many that at least a few of them *must* be real. They can't all be impostors, can they?"

This prompted Jasper to speak for the first time since the third course. "Father is right, for once. They're all crooks. Every last one of them."

"I should hope not," Mrs. Willoughby said with a sigh. "I prefer to think that some are performing a valuable service by connecting people with loved ones they've lost. I've considered going to see one myself several times, only to have your father talk me out of it."

"Because it's quackery!" Mr. Willoughby interjected.

Violet clucked with sympathy. "I had no idea, Mother. Who do you want to contact?"

Mrs. Willoughby bowed her head, in either sadness or shame. It was difficult to tell. "Joseph," she said.

The rest of us grew quiet at the mention of the Willoughbys' lost son. Jasper's twin brother had succumbed to scarlet fever when both were five. Violet spoke about him only in passing. We were both alike in that regard — never letting each other see how much we'd been injured by our pasts.

"I miss him so much sometimes," Mrs. Willoughby admitted. "And I can't help but wonder what it would be like to talk to him one last time."

Across the table, Thornton Willoughby glared at me as if I had been the one to breach family protocol and mention the boy's name. "I must say, you would be wise to take that assignment, Edward. The more flimflam artists who are exposed, the better off this city would be. Your newspaper would be doing a valuable service."

With that, he slurped down the remainder of his coffee and placed his cup solidly on the table — the signal that lunch was officially over. I thanked the Willoughbys for a lovely meal and got a reminder from Violet that we were to have dinner on Sunday night at the home of her friend Bertram Johnson. Then I took my leave, heading back to the *Bulletin* building the same way I'd come. When I reached Eighth and Chestnut, I again encountered the boy with the leaflets, still commandeering the corner.

"Sit with Mrs. Collins, world-renowned

medium!" he shouted. "Speak once more to loved ones who now rest in the hereafter!"

The couple strolling directly in front of me, a gray-haired man and woman, stopped at the boy and took a leaflet. The man's suit was similar to my own. The woman's dress, unlike the gay colors on display up and down the street, was black.

"Does she truly have the gift?" the woman asked as her gaze flitted across the leaflet. "Can she really help us speak to the dead?"

"Mrs. Collins?" the boy said. "She's world famous, ma'am. Presidents and kings have sat with her and departed fully satisfied."

The woman turned to her obviously unimpressed husband. "Perhaps she will be the one. The one who can let us talk to Stephen."

The hope in her voice stabbed at my heart. Stephen most likely had been struck down during the war, like so many others. I had known dozens of men just like him. I had met their mothers and spouses and lovers, as well. All those sad-eyed women trapped in the unforgiving grip of grief.

"I don't think so, dearest," the man gently said. "We must continue on our way."

"But can't we even attempt it?"

"We have," her husband said. "Many times."

"Then we must try again." The woman clutched the leaflet as if it were a Bible, so firm she was in her belief. "Certainly no harm

50

will come if we try one last time."

Her husband took the leaflet from her hands and thrust it back at the boy. He moved forcefully onward, giving his wife no choice but to follow. Watching them depart, I thought of Mr. and Mrs. Willoughby and wondered if a similar exchange would take place if they happened upon this boy. I was reminded of Marjorie Willoughby's bereavement, so palpable that it silenced the rest of us at the table. How many grieving mothers like her sought out people such as Mrs. Collins? How many had squandered their hard-earned money on nothing more than a hoax?

It occurred to me that Hamilton Gray's idea might not be so ridiculous after all. While it would be impossible to rid the city of mediums entirely, I began to see the value in exposing at least one or two of them in the *Evening Bulletin*. It could certainly serve as a warning, for Philadelphia's citizens and charlatans alike.

As I approached the boy, he called out dramatically: "The skeptic has returned! Changed your mind about Mrs. Collins's gifts, sir?"

"I have," I replied. "I would like to attend a séance this evening, if possible."

"There's one at eight o'clock. Mrs. Collins will be pleased to have you. I guarantee it will be an evening you won't soon forget."

51

I patted the boy on the head and gave him a penny. "I certainly hope so."

IV

Mrs. Lucy Collins lived a few blocks west of Broad Street, in a perfectly respectable neighborhood of upper-class homes. Stepping out of my hired hack, I took a moment to study the house in front of me. It was large, but subdued; elegant, but not boastful. It made me wonder if Mrs. Collins was a woman of means. More likely, the illusion had already begun. I imagined the house full of empty rooms, with only the front parlor furnished to give the impression that someone actually lived there, much like a false storefront constructed to disguise illegal activities going on behind it.

Inside the home, I found four others waiting in the parlor, including the woman in black I had seen on the street that afternoon. Her husband, I noticed, was conspicuously absent. As I hung my coat and hat on a nearby rack, we exchanged a look of recognition before she turned away, eyes downcast.

The remaining visitors were strangers. One was a squat, pink-faced man who, despite the cool temperature of the room, had broken out into a sweat. The other two were an elderly couple seated on a floral love seat against the wall, their hands clasped in solidarity.

"Is this your first time sitting with Mrs. Collins?" the husband asked me by way of greeting.

"It is," I replied. "I hope I'm not disappointed."

The man offered a nod of understanding. "It's our first sitting, too, but we've heard nothing but excellent things about Mrs. Collins. The name's Rowland. Pierce and Millicent Rowland."

"I'm —" I fumbled for a name, trying to yank one from thin air. Inspiration struck when I noticed that Mr. Rowland was wearing a silk necktie the color of a grassy meadow. "Green. Mr. Carlton Green."

As we shook hands, Mrs. Rowland asked, "Who are you trying to contact, sir? We're here to speak to our daughter, Mary."

"I'm hoping to hear from my sister —" I again struggled to conjure up a fictitious name. "Daisy."

Mr. Rowland turned to the pink-faced gentleman, now sweating more profusely. "And you, sir? Who are you trying to contact?"

The man mopped his brow with a handkerchief before saying, "I long to speak to my late wife, Katherine. Today would have been her birthday."

"I'm very sorry for your loss," said Mr.

Rowland.

"Thank you," the gentleman replied, extending his hand to Mr. Rowland. "I'm Mr. Peter Spencer."

Mrs. Rowland offered him a warm smile and said, "It's a pleasure to meet you, Mr. Spencer."

While the three of them chatted among themselves, I roamed the parlor, examining the décor. The room was tastefully appointed, with enough subtle flourishes to make it comfortable. Evenly spaced gaslights flickered from the walls, surrounded by wallpaper striped a soothing shade of yellow. Potted palms sat in the corners and lace curtains hung at the windows.

Pushed against the wall opposite the Rowlands was a narrow mahogany table, upon which sat a small lamp and an elaborate arrangement of daffodils and other spring blooms. The vibrant yellows of the daffodils contrasted nicely with a single ivory lily at the front of the arrangement. Half opened, the lily's petals had a shine to them, as if they had been coated by fresh dew.

Hanging above the table was an oil painting of a stern-looking man with shifty eyes and a disgruntled mouth. He stared at those of us in the parlor with disdain, the black-eyed Susan painted onto his lapel doing nothing to lighten his apparent mood.

As I leaned in to further examine the paint-

54

ing, the door to the adjacent sitting room suddenly opened. A voice floated from the room, announcing, "Please, come in."

The five of us entered a room as dim and stark as the parlor was bright and comforting. Heavy curtains covered the windows, blocking out whatever moonlight there might have been outside. Situated along one wall was a small side table. Against the opposite wall sat a massive wooden cabinet into which strange symbols and odd faces had been carved. The center of the room was dominated by a round table covered with a black cloth that brushed the floor. Sitting like a centerpiece on the table were four glass domes. Inside each dome was a small bell that dangled from a miniature tripod made of wood.

Mrs. Lucy Collins herself stood beside the table, wearing a purple dress and white elbow-length gloves. She looked very much like the image on the leaflet, only the illustration hadn't fully captured her beauty. The face — narrow cheeks, sharp chin — was the same, of course. So was her hair, styled in a similar waterfall of curls.

Yet there was a glow to her that the image just couldn't convey. It was centered in her green eyes, which sparkled with an intensity that I had never seen before or since. They looked like emeralds, those eyes, bright and mesmerizing. It was as if Mrs. Collins had arrived in Philadelphia after stepping out of a Vermeer painting, the delicate lightness of his brushstrokes still intact.

At first glance, I found myself utterly transfixed. Which was her aim, I had to remind myself. She was, after all, just like the proverbial wolf in sheep's clothing.

When she spoke, I detected a hint of Virginia in her voice. "Welcome and good evening to you all. Once you make your payment, we can begin."

She gestured to a silver tray on the side table. Above the tray was another oil painting, a pastoral scene of trees and a pond with a flock of geese in the distance.

"And how much," I said, "are we to pay for the privilege of your company, madam?"

"Ten dollars, sir."

Ten dollars! I was stunned, and for a moment considered leaving. That was a half-week's pay, with no guarantee the *Bulletin* would compensate me for it later. Yet the others placed their hard-earned money on the tray without hesitation, Mr. Rowland leading the charge. Despite wanting more than anything to storm out, my conscience wouldn't let me watch them waste their money without doing the same. I was supposed to be doing this, after all, for their benefit.

With great reluctance, I paid the sitting fee. As soon as my money hit the silver tray, Mrs.

Collins closed the door. "Now," she said, "let's all have a seat. Anywhere you prefer."

She sat opposite the door, directly in front of a small side table topped with an oil lamp. I took a seat directly to her right. My thinking was that the closer I sat to her, the more likely I'd notice the tricks she most certainly had planned. Mrs. Rowland sat next to me, followed by her husband. The woman in black — since I never did catch her name, I mentally referred to her as Stephen's mother — took a seat beside Mr. Rowland. Mr. Spencer sat between her and Mrs. Collins.

Once everyone was settled, Mrs. Collins said, "Before we begin, I'd like everyone to take a moment to study the bells on the table. Each one represents the loved one you're trying to reach. If their spirit is present, the bell closest to you will ring."

All of us did as we were told, staring dumbly at our respective glass-encased bells.

"Now, please direct your attention to this cabinet," Mrs. Collins said, pointing to the wooden monstrosity against the wall. Twice the size of an average armoire, it loomed in the darkness like a crypt. The curious symbols etched into it — moons and stars, mostly, but others I couldn't identify — alternately brightened and faded in the flickering of the room's single lamp. The faint, shifting light transformed the cabinet's carved faces into open-mouthed demons, then benevolent angels, then back again.

"My spirit cabinet was passed on to me by my grandmother, who also possessed the gift of conversing with the dead. Carved by Italian monks during the Renaissance, it holds special powers. I mention this only because if a spirit intends to manifest itself this evening, it will do so in that cabinet." Mrs. Collins offered a slight smile. "But I offer no guarantees that such an event will occur."

She set her hands palms down on the table and instructed Mr. Spencer and me to each place a hand on top of her wrists. Beneath her silk gloves, her arm felt small and delicate, like a child's.

"I trust you both will be honest gentlemen," she said. "Speak up if you feel my hands or arms move at any point in the séance. I don't want anyone to think there's trickery involved in whatever may happen here this evening."

At this, I suppressed a smile of my own. Of course there'd be trickery involved, and I was certain I'd be able to see right through it.

Mrs. Collins next told everyone to hold hands, forming a chain around the table. Beside me, Mrs. Rowland removed her gloves and placed them on the table before linking hands with me and her husband.

"Circles are powerful, yet soothing," Mrs. Collins informed us. "Those in the spirit realm are drawn to them. But, in order for spirits to appear, I must have absolute silence, stillness, and near darkness."

Her arm wriggled beneath my hand as she said, "Pardon me for a moment, gentlemen, as I dim this lamp."

She turned to the table behind her and lowered the lamp until only the faintest of glows remained. The table became invisible, as did the room around us. Everyone at the table had been turned into shadows, barely perceptible. The only things that could clearly be seen were the bells at the table's center, their glass domes reflecting what remained of the lamplight.

Mrs. Collins returned her hands to the table and Mr. Spencer and I placed our palms on top of her wrists once more.

"Now," she said, "if we're all ready, let's begin."

For something that allegedly required silence, the séance began with an absurd amount of talking. Mrs. Collins proceeded to spout hokum about the spirit realm and how we were summoning them in friendship and curiosity. She mentioned someone by the name of White Sparrow, a long-dead Chero-kee woman who served as her guide between this world and the spirit one. She told us to think good thoughts so that our vibrations would be felt by White Sparrow on the other side. Never before had I heard so much rub-bish in such a short period of time, and it took all means of willpower to keep from

59

laughing uncontrollably in the darkness.

After that came a long period of silence, five excruciating minutes at least, in which we all waited for our vibrations to be received. Just when it seemed as if I'd fall asleep from sheer boredom, Mrs. Collins broke the quiet with a sudden, half-gasped, "I sense something. A presence. A *familiar* presence."

She moved slightly beside me, and I saw the barest shadow of her face tilting upward as she called into the room. "Is there a visitor from the spirit realm present? Please, signal to us that you are here."

Somewhere in the darkness — from which direction, I couldn't tell — a light rapping noise was heard. To my right, Mrs. Rowland inhaled slightly. Across from me, Mr. Spencer's breathing grew more rapid.

"Spirit," Mrs. Collins said, "is it possible for you to answer questions for those of us gathered here? Rap once for no, twice for yes."

One rap emerged from the gloom. After a dutiful pause, another one arrived.

"Thank you, spirit," Mrs. Collins replied. "Is your name White Sparrow?"

Two raps, this time in quick succession.

"I welcome your presence once more, my old friend. Are you again here to serve as a guide between this place and the other side?"

Another two raps followed.

"Wonderful! Are there other spirits with

you? Ones who know and wish to contact those of us present?"

This time, instead of two raps, we heard an elaborate stream of them, like a rapid drumbeat.

"I believe that's a resounding yes," Mrs. Collins told us. Then she said to the ether, "Please ask one of the spirits with you to make their presence known by indicating who they wish to contact."

Another lengthy silence followed, filled with anticipation. At last, the bell nearest Mr. and Mrs. Rowland began to move of its own accord inside its glass dome. Mrs. Rowland gasped again as the bell rang — a quiet tinkling in the darkness.

"Does that mean someone wants to speak to us?" she asked.

"Are you Mr. and Mrs. Pierce Rowland?"

"We are."

"White Sparrow has ushered in a spirit that wishes to communicate through me," Mrs. Collins said. "I see a girl. So pretty . . . yet she died so young. I sense . . . an illness of some sort. And this girl, she's a relation to you, no?"

I felt Mrs. Rowland's hand trembling in my own. "Our daughter."

"Mary is her name, yes?"

"That's right. Is she here?"

"Yes. She's here," Mrs. Collins said. "She can feel your presence. Your warmth. Your love. She says that . . . while her illness tormented her when she was alive, she is now at peace and happy. She wants you to know that, so you may no longer worry if she suffered during her last days. She says . . . that your care comforted her greatly and that she loves both of you very much."

Mrs. Rowland began to weep in the darkness next to me. Her husband whispered to her, "You see, Millicent. She's at peace at last. Our dear girl has found peace."

The evening progressed in a similar manner for half an hour or so. The bell next rang in front of Mr. Spencer, who was informed that the spirit of his beloved wife was present. She, of course, knew he came to wish her a happy birthday and that she was patiently waiting for him in heaven, which made him, too, break into tears. Stephen's mother also wept when the spirit of her son inevitably rang the bell in front of her. Mrs. Collins told her that even though he died on the battlefield, Stephen had no regrets about joining the Union Army. He willingly gave his life for his country and his parents should feel proud of what he did, not sad that he is gone.

"But I miss you so much, darling," Stephen's mother said, her tear-wracked voice filling the room. "You can't fathom the depths of my grief."

Mrs. Collins paused, as if listening to a response no one else could hear. "Stephen says he does know," she said, "for he is with you always. You might not see him or hear him, but he is there . . . keeping watch over your husband and yourself."

At long last, the bell in front of me rang, prompting Mrs. Collins to ask, "Is there a Mr. Green present?"

I was thankful that the darkness obscured my face, because at that moment I was grinning from ear to ear. Although her show had been surprisingly convincing throughout, I now had tangible proof that Mrs. Collins was nothing more than a scam artist. Surely, if a legitimate spirit were trying to contact me, it would have used my real name.

"I'm Mr. Green," I said, continuing the ruse.

"A young woman is present," Mrs. Collins said. "She left this earth too soon. She says . . . her name is Daisy and that you were siblings."

"Yes. Daisy was my sister. How I long to see her again."

Mrs. Collins continued, saying, "Daisy wants you to know that her illness didn't darken her spirit."

I was forced to make an immediate decision. Did I go along with what Mrs. Collins was telling me and pretend it was all true? Or should I attempt to trip her up a bit, hoping this séance of hers tumbled like the house of cards it really was?

I chose the latter.

"Illness?" I asked. "Daisy was killed in a carriage accident."

"But she was ill, too," Mrs. Collins said, not skipping a step in the faux waltz the two of us were dancing. "Terribly ill. She didn't have the heart to tell you. She says . . . the carriage accident was actually a blessing in disguise, because it prevented her from suffering due to her illness."

"I'm so relieved," I said, attempting to sound as emotional as, say, Mr. Spencer or Stephen's mother. "The last thing I wanted was for my sweet sister to suffer."

"She knows that and she thanks you. She says . . . that you were the most kind-hearted brother anyone could ask for and that she cherishes the time you had together."

Once again, Mrs. Collins covered herself well. She seemed quite unflappable, which is why I decided to test her further and have a bit of fun in the process.

"And what about Reginald?" I asked. "Is there news of him?"

"Daisy says that Reginald is with her," Mrs. Collins replied, "and that he sends his regards."

"Reginald was her beloved horse," I said. "Can animals really speak in the afterlife?"

Instead of a response from Mrs. Collins, I heard a shriek from Mrs. Rowland. "Something just touched me!"

"What was it?" her husband asked.

"I can't say with certainty —"

I heard a second shriek, this time from Stephen's mother. "I felt something as well! It just brushed past me!"

Soon I, too, felt it. It was a rush of air blowing past my ear. A second followed, traveling in the opposite direction and brushing the back of my neck so closely that the hairs there stood on end.

"A brave spirit has come closer," Mrs. Collins announced. "Spirit, make your presence known to us."

Mrs. Rowland shrieked again. She gripped my right hand tightly, her fingernails digging into my flesh. At first, I wondered if she was suffering from an attack of some kind, but then I saw what caused her to cry out. The others did, too, and reacted in a similar fashion.

The focus of our attention was Mrs. Rowland's gloves, which had started to rise off the table. They stayed clasped together a moment, fingers pointed upward as if they were in prayer. But soon they separated, floating off in opposite directions, barely visible in the faint glow of the lamp.

"The spirit is attempting to manifest itself," Mrs. Collins said as the gloves twisted and twirled in midair. "So that we might see its ghostly form."

Just then, the table began to rock back and

forth. Jostled by the movement, the bells rang wildly within their glass domes. The gloves dropped back in front of Mrs. Rowland as the table pitched violently. Those of us seated at it began to inch backward in our chairs, but Mrs. Collins stopped us.

"Keep holding hands!" she ordered. "We mustn't break the chain!"

The table lifted off the ground. My hands — one remaining on Mrs. Collins's wrist, the other still clutching Mrs. Rowland — rode with it, stopping until they were about chest high. The table simply floated there, rising and lowering at random. Then it fell to the floor with a hearty *thunk,* the bells clanging in disharmony.

That was immediately followed by a noise coming from the cabinet on the other side of the room. Rustling, it sounded like. Or perhaps a hoarse whisper. The cabinet door flew open, setting off another cry from Mrs. Rowland. But in the gloom I saw no one inside it, despite the whispers that were only growing louder.

The noise spurred Mrs. Collins to say, "Spirit, is that you?"

The response, which we all heard quite clearly, was a drawn-out hiss. *"Yesssssssss-sssssss."*

"Spirit," Mrs. Collins said. "If you are able, show yourself!"

Mrs. Rowland let out another shriek, more

shrill and terrified than the previous ones. "Look!" she gasped. "Everyone look!"

That was the moment I saw a figure appear inside the once-empty cabinet. A glowing, ghastly shade of white, it appeared to be half in this realm, half in the other. Its shape was that of a man, although I saw right through it to the darkness behind him. The figure, possessing arms but no legs to speak of, hovered in front of us. It turned its skull-like head back and forth, surveying us with sunken, eyeless sockets.

"Oh, spirit!" Mrs. Collins said, her voice pitched to excitable heights. "Tell us your name and who you have come to see!"

As the manifested spirit raised one of its spindly arms and pointed an extended index finger at the table, Mrs. Rowland squeezed my hand tighter than before. Once again, my first instinct was that something was wrong with her, and this time I was right. She swayed to the left, bumping into my shoulder before collapsing facedown onto the table.

"Mrs. Rowland, are you ill?" I asked — a stupid question, considering that she clearly was.

I stood, removing my hand from hers. Her husband did the same as he pulled her back into her seat. Within seconds, Mrs. Collins had brightened the lamp behind her, filling the room with much-needed light. I looked toward the cabinet and saw that it was now empty. The spirit was gone. Indeed, all of them were.

"Millicent, my dear, say something!" Mr. Rowland fanned his wife's face. "What's wrong?"

Blinking in the newfound light, I could tell clearly that poor Mrs. Rowland had fainted. I had witnessed it enough times in the ink-fumed *Bulletin* offices to know, and regretted not bringing along my smelling salts. Luckily, Mrs. Collins had her own, contained in an ivory snuffbox that she whisked from the folds of her skirt. One hearty sniff later and Mrs. Rowland was conscious.

"Oh dear," she said groggily. "Whatever happened?"

Her husband did the honors of answering. "You fainted, darling."

"And the —" Her gaze moved to the cabi-net, where the very thing that caused her to faint once floated.

"It's gone," Mrs. Collins said. "It departed as soon as we broke the circle. All of the spirits have now left us."

Mrs. Rowland looked genuinely apologetic as she said, "I didn't mean to make it go away. It was just so . . . startling."

"It's perfectly fine," Mrs. Collins assured her. "We've all had a very exciting night. As far as séances go, this was one of the finest I've ever presided over."

There was general agreement that, yes, it

was an evening to remember, and then everyone prepared to take their leave. The Rowlands and Mr. Spencer departed first, the two men assisting Mrs. Rowland to a waiting carriage. Soon, Stephen's mother left, holding back more tears as she thanked Mrs. Collins effusively for letting her hear from her son one last time.

Then it was just the medium and myself, eyeing each other across the empty room.

Mrs. Collins, her face flushed from all the activity of the séance, looked even prettier with some color in her cheeks. She seemed so warm and genuine that I felt a pang of guilt as I said, "Those were some very impressive tricks."

She laughed gaily. "Tricks, Mr. Green? Whatever are you talking about?"

"There's an interesting invention called the Aurolese phone," I said. "It's a listening device for women with a hearing impairment. Some are shaped like a small lily so a lady can wear it behind her ear without drawing attention to the fact that she needs a listening aid."

Mrs. Collins, still smiling, said, "I've never heard of such a thing."

"That's very strange, then. Because there's one sitting in the vase of flowers in the parlor. I assume the tube attached to it, modified to be longer than average, runs through the wall and into this room."

I approached the painting on the wall. From a distance, it looked like fine art. Up close, however, it was easy to see the sloppy brushstrokes and haphazard technique.

"It's hidden behind this painting," I continued. "Also behind there is a hole in the wall. A hole of similar size is in the painting that hangs in the parlor, carefully obscured by a flower on the subject's lapel. This allows you to not only see who's about to attend your séance, but also to overhear who it is they've come to contact."

"That's a ridiculous theory," Mrs. Collins replied, although the flicker of fear in her eyes told me she thought otherwise.

"Is it? In the parlor, the Rowlands, Mr. Spencer, and I all talked about who we wished to hear from tonight. And, lo and behold, those were the so-called spirits who arrived during the séance. Only the person who contacted me? My dear sister Daisy? She doesn't exist, Mrs. Collins." I offered her a sardonic smile. "Neither does Reginald the horse, for that matter. By eavesdropping, you also knew to place only four bells on the table, even though there were five of us present."

"Mr. and Mrs. Rowland were both here to speak to their daughter," Mrs. Collins said. "Necessitating only four bells."

"Indeed, they were," I replied. "But we were all strangers to you. There are only two ways you could have known they were a couple. One was by spying on us. The second is that they were both in on the scheme. It turns out, both ways are the truth."

"You're mad," Mrs. Collins said, chin raised in indignation.

"Oh, but I'm not. You needed someone to start the conversation in your parlor. Who better to get people talking than an innocent couple who claimed to be there to contact their deceased daughter? Mrs. Rowland also acted as a stage director of sorts, didn't she? With her shrieks and gasps indicating that something was happening. She's the one who directed our attention to the floating gloves. While that was going on, I have no doubt that some other trick was being set up. When the grand finale occurred, it was Mrs. Rowland's fainting that ended the show."

"I refuse to stand here while you accuse me of fraud," Mrs. Collins said, her voice raising an octave. "I've never met the Rowlands before tonight. And as for tricks, well, what about the bells?"

"You manipulated them, of course."

"Those bells were manipulated by spirits. They're encased in glass! You saw with your own eyes that I didn't touch them."

"No, you didn't. But you did make them ring somehow."

"I think you should leave now," Mrs. Collins said, adding, "before you make a further fool

71

of yourself."

"I will in just a minute. Although I'm no fool. But I suspect you already know that, Mrs. Collins."

I moved to the table and crouched down until the bells were at eye level. All four of them were the same size, each one hanging from the center of identical tripods. A quick tap of each dome revealed them to be made of impenetrable glass.

The obvious trick would have been to tie a string around the clapper of each bell. The strings would then run through holes in the table to a spot near Mrs. Collins's seat, where she could pull them at will. Only no strings hung from the bell clappers. I would have been able to see them.

Mrs. Collins, no doubt noticing my furrowed brow, said, "Not so sure of yourself now, are you, Mr. Green?"

I ignored her, instead examining the four tripods. The legs of each met just above their respective bells and were topped with a wooden cap. Two legs of every tripod had a rounded bottom, while the third leg remained flat against the table.

"Hollow legs," I said, suddenly realizing the trick. "One leg of each tripod is hollow. The strings are attached to the top of the bells and run through each tripod's hollow leg to a spot beneath the table. Very inventive, Mrs. Collins."

"*You're* the inventive one, Mr. Green." The edge in Mrs. Collins's voice had grown sharper. "Clearly you've forgotten that you had your hand on one of my wrists the entire séance. Mr. Spencer did the same with my other wrist. At any point, did you feel my arms move?"

"I did not," I replied. "There was no movement at all, which doesn't come as a surprise, seeing that it wasn't your wrist I was touching."

"Then what was it? Do tell."

"It was a prosthetic arm," I said, "wearing the same pair of gloves you have on now, kept hidden under the table and placed there after you dimmed the lamp. Mr. Spencer was touching a similar prosthetic, allowing you to have both hands free during the entire séance. After Mrs. Rowland fainted, you removed them from the table before brightening the lamp again."

Mrs. Collins huffed, wordlessly indicating that I was right.

"What you couldn't do yourself — such as the rapping and the brushes of air we felt — was the work of another accomplice."

That same accomplice, I figured, had made Mrs. Rowland's gloves float in the air after she unclasped hands with her husband and both of them attached very thin wires to the gloves. The wires were affixed to two wooden sticks, which the accomplice used to manipulate the gloves like a puppeteer.

"As for the table's movements," I said, "I have a feeling that if I examine the base of the table, I'll see a mechanical device that allows you to raise and lower it using only your feet."

Mrs. Collins had started to look queasy by then, yet she refused to admit defeat.

"Are you quite finished?" she asked. "Because I would like you out of my house, sir. Immediately."

"So, that's it?" I replied. "No rebuttal? No words in your defense?"

Mrs. Collins folded her arms across her chest and glared at me. "I feel no need to defend myself. In fact, it is you, sir, who should be accused of dishonesty. You came here as a skeptic and intend to leave that way, despite what you witnessed tonight."

"My dear Mrs. Collins, the only thing I witnessed is a swindler who took a great deal of money out of the hands of unsuspecting people."

"A swindler, am I? Allow me to share with you the many flaws in this grand accusation of yours. Take that poor, grieving mother who lost her son. If I was listening to you in the parlor — and I most certainly wasn't — how could I possibly know about Stephen, who died during the war?"

She was correct in that regard. While the rest of us were chatting in the parlor, the woman didn't speak a word. Still, it wasn't difficult for me to figure it out.

"She mentioned her son to her husband this afternoon on the corner of Chestnut and Eighth," I said. "I heard them talking about him and assumed, like you, that a son of parents their age was struck down in battle. I'm certain the boy you hired to hand out your leaflets heard them as well. I'm also certain that same boy is around here somewhere."

I approached the cabinet where the spirit had manifested itself. Up close and in better lighting, it looked far less exotic — more amateurish than ornate. The symbols had been haphazardly notched into the wood, most certainly by an inexperienced hand. The carved faces were nothing more than clay figures pasted onto the cabinet's corners and painted brown.

"I will ask you for the final time to leave my house, Mr. Green," Mrs. Collins said.

"*This* was your finest illusion, by the way," I replied. "Quite convincing."

Standing at the open cabinet door, I clearly saw the large pane of glass that had been placed diagonally inside it. I rapped on the glass to indicate to Mrs. Collins that I knew it was there.

"The Pepper's ghost illusion," I said. "Works every time."

Poking my head into the cabinet, I looked

to my left, where a small nook sat just out of view from anyone in the main séance room. The nook had been draped with black cloth. In its center, sitting on a stool also painted black, was a figure cobbled together out of wood, leather, cloth, and parts of a model skeleton most likely stolen from a local hospital. All of it had been painted a silvery blue, which appeared white when reflected on the pane of glass. Behind it was a lantern, turned on when it was time for the "spirit" to appear.

A boy dressed from head to toe in black huddled beside the figure, his face darkened with charcoal. I recognized his eyes as he glared back at me. It was indeed the boy from the street corner.

"You can come out now," I told him. "Your act has been discovered."

"Come on out, Thomas," Mrs. Collins called to the boy. "It's all right."

The boy burst from the cabinet, head lowered. He rammed his skull into my stomach so hard that I stumbled backward. All the breath stored in my lungs escaped in one rough grunt. The boy, meanwhile, began to pummel me from every direction. While beating me about the head and shoulders, he yelled a torrent of profanity no child his age should even know, let alone utter.

"No-good devil! Dagnabbed whore stuffer! Goddamned cock biter!"

The boy ceased his attack only after Mrs. Collins forcibly pried him off me. Even then he still threw punches, his tiny fists slicing the air.

"I knew he was trouble!" he shouted. "Knew it as soon as I laid eyes on the son of a bitch!"

Mrs. Collins held him tight against her side. While it appeared that she was comforting him, I believed her grip was mostly to keep him from lunging at me again. "Hush, Thomas. Everything will be fine. You go on up to bed."

Young Thomas glared at me. "I'm not leaving you alone with that filthy, rotten heap of shit. Leave him alone with me and I'll kick him clean to hell, I will!"

"I have half a mind to do that myself." Mrs. Collins, too, shot a withering look my way. "But don't worry about a thing. I can handle Mr. Green on my own."

She released the boy, who immediately ran toward me and kicked me in the shin.

"Ow!" I yelled as pain shot up my leg.

"Next time I'll be aiming for your balls," the boy warned. "If you've got any, that is."

With that, he exited the room with an impish strut, leaving me to stumble to the nearest chair and collapse into it.

"Forgive my brother," Mrs. Collins said. "He has a bit of a temper. I told him he needs to learn how to control it."

"He needs to be caged," I said as I rubbed my throbbing leg. There was going to be a bruise there in the morning. I just knew it.

"He's only trying to protect me. But, as I said, I can take care of myself. So let's be quick about this. How much would you like?"

"How much would I like of what?"

"Money, of course," Mrs. Collins said. "How much will it take for you to keep quiet about this? I can give you one hundred dollars right now if you agree to walk away and not tell a soul what happened here tonight."

There were a great many people in this city who would have agreed to that offer in an instant. It was an astounding amount for anyone. But, as I had told Mr. Willoughby at lunch, my inheritance provided me with all the money I needed.

"I'm not looking for a bribe," I said. "For that matter, I'm also not Mr. Green. My real name is Edward Clark, and I'm a reporter for the *Evening Bulletin.*"

Mrs. Collins seemed to crumple at the mention of the newspaper. She staggered backward a moment, fumbling for a chair. Upon finding one, she plopped into it, arms dangling, the once-voluminous skirt of her dress stretched flat across her lap.

"A reporter," she said. "I suppose you intend to write about this? An exposé detailing the tricks employed by the city's mediums?"

"That's exactly my plan."

"Then I'll make it two hundred dollars."

"Keep your money."

"Three hundred," Mrs. Collins quickly added. "That's the highest I can go."

I'm sure I looked as bug-eyed as a housefly on an apple dumpling. "Do you really have three hundred dollars that you can part with at the snap of a finger?"

"What I do pays very well, Mr. Clark."

"Clearly," I said. "But don't you feel the least bit guilty? You're taking money from people — huge sums of it, I might add — and offering them nothing but illusions in return."

"I offer them comfort, Mr. Clark. These *illusions* that you seem to know so much about are only a means to that end."

"But you're using tricks to make people believe things that aren't real."

"I'm doing no such thing," Mrs. Collins said. "They believe these things because they *want* to believe them. People come to me out of desperation. They're grieving and lonely and have lost someone very dear to them. Take Mr. Spencer, for example. Or that poor woman who lost her son. All they wanted was the comfort of knowing their loved ones are in a better place. I could have been honest and told them I haven't a clue what happened to his wife or her son."

"That would have been the decent thing to

do," I said bitterly.

"Then they would have gone to another medium and paid more or less the same amount for similar results."

"So you decide to exploit their grief yourself and make a tidy profit in the process."

"Yes," Mrs. Collins replied. "If that's what I must do to support my brother and myself, then yes, I'll do it."

"And what of Mr. Collins?"

"He's long dead," she said. "The sole thing he left me is that wretched portrait hanging in the parlor. Trust me, I was all too happy to drill that spy hole through his heart."

"Surely there's a better way to make a living."

"By all means, Mr. Clark, educate me," Mrs. Collins shot back, fire in her eyes. "Tell me how a woman with no husband and no means is supposed to support herself. Servitude? Begging on the streets? Or perhaps you would prefer that I whore myself?"

"A whore, at the very least, has some honesty about what she does."

I stood, unable to spend another minute in her company. My blood was practically boiling as I stormed out of the séance room and into the parlor. Mrs. Collins followed, not content to let me have the last word.

"Wait just a minute, Mr. Clark!" she called out.

But I refused to stop, grabbing my coat and

top hat from the rack in the parlor without even slowing. I was unwilling to hear what she had to say, and afraid of what my response might be. Mrs. Collins seemed to bring out the worst in me.

"I will not discuss this any further," I snapped. "You can expect my report of this evening's activities to appear in the *Bulletin* within the week. Hopefully, that will give you enough time to pack your things and move on to another, more gullible location."

I was outside now, standing on the stoop just beyond the front door. Behind me, Mrs. Collins rushed through the parlor to stop me.

"Five hundred dollars," she said breathlessly. "That's my final offer. Please take it, Mr. Clark, and we can end this nonsense right now."

I turned slowly, smiling at her as I placed my hat atop my head. "Mrs. Collins, all the spirits in the world couldn't convince me to take your filthy money. Besides, you'll be needing it. I hear being chased out of town by a horde of angry customers can get quite expensive."

Mrs. Collins gave me a look of pure hatred as she slammed the door in my face. The resulting breeze was so strong that my hat flew off my head, tumbled down the walk, and plopped into the muddy street.

■ ■ ■ ■

Book Two:
Voices from the
Great Beyond

■ ■ ■ ■

I

That night, I dreamt of ghosts.

Not the random, faceless ghosts of your average nightmare, but men I once knew. Close friends who perished in battle, looking the way I had last seen them. There was Davies, one arm missing, his shoulder nothing more than shards of bone and shreds of sinew. And Cole, shriveled to a walking skeleton by hunger and disease. And Duncan, the gunshot wound to his throat gaping like a second mouth. They and dozens more spent the night stomping through my bedroom like some endless phantasmagoria. Some were oblivious to my presence, merely shuffling out of one wall and disappearing into another. But others stared as they passed, contemplating me with dead eyes, jealous that I, through some whim of fate, managed to survive when they did not.

I was grateful when dawn arrived, for the sunlight streaming through the windows prevented me from having to close my eyes again and risk seeing more disturbing visions. Even though it was early, I crawled from my bed and prepared my own bath. This was usually a task for Lionel, who woke before I did. But, since it was Saturday, he slept an hour later, for that was my habit as well. On that morning, I didn't mind doing it myself. The work, coupled with the early morning chill, woke me further and helped chase away the memories of my horrible dreams.

After bathing and dressing, I headed downstairs, not exactly an easy task. Sometimes, usually early in the morning or after a late night out, it seemed like my house consisted of nothing but stairs. I understood why Violet wouldn't even consider living there when we got married. It was not a home for the faint of heart or those leery of heights.

The house was a tall and narrow affair planted in the center of Locust Street, directly opposite the southern edge of Rittenhouse Square. Four stories high and only slightly wider than a pair of railroad cars, it had a wobbliness to it that brought to mind a too-high stack of books that could topple at any moment.

Still, I loved it like no other place. The dining room and parlor on the first floor were cramped and cozy. The same could be said of the second level, which housed my study, a guest bedroom, and a sitting room used only by intimate acquaintances. The fourth floor was the butler's quarters and attic space — places I rarely ventured. But the third story was mine alone. My bedroom and bath were there, as was another sitting room that contained a single chair reserved for yours truly. The windows of my bedroom over-looked the square, and during the summer, the trees there seemed to stretch across the street, making it feel like I was sleeping among their branches.

Oh, but those stairs! There was a formal staircase, decorated with mahogany banisters and carpet as green as the forest floor, that led visitors to the second story. But the one I used most often rose in a tight spiral from just outside the kitchen on the ground level to the fourth floor. It was a dizzying descent, especially after a poor night's sleep, but I always managed to make my way down in one piece.

That morning, Mrs. Patterson was already in the kitchen, preparing my breakfast. She rubbed her eyes upon seeing me, as if she couldn't believe I was really awake at such an hour.

"Is everything all right with you, Mr. Clark?" she asked. "The sun's hardly up and I ain't near done with your breakfast yet."

But she had put on a pot of coffee, a drink that I found indispensable after it was intro-duced to me during the war. Pouring myself a cup, I inhaled deeply, the smell reminding me of sitting around the fire with some of the very same men who had haunted my dreams during the night.

"I didn't sleep well," I told Mrs. Patterson. "I figured it was best to get up and moving instead of tossing and turning some more."

"A half night's sleep is better than none," Mrs. Patterson replied. "My father always said that."

"I would have gladly settled for half," I said. "But I only got a quarter at best."

I spent the next half hour sipping my coffee and perusing the *Evening Bulletin,* which had already been well read by Lionel the night before. I was pleased that my article on the death of Sophie Kruger ran in a prominent spot, even though, true to his word, Mr. Gray had excised all mentions of Mrs. Kruger's premonition involving her daughter.

Soon Lionel was up and about, apologizing profusely for not waking sooner. He was new to the job — the cousin of a friend of Mrs. Patterson's niece who needed work — and unaccustomed to the rather detached way I ran the household. Mrs. Patterson, on the other hand, had been with me since I bought the place. She had no qualms about letting me pour my own coffee and knew I had no preference for the way the bacon was cooked. That morning, she had prepared it the way she liked it: practically blackened.

I was on my second cup of coffee and

fourth piece of bacon when the bell rang at the front door. Lionel, giving me a stricken look, asked, "Do you think Inspector Barclay ordered another policeman to come round?"

"I hope not," I said. "I'd prefer to not spend my Saturday morning in the company of a corpse."

When the bell rang again, more urgently this time, I began to suspect Lionel was right and that Barclay *had* summoned me to another crime scene, even on my day off. But once Lionel answered the door, he returned to the dining room looking perplexed.

"Mr. Brady is here to see you, sir."

"Brady? I don't know anyone by that name."

"But you most likely do," Lionel said. "He says he's Mathew Brady, sir."

"The photographer?"

"That's what he says."

Suddenly I became the one who was perplexed. I had no idea why the nation's most notable photographer was standing at my door. It wasn't as if I were President Grant or one of the many other important men who have sat before his camera.

"I suppose I should see what he wants, then," I said.

At the door, I found Mr. Brady on the sidewalk outside, dressed in a gray morning suit. His curly hair and powder white beard lent him a professorial quality, as did the wire spectacles perched on his nose. Next to him, sitting atop a waist-high wooden tripod, was a box camera.

"Are you Mr. Clark?" he asked.

"I am, but —"

"Mr. Edward Clark?"

"Why, yes. I am honored to meet —"

He ducked behind his camera and interrupted once more with a "Hold still, please." He then proceeded to remove the cover over the camera's lens while I remained frozen in place like an imbecile. After ten seconds or so, he recovered the lens and reappeared from behind the camera.

"Thank you very much, Mr. Clark," he said. "Have a pleasant day."

With that, he departed, collapsing the tripod and carrying the camera over his shoulder to a waiting carriage.

"W-wait! Why did you — ?"

My voice faded when it became clear that Mr. Brady would provide no answers. He simply climbed into the carriage with his equipment, and off it went. Dumbfounded, I returned indoors, finding Lionel and Mrs. Patterson waiting in the front hall.

"What did he want?" Lionel asked.

"He . . . well, took a photograph."

"Of *you*?" Mrs. Patterson said, voice thick with incredulity.

I bristled at her tone. "Yes, of me."

"But why?"

To that question, I had no suitable answer. In fact, I had to wait several hours to discover the reason behind Mr. Brady's surprise visit.

By then it was almost noon, and I was in the sitting room on the third floor, in the middle of a private fitting with my tailor. Despite Violet's predictions, my store-bought sack suit days had yet to arrive. The tailor, Mr. Brooks, having just measured my chest and shoulders, was moving on to my waist when the doorbell rang again. Lionel answered it at once, no doubt hoping for another appearance by Mathew Brady. Instead, I heard a familiar and unwelcome voice rise from the doorway.

"I demand to see Edward Clark and I refuse to be turned away, so you might as well let me in this instant."

It was, without a doubt, Mrs. Lucy Collins. Somehow she had tracked me down, and it was clear from her tone that she had come to continue our argument from the previous night. Still, Lionel did his best to fend her off.

"Mr. Clark is otherwise engaged, ma'am, and not fit for company."

"I don't care if he's busy," Mrs. Collins said. "I intend to speak to him, and that's that."

I heard what seemed to be a slight scuffle, followed by the sound of angry footsteps on the main staircase. Beneath me, Mrs. Collins

91

stomped her way across the second floor, calling out, "Show yourself, Mr. Clark! There's no use hiding from me!"

It didn't take her long to locate the spiral staircase at the back of the house. Her boots rang out her ascent, followed by the rustling of her skirt on the railing. A moment later, she was on the third floor, pushing into the sitting room and seeing me standing there in nothing more than a pair of white long johns.

If my state of undress surprised Mrs. Collins, she certainly didn't show it. Nor, I must add, did she immediately avert her eyes and excuse herself from the room, as a true lady would have done. Perched on a wooden step stool and in practically no clothing, I remained upright, using only the shocked Mr. Brooks as a makeshift human shield.

"Mrs. Collins!" I said. "This is highly inappropriate."

"The first thing you should know about me, Mr. Clark," she replied, "is that I don't give a damn about propriety. The second is that you should never, ever try to engage in a battle of wills with me, for I will always win."

After hearing that, one could hardly blame Mr. Brooks for being absolutely scandalized. Lionel looked the same as he reached the third floor, breathless and battered. I suspected Mrs. Collins had performed on him a maneuver similar to what her brother did to me the night before.

"I'm sorry, sir," Lionel said. "I tried to stop her —"

"It's all right," I told him, still partly hidden behind Mr. Brooks. "I believe Mrs. Collins and I have a business matter to discuss. Please escort her to the parlor while I get dressed."

Lionel offered an exasperated nod. "Yes, sir."

"I'm not going anywhere," Mrs. Collins announced. "This is a very important matter, and it needs to be addressed immediately."

"Whatever it is," I said, "surely you can wait outside long enough for me to clothe myself."

Mrs. Collins shook her head. "By all means, dress yourself. But I'm not budging."

"Suit yourself."

I stepped out from behind Mr. Brooks to reveal my entire underwear-clad body, the boldness of my gesture surprising even me. There was something about Lucy Collins that inspired bold gestures. It was, I suppose, a desire to match her in brazenness.

Yet I soon realized that she refused to be matched. Instead of being shocked into retreating, as was my hope, Mrs. Collins merely looked me up and down, as if appraising my manliness. Her gaze — as forthright as a sailor's — made me blush.

Quickly, I grabbed my trousers, pretending that her presence didn't bother me. "Are you enjoying the view?"

"I've seen worse," Mrs. Collins replied.

I reddened even more. With my cheeks burning and my hands trembling, I managed to step into my trousers, almost falling over in the process.

"For heaven's sake," Mrs. Collins said with a huff. "If you're going to take this long, then I'll wait in the parlor. But be sure of this, Mr. Clark: You'll want to hear what I have to say."

Lionel quickly led her out of the room. Once they were gone, I dismissed Mr. Brooks, saying that I would call on him next week at his shop, where it was less likely we'd be interrupted. I then finished dressing and descended to the first-floor parlor, where Mrs. Collins sat with a leather satchel in her lap.

"Thank you for allowing me to put on some clothes," I said with pronounced sarcasm. "It must have been difficult to wait, seeing how your vitriol is stronger than your sense of decency."

"You flatter yourself, Mr. Clark. You could have been as naked as the moment you were born and I wouldn't have cared a whit."

She flung open the satchel and removed a photograph, which she thrust into my hands. It was an unflattering image of a baffled man in front of an open door. It didn't take long to realize that the baffled man in the picture was me, standing just outside my house.

"You're the one who sent Mr. Brady here

this morning?"

"He's an acquaintance of mine," Mrs. Collins said. "He's staying in the city for a few weeks and, since I know he's experiencing some money troubles at the moment, I hired him to photograph you. It isn't one of his finest works, but it will get the job done."

"And what job is that?"

"I intend to show this photograph to every medium in the city, exposing you the same way you intend to expose them," Mrs. Collins said, leaning forward in her chair. "Once they get a good look at this photograph, I dare say no medium will let you into their séances, no matter what fictional name you use."

"You wouldn't dare," I said, struggling to keep my voice calm.

"Trust me, Mr. Clark, I'm capable of far worse."

"Considering the sheer wickedness of this plan, I highly doubt that."

Feeling like a fox that's been outmaneuvered by a hen, I stared at the photograph. My face was fully visible in it, clear to anyone who gave it even a cursory glance. Even if I attempted to wear some sort of disguise, there was a good chance any medium who saw the photograph could recognize me from it.

"I presume you're more willing to bargain now than you were last evening, aren't you, Mr. Clark?"

I thought it through for a moment, trying to find some way in which I could gain the upper hand. It was hopeless. Mrs. Collins had me cornered.

"All right. Let's say for the moment that I agree not to write about how you're nothing but an unrepentant fraud," I said. "You can continue your shameful séances and I'll be able to pursue other mediums. Is that what you want?"

Mrs. Collins yanked the photograph from my hands and stuffed it back into the satchel. "That's not quite good enough. I need something else out of this bargain."

"But you'll still retain your customers," I said. "What else could you possibly want?"

"*More* customers, of course," she replied, those green eyes of hers glistening with mischief. "Here's my proposal, Mr. Clark. I'm going to join you in exposing the city's other mediums. Between the two of us, I'm certain we'll be able to spot every trick there is. Once all of the other mediums are run out of town, *I'll* be the one their formerly devoted customers turn to for all their spiritual needs."

I had to admire Mrs. Collins for coming up with such a brilliant plot, even as I feared her ruthlessness. Yet I knew I couldn't help her create a monopoly on the city's séances. My conscience just wouldn't allow it.

"Letting you off the hook for the sake of

this assignment is one thing," I said. "But letting you join me in an effort to ruin your competition is quite another. I won't allow it. Nor will my editor."

"I thought you would say that. Which is why I spent most of the night doing research about you, Mr. Clark."

"Research? Really? And what did you think you would find?"

"I kept wondering about how you knew so much about tricks and illusions. Your knowledge goes beyond that of a mere amateur, Mr. Clark, as you're well aware. Now, I know why. It's because of *this.*"

Mrs. Collins once again opened her satchel. This time, she pulled out a newspaper and, like the photograph, thrust it toward me. It was an issue of the *Philadelphia Times,* yellowed with age.

"FAMED MAGICIAN KILLS WIFE DURING SHOW," the headline said in big, bold letters. Below that, in only slightly smaller type, it read, "The Amazing Magellan apprehended for wife's stagebound death."

A seed of fear formed in my stomach. It quickly took root, expanding inside me and curling around my organs.

"You must have been very young when it happened," Mrs. Collins said.

I managed a single nod and a sputtered, "T-ten."

"A tragedy, really," Mrs. Collins continued.

"But the newspapers would have a field day knowing someone involved in that day was still alive and living right here in Philadelphia."

The fear in my gut gripped me fully then, so much so that I could scarcely breathe. Despite her earlier warning, it was clear I had underestimated Lucy Collins by miles. She had been absolutely correct — she was indeed capable of far worse than simply showing my photograph to mediums.

"Please," was all I could manage to say. My mouth was so dry with terror that my voice emerged as a croak. "This must remain a secret. At all costs."

"And it can," Mrs. Collins replied. "But first, you must agree to the partnership I proposed. Otherwise, everyone in this city will know about your past. They'll know, Mr. Clark, who you *really* are."

I despised her at that moment. Despised her as much as one could a veritable stranger. I wanted to tell Mrs. Collins to leave my house and to continue walking straight to hell.

I almost did, too. The only thing that stopped me was the thought of Violet and how she'd react when word got out about my true identity. She would be crushed, I knew. And I refused to cause her such pain if it was in any way avoidable.

In this case, it was.

I therefore had no other choice. If I went along with Mrs. Collins's plan, my secret could remain just that.

"Fine." I addressed the wall instead of Mrs. Collins, simply because I couldn't bear to look at her or the newspaper in front of me. "This evening, then. We'll visit the medium of your choice."

Mrs. Collins, a satisfied smile creeping across her face, snatched the newspaper and stuffed it back into her satchel.

"I thought you'd see it my way, Mr. Clark. I already have the perfect medium in mind. I'll stop by in my coach promptly at seven."

"Fine," I said again, having little energy to utter much else. "Good day, Mrs. Collins."

"And a very good day to you, Mr. Clark. I'll see myself out."

So she did, leaving the parlor without a backward glance and probably filching some of my more expensive knickknacks on her way to the door. I stayed seated, not caring one way or the other. I was too stunned to care about anything other than how her knowledge of my life had the potential to utterly ruin me.

Despite my agreement with Mrs. Collins, I knew that she wasn't to be trusted. I knew there might come a day when she'd break our pact, revealing everything.

What would I do if that happened?

I had two options, both equally disheartening. I could admit to everything and face the repercussions, however harsh they might be. Or I could flee the city, without warning or explanation, heading westward until I came to a place where no one had heard of the Amazing Magellan.

Yet this no longer affected just myself. I had Violet to think about now. Poor, innocent Violet, who had no idea what she was getting herself into when she agreed to marry me. Would she still love me if she learned the truth? Or would her family forbid our union and whisk her away? The thought of losing her filled me with dread.

The longer I remained in the parlor, the more I felt my past pulling at me like invisible ropes tied around my wrists and ankles. Eventually, the tug was so strong that I had to stand and move unsteadily out of the room. Too shaken and shamed to face either Lionel or Mrs. Patterson, I headed up the back steps, twisting my way to the fourth floor. It was always dark up there, so I grabbed a lamp along the way, letting it spring to life outside the door to the attic. Then, fortifying myself with a deep breath, I entered.

The attic felt, for lack of a better word, haunted. Everything up there was dark, dusty, and still. Each crumbling crate and dust-grayed trunk acted like a tombstone, marking the resting place of some memory or another.

100

Many of the items stored in that lightless space beneath the eaves once belonged to the previous owner. Collections of romantic poetry. Dusty instruments with broken strings. Silk dresses that had become feasts for moths. But there were a good many of my own possessions, as well — childish items I had outgrown decades ago. I was inundated with memories as I passed crates of adventure tales and toy soldiers and shells gathered during visits to the seashore. Soon I was at the rear of the attic, not only the darkest corner of the house, but the place where my blackest memories were stored.

It was there that I sat upon a chest of old clothes, raised my lamp and gazed at an object I hadn't viewed in years. It was a poster, propped against the wall and coated with an inch of dust. I wiped the grime away with my palm, revealing the image of a dashing man dressed in a black tuxedo and a cape lined with red silk. He held a silver hoop, through which a woman passed, floating on air.

The Amazing Magellan.

The floating woman was his equally amazing wife, Annalise.

And that poster was an advertisement for what ultimately became their final performance.

II

I'm going to assume that you've never heard of the Amazing Magellan.

The infamy of Magellan Holmes — his real name, by the way — has long faded. But for a time, he and Annalise were one of the most famous couples in the nation. Everyone knew their names.

On Independence Day in 1854, Magellan and Annalise took to the stage of the Walnut Street Theatre for what would be the thirteenth and final time. Anticipation for the performance had been building for weeks, with all of Philadelphia jostling for a seat. Tickets were being resold for ten times their worth. Confidence men made small fortunes hawking fake ones. Those who didn't have tickets attempted to sneak into the theater through back doors and upper windows. One woman was even caught trying to smuggle her husband inside the theater beneath her voluminous hoopskirt. Yet for each attempt that was foiled, another was successful, and by the time Magellan and Annalise stepped onto the stage, the crowd inside the theater was almost twice as large as seating allowed.

This, of course, was no ordinary performance. It was Magellan's return to his hometown of Philadelphia after three years spent traveling the globe. During his time away, he had performed for kings, czars, and maharajas, leaving each royal and dignitary he met awestruck by his singular illusions.

The longer he was away from home, the greater his legend grew. Rossetti painted him. Whitman wrote about him. Newspapers and periodicals at home and abroad detailed his every trick. No less a publication than *Scientific American* proposed that he be studied by physicians at Princeton University.

When he left Philadelphia, he was known simply as Magellan Holmes, magician. By the time he returned, he had been given a new, more flamboyant name — the Amazing Magellan.

While he was abroad, everyone, it seemed, had learned of his accomplishments. People spoke in awe about how he made the hats of the ladies in the audience float on their own accord and hopscotch around the theater, landing from head to head to head. How he caused the lovely Annalise to fly over the crowd, letting skeptics reach out to feel for hidden wires and lifts. How he could make objects levitate — heavy things that grew in proportion to his fame. Horses. Carriages. Elephants.

But that alone isn't what turned the good people of Philadelphia into hucksters and fools. From the moment his homecoming performance was announced, there was talk that the Amazing Magellan was planning his most jaw-dropping feat yet. Something that the audience had never seen before and would never forget.

To prevent even the slightest bit from being revealed, Magellan made sure this grand new trick required no stagehands in the wings. It would just be him and his wife. Together, they practiced for weeks, going over every aspect until it was, in his mind, the most perfect illusion ever devised.

The performance on that steaming Fourth of July began small, with the Amazing Magellan warming up the lucky audience with a few standard illusions. Pulling rabbits out of hats. Vanishing inside a wooden cabinet. Fiddling about with a twist of rope until it suddenly straightened and pointed upward on the tip of his finger. Soon, though, he went into the more amazing feats that had prompted his new name. The crowd greeted each one wildly, thrilling especially to the floating ladies' hats, which climaxed with dozens of them bouncing around the theater, and the levitating object, this time a hippopotamus.

But soon, the moment came for his brand-new illusion — the one the audience had been waiting for. The crowd watched with rapt attention as stagehands wheeled out a large tank made of glass on all four sides and filled with water. Standing at the edge of the tank, the Amazing Magellan was constricted in all manner of ways. Rope was wound around his arms and legs. His wrists were confined by iron manacles and fixed into place with a padlock. Chains heavy enough to tow a Pullman car were slung over his shoulders and crisscrossed his chest. Once he was soundly ensnared, the stagehands retreated to the back of the theater. Magellan Holmes then told the crowd that he was about to immerse himself in the water and have a red velvet curtain pulled around it for thirty seconds. About what was to happen after that, he would say no more.

The illusion was supposed to proceed in this manner: After Magellan dropped into the water like a two-ton rock, Annalise would stand in front of the tank and draw the curtain around them. Thirty seconds would pass, during which the audience neither saw nor heard a thing from the stage. When time was up, the Amazing Magellan would appear suddenly in one of the theater's box seats, as if he had been sitting there enjoying the show all along. He would then jump to the stage, open the curtain, and reveal Annalise inside the tank.

But that was only the first half of this two-act illusion. The second portion would involve the glass-walled tank rising five feet off the stage with nothing supporting it. Annalise, still submerged in water, would swim around the tank, as beautiful and transfixing as a mermaid. When the tank slowly returned to the stage, she would remain at the same height, swimming first in water, then in nothing but air.

It was an ingenious illusion — certainly one of the greatest ever devised. Unfortunately, it was never seen in its entirety.

Not on that steamy night in July.

Not ever, in fact.

The audience indeed saw the water-filled tank being wheeled onto the stage. They watched the Amazing Magellan remove his cape and tuxedo, revealing a purple bathing suit underneath. When he was being tied, chained, and otherwise weighted down, he stared at the crowd, the perspiration on his face brightened by the gaslights lining the stage's edge. Then the stagehands left and Magellan Holmes hopped into the water, sinking immediately. Standing at the bottom of the tank — eyes open, a triumphant smile playing across his lips — he nodded first to the audience, then to his wife. On cue, Annalise stood in front of the tank and pulled the curtain closed.

A deep hush fell over the theater as every man, woman, and child looked to the stage. Watching. Waiting.

A man in the third row opened his pocket watch and began to silently count the passage of time.

Five seconds.

The crowd leaned forward, listening intently. Was that a noise coming from the stage? A splash of water? A clank of chain?

Ten seconds.

A few stared at the red curtain until their eyes hurt, straining to see even the faintest rustle, of which there was none.

Fifteen seconds.

A man in the balcony coughed, startling those seated around him. A woman nearby, index finger pressed to her lips, turned to shush him.

Twenty seconds.

More sounds rose from the audience. Shiftings and tappings and the cracking of knuckles as nervous hands gripped armrests.

Twenty-five seconds.

All noise ceased once more as everyone began to hold their breath, bracing themselves for the incredible, the stupendous, the amazing.

Thirty seconds.

The man in the third row snapped his watch shut with a tinny *click* that echoed to the farthest reaches of the balcony. Onstage, the red velvet curtain remained closed.

When it stayed that way for several minutes, the mood of the audience shifted. Anticipation turned to boredom, which soon became discontent. It was only after a chorus of boos arose that a single stagehand approached the curtain and whipped it open.

There was a collective gasp as the audience

took in the gruesome sight displayed on that stage. A woman near the back screamed. Another fainted. Several men, so shocked by what they saw, stood and peered at the stage to make sure their eyes weren't playing tricks on them.

Onstage, Annalise Holmes was in the tank of water, floating lifelessly. One of the ropes that had once bound her husband was now drawn tightly around her throat. The Amazing Magellan was nowhere to be found.

More stagehands rushed from the back of the theater, bearing hammers and fire axes and sharpened bars of iron. They beat upon the tank until its glass resembled a hundred frozen cobwebs. When the tank wall facing the audience shattered, a cascade of water and glass shards rushed over the stage and into the crowd. Annalise was carried with it, flopping onto the stage like a fish tossed onto dry land. As the shocked and soaked patrons ran from the theater, a stagehand placed an ear against the water-slicked flesh over Annalise's heart, checking for signs of life. There weren't any.

While this was happening inside the theater, another drama was taking place directly outside it. News of the tragedy traveled instantly, being passed from an usher to a ticket taker to people passing on the street. Within minutes, the crowd rushing to the theater collided with those fleeing from it —

a conflagration of humanity that filled Walnut Street. To avoid running down pedestrians, carriages traveling the thoroughfare were forced to quickly stop, horses rearing, passengers jostled.

By the time the police finally arrived, the scene outside the theater had devolved into utter chaos. Panic seemingly spread like smallpox, hopping from one person to the next. Women shoved. Children fell into the muddy street. Men started to throw punches. And for a moment it seemed that the melee going on outdoors had eclipsed the very event that had prompted it.

That all changed, however, after a lone man entered the fray. When people saw him, they stopped their pushing, their yelling, their general unruliness. A hush spread through the crowd, radiating outward from the man like water into which a pebble had been dropped. Soon everyone on the street, just as they had done so in the theater, fell silent.

The man was the Amazing Magellan, reappearing at last.

The manacles around his wrists were gone. Police inspectors later found them behind the theater, just outside the stage door. The ropes, too, no longer bound him, although one snaked around his right ankle, trailing behind him. The chains, though, remained, weighing him down and digging into the skin of his shoulders until they were raw and bleeding.

Stumbling in a daze, his eyes unfocused, he cried out, "She's gone! My love is gone!"

When a group of policemen approached, he let himself be taken into custody. A new set of manacles was placed around his wrists and he was led to a waiting wagonette.

He was never seen in public again. The Amazing Magellan had, intentionally or not, pulled off his greatest trick.

He had vanished for good.

Since then, little is known about what really happened backstage at the Walnut Street Theatre. Because all the stagehands had been dismissed prior to that final illusion, there were no witnesses. Still, whispers persisted throughout the city that Magellan Holmes had grown unhappy in his marriage. Some said he had met another woman while overseas and wanted to begin a new life with her. The grand new illusion he had been working on was merely a ruse, designed to give him just enough time to strangle his wife and flee the theater.

These stories seemed to match official accounts by the police, who claimed to have proof of his plan in the form of the iron shackles found outside the stage door. They claimed two people in a nearby alleyway — a man and a prostitute, rumor had it — witnessed Magellan running past, yanking away the ropes tangled around his limbs. The only thing that kept him from getting away was the unexpected crowd in the area. They came from all points of the city, filling the streets and forcing Magellan to run first one way, then the other, until he was suddenly and unluckily back at the theater.

It came as no surprise to anyone when word got out that Magellan Holmes had confessed to the willful murder of his wife.

Many assumed he would hang for his crimes, but that day never came. The scuttlebutt around the city was that a stay of execution had been signed by President Franklin Pierce himself, an admirer of the magician since his performance at the White House. Yet others said he was spared the noose because the police wanted to prevent any embarrassment — they didn't know if it was possible to hang a man who could levitate. And so the Amazing Magellan was ordered to spend the rest of his days incarcerated at Eastern State Penitentiary, on the northwestern edge of Philadelphia.

Forgotten amid all this drama, like a lone card that had fallen out of a playing deck, was Columbus Holmes, the ten-year-old son of Magellan and Annalise. He had been by his parents' side during their trip around the world, seeing Paris and London, Munich and Rome. He had shaken hands with Czar Nicholas and bowed before Queen Victoria.

And he had been in the audience at the

Walnut Street Theatre on that infamous Fourth of July, witnessing the entire scene.

For a few months after the crime, his image was everywhere. People gazed upon newspaper illustrations of the dark-haired, serious-faced boy and wondered what would happen to him now that he was essentially an orphan. But as Magellan Holmes sat in prison and the entire incident became a distant memory, no one attempted to find out more.

If one were to bother, it could be discovered that Columbus Holmes was sent to stay with his only living relative — his father's maiden aunt in Buffalo. Not wanting to be reminded of her shamed nephew or his crime, she, in turn, shipped Columbus off to an elite all-boys school in New England, where he became an outcast among his classmates.

When that cold and unloving aunt died, Columbus returned to the house in Buffalo only long enough to sell it and most of the possessions contained within its walls. By then, the War Between the States had broken out, and he enlisted in the Union Army, succumbing to dysentery before ever seeing battle. Because there was no one left to receive his body, he was buried in an unmarked grave somewhere in the foothills of Virginia.

The lineage of Magellan Holmes ended there.

But a strange thing happened to Columbus

Holmes during his final days on earth. In a bustling and chaotic field hospital, he was placed beside another sick young man of the same age, also without any relatives. When dysentery claimed the life of that soldier, a harried and war-weary doctor misidentified the young man, confusing him with Columbus. It was, truth be told, an easy mistake to make. The field hospital contained a great many sick and dying men, with little in the way of identification, and the two ill soldiers did bear a slight resemblance to each other, which their unshaven faces made all the more prominent.

Delirious with fever and on the verge of death himself, Columbus Holmes nevertheless sensed an opportunity in the doctor's error. Since the death of his mother, he had longed to change identities, to be known as anything other than the son of the infamous Magellan Holmes.

This was his chance.

So when he heard that confused doctor misidentify the dead soldier lying next to him, Columbus chose not to correct him. Nor did he say anything when two men carted away the corpse that suddenly bore his name. When someone else arrived to discard the young man's things, Columbus handed him his own meager possessions.

As the days passed and Columbus regained his health, he expected someone in that field hospital to realize the mistake that had been made. But it was a crowded, disease-ridden place, with more wounded arriving every day. No one noticed that the sickly young man once known as Columbus was answering to a new name.

Once he had fully recovered, the former Columbus Holmes walked away from the field hospital a new man. He was assigned to a new unit — his old one having long moved on — and earned the trust of his comrades. He marched with them into battle and fought bravely by their side. At war's end, he followed one of his new friends back to Philadelphia, where he bought a house, got a job, and began a new life, all using the name of a soldier who lay buried in the Virginia soil.

That poor dead soldier's name was Edward Clark.

Now it is mine.

III

Later that evening, I found myself riding in Mrs. Collins's impressive coach. To where, I did not know. The streets were filled with people from all walks of life emerging outdoors to enjoy the crisp spring air. Couples on their way to dinner strolled arm in arm down the crowded sidewalk, passing a lone lamplighter who paused every few steps to brighten the quickening dusk. If those along the street happened to peek into the windows of the coach, they probably would have assumed Mrs. Collins and I were just like them. A happy couple heading out for an enjoyable evening of food, drink, and entertainment. If they had looked closer, though, they would have seen Mrs. Collins and I sitting a good deal apart. Those who were particularly observant might have also noticed the ruthless gleam in her eyes and the panic in my own.

Also making me nervous was her brother, Thomas, who happened to be our coachman for the evening. I would have preferred someone older than ten at the reins of a pair of Cleveland Bays, which looked strong enough to drag us all the way to Ohio if they had a mind to. Yet up top he sat, cap askew and a wad of chewing tobacco wedged in his cheek. On the bright side, his perch kept him out of earshot, which allowed me to speak freely.

"How did you learn who I was?" I asked Mrs. Collins.

She waved the question away as if it were a pesky mosquito. "If you're concerned that I'm going to start telling others, don't be. Simply carry on with the plan and your secret is safe with me."

"But I must know. If you found out without much effort, then others can as well."

"I assure you that I learned of it quite accidentally," Mrs. Collins said.

"From whom?"

At this, she offered a sly smile. "From *you,* naturally."

"I told you no such thing!"

"Not in words," Mrs. Collins said. "But the expression that was on your face told me everything I needed to know."

I thought back to earlier that day, and how I had reacted to seeing the newspaper article about my mother's death and my father's arrest. My shock had been so great that I never bothered to deny Mrs. Collins's claim. I simply assumed she somehow knew I was the son of Magellan Holmes. But that clearly hadn't been the case.

"You tricked me into admitting the truth," I said, disbelief heavy in my voice.

" 'Trick' is such a strong word," Mrs. Collins replied. "I merely baited the hook. You chomped down on it all on your own."

"So you had no idea about my true identity?"

"I had a *suspicion,*" she said. "As I mentioned earlier, I knew you had to be a magician, a medium, or someone closely acquainted with one. You knew too many tricks of the trade. So this morning, I visited a few of the newspaper offices in the city."

I found myself hoping that *my* newspaper hadn't been one of them.

"Of course I didn't go to the *Bulletin,*" Mrs.

116

Collins was quick to add. "They're the ones who sent you to me, after all, and would have been very unhelpful. But the others were quite accommodating when I asked about notable magicians in the city. A gentleman at the *Times* produced a box full of articles about Philadelphia's famed magicians. Among them was one about the Amazing Magellan's arrest. It included an illustration of his son. A son who would be around the same age you are now. One who, as it would happen, bore a slight resemblance to you."

"And you recognized me from that?"

"No," Mrs. Collins said. "You look far different now, of course. But there was enough of a resemblance for me to make an assumption about your identity. Lucky for me, that assumption was correct."

"So if I had denied everything, you would have then left me alone?" I asked.

"Hardly. I would have found another way to get you to do my bidding. I'm quite good at that, as you'll soon learn."

"I think I already have."

"What I don't understand," Mrs. Collins said, "is why you changed your identity in the first place. Certainly no one would think any less of you because of what your father did."

Ah, but here she was wrong. People *would* think less of me. I knew because they had done so in the past. My father's aunt, for one, had wanted nothing to do with me. The school she had banished me to was even worse. Boys can be cruel to begin with. Put the son of a confessed murderer in their midst and they'll become absolutely savage.

I'm ashamed to admit that I joined the army not out of a strong desire to keep the union whole, but to be among men who might not know who I was and would therefore have no reason to pass judgment. But anonymity wasn't enough. I wanted to rid myself not only of my father's deeds, but his name as well. I couldn't bear to be Columbus Holmes, a name I had always disliked. It was too ornate, too showy. I longed to be a David or a Franklin. A name that blended easily into a crowd. A name that wasn't associated with the death of my mother. So when the opportunity to acquire a new one presented itself, I grabbed it without hesitation.

"People will always judge," I told Mrs. Collins. "The sins of the father always reflect poorly on the son."

"Speaking of your father, what does *he* think about this change of identity?"

"He doesn't know," I said. "I haven't seen Magellan Holmes since the day he was arrested. The night my mother died, he became dead to me as well. Now please, Mrs. Collins, if you don't mind, I don't want to discuss this any further."

"Then I won't bring it up again," she

replied. "Except to say that, since I know your real name, I'll allow you to start using mine. Please call me Lucy. Mrs. Collins sounds like someone who's nearing seventy."

"But wouldn't the use of our first names imply a familiarity with each other?"

She blinked at me demurely and asked, "Are you saying you *want* to be familiar with me, Edward?"

"Hardly," I said. "Which is why I wish to be addressed as Mr. Clark."

"Wish all you'd like, *Edward.* But seeing that we're going to be spending plenty of time together, we might as well become better acquainted."

I crossed my arms over my chest and expressed my displeasure with a huff. While I had the urge to throw open the coach door and jump into the street, I knew such an act would prove useless. Any escape I made would only be temporary. Lucy Collins, I was certain, would surely track me down again. There was no way around the fact that I was, for the moment, trapped.

"Fine," I said. "So tell me, *Lucy,* what made you turn to Spiritualism as a way to earn a living?"

"Desperation." Lucy Collins gazed out the coach window, her face the very picture of stoicism. "There aren't many opportunities for women like myself. Marriage is considered the easiest way to keep a roof over your head and food in your stomach, although it's more like indentured servitude, if you ask me."

"It sounds like finding another husband isn't high on your list of priorities."

"I would prefer to be hanged than endure another marriage. I'm perfectly happy in my current situation."

"Deceiving people," I said.

"*Helping* them," Lucy replied. "And for your information, what I do is far more difficult than you think. Customers arrive with different needs. My task is to understand what those needs are and then fulfill them. It's hard to keep up."

I furrowed my brow. "Keep up with what?"

"The latest tricks, of course. If one so-called medium devises a new way of doing things, it soon becomes expected of every medium. Those bells on the table, for instance. They were the invention of Norma Workman, a medium in Boston. They proved so popular that soon every medium in Boston and beyond had them, lest their customers think they were charlatans."

"But you *are* charlatans," I reminded her.

Lucy continued as if I hadn't said a word. "It was the same way with spirit guides. When I first started, no medium had a spirit guide. They just got on with the séance and no one was any the wiser. But when a medium right here in Philadelphia claimed to have a spirit guide that could connect her to the other side, well, then everyone needed one. First, it was in vogue to have young children as spirit guides."

"Morbid," I said.

Lucy nodded. "But popular. Especially with mothers. When that got old, someone concocted an Indian guide. Soon everyone had to have one of those as well."

"And thus, White Sparrow was born?"

"Indeed," Lucy said with a wicked smile. "And she has been quite lucrative for me."

"So, who is this Philadelphia medium to blame for all the spirit guides?"

Lucy's grin widened until she resembled a cat that had just wholly consumed the proverbial canary. "Why, the very one we're visiting tonight. Mrs. Lenora Grimes Pastor."

The name required no further explanation on Lucy's part. Mrs. Pastor's reputation loomed so large throughout the city that even I had heard of her. I wasn't surprised in the least that Lucy had chosen her biggest rival as our first target. She was nothing if not enterprising.

There were a great many convincing mediums in Philadelphia and beyond. What made Mrs. Pastor so unusual was the ardent devotion of her admirers. Those who had sat with her swore she was directly connected to the Great Beyond. When she fell into one of her trances, they said, voices that weren't hers emerged from her mouth, speaking truths that she couldn't possibly have known.

It was nothing but mimicry, of course. Yet Mrs. Pastor was a fine enough mimic to have some of her grandest exploits written about in the newspapers. A trip to Illinois a few years prior had generated many headlines, mostly due to the fact that she was there to conduct a séance at the request of Mary Todd Lincoln. Those who attended were convinced beyond a doubt that the voice of President Lincoln himself had emerged from beyond the grave and through her tiny frame.

Because of her notoriety, I wasn't surprised to see that the Pastor residence was located near Fairmount Park, in the well-to-do western edge of the city. What did surprise me, however, was the exact address of the home. Instead of residing in one of the mansions that encroached on the northern end of the park, the Pastors had chosen to live on Taylor Street, an inconsequential lane in the shadow of the hilltop reservoir at the park's southern tip. When Thomas drew the coach to a stop, I saw a narrow three-story structure as modest as it was sensible. It certainly didn't look like the residence of Philadelphia's most famous medium. I had expected something more extravagant, similar to the mansions along Girard Avenue. Compared with those behemoths, Mrs. Pastor's home looked like a shack.

"We're here!" Thomas yelled down to us.

"Get out while the gettin's good."

I exited the carriage first, holding the door for Lucy.

"Thank you, Thomas," she said.

"Yes," I added absently. "Many thanks."

Thomas spat at me, the dollop of tobacco juice landing next to my foot. I glared first at the boy and then looked to his sister. Lucy, either ignorant of his actions or simply unconcerned with them, headed promptly toward the house.

That evening, Taylor Street was a model of calm and quiet. The only noise came from the northeast in the form of the Pennsylvania Avenue trolley, and the only other sign of life was a male pedestrian in the distance, approaching from the opposite direction.

"Are you to be Mr. Green again this evening?" Lucy asked as I joined her on the sidewalk.

"I suppose. The name worked well enough last night."

She looped her arm through mine. "Then I shall be your wife, Edith. Childhood sweethearts, we've been married for a decade and remain madly in love."

"That will be hard for me to pull off," I said. "I'm a reporter, not a thespian."

"Then what shall our story be?" Lucy asked.

"It was an arranged marriage that has yet to be consummated because I find myself miserable in your company."

Lucy shook her head and said, "While certainly accurate, I'm afraid no one would believe that for a moment."

"Why not?"

"Because," she replied, "few men can resist my charms."

"Count me among the lucky few."

"Come now, Edward," Lucy purred. "Don't you find me even the slightest bit charming?"

"Charming like a snake."

"I'll just have to try harder." She tightened her arm around my own until she was pressed right against me. "Now, Mr. Green, are you ready to attend a séance?"

I tried to once again get into the mind-set of being another person. Speaking from past experience, it wasn't easy. In the first few weeks of being Edward Clark, I sometimes found myself not responding when being addressed. The same had almost happened the night before, when I was pretending to be Mr. Green. Since I was in the midst of keeping track of several identities, I could be forgiven for being momentarily confused when I heard a familiar voice call out to me.

"*Edward?* Is that you?"

I turned to see a bedraggled Jasper Willoughby slouching up the sidewalk toward us. My future brother-in-law looked no more alert than the last time I had laid eyes on him.

"Jasper," I said, quickly yanking my arm from Lucy's grip. "This is quite the surprise. What brings you to this side of the river?"

"It's a lovely evening. Perfect for a stroll in the park. And what are you doing in this part of town?"

Jasper briefly eyed Mrs. Pastor's place with a mixture of regret and what could only be described as annoyance. But then his gaze — aflame with curiosity — settled on Lucy Collins, and a whole new concern revealed itself.

"And who might this be?" he asked, innuendo thick in his voice.

"This is Mrs. Lucy Collins. She's —" I found myself at a loss for words. She certainly wasn't a friend, but telling Jasper she was the woman blackmailing me into helping her ruin her rivals wasn't the best introduction, either. Lucy, fortunately, interjected.

"I'm assisting Mr. Clark with his assignment this evening."

"Assignment?" Jasper said. "Has there been a murder, Edward?"

"We're about to attend a séance here. Part of that scheme by my editor that I mentioned at lunch yesterday."

"But I thought you despised the idea."

"I do," I said. "Sadly, I have no choice in the matter."

After that, there seemed to be nothing left to say. A rope of distrust hung between Jasper and me, invisible yet keenly felt. We stared at each other a moment, each of us wondering what the other was really up to. Our silence was broken only by Lucy, who extended a hand and said, "And you are?"

"Jasper. Jasper Willoughby."

"Of Willoughby Hats?"

Jasper gave a half nod, vaguely annoyed to be recognized in such a manner. "That's correct."

"And how do you know Mr. Clark?"

"He's engaged to my sister."

The mention of a fiancée prompted Lucy to mischievously arch an eyebrow. It was yet another piece of knowledge she could use against me, if she so desired. "That's fascinating."

"Is it?" Jasper asked, now with confusion added to his suspicion.

"Mr. Clark rarely speaks about his fiancée," Lucy said. "But I'm sure she's lovely."

"She is," I said, speaking to Lucy but looking directly at Jasper. "I adore her."

My message was none too subtle, but I wanted to make it clear to the youngest Willoughby that I was not stepping out with another woman behind Violet's back. It seemed like he believed me. At least I hoped so.

"Well, I suppose we all should be going our separate ways," Jasper said, giving another of his not-quite nods. "Enjoy your séance . . . if such a thing is possible."

Lucy waved good-bye to him, saying, "You can, and we most certainly will."

Once Jasper fully vanished from view, Lucy let out a low, impressed whistle that made her sound more like a sailor than a widow.

"So Edward Clark is engaged! No wonder you're resistant to my charms."

"I'm resistant because there's nothing charming about you."

Lucy ignored the slight, instead offering me a sly grin. "And your fiancée is a Willoughby, to boot. I never pegged you as a social climber, Edward. How much do you think the family's worth?"

"I don't know and I don't care. And they're off-limits to you. All of them."

"I suppose I can leave one wealthy family alone," Lucy said. "It's not as if I'll be lacking customers once all this is through. Besides, I understand wanting to keep a wealthy mark all to yourself."

"*Mark?* If you're implying that I'm a common con artist, then you're sorely mistaken."

"Of course," Lucy replied as she slipped her arm through mine again. "I'm sure Miss Willoughby knows all about Columbus Holmes."

I offered no reply, letting her draw her own conclusion.

"That's what I thought," she said.

"The situation is more complicated than

that," I said. "Yes, I'm withholding the truth, but my engagement to Miss Willoughby is in no way a con."

By that point, we had reached the door to the Pastor residence. And while I wanted nothing more than to go inside and get this miserable task over with, Lucy stopped me before I got the chance.

"We're more alike than you think, Edward," she said. "You don't see it now, but someday you will. And the sooner you do, the better we'll get along."

With that, Lucy Collins took a deep breath and gave the front door a hearty rap.

IV

When the door opened, it revealed one of the most imposing men I had ever seen. Standing a shade over six feet, he was built like an ancient oak — wide and solid. His skin was the color of blackstrap molasses, contrasting starkly with the whiteness of his shirtfront.

"You both here to sit with Missus Pastor?" he asked in a deep, unhurried voice.

"We are," I said, feeling miniscule in his presence. "Unless there's no room for us tonight."

The man flashed us a reassuring smile. "Here there's always room. Missus Pastor don't turn no one away."

The door widened more and we stepped

into a foyer. Again, it was more modest than I was expecting. The walls were white, the floor was unvarnished, and the only furniture to speak of was a plain wooden rack for our coats and hats.

"Missus Pastor is in here," the man said, pointing out a sitting room to our left. "She's about to start, so you best jump in and grab a chair."

The sitting room was noticeably less stark than the foyer. The walls there were still white and unadorned, but a surprising amount of furniture cluttered the floor. Small tables had been placed everywhere, each bearing several oil lamps that cast a warm glow over the premises. Scattered on top of the tables and around the floor were musical instruments of every shape and size. I noticed a harp as tall as myself sitting in a corner, as well as smaller pieces like drums, fiddles, and a bugle placed upright on its bell.

In the center of the room was a half circle of wooden chairs built more for function than form. Four of them were already taken. An older man and a noticeably younger woman sat beside each other, he in a formal gray suit, she dressed resplendently in a satin gown of deep purple. Seated a chair away was another woman, shrouded in a black dress. A parted black veil, hanging from a bonnet of the same color, swept her shoulders.

The chair closest to us was occupied by

another gentleman. He possessed a face that looked as if it had been carved from a potato, and his hair circled the back of his scalp like a crown of laurels. He seemed exceedingly familiar to me, although I didn't know how.

Lucy Collins, naturally, knew exactly who he was.

"That's Mr. Barnum," she whispered.

"P. T. Barnum?" I whispered back. "The showman?"

"The very one."

"I wonder what he's doing here."

"All I know is that, before the evening is through, he'll be looking for a new medium."

Lucy sat down beside him and touched his arm. "Pardon me, but you're Mr. Barnum, are you not?"

"No names, please."

This was spoken by a tiny woman propped up in an upholstered armchair twice her size. She was so small that her black muslin dress appeared to be swallowing her whole. Her graying hair, kept in place by a black bonnet, only furthered the impression that she was a mere child dressed up as an adult. While her face was doughy and the very definition of plain, there was an unnerving keenness to her eyes. They were friendly yet stern at the same time, like an instructor's when you knew you were his favorite pupil. I had no doubt that this was the famous Lenora Grimes Pastor.

Beside her was a man dressed in a severe black suit that, in contrast to Mrs. Pastor's oversize dress, was several sizes too small for him and his bulging stomach. The watch chain leading from his waist to his jacket pocket stretched to the breaking point when he turned to Lucy and me.

"My wife prefers to make introductions at the *end* of the séance," he said, a Southern accent sweetening his voice. "Lest anyone doubt the spirits who may later make themselves known."

Mrs. Pastor looked my way, her voice far friendlier than that of her husband. "You may stand, if you wish, but I suspect you'll be more comfortable in a chair like the others."

I quickly took a seat between Lucy and the mourning woman in black. I couldn't agree that it was any better than being on my feet — the chair's construction offered little in the way of comfort — but Mrs. Pastor nodded approvingly.

"Now that all the chairs are occupied," Mr. Pastor said, "perhaps it's time to begin."

His wife spoke up. "I think some refreshment is called for, don't you, Robert? I, for one, would adore a lemonade. Stokely, would you mind sending Claudia in with cups for everyone?"

The tall dark man, who had been standing by the doorway, nodded. "I'll go on and do that right now, Missus Pastor."

His departure gave the medium a chance to survey the small group gathered in her sitting room. She smiled, seeming genuinely pleased that we had all come to see her. I would have believed it, too, if I hadn't known better. I was certain that everything Mrs. Pastor said and did was completely rehearsed. Every word. Every gesture. The goal was to get those of us present to believe that what we were about to witness was real — and then to pay accordingly.

"I see two new faces," she said, obviously referring to Lucy and me. "Do you have any questions before we start?"

I meekly raised my hand. "Only about payment."

"Sir, my wife doesn't accept payment for her services," Mr. Pastor said, a touch of resignation in his voice. "But if you wish to contribute when we're finished, Stokely will come around with a donation box."

"I feel it's a sin to profit from the gift God has given me," Mrs. Pastor added while shooting a stern look in Mr. Barnum's direction. "But I also understand the desire to make payment for services rendered, such as they are. Hence the donation box. All monies collected will be donated to the Quaker school currently being built in Germantown. Your generosity will be most appreciated."

Of course, I knew that nothing would go to the creation of this school, which was most likely a complete fabrication. They were merely preying on innate human kindness. By pretending not to accept payment, the Pastors in all probability collected even more. It was a brilliant move, one that I was certain Lucy Collins would note and use in the future.

A servant girl entered the room bearing a tray full of silver cups. She made her way first to the Pastors, where a narrow table stretched in front of their chairs. She placed a cup in front of Mrs. Pastor before letting Mr. Pastor take one. The others chose cups from the tray and placed them on nearby side tables. In the case of Lucy and me, there was nothing available, forcing us to hold the cold, sweating silver.

"Thank you, Claudia," Mrs. Pastor said. "Please tell Stokely that we're about to begin and that there should be no further interruptions. And be sure to lock the door on your way out."

"Is that necessary?" I asked.

"Quite," Mrs. Pastor said.

"It helps us avoid interruptions," Mr. Pastor explained. "We don't want anyone barging in and waking Mrs. Pastor from her trance. It could be quite dangerous."

The servant girl left the room, and I got a better look at her as she passed. She was a mousy young thing, with a slender frame and long auburn hair that hung down her back in a thick braid. She appeared nervous, as if afraid of the spirits that Mrs. Pastor planned to summon. I assumed it was yet another part of the show. Quite honestly, it wouldn't have surprised me to learn that the girl practiced her worried glances in the mirror each night.

Once she had closed the door behind her, I heard the sound of a key being slid into place, followed by a light click. We were all now locked in.

Mrs. Pastor took a sip of lemonade and settled back in her chair. She crossed her arms over her chest and closed her eyes.

"It is time to begin," Mr. Pastor said. "In a few moments, my wife will enter a trance. When she next speaks, it will be the voice of her spirit guide."

I felt the sharp poke of an elbow against my arm. It came from Lucy, who gave me an *I-told-you-so* glance.

"During that time, no one should address my wife directly," Mr. Pastor continued. "If her name is uttered, the trance, and her connection to the spirit realm, may be broken."

"May we speak at all?" I asked.

"You may. And if a spirit using my wife as a vessel addresses you, feel free to engage it in conversation. That is, after all, why you are here. Are there any further questions?"

Lucy piped up with one. "Shouldn't we turn off the lamps? Doesn't the room need to be darkened?"

"There's no need for that," Mr. Pastor said. "My wife prefers it if the room is well lit."

As did Lucy and I, for it made our task there easier. If there was going to be trickery taking place, the light would make it far more difficult to convincingly pull off.

Mr. Pastor picked up a tambourine that had been propped against a leg of his chair. "Now, let us begin."

He held the tambourine in front of his wife, shaking it until it sounded like a slab of bacon tossed onto a hot pan. Using an open palm, he struck the center of the instrument one, two, three times. Then he set the tambourine down on the table in front of him.

All eyes were on Mrs. Pastor, who remained reclined in the chair, her head now lolled backward. With her eyes closed tight, she didn't move or appear to be conscious.

"She's entering her trance," Mr. Pastor assured us. "Soon, the spirits will show themselves."

He was wrong on that matter. A great deal of time passed where the only activity consisted of watching Mrs. Pastor seemingly nap in her chair. According to my watch, this lasted for ten minutes or so, during which a general restlessness descended upon the room. The mood was personified best by Mr. Barnum, who looked to the ceiling before letting out a languid sigh.

"It's taking quite a bit longer tonight," the

woman dressed in black said to no one in particular.

"It is indeed," Mr. Pastor replied.

"I wonder why that is," the woman in black mused. "I so hope it's because she's traveling a great distance to reach Gerald. The Orient is so far away."

Another ten minutes passed without anything happening. Finally, we heard a noise directly in front of Mrs. Pastor. Once more, the sound of frying bacon filled the room.

It was the tambourine being shaken again. Only this time, no one was touching it; both of Mr. Pastor's hands rested on the arm of his chair. Still, the tambourine continued to move, rattling against the table's surface.

"That's most likely Philip," Mr. Pastor said. "He is my wife's young spirit guide. Philip, is that you?"

Without warning, the tambourine rose into the air, producing gasps from the others. I, however, dismissed the floating instrument as an illusion, for that was the only explanation. It was being lifted by a thin wire, no doubt by someone hidden upstairs manipulating the instrument through a small hole in the ceiling.

The instrument's shaking was accompanied by the voice of a young boy, which said, *"Am I alone?"*

I immediately checked my surroundings, searching for the little boy hidden, like Lucy's brother Thomas, somewhere in the room. Only there appeared to be no place to hide. The room contained only one door, the locked one that led to the entrance hall. The walls looked completely flat and solid, betraying no sign of a hidden antechamber. The floors and ceiling, too, appeared the same way. If there was a child hidden somewhere, he needed to be extremely small and exceptionally good at disguising himself.

My gaze moved to Lenora Grimes Pastor. While she looked to be sleeping, I noticed her lips moving as the boy's voice said, *"Hello? Is there someone else there?"*

The voice, I realized, was coming from Mrs. Pastor herself. Only that was impossible. I had heard her speak, and the voice escaping her lips sounded nothing like the one she had used earlier. Of course, she could have been a talented mimic, able to change her voice at will. But there was something about the sound of this boy that made me think otherwise. There was a distance to it, as if he was using a tin can to amplify the sound.

"Philip," Mr. Pastor said. "It's good to hear your voice again."

"Who am I speaking to?"

"It's Robert Pastor, son."

"Hello, Mr. Pastor. Are you alone?"

"No, my boy. There are friends here. A gathering of friends who would most enjoy hearing from *your* friends. Are any of them present?"

"There are, Mr. Pastor. Many of them."

"Then tell them to show themselves."

Noises began to drift out of the other instruments scattered around the room. It began with a few invisible plucks of the harp and was soon followed by clanks, toots, and bleats from everything else. Their sounds swelled into a discordant song that filled the air.

Then, to my astonishment, all of them joined the tambourine in flight. A cowbell sitting next to my chair suddenly rose to the level of my shoulders. Unlike the bells at Lucy's séance, this one wasn't encased in glass nor was it attached to a string. I ran my hand all around it, feeling nothing that could have kept it suspended.

Lucy, watching my examination, gave me a wide-eyed stare. "How is she doing this?" she whispered.

I shrugged, also dumbfounded. "I have no idea."

By that point, all the room's instruments were spinning about, still being played by invisible hands. Mr. Barnum looked amazed to see a violin, bow scraping along the strings, hover before him. A drum floated behind Mrs. Pastor's chair, a pair of sticks thrumming a steady rhythm. Even the harp, which must have weighed as much as two men, rocked back and forth in midair, its strings quivering out an aimless tune.

Then the noise stopped, just as suddenly as it had begun. The instruments, however, remained unencumbered by gravity. They drifted around the room in silence as the voice of Philip piped up again.

"Do you see them?" he asked.

"We do, Philip," Mr. Pastor replied. "Well done. Now, do any spirits wish to address someone in this room?"

"Yes," Philip said. *"I'll fetch one. Good-bye, Mr. Pastor."*

Then he was gone. I could feel it, although I was at a loss to explain how or why. It was as if someone had closed an open window, shutting out a cooling breeze. Within seconds, however, a new presence entered the room. A different window had been opened.

Mrs. Pastor stirred in her chair, and for a moment I thought she was going to emerge from her trance. Instead, her head shifted to the left. When she opened her mouth, a different voice came out of it.

"Has someone called upon me?"

Hearing the voice, the woman in purple satin straightened in her chair. "Henrietta? Is that you, darling?"

"Leslie?" the voice said. *"Have you paid me another visit?"*

"I have, my dear sister. How good it is to hear your voice again."

139

I spent the next several minutes listening to the two women — one alive, the other very much dead — conversing as if they hadn't been separated by mortality. From their exchange, I gathered that Leslie, the woman in purple, had lost her younger sister several years earlier and that the two had been very close. For the most part, they discussed other family members that had moved on to the hereafter. (*"Mother and Father are doing wonderfully,"* Henrietta assured her sister. *"They long to see you again."*) Despite the undoubtedly strange circumstance in which it was taking place, the conversation verged on the tedious. I was beginning to feel like a stranger seated between two old friends at a dinner party when, from out of nowhere, the spirit of Henrietta said, *"Is your husband with you?"*

"Eldridge? He's right here."

The woman rested a hand on the arm of the gray-suited man beside her. Her husband shifted in his seat, clearly uncomfortable at being mentioned by someone no longer alive.

"I do so wish you were alone," Henrietta said. *"I have something of dire importance to tell you."*

"Then by all means, reveal it."

There was no immediate response in return. The woman in purple leaned forward, the satin of her gown rustling in the newfound silence. "Henrietta? Are you still there?"

"*I am,*" was the spirit's response. *"But not for much longer."*

"Please tell me what's so important."

"I can't. Not with your husband present."

"Retta, please." Leslie was standing now, speaking directly to the motionless form of Mrs. Pastor. "You must."

"Do you trust Eldridge?" her sister's spirit asked.

The woman nodded. "Implicitly."

"Don't."

That was Henrietta's last word before she left. As with Philip, I got that same sense of a window being slammed shut. The woman in purple, this poor Leslie so desperate to speak to her sister, felt it, too.

"Henrietta?" she called out. "Are you still there?"

No response emerged from the still-sleeping form of Lenora Grimes Pastor. Yet the woman continued to call out her sister's name, each utterance weaker than the last.

"Henrietta? Retta? Please come back, Retta. You must tell me more."

Finally, the woman in purple sank slowly into her chair. Her husband, the one allegedly not to be trusted, tried to comfort her. Twisting away from his grasp, the woman covered her face and began to weep. Already, it appeared, she was taking her dead sister's words to heart.

Another silence followed, in which the only

sounds that could be heard were the muffled sobs of the woman in purple and the floating instruments as they bumped off the ceiling and brushed against the walls. It was soon broken by the voice of young Philip.

"Hello? Mr. Pastor?"

"Yes, Philip."

"There's someone here," the boy said. *"Someone who would like very much to address a woman in your party."*

The woman dressed in black perked up in her chair. "Gerald? Is his name Gerald?"

"No, ma'am," young Philip replied. *"He frightens me, Mr. Pastor. I don't want to let him speak."*

"You don't have to, Philip. As my wife's spirit guide, you're not required to do anything you don't want to."

"I might not have a choice, sir." The boy's voice contained a palpable fear that sent shivers rushing across my body. *"He says . . . he says he intends to hurt me if I don't. Please don't let him hurt me, Mr. Pastor. Please!"*

A strong, ice-cold breeze swept through the room. It felt exactly like the January wind that sometimes whipped off the frozen Delaware. I ran my hands up and down my arms in an attempt to warm myself. Others, I saw, were doing the same. Even Mr. Pastor had taken notice. He looked around the room with wide, frightened eyes, an act that produced a great deal of unease.

Mrs. Pastor began to thrash in her chair as a new voice — male this time — emerged from her mouth. Only "emerge" isn't the best way to describe it — it was more like a burst of sound, filling the room and shaking the instruments as they swirled all around us.

"Jenny Boyd!" it roared.

Next to me, Lucy Collins gasped. The silver cup she had been holding dropped from her hands and clanged onto the floor, splashing lemonade on her shoes and dress. She paid it no mind.

"It's me, Jenny," the voice intoned. *"Declan. Don't say you've forgotten me, because I know you haven't."*

Lucy's eyes were closed and her lips were moving, mouthing something I couldn't hear. I looked to her hands, which contained a string of rosary beads. I hadn't a clue as to where they had come from. Hidden in the folds of her dress, presumably. But now they rattled in her hands as her thumbs rolled over the wooden pearls.

"I know you're there, dolly," the voice continued. *"You can't hide from old Declan. No matter how many names you use or cities you run to. You know I'll find you."*

I heard an intake of air, as if this Declan person was inhaling deeply. He sounded like a man who studied flora relishing the scent

143

of a beloved flower.

"I smell you, Jenny," he hissed. *"That's how I know it's you. You smell the same way you did the night I died. When you killed me."*

Lucy let go of the rosary, dropping it into the puddle of lemonade at her feet. Her hands now free, she used them to cover her ears.

"Make it stop!" she shouted. "For God's sake, someone make it stop!"

Her outburst, it seemed, was strong enough to silence the voice coming from Mrs. Pastor, for we heard it no more. In addition, the bitter cold dispersed with it. In its place was comforting warmth that seeped into the room, as if the entire house was being slowly submerged into a steaming bath. While a bit of the previous chill lingered at the base of my spine, I found myself soothed by this newfound heat.

"Hello?"

It was yet another voice, softly exhaling from Mrs. Pastor's lips. A woman's voice, as gentle as the warmth that had been brought with it.

Only hearing it provided me with no comfort. Another shiver entered my body, far more violent than the previous ones. It made me start to tremble uncontrollably.

I let out a strangled cry of surprise, which made Lucy take a moment out of recovering from her own bout of fear to notice mine.

144

"Edward," she whispered. "What's the matter?"

The shivering prevented me from speaking. Even if I had been able to talk, I doubt I could have explained my dread. The fear was so great that it seemed to take control of my bones, rattling them.

For it wasn't just any voice emanating from somewhere deep inside Mrs. Lenora Grimes Pastor.

It was, you see, the voice of my mother.

V

Although fifteen years had passed since I'd last heard Annalise Holmes speak, I recognized her voice at once. How could I not? I had spent the first ten years of my life listening to it. It was the voice that had pointed out the Arc de Triomphe to me in Paris and gently encouraged me to ride an elephant in Bombay. It was the voice that woke me in the mornings and lullabied me to sleep at night.

Logic would dictate that hearing it again after so long an absence would have filled me with a sense of joy and wonder. It's common, for example, to hear someone who has just lost a loved one say, *"If only I could hear their voice one last time."* But there was nothing logical about the situation. It was strange, unexpected, and unknown, and I responded accordingly — with fear.

145

All the while, the voice of my mother continued to emerge from someone who wasn't her.

"Columbus," it said. *"You are there, aren't you, my dear, sweet boy? Tell me that you are."*

I swallowed and tried to speak, but it was more difficult than you can imagine. My throat was so dry it felt as if I had just swallowed a bucket of sand. My voice, when it finally did emerge, was a hoarse, scratching sound.

"Mother," I said.

"Columbus, it is *you!"* There was joy in my mother's voice. Joy that I wished I had shared. But I was still too terrified to take any pleasure from our conversation. *"My boy, my sweet boy, how I've missed you."*

"I've missed you, too," I said. "So very much."

"I know, dear Columbus. I know."

The more she spoke, the more my fear subsided. I felt it draining from me, as if it was retreating into the musical instruments floating all around. The fear swirled into the bell of the bugle and filled the top of the drum like it was a mining pan. Soon it was gone, replaced by a sorrow as deep and unfathomable as the sea.

"Mother," I said. "I wish more than anything that you were still here. I wish that I could at least have been able to say good-bye to you, but you were taken from me."

"But I'm here," my mother replied. *"I'm always with you."*

Something touched my cheek, barely grazing the skin. It was light — so light I could barely feel it. And soft. More a puff of air than a touch. But its warmth, its gentleness made me think that it truly was my mother and not just some cruel parlor trick.

I realized I was crying, although I had no idea when it began. My cheeks were soaked with tears, and when I tried to wipe them away, I noticed there was a handkerchief in my hand. On the edge of my vision, I saw Lucy Collins nod. Such a resourceful woman. Always prepared.

"Tell me wonderful things, Columbus," my mother said. *"Are you well? And happy?"*

"Not without you. But I try to be. I truly do."

"Is there someone special in your life? Someone you love and who loves you in return?"

"Yes," I said. "Her name is Violet."

"Such a pretty name," my mother replied with satisfaction. *"Is she a pretty girl, too?"*

"Yes, she's lovely."

"Have you wed yet?"

"Not yet," I said. "Soon."

"Promise me you'll always try to make her happy, Columbus. Make her happy and she'll do the same for you. That's all you need. Love

147

and happiness. Your father and I always understood that."

I was stunned by the way she so casually
mentioned my father. Did she remember
nothing about how she died? Had she no
recollection of the man who killed her?

"I don't want to talk about him," I blurted
out. "Not even with you."

"My sweet boy, why ever not?"

I looked around the parlor, eyes darting
among everyone else present. They all sat in
rapt attention, probably by this time wondering who I really was and what I was talking
about.

Hoping not to give too much away, I said,
"It's . . . it's hard to speak of him, Mother,
knowing what he did to you."

I detected confusion in my mother's voice.
"Did to me? Your father?"

"Yes," I said. "He killed you. In front of all
those people."

In the furthest reaches of my mind, I
understood that I was revealing my secret to
everyone in the room. But I honestly didn't
care. In another part of my consciousness,
they didn't even exist. It was just my mother
and I, speaking to each other as if nothing
bad had ever happened.

"Your father did this, you say?"

"Yes, Mother," I replied. "He destroyed
everything. He took you away from me."

My mother's voice grew concerned. *"But*

that cannot be."

I wondered how much those in the afterlife knew about what was happening here on earth. Did she know, for instance, that my father was now rotting away in prison? Was she aware that I had renounced my given name out of anger and humiliation?

"It is," I told her. "I haven't spoken to him since you left us."

"You must listen to me, Columbus," my mother said. *"You must listen closely and obey."*

I leaned forward, twisting Lucy's handkerchief in my hands. "I will, Mother. I will."

"You must see your father as soon as you can. You must speak to him and tell him of this meeting. He might not believe you at first. But tell him this word and he will."

As dishonorable as it seemed, I had no intention of seeing my father, despite what she was saying. Deep down, I knew it was something I'd never be able to do. Still, I asked, "What word is that?"

"Praediti."

A rush of air swooped from the back wall toward where Mrs. Pastor was reclining. It was a forceful gust, reminiscent of a breeze in early March, before lion has been replaced with lamb. The instruments, still suspended, spun in this strange wind, careening off one another and crashing into the walls. Many of the lamps were snuffed out, plunging the room into a web of half shadows.

I stood, the wind pummeling my back and trying to propel me forward in wicked, brutal shoves. I resisted, my heels scraping across the floor as I shouted to be heard over the gusts.

"Don't leave me yet, Mother! Tell me what that means!"

Accompanying the wind was a watery, sucking sound. Upon hearing it, I looked to Mrs. Pastor, barely visible in the new dimness. She was sitting up, eyes open wide, mouth agape. She looked terrified, and rightly so, for it appeared that the wind was being swallowed into her mouth.

Everyone else in the room responded to the gusts the only way they could — by tightly gripping the seats of their chairs and holding on for dear life. The woman in purple let out a frightened yelp that got instantly swallowed by the breeze. More lamps were extinguished until only the one next to Mr. Barnum remained lit. It flickered perilously as the last bit of wind rushed past.

Just like that, the breeze was gone, leaving the room in an all-too-brief stillness. Mrs. Pastor closed her mouth. Her eyes followed suit as she fell backward into her chair. The instruments over our heads immediately ceased their movement.

Then they fell.

This time, there was no gentle glide similar to the way in which they had been raised.

Instead, they rained down all around us. The tambourine plummeted once more onto the table. The cowbell flew past my head so quickly that I felt the brush of wind its fall produced. The harp, lightweight only a moment before, smashed deep into the floor and sent splinters of wood flying.

All of us covered our heads, trying to keep from being hit by both instruments and debris. I grabbed Lucy and tossed her onto the floor, covering her body with my own while using my arms to shield my head.

Mr. Barnum tried and failed to duck out of the path of a falling violin, and was struck on the head. He fell from his chair, knocking over the table and lamp next to him. The lamp shattered, sending a stream of oil across the floor that quickly burst into flames.

Someone — I had no idea who — screamed at the sight of it. As the fire grew, I saw someone rush to Mrs. Pastor, visible only as a darkened form standing between her and the flames. By that point, all of the instruments had landed, giving me the chance to tear off my jacket and pound out the fire now running across the floor. Lucy, I noticed, had rushed to Mr. Barnum's aid, using the handkerchief I had dropped to blot a bloody mark on his head.

It wasn't until the fire was fully smothered that a realization crashed over me, one more heavy and crushing than the harp that shattered the floor.

My mother was gone.

I sat up, listening for her voice and trying to detect the familiar warmth of her presence. I sensed nothing. She had been taken from me a second time. Once again, I hadn't been given a chance to say good-bye.

But losing her now didn't hurt as much as the first time. Shortly after her death and my father's arrest, I read an adventure story in which the villain fell from a cliff, grasping at nothing before meeting his doom. It was supposed to be a triumphant moment in the story, the happy ending such tales require. Yet I had felt nothing but sympathy for this villainous man. I knew what it was like to be in continual descent, helpless and frightened.

This time around, there was no dizzying fall. All I experienced was the moment of impact, which left me breathless and aching. In my mind, I heard the voice of my younger self crying out to her.

Come back! Please, come back!

Only it wasn't my voice doing the shouting. It belonged to someone else, and I wasn't the only person who heard it.

Lucy and Mr. Barnum relit one of the fallen lamps and held it aloft to brighten the room. Its glow fell upon Mrs. Pastor, still sprawled in her chair. So shocked was I by the depth of her trance that it took me a moment to notice her husband standing over her and shouting, "Lenora! You must come back!"

I rushed to Mr. Pastor's side and grasped him by the shoulders. "Does it usually take her this long to awaken from her trance?"

He shook his head. "I don't know what's wrong. This has never happened before."

Mr. Barnum joined us, also looking worried. "Perhaps she fainted."

Robert Pastor knelt before his wife, lightly slapping the back of her hand before moving on to her cheeks. When that failed to rouse her, I reached for her free hand and touched the inside of her wrist. Feeling nothing there, I asked Mr. Pastor for permission to check her heart.

"By all means, check," he said.

I pressed an ear against Mrs. Pastor's chest. She was so tiny that I felt like a child playing doctor with a rag doll. And just like that doll, Mrs. Pastor failed to produce a heartbeat. For one final test, I placed my open palm in front of her nose and mouth. I waited, hoping to feel the slightest hint of breath on my skin. When a count of twenty passed and I felt nothing, I knew the worst had happened.

"I'm so sorry," I said. "She's no longer with us. Mrs. Pastor is dead."

■ ■ ■ ■

BOOK THREE:
AFTER THE SUDDEN
DEATH OF LENORA
GRIMES PASTOR

■ ■ ■ ■

I

Once I announced Mrs. Pastor's fate, her husband sent the servant Stokely to fetch the family physician, Dr. Whitman. Within minutes of the good doctor's arrival, he confirmed that Mrs. Pastor was indeed deceased. That, in turn, brought a policeman by the name of Queally who, seeing a thoroughly ransacked sitting room, a group of strangers, and one corpse, quickly summoned an inspector.

That inspector just happened to be my old friend William Barclay. When he swept through the door and saw me, his face was so wonderfully shocked that I almost wished Lucy's photographer friend Mr. Brady had been there to preserve it. Yet Barclay didn't betray his emotions to the others. He merely nodded in greeting before moving directly to the body of Lenora Grimes Pastor.

While he inspected the scene, Queally gathered the names of all the witnesses to Mrs. Pastor's death. Just as she had wished, the introductions were made after the séance had ended.

Queally began with the deceased's husband, Robert Pastor, who took a good deal of time to provide the most basic information. When Mr. Pastor spoke it was in a dull murmur — clearly the result of shock. As for the séance guests, Queally asked all of us to provide our names. The woman dressed in black at first only identified herself as Mrs. Gerald Mueller. When Queally asked her to clarify, she also gave her first name, Elizabeth. Next were the woman in purple, Leslie Dutton, and her husband, Eldridge. They were followed by Mr. Barnum, whose name elicited in Queally a reaction similar to what mine had been.

"P. T. Barnum?" the policeman asked.

"Yes, that is my name."

"*The* P. T. Barnum?"

"The very same, my boy."

For a moment, Queally was in awe. "I enjoyed your museums very much, sir."

"Many thanks," Barnum replied. "It's a shame they keep burning down."

Queally then moved on to Lucy Collins and me, asking us to identify ourselves. As I spoke my name — Edward Clark, not Columbus Holmes — I noticed Barclay momentarily look away from Mrs. Pastor's corpse and give me a disappointed stare. I had no doubt he wished I were anywhere but there.

Once all the introductions had been made,

Stokely led Mr. Pastor upstairs so he could grieve in private. The rest of us were whisked to the dining room to sit and await further questioning. A pall quickly settled over the room, bringing with it an oppressive silence that was occasionally broken by the sound of the women weeping. Mrs. Collins, I hasten to add, was not one of them.

Whether in tears or not, everyone present was in a daze, myself included. Between conversing with my dead mother and watching Mrs. Pastor die before my very eyes, I was surprised I could still sit upright. Glancing in the wide mirror adorning the wall opposite my chair, I saw a slack-jawed and chalk-skinned man staring back at me.

Similar expressions could be found on most everyone else at the table. Lucy looked to be lost in thought, her eyes dim and lifeless as she stared at the white tablecloth in front of her. The Duttons sat side by side in such a stiff manner that they brought to mind two candlesticks. When Mrs. Dutton began to weep again, her husband made no motion to comfort her. In fact, he appeared to be on the verge of tears himself, looking forward while absently caressing his gold watch.

The one who cried the loudest, though, was Elizabeth Mueller who, with her black dress and ghostly pallor, was already prepared for mourning. Dabbing at her eyes with a handkerchief, she said, "This is horrible. Tragic and horrible."

"Were you and Mrs. Pastor close?" asked Mr. Barnum, the only one in the room who seemed capable of responding.

"I sat with her often over the past year, always expecting to hear from my dear Gerald," Mrs. Mueller replied. "Each time she went into her trance, I prayed that the first voice I'd hear would be his. But it never was. I've seen so many people make contact with their loved ones, only to be denied myself. But I never gave up hope. I knew that one day Mrs. Pastor would be able to reach him. But now she's gone, and I know that I'll never hear from my Gerald again."

She began to cry with more intensity, her sobs echoing through the dining room. When it became too loud for the rest of us to bear, Mr. Dutton slammed his fist against the table.

"Stop that at once, you silly woman!" he snapped. "I've never witnessed something so selfish. Weeping because you can't contact your husband! The rest of us are grieving because there's a dead woman in that sitting room. A woman we admired. Who had a gift and used it to help people."

Mrs. Dutton clutched at his arm, trying to calm him. "Eldridge, please stop."

"I will not stop!" Eldridge Dutton pulled away from his wife before fixing Mrs. Mueller with a hard stare. "I know why you're so keen to speak to your precious Gerald."

"I'm certain you do," Mrs. Mueller replied, staring right back. "And I know why your wife's deceased sister told her not to trust you. Indeed, it's the very same reason you're so broken up about what just happened to Mrs. Pastor."

Thankfully, Mr. Barnum stood before either of them could utter another word. The wound on his head, no longer bleeding but still ragged and raw, lent him an air of gravity. It was something I'd first noticed during the war. People always seemed to stop and listen carefully to the walking wounded.

"Both of you stop this nonsense at once," he said. "We find ourselves in a very upsetting situation, and the only way we'll get through it is if we let each other grieve in our own way."

After that, the room fell silent again, remaining that way until Queally eventually entered and announced, "Inspector Barclay would like to speak with each of you individually for a moment."

"But why?" Mrs. Dutton asked. "Does he know the cause of Mrs. Pastor's death?"

"Only the inspector can answer that, I'm afraid," Queally said. "You'll each get an opportunity to ask him whatever questions you may have. But for now, he would like a moment of Mr. Barnum's time."

Queally then departed, taking P. T. Barnum with him and leaving the rest of us to ponder

161

what was being said in the next room. This went on for an hour or so, with Queally entering the room and escorting another person out of it. After Mr. Barnum, it was Mrs. Mueller's turn, followed by each of the Duttons.

Soon it was just me and Lucy. We eyed each other across an expanse of white tablecloth, unsure of what to say.

"How are you feeling?" I asked after several moments of silence.

"Wonderful," Lucy replied with forced cheer. "And how are you, Mr. Clark?"

So it seemed we were no longer on a first-name basis. Still, I said, "I must admit I'm shaken by what happened tonight."

"Whatever for? Clearly, Mrs. Pastor had a health issue none of us knew about. Now the city has one less person pretending to be a medium. Isn't that your goal?"

"That's a horrible thing to say."

"I'm only speaking the truth," Lucy said. "We both know that Mrs. Pastor was a skilled mimic who met an unfortunate end in the act of fooling us all."

"We know no such thing."

"Just because you weren't able to detect her illusions doesn't mean they didn't exist. I'm certain there's a simple explanation for everything that occurred tonight."

"If there is, I'd love to hear it," I said.

Unlike Lucy, I wasn't certain about anything I had witnessed that night. I wanted to believe, deep down in my soul, that it had all been the work of a skilled charlatan. Had circumstances been slightly different, I might have done just that.

Yet I had heard my mother. I'd spoken with her as if she had been standing right there in front of me. That it was her voice, I had no doubt. Not even the best mimic in the world could have matched her warm tone. What I didn't know was how it was possible, nor did I understand what any of it meant.

"Don't tell me you're suddenly a believer in the supernatural," Lucy said.

I shook my head. "I don't know what to believe."

Indeed, I didn't. I was torn by two very different emotions. One, wholehearted and pure, was the belief that Mrs. Pastor had somehow summoned the spirit of my mother. The other — dark and cynical — was that the act of summoning spirits was impossible. These two warring thoughts tugged me in opposite directions, leaving my mind reeling and my body spent.

Lucy Collins pretended not to be feeling the same way, although I could tell from the paleness of her face and her trembling hands that she, too, was conflicted by what had transpired that night.

"I remain firm in my belief that it was a hoax," she said. "You only think you heard your mother —"

"I *did* hear her!" I said, leaping from my chair. "And you heard someone, too."

Lucy also rose, keeping pace with me as I walked the length of the table. "I heard nothing out of the ordinary."

"No? Then who is Declan?"

"I have no idea who you're referring to."

"During the séance, the man named Declan upset you greatly. Are you this Jenny Boyd he spoke of? Did you" — I lowered my voice, in case Barclay or Queally was within earshot — "*kill* him?"

Lucy stopped pacing, curled her hands into fists, and placed them on the table. Leaning forward, she glared at me until I was caught in her green-eyed gaze, unable to move.

"You listen to me, Mr. Clark," she said, her voice as hard as granite. "If you utter the name Jenny Boyd to anyone, I will expose you instantly. Within an hour, everyone in Philadelphia will know who you are and what your father did. Do I make myself clear?"

I nodded. "Clear as creek water."

"I thought so. As for our arrangement, consider it finished. You may continue with your witch hunt of the city's mediums while I carry on with my practice. Are we in agreement?"

Queally suddenly entered the room again, announcing, "Mrs. Collins, the inspector would like to see you next."

Lucy remained where she was, staring me

164

down. "Mr. Clark, do we or do we not have an agreement?"

I can't put into words how much I loathed her at that moment. Using my past to blackmail me into silence was a despicable act, made worse by the possibility that she was a murderer in addition to being a charlatan. I felt the urge to run to Barclay and declare my true identity, just to spite her. Still, all I could say was, "Yes, we do."

"Good," Lucy said. "I suppose this is goodbye, then."

I crossed my arms and huffed. "More like good riddance."

Lucy ignored the barb and turned to Queally. "Sorry for the delay," she said. "I'm ready to see the inspector."

With that, she and the policeman left the room. I won't lie: It was a relief to see her go. Twenty-four hours caught in the orbit of Mrs. Lucy Collins was twenty-four too many.

Yet the room seemed to dim immediately after her exit, as if her mere presence had brightened it somehow. I chalked that up to the abrasiveness of her personality. The more grating something — or someone — is, the more you notice their absence. It was very similar to how you can still feel the poke of a pebble once you've removed it from your shoe.

Roughly ten minutes after Lucy departed, Barclay entered the dining room. As expected, he didn't appear happy to see me.

"Would you mind telling me," he said, "what the devil you're doing here?"

I explained in the best manner that I could, telling him about my unusual assignment for the *Bulletin.* I stressed that I was simply there to observe the séance and look for signs of trickery.

"Did you find any?"

Again, I felt the pull of conflicting opinions. Rather than try to explain them to Barclay, I chose an answer that caused me no doubt whatsoever.

"Not that I could see. It all certainly *looked* real. Did the others say the same?"

Barclay didn't provide an answer, opting instead to pose another question. "Who was that woman you arrived with?"

"Mrs. Collins?"

"Yes. Is she a friend of yours?"

"An acquaintance," I said. "She's a medium — a fake, I might add — who agreed to help me with my assignment."

"And does Miss Willoughby know about this acquaintance?"

I looked at Barclay, seeing the same expression that had been on the face of Violet's brother. The idea that he thought I might have been acting indiscreetly with another woman appalled me.

"You know me better than that, William," I said. "I met her only yesterday. When she offered her assistance, I accepted."

"I'm sorry," Barclay said. "I know you would never do anything that would hurt Violet. But I'm curious to hear how much you know about this Mrs. Collins. Someone told me she appeared quite agitated during the séance."

"Who told you that?" I asked quickly.

This time, Barclay didn't sound apologetic at all. "You know I can't divulge that. But they told me that a voice was heard. A frightening one, they said. He addressed someone in the room named Jenny Boyd and accused her of killing him. From the way she reacted, they assumed Mrs. Collins was really this Jenny he was speaking of."

I had no choice but to lie. If I wanted Lucy to keep her end of the bargain we had struck, then I needed to uphold mine.

"They're mistaken," I said. "Mrs. Collins was simply upset by the way the voice sounded. It *was* frightening. Very much so. If she hadn't cried out for it to stop, I likely would have."

Barclay crossed his arms, watching me with his head slightly cocked. He appeared to be digesting what I had told him, sorting through it, trying to find a nugget of falsehood.

"I imagine it was upsetting," he finally said. "The whole evening must have been an ordeal for you."

I exhaled, relieved that he believed me.

"Yes. It was."

"And what of the voice that spoke to *you*?"

Of course, one of the others present had mentioned the conversation with my mother. In all likelihood, everyone but Lucy Collins made a note of it. None of them, naturally, could have predicted the uncomfortable situation it now put me in.

Faced with lying to Barclay for a second time in as many minutes, I chose to tell the truth — within reason.

"It was my mother," I said.

Barclay's face took on a queer expression, as if he simply couldn't fathom what I was telling him. "Do you truly believe that, Edward?"

"Yes," I said. "And no."

"Which one is it?"

Exhaling a frustrated sigh, I said, "I don't *know*."

I was incapable of uttering a more truthful statement. The evening had been so unexpectedly bizarre that it was hard for me to conclude what was real and what wasn't. All I had to guide me was the feeling in my gut. That feeling, I might add, told me with quiet insistence that what I had witnessed was real. That my mother truly had contacted me from beyond the grave.

"It certainly sounded like my mother," I said to Barclay.

"I was told she called you by a different

name. Columbus, I believe it was."

"A childhood nickname," I quickly replied. "After Christopher Columbus. It seems I was always exploring."

"What did the two of you talk about?"

Barclay's tone told me that he already knew the answer, so lying was of no use. "We spoke of my father."

"What about him?"

"You've certainly heard this already, William. I see no reason why you need to hear it again."

Barclay's hand had already surreptitiously crept to his beard. Now it was making its way to his mustache, tugging ever so slightly on it. His entire head tilted with it — an unconscious expression of his confusion.

"I want to hear it from you," he said.

His request forced me to utter the biggest falsehood I had told all night. While admitting that I spoke of my father killing my mother, I untruthfully told Barclay that it was in relation to the sinking ship on which they had reportedly died. I said my mother, who was deathly afraid of sailing the high seas, had been all but forced by my father onto a vessel that met its fate in the deep waters of the Atlantic. I said — with utter conviction this time — that I had always blamed my father for her death.

Barclay, to my guilt-filled relief, believed every word. Making matters worse were his eyes, which darkened with pity for my tragic situation. There was such sympathy in them that I longed to look away. But I couldn't. I was forced to continue to accept his sympathy, to feel its warmth spread toward me, and to know I was unworthy of it. I had betrayed the trust of my closest friend, and it made me feel hollow inside.

"I'm sorry for all the questions," Barclay said.

I accepted his apology, knowing full well I was the one who should have been asking for forgiveness. I should have been on my knees, exposing my darkest lies before begging for absolution. Instead, I exploited Barclay's sympathy for my own gain — an act of selfishness that would have made Lucy Collins beam with pride. Perhaps she had been right all along. Maybe we were more alike than I ever could have imagined.

"You haven't told me why *you're* here, my friend," I said, desperate to change the subject. "As someone who witnessed it, I can say there's nothing suspicious about Mrs. Pastor's death."

Barclay cocked an eyebrow. "So you don't call ghostly voices, floating instruments, and strange winds suspicious?"

"All of that was stranger than anything I've ever encountered," I admitted. "But as for the death itself, Mrs. Pastor certainly succumbed to natural causes."

"I suspect you're right," Barclay said. "But when I spoke to Robert Pastor, he told me that his wife was in good health. Her physician concurred. Because of that, Mr. Pastor has requested that the coroner conduct an autopsy on his wife's body."

It was a startling request, to be sure. While the process of an autopsy had proved to be useful, few people wanted their loved ones sliced up like some macabre science experiment, even if such desecration of the human body could yield a proper cause of death. Yet I could see why Mr. Pastor wanted answers. Barclay, however, could not.

"It seems a waste of time, if you ask me," he said. "But Mr. Pastor wants to know why his wife died. We shall do our best to fulfill his request."

It was past midnight by the time I returned home. Mrs. Patterson had left long ago and Lionel had retired to his quarters, leaving the place dark and eerily still. Although I was alone for the first time that night, I got the sense that someone else was present. As I crept up the stairs, I cast sidelong glances at the shadows, expecting to see someone — or something — hidden among them. Halfway up the staircase, I thought I spied a flash of white rushing past me, just on the edge of my vision. Yet when I twirled around to get a better look, nothing was there.

On the third floor, I fired up every lamp I encountered, hoping the brightness would chase away that unnatural feeling. It helped, but only so much. I still sensed that someone was watching me, although that was impossible. Yet the feeling was enough to keep me awake, even after I discarded my clothing, crawled into bed, and closed my eyes.

In addition to the sense that I wasn't alone, a mad torrent of thoughts and theories rushed through my head. I kept thinking about all that had happened, both before the séance, during it, and after. Had it really been my mother who spoke to me? It had certainly sounded like it. And during our conversation, I had truly believed it was her.

That train of thought carried me to the subject of ghosts, spirits, and voices from the Great Beyond. I had never believed in such things. Not even as a child, when imaginations run wild and anything seems possible. Yet the events of that night made me reconsider my stance. Maybe spirits really *did* exist. Maybe it *was* possible for them to reach out to those they loved. And maybe, just maybe, that's what my mother had managed to do that night.

Yet now that some time had passed, small doubts began to creep into my thinking. Perhaps it had all been a hoax. Perpetrated not just on me, but also on Lucy and the others present. Perhaps Mrs. Pastor had somehow been aware of my true identity. If so, there was a chance — albeit a small one — that she could have mimicked my mother's voice.

When those thoughts subsided, new ones emerged. My mind briefly focused on Violet, Barclay, and the guilt I felt from lying to them. My relationships with both of them had been built on nothing but lies. And it was only a matter of time, I feared, before the truth would come out and crush both of those tenuous structures under its weight.

Finally — and quite surprisingly — my thoughts turned to Mrs. Lucy Collins and if I'd ever see her again.

The rational part of me quite rightly wanted never to lay eyes on her again. She was nothing but trouble, that much was certain. Yet a small, irrational piece of me had enjoyed being in her presence. She was disagreeable, to be sure, yet that's what kept me alert and on my toes. Rare was the person who could do that.

Besides, unlike with Violet and Barclay, there were no lies between us. Lucy Collins knew all of my secrets. Strange as it seemed, she was the only person in this city who knew the real me.

After Lucy faded from my thoughts, I opened my eyes and checked my watch, which sat on the bedside table. An hour had passed and I'd slept not a wink. In order to get any rest, I knew I needed to make sense of things. Consequently, the only way to do that would be to write everything down. So I crawled out of bed and settled into a nearby chair, pen and paper at the ready. Then I began to write, scribbling furiously until the sun rose and swept the watchful shadows from my room.

II

To say my editor was happy with what I wrote would be a gross understatement.

The usually emotionless Hamilton Gray was over the moon. Ecstatic. Downright giddy, as a matter of fact.

"Astounding," he muttered continuously while reading my account of Mrs. Pastor's death. "Absolutely astounding."

It was the morning after my long, sleepless night — a warm Sunday that found most of the city's residents worshipping at one church or another. Mr. Gray and I, however, attended the Church of Journalism, which wasn't divided into denominations, didn't require tithing, and certainly didn't have a day of rest. For us, news — or at least the selling of it — outweighed God and all the angels in heaven.

When Mr. Gray finished reading my article, a smile stretched from one ear to the other. I couldn't recall ever having seen him so joyful. "My boy, you have made this newspaper proud."

"I assume the article is adequate?" I said.

Mr. Gray pressed the pages to his chest, literally hugging them. "Adequate? It's *brilliant*. The *Public Ledger* and the *Times* shouldn't even try to outdo us. But try they will, and they'll only look foolish in the end."

I was well aware of what this meant for the *Evening Bulletin*. While it was true that every paper in the city was preparing to report on Mrs. Pastor's death, mine would be the only one with intimate knowledge of what had transpired when she passed away. The only thing readers in Philadelphia enjoyed more than a good story about murder and mayhem was a firsthand account of it. That's exactly what they were going to get.

What they wouldn't read about, however, were my secrets.

The piece I had written for the *Bulletin* was mostly an accurate account of what I saw at Mrs. Pastor's home. I mentioned the floating instruments, the otherworldly voices, the wind that rushed through the room right before she died. I chronicled my quick, yet chaste, examination of the body before concluding she was dead, and the aftermath of that pronouncement. But readers of the *Bulletin* saw no mention that Annalise Holmes was one of the voices to come out of Mrs. Pastor's mouth, nor did they know about the other ghostly visitors during the séance. By not revealing what I knew about the others, I hoped they, in turn, would refrain from revealing what they knew about me.

Fortunately, Mr. Gray was too enamored of the more dramatic portions of my article to question whether anything was missing.

"Was P. T. Barnum truly in attendance?" he asked.

"Yes. He was very much present."

"Astounding," Mr. Gray muttered again. "Our readers will simply not believe what they're reading."

"The only downside, I suppose, is that our exposé of the city's mediums has stopped before it could begin in earnest," I said. "After this, it will be impossible to conduct the investigation in anonymity."

Mr. Gray squeezed the pages a little tighter. "Our readership will have increased so much that it no longer matters. If Mr. Peacock wishes, I'll have someone else continue it. As for you, Clark, Mrs. Pastor's death is the only thing you'll be writing about."

"I doubt there'll be much more to write, sir."

"There'll be the report from the coroner, I assume. Don't you find it strange that an autopsy has been requested in this matter?"

"Not at all," I replied. "I gathered that it's unclear what caused Mrs. Pastor's death."

"What if it was murder?" Mr. Gray said,

his eyes agleam at such a prospect. "The city's greatest medium killed during one of her own séances. Oh, you couldn't create a better story."

"I hope that it's not. For the sake of her loved ones."

Left unspoken was how I wished it for my own sake as well. While I wrote about killings almost daily, it was not my desire to also have witnessed one.

After reading the story again, Mr. Gray declared it the best thing I had ever written, congratulated me on a job well done, and sent me home. On my way out of the building, I spotted a few colleagues arriving for the Sunday afternoon shift. They nodded politely, but in their eyes I glimpsed what seemed to be unbridled envy. No doubt they had heard about what happened to Mrs. Pastor and were jealous that it was me, and not them, who had been there to witness it.

I made the journey home on foot, enjoying the sun on my face and the relative quiet of the city's streets. There was a slight breeze blowing down Chestnut Street, carrying with it the sound of an organ being played and a congregation giving full voice to a hymn I faintly recognized.

I am, sad to say, no longer a religious man. Once you have seen what I have — battalions of fearful, angry men racing across a battlefield with the sole intention of slaughtering each other — you begin to doubt that a benevolent god exists. Yet, as a young child, I was a frequent churchgoer, often found with my mother in the front pews of the First Reformed Church on Race Street. My father never attended, adhering to Mr. Karl Marx's theory that religion was the "opium of the people." My mother, however, had been a devout woman who insisted I put on my best suit every Sunday and sit through fiery speeches spoken in a packed, sweltering church. While the sermons were wasted on me, I learned to love the music of the lord. Even now, I remember the words and melodies to many hymns of my youth. Whenever I think of them, I hear my mother's clarion voice singing along.

Of course, I thought of her on that lovely Sunday morning, thanks to the hymn I heard floating down Chestnut Street. I still wasn't entirely convinced it had been my mother I'd spoken with the night before. A nagging, doubting part of my brain kept telling me it had been the cruelest of tricks. Yet the rest of me disagreed. My brain could think whatever it wanted, but my gut, my heart, and my soul told me otherwise. And listening to that hymn, I started to slowly but surely believe that my mother had somehow spoken to me.

It didn't matter that our conversation from the previous evening had become hazy and half forgotten. I remembered her telling me

178

to visit my father, which I knew I would never do. I also recalled that strange word she had said — Praediti. But everything else was vague, like a dream that had quickly dissipated upon waking.

While I didn't remember most of her words, the sound of her voice — that warm tone that had brought me to tears — began to haunt me. I thought I heard it standing out from the other voices singing the hymn that was slowly fading in the distance. Before the song vanished completely, I stopped on the sidewalk and turned, trying to face the direction it was coming from.

That's when I noticed a man in a black suit following me.

At first glance, there was nothing unusual about him. He walked about half a block behind me, strolling leisurely, as many men do on bright Sunday mornings. His morning suit was clean and pressed, again not out of the ordinary. While he was too far away to get a good look at his face, the way he moved — back rigid, facing forward — gave me pause. He seemed like someone trying very hard to give the impression that he was *not* looking at something. When, in truth, he was looking at *me*.

I turned away from him and began to walk again, keeping my pace to a crawl. Glancing over my shoulder, I noticed that the man had also slowed. He barely shuffled along, head still raised, eyes pretending to look beyond me. Yet when I began to move faster, another backward glance revealed that his pace had quickened as well. Not noticeably fast, mind you. Just enough to keep an equal distance from me.

My first instinct was to confront the man and demand to know why he was following me. But a single seed of doubt prevented me from accusing him of it. If I was wrong, I didn't want to appear rude or, worse, insane.

Instead, I decided to be more discreet. Looking to my left, I saw that I had reached a dry goods store, closed for the Sabbath. Its wide windows faced the street, behind which were flour sacks piled into tidy pyramids and elaborate stacks of tin cans. I stopped directly in front of a window, pretending to peer inside. In reality, I could see the street behind me reflected in the glass.

Then I waited.

The stranger in the black suit slowed again, proceeding at a pace that even a turtle could have surpassed. When he realized I wasn't going anywhere, he picked up his pace. As he approached, I resisted the urge to turn and face him. Instead, my gaze remained steady on the reflection in the window.

The man soon appeared on the left side of the glass, walking swiftly. He still faced forward, chin slightly raised, like a commander marching in front of his troops.

I lost sight of him briefly as he passed directly behind me, my reflection blocking out his own. When he slipped into view again, a chill of dread shot through my entire body.

The man had turned his head while behind me and was now staring directly at me in the glass.

Never before had I seen a more ghastly countenance on a man still living. Wide of forehead and narrow of chin, the stranger's cheekbones jutted out on both sides of his face. His skin was as white as talcum powder, which set off tar black eyes devoid of emotion. Aimed squarely at my face, those two dark orbs studied me, taking in everything at once.

Yet the most startling thing about the man's appearance was his nose.

He didn't seem to have one.

In its place was a dark crevasse divided by a thin strip of cartilage. It was as if his nose had been lopped off long ago, leaving large, unnatural nostrils ringed by flaps of white skin that vibrated slightly as he breathed. The result was as appalling as it was fascinating. And as the man continued walking past me, I couldn't help but stare, inadvertently making eye contact with him in the window's glass.

As his eyes met my own, the stranger gave me what could only be called a smile, although it contained neither warmth nor mirth. The slight upturning of his pale lips suggested something more sinister than friendly.

In an instant, the smile was gone, as was the entire reflection of his face, for he had turned forward again and quickened his pace. I stayed where I was, listening to his footfalls on the sidewalk. When I counted twenty of them, I slowly turned around.

To my surprise, he was no longer on the street. Apparently, I had waited too long, giving him just enough time to round a corner or duck into a nearby building.

Left alone once more, I continued my walk home.

The streets filled considerably in the next fifteen minutes as the city's churches released their congregants. Pedestrians in their Sunday best, momentarily cleansed in the spirit of the lord and free to engage in another week of sin, soon surrounded me. I took no comfort in the growing crowd. In fact, it made me more nervous than if I had been alone. At least then I could have seen if the noseless man was following me again. But now each person joining the fray only further hindered my lookout for those dark, prying eyes. Still, I at least tried, constantly checking over my shoulder to make sure the man wasn't behind me once more.

I did this for the remainder of my trip, not stopping until I was safely home and locking the door behind me. Once inside, I leaned against the door, breathing heavily. My hands shook. My heart, normally so sedate, thrummed so hard in my chest that someone listening to it would have thought I had sprinted all the way from Chestnut Street. Closing my eyes, I tried to picture anything other than that man's horrific, noseless face.

I couldn't.

His image continued to haunt me, and although I knew he hadn't followed me home, I couldn't shake the dreadful feeling that I would be seeing him again very soon.

III

In the afternoon, Violet and I set out in her father's brougham for a long, relaxing ride before meeting friends at a dinner party. I felt rather unchivalrous about having my fiancée pull up to my doorstep instead of the other way around, but I knew Violet didn't mind. I also understood that her father liked it that way. Although we were betrothed, Mr. Willoughby preferred not to leave his daughter alone with me until we were properly man and wife. So we were often accompanied by either one of her parents or a member of their household staff.

That afternoon, our chaperone was the coachman, a stout fellow called Winslow. He rode up top, giving Violet and me a modicum of privacy inside the enclosed brougham.

Still, we knew we remained within earshot, and were thus on our best behavior.

"You look tired, Edward," Violet said.

"That's because I didn't sleep a wink," I replied.

"Oh, please don't become like Jasper. I doubt last night saw an hour's worth of sleep between the two of you. He came home late again, knocking things about in the next room until the sun came up. Little does he realize that it affects my sleep as well."

The mention of her brother produced a flare of panic in my rib cage.

"Have you spoken with Jasper at all today?"

"No," Violet said. "He was sleeping all morning. He didn't even come down for lunch. I do worry about him sometimes."

As did I. I'd have some explaining to do if he eventually told Violet about seeing me on the street with Mrs. Collins. I considered telling her about it myself, but decided against it. It wasn't as if I'd be seeing Mrs. Collins again. Also, I had a feeling that Jasper would stay quiet about it as well. I had no idea what he was doing out and about alone on a Saturday night, but whatever it was, I assumed he didn't want his sister to know.

"I'm certain it's just a phase," I said. "He's still young and carefree."

"I hope you're right."

Violet reached out to me with a gloved hand. I held it in both of my own, caressing the satin stretched across her delicate palm. We rode in silence for a while, hands still clasped as we gazed at the city slipping slowly past us. The brougham traveled north, taking me once again to Chestnut Street and the building that housed the *Evening Bulletin*.

By then the presses were rumbling away, I knew, churning out thousands of newspapers with my name on the front page. I supposed I should have been excited by that prospect. It was, after all, the high point of my writing career. Yet I felt uneasy knowing that my impending notoriety could lead others as enterprising as Lucy Collins to learn who I really was. But nothing could be done about it at that point. With the presses rolling, whatever was being printed on those warm pages couldn't be wiped away.

Violet, naturally, had heard about what happened to Mrs. Pastor, yet she didn't broach the subject other than to offer sympathy that I had been there to witness it. I appreciated her silence on the matter. Anyone else would have pestered me for tawdry details, curious about what I had seen and heard. But not my Violet. There wasn't a curious bone in her body, which was one of the things I loved about her. She was comfortable with what she comprehended and saw no reason to muddy the clear waters of her knowledge.

In my youth, if someone had asked me what type of woman I wanted to marry, my ensuing description would have been nothing like Violet Willoughby. Back then, I would have talked about someone very much like my mother. Keen of mind. A touch of mystery. Eager to explore the world.

Violet was none of those things. She was intelligent, but not overtly so, which was how she had been raised. Her mystery was the kind all women possessed, in that it was impossible to quite know all of her thoughts and desires. As for travel, sweet Violet had told me she felt no need to see the world, since everything she knew and loved was right here in Philadelphia.

Instead, Violet had characteristics above and beyond those I desired as a boy but now saw value in as a man. Her kindness was unparalleled, and her disposition was sunnier than a June morning. She was never cross, nor was she ever blue. A great deal of that, I was certain, came from wealth. To Miss Willoughby, every day was an occasion to put on beautiful dresses, visit with friends, and enjoy the good fortune that had been bestowed upon her. While that may have seemed trivial to most, there was something admirable about a young woman who loved life. That joy, after all, was what had initially drawn me to her.

Violet and I had met the previous August, at a dance for war veterans hosted by a group of society ladies. Attending such an event was the last thing I wanted to do, but Barclay insisted I go. He felt I was becoming too much of a recluse — which, in truth, I was — and that a night out among lovely young women and fellow soldiers might do me some good. On that matter, I disagreed. I had no expectations that spying a pretty girl on the dance floor could or should erase those horrible memories that had been forged on the battlefield.

The dance, just as I had expected, was a sorry affair despite attempts to keep things festive. The hall was festooned with red, white, and blue bunting. A small orchestra had been set up in the corner, playing the airiest waltzes and reels. Along one wall was a table offering punch, coffee, and a variety of cakes and pies. Yet the air inside the hall was thick with humidity and sadness. It was far too hot for a dance, to be sure, and a fair number of both sexes wilted in the heat.

Then there was the uncomfortable fact that many of those in attendance were battle scarred and weary souls. Some bore their wounds quite literally, such as one man missing an arm whom I saw dancing with a lovely brunette. The girl smiled bravely and looked him square in the eyes, but her free hand, not knowing where to be placed, fluttered around his pinned-up sleeve like a confused bird. Others were physically unharmed, but the events of the war still haunted them. I could see it in their glassy eyes, in their stooped shoulders, in the hollow words they spoke. I knew the signs because I was one of them, shuffling through my life without any attempt to actually live it.

I decided to leave the dance after less than an hour. It was all I could possibly endure.

Stepping out of the hall, I was stopped by a pretty young woman in a light blue dress. She stood in the doorway, her yellow hair elegantly piled atop her head and held in place by a bonnet adorned with white rosebuds. Her pale skin was offset by cheeks gently kissed by rouge paper. She looked lovely — a shimmering vision emerging from the still air of that suffocating hall.

Only she was scowling at me.

"Pardon me, sir," she said, "but are you leaving?"

"I am," I replied.

"Why so soon?"

"I'm feeling unwell. I'm afraid I need to go home at once."

Her response was surprisingly indignant. "You look perfectly fine to me."

"I can assure you, miss," I said, "that I am nowhere close to being fine. The same could be said about the rest of the men in there."

"I know," the woman replied. "All of us know that. And, I must say, it's very rude of you to leave after so many people put so much work into trying to help you. Why, did you even have a piece of cake?"

I stared at her a moment, blinking incredulously. *"Cake?"*

"Yes," she said, suddenly rambling. "There's a divine chocolate cake that Mrs. Tracy baked herself. And a lemon cake. That's from Miss Cecilia Hughes. I brought a cinnamon cake, although I can't take credit for baking it. Our cook did that, but I asked her to make the best one she possibly could because it was for men like you."

Rather than finding it endearing, her stream of words only furthered my foul mood. By that time, I had had my fill of stuffy rooms, of forced cheer, of pretending that the horrors of the war had never happened. Listening to the girl babble caused something inside me to snap.

"Do you really think cake, cinnamon or otherwise, will help men like me?" I asked. "You can't begin to understand the things we've witnessed. I have seen friends, standing at my side, struck down by bullets that could have been meant for me. I have seen men turned to pulp by a single cannonball. I have seen them bite through chunks of wood two inches thick as a field doctor sawed through the bones of their leg. So, miss, despite having witnessed all of these things and despite having to see them again in my nightmares, you think it can all be forgotten with a dance or two and a bit of dessert?"

If the young woman had been hurt by my tone, she didn't show it. Indeed, she displayed no emotion as she took a step forward and said, "No, sir, I don't think that. I understand you all have been through a terrible ordeal and that many of you will never recover from it. I also understand that whatever we ladies do, it will never be enough to properly repay you for the bravery you have shown. I know all of these things. Yet I still see no reason why that prevents you from enjoying a piece of cake."

Her response, so naive yet filled with logic, caused me to do something I hadn't done in months — I laughed. It erupted from the pit of my stomach, loud and boisterous, the sound and sensation at once foreign yet familiar to me.

"Are you mocking me?" the woman asked.

"Not at all," I said, clutching my stomach. "I'm agreeing with you. There honestly isn't any reason at all why I shouldn't be able to enjoy some cake."

She gave me the once-over, eyes scrunched in confusion. "So . . . would you like some?"

"I would love some."

She led me back inside, where I had a piece of the cinnamon cake she had brought. After that, I moved on to the lemon cake, followed by a slice of Mrs. Tracy's chocolate one, which was indeed divine. In total, I ate four pieces of cake, not because I was hungry — I

190

was, in fact, making myself sick — but because I was afraid that if I stopped, the lovely girl next to me would lower her cake knife and leave to convince some other fellow to remain at the dance. But she stayed by my side, even after I forced down my final slice of dessert. Then we danced, the cake sloshing uneasily in my belly. When the dance was over, I asked the girl her name.

"It's Violet," she told me. "Violet Willoughby."

"I'm Mr. Edward Clark. And I must say, Miss Willoughby, that it is a great pleasure to meet you."

"Likewise, Mr. Clark."

"Forgive my boldness," I then said, "but could I ask for permission to call on you sometime?"

"Of course you can," she replied. "As a matter of fact, I've been waiting for you to ask that since your first slice of cake."

I came around to her house a week later, then the week after that. Soon I was making the journey across the Schuylkill River each Friday night and Sunday afternoon, with a few additional visits during the week. I found myself lighter in Violet's company, and much happier. Even Barclay noticed it and, after a few months, told me I should consider marrying her. I took his advice to heart, proposing to Violet in front of her parents' house on Christmas Eve as snow drifted from the sky and melted against her tear-stained cheeks.

"You're very quiet this afternoon," Violet remarked, bringing me back to the present. "What are you thinking about?"

"You," I told her.

"That's a coincidence, for I've been thinking about you as well. You see, I have a surprise planned."

"What kind of surprise?"

"It wouldn't be one if I told you, Edward. You'll see when we get there."

I looked out the window, having at first no idea where we were. We had definitely left Chestnut Street and were heading north. After traveling another block, I saw a street sign indicating that we were on Broad, just above Girard Avenue. It wasn't until Winslow brought the brougham to a stop that I realized where we were.

"Surprise!" Violet said, throwing open the door and gesturing to the white house before us. "Our future home."

Even without her pointing it out to me, there was no way I could have missed noticing the structure in front of us. Immense in every possible way, it clearly was built to be noticed. Three floors high and equally as wide, the house sat, solid and squat, in the center of a lawn that flowed like an ocean swell to the edge of Broad Street.

"Would you like to see the inside?" Violet asked, giving my arm a squeeze.

"Of course," I said, although I found the prospect somewhat daunting. I assumed I would compare its interior to my own tall and rickety home, feeling small as well in the process. Still, I followed Violet up the flagstone walkway that cut through the lawn, my neck craning as I examined the house from foundation to roof.

Although in fine condition, the house gave off an aura of abandonment. The shrubs bordering the property were a bit too unruly, and the trees in the yard seemed slightly too gnarled and bedraggled. As we got closer, I noticed chips in the paint not visible from the street and a crack or two in the windows. When we stepped onto the front porch, the wood beneath our feet sighed from the weight.

Instead of producing a key from her silk purse, Violet approached one of the windows that flanked the front door. She pulled back a shutter, the wood protesting the movement with an irritated creak, and revealed a small key hanging from a nail.

"We leave it for the caretaker," she explained. "He looks in on the place every month."

"You mean no one from your family ever checks on the house?"

"Of course not," Violet said as she moved to the door and slipped the key into the lock. "We're all much too busy for that."

"Then what prevents the caretaker from moving in himself without your knowledge?"

She gave me a patient sigh before pointing to the street. "Because the caretaker is right there. It's Winslow. And I'm certain we would be able to deduce that he's been living here."

With the door unlocked, Violet gave it a mighty push, revealing an entrance hall larger than the entire first floor of my house. It was a grand home, built for grand people. I felt out of place the moment I tiptoed inside.

Violet, to that very manor born, strode through the door with confidence and asked, "What do you think?"

I surveyed my future home. To the left, a front parlor sat on the other side of a graceful archway. A dining room, glimpsed through a similar arch, was to the right. In the center was a curved staircase that swept upward to the second floor.

"It's . . . big," I said.

"Not too big, though. The perfect size for a family."

Roaming the first floor, I recalled Mrs. Willoughby saying that their growing family was the reason they left this house for a different one. Yet it seemed like more than enough space for the family, even with the addition of twin boys. I imagined that a twenty-person clan could have lived comfortably inside the place, let alone a family of five.

What I couldn't imagine was living in such a home myself. I was accustomed to a sort of comfortable confinement, a world of small rooms stuffed with well-worn furniture. The old Willoughby home, by contrast, boasted rooms of imposing width and height. Walking through it, I felt like a storybook character exploring the residence of a giant.

I didn't tell any of this to Violet, of course. She seemed so eager to show it off, so desperate for me to like the place, that when she prodded me for compliments, I found myself offering them freely.

"I think it will make a wonderful home," I said.

While the Willoughbys had taken most of their furniture with them during the move, a few pieces littered the first floor. In the dining room, for example, I saw a few wooden chairs waiting for a proper table to surround. I discovered a sofa and a wingback chair in the parlor, covered with white canvas. On the wall, facing the window, was a painting so sun paled and coated with dust that I couldn't make out what it depicted.

"Let's have a look at the upstairs," Violet said, pulling me toward the grand staircase.

On the second floor, the hallway stretched from one end of the house to the other, dotted with doors on both sides. Some of them were closed. Those we didn't bother with. Others were wide open, including one for what looked to be a child's bedroom. Poking my head inside, I saw two beds side by side, their headboards pushed against a wall painted light blue.

"How long has it been since you've lived here?" I asked Violet.

"It must be going on fourteen years now, but it feels like a lifetime ago. Now, let's go see the third floor. The nursery is up there. You can see where I spent my childhood."

She moved farther down the hall, heading to another, more modest set of stairs at the end of it. I remained on the threshold of the bedroom, looking inside. The twin beds were covered with white sheets, making them look as if they belonged in a hospital ward instead of a child's room. A coating of dust clung to the cloths, turning them gray. There was dust everywhere, in fact, dirtying the walls and weighing down the cobwebs in the corners. Almost a quarter of an inch of dust covered the floorboards, save for several indentations where it had been tamped down.

I looked closer, seeing that the indentations were none other than footprints. They were scattered around the room in all directions, as if someone had been roaming it fairly recently. Judging from the lack of footprints in other parts of the house, I couldn't imagine it was Winslow who had been doing the walking.

I was about to ask Violet if she was certain

no other people were coming and going in the house, but never got the chance.

For at that very moment, she began to scream.

The sound sent me bolting down the hall to the staircase at its end. I took the steps two at a time, almost running directly into the wall at a narrow landing where the stairway turned. All the while, Violet's screams echoed down the steps, filling my ears and making my heart pump with fear.

When I reached the top step, I saw her running toward me in full panic.

"Bees!" she cried out. "They're everywhere!"

At first, I didn't understand what she was talking about. Then I spotted a honeybee crawling on the yellow lilies affixed to her bonnet. Another inched its way along the brim, while two more scurried over her shoulders. I swatted them away while at the same time pulling Violet to the landing.

"I've never seen so many in my life!" she said, tears springing from her eyes. "Oh, Edward, it's horrible!"

"Stay right here," I told her before ascending the steps again.

I heard the bees before I reached the top — a monotonous humming that engulfed the room above me. Climbing one last step, I finally saw them.

There were thousands of bees inside that

old nursery, filling it. Several hundred flew about the room, careening from wall to wall and floor to ceiling. The rest swarmed over every conceivable surface — great, writhing bunches covering the walls and the discarded furniture. Several large hives drooped from the ceiling and spread across the rafters, connected to each other.

The entire nursery had been transformed into a colossal beehive.

Gathering my wits about me, I stepped into the room only long enough to grab the handle of the door Violet had unwittingly opened. Then, keeping my head down and swatting the air like a madman, I slammed the door shut. A few bees escaped in the process and either flew on down the stairwell or returned to the door, bumping against it in agitation. Not wanting to anger them further, I quickly took my leave.

I found Violet at the bottom of the steps, leaning against the wall for support. She looked paler than usual, and for a moment I feared she might faint. But she regained her strength quickly and managed to stand on her own. She even surprised me by lifting her chin and saying, "I suppose we have some work to do before we move in."

"Yes," I replied. "But first, the bees must move out."

"I wonder how so many got inside."

"A window, probably," I said. "Or perhaps

there's a hole in the roof that one found and then the others followed."

I offered Violet my arm and led her through the hallway and down the grand staircase. She still looked a bit shocked, so we descended slowly. In an attempt to lift her spirits, I said, "My mother once told me that bees are nothing to be afraid of. In fact, she said they're a sign of good luck, because they create sweetness wherever they go."

Violet, brave girl that she was, summoned a smile. "Then, Edward, we must be the two luckiest people on earth."

IV

As luck would have it, the dinner party was located just around the block. It was at the home of Mr. Bertram Johnson — Bertie to his friends — who had known Violet since they were both children. The backs of their houses had faced each other, their rear lawns running together. At the halfway point, separating one property from the other, was a thin strip of trees and shrubbery. In the summertime, Violet, Bertie, and their various siblings and friends played there until far into the evening, when fireflies would flit between the branches.

I learned this as we strolled to Mr. Johnson's house, having left Winslow and the brougham behind. I assumed that a walk would do us both some good after our honey-bee scare. It seemed to, because Violet chattered nonstop the entire way.

"They were such wonderful times," she said with a sigh. "That's why that house means so much to me. It was the place where we were all the happiest."

But now it was infested with stinging insects, which poor Winslow apologized profusely for overlooking. He told Violet he had neglected to check on the nursery since the previous summer.

"And what about the twins' old bedroom?" I had asked. "When was the last time you were in there?"

"Not for a very long time, sir," he had replied. "I don't dare set foot in there."

For her part, Violet was very forgiving of Winslow and seemed a hundred times more vibrant as we climbed the porch steps to Bertie Johnson's front door. As it opened, I prepared for the deluge of hugs, kisses, and gossip that would surely commence when Violet saw her friends. They all adored her, which was wonderful to see. About me, however, they remained completely ambivalent. They were nothing but cordial, yet no matter how many times I met them, I got the sense they thought Violet should be with someone more appropriate, more handsome, more fun.

Someone, for instance, like Bertram Johnson.

Bertie was one of those rare men who inspired admiration and envy in equal measure. A tall and strapping twenty-three, his social skills were unparalleled. I'd seen him be boisterously crude among other men and delicately sincere with members of the fairer sex. That easygoing manner made everyone, from the youngest child to the oldest widow, feel comfortable in his company. In any social situation, Bertie was the sun and the rest of us had to simply be content to orbit him.

On that night, Bertie answered the door himself, smiling widely as he ushered us inside. He gave Violet the briefest of welcomes before turning to me and saying, "And here he is, the man of the hour!" The pat on the back that followed was so jovially forceful it almost knocked me to the floor.

"It's good to see you, too, Bertram," I said, not yet a close enough acquaintance to call him Bertie. "And thank you for that warm welcome."

"You've earned it, Edward," he replied.

"How so?"

"Why, with this, of course."

Clutched in his other hand was a copy of the *Evening Bulletin,* fresh off the presses on Chestnut Street. The other half dozen people in attendance also had copies, which they read together while pressed shoulder to

201

shoulder. Seeing my arrival, they soon clustered around me, pumping my hand and congratulating me on writing such an exciting article. Bertie slapped me on the back two more times, impressed. He even began dinner with a toast dedicated to me.

I was, quite unexpectedly, in fashion.

Talk of Mrs. Pastor's death continued for the next hour. All through dinner, I was peppered with questions about the incident. Could Lenora Grimes Pastor really summon the voices of the dead? What was it like when she passed away? Did she immediately turn into a spirit and ascend toward the heavens?

I answered them the best I could. Mostly I recounted what was already in the *Bulletin* article, my audience not caring that it was the exact same story they had just been reading.

The only two people not weighing in on the topic were my fiancée and our host. Violet, displaying patience that deserved sainthood, smiled brightly throughout dinner, even though I knew she had no interest in all that talk of Mrs. Pastor. At one point, I looked across the table and caught her yawning discreetly into her glove.

Bertie, however, was more vocal in his desire to at last change the subject. I got the sense that, eager as he was to make a show of my arrival, he had grown tired of having a mere moon such as I eclipse his sunlight. For that, I couldn't blame him. Even I was bored with the sound of my voice.

"Violet was telling me about a discovery you two just made at her old house," he said. "Something about bees in the nursery."

"The place was overrun with them, Bertie," Violet added. "I've never been so frightened in my life."

"Remember that summer when a nest of bees moved into the big oak?"

Violet giggled at a memory only the two of them shared. "Of course I do! You were stung so many times we lost count."

More reminiscences between them followed, with the rest of us nodding out of politeness and pretending to be amused. It was a stark reversal from moments earlier, one that, intentionally or not, showed the rest of us how lopsided the conversation had been. But by the time dessert arrived, others had started to recount their own childhood memories, restoring balance to the table. The questions about Mrs. Pastor had finally come to an end, and I prepared for the inevitable waning of my popularity.

Instead, the opposite happened, as the after-dinner drinks brought with them a new round of inquiries.

"Were there really instruments floating around the room?" asked a red-haired friend of Violet's whose name constantly eluded me.

"Or did you just create that for dramatic effect?"

"They were indeed floating," I said. "I don't know how, but they were."

"Do you really think those were spirits speaking through Mrs. Pastor?" asked her companion. Walter, I believe his name was.

"It's hard to say," I replied. "But it certainly felt like they were."

Another guest chimed in with, "And what of Mrs. Pastor? Maybe she's now using a medium of her own to be heard."

"I have an idea," the red-haired girl said. "We should contact her ourselves and ask."

"And just how should we go about doing that?" Walter asked.

"We could ask Edward," Bertie suggested, a bitter edge to his voice. "Since he's been to a séance, he should know what to do."

"My séance days are over," I said. "I'm afraid I'd be of little help."

"See," Bertie told the others. "If the expert himself can't be of assistance, then we should stick to parlor games. Now, who's up for a game of the minister's cat?"

I seconded Bertie's suggestion, only in an attempt to get into his good graces again and not because I had any desire to play. But no one else expressed much enthusiasm for games of any kind. Finally, the red-haired girl snapped her fingers.

"I know," she said. "Table tipping. That's

how we can contact Mrs. Pastor."

Everyone agreed this was a fine idea. Everyone, that is, but Bertie and me. For the host, it was one more portion of his party taken up by talk of mediums. As for me, I found table tipping as juvenile as skipping rope. It was something children did to frighten themselves on stormy nights. It was definitely not an activity for adults sipping Madeira. Besides, after the night before, I was beginning to think it was best to let the dead rest in peace. But we were overruled by the majority, including Violet, who perked up immensely at the idea.

"This is so exciting," she whispered as I led her into the parlor. "I've never tried table tipping."

"It's all foolishness, you know," I said.

"Perhaps," she replied, "but it's exciting nonetheless."

She took a seat at a round table that had already been stripped of candlesticks and linen by the other guests. I sat beside her, with the red-haired girl and Walter to my left. Bertie took a seat on the other side of Violet, clearly annoyed at having to go along with the idea. Thus situated, we all placed our hands palms down on the table.

"Who should do the speaking?" the red-haired girl asked.

"You do it, Marybelle," Violet answered. "You've done this before, haven't you?"

"Of course," said the seemingly impossible-to-remember Marybelle. "Many times. We all must stay completely quiet and make sure that no one wobbles the table by accident."

"Does that mean we're allowed to do it on purpose?" Bertie asked with a sly grin.

"Of course not," Violet replied. "And don't you dare try it, Bertie."

"I won't," he said. "I promise."

Satisfied that Bertie intended to keep his word, Violet nodded to Marybelle to begin.

"Spirits of the Great Beyond," the red-haired girl intoned, sounding very much like Lucy Collins, "can you hear us?"

The table shook a moment and tilted slightly in Marybelle's direction.

"That means yes," she informed us before asking the spirits another question. "Is there a spirit present who would be amenable to speaking to us?"

Again, the table tilted toward her. Once more, I was reminded of Mrs. Collins, because it was obvious Marybelle and Walter were manipulating the table themselves. Yet no one noticed or cared, because the charade continued unabated.

"Would the spirit who wishes to speak to us please announce its presence?"

The table tilted more forcefully this time, rocking back and forth. Now, it appeared, Bertie had joined them in jostling it.

"Thank you, spirit," Marybelle said. "May

I ask, are you a gentleman?"

When the table didn't move in response, she looked at us and shook her head. "Then you are a lady?"

The table bucked, continuing to do so as Marybelle asked a series of obvious questions designed to lead us to only one answer. *Have you met someone sitting at this table? Was that person Edward Clark? Are you recently deceased? Did your death occur last night?*

Finally, she asked, "Spirit, is your name Lenora Grimes Pastor?"

In response, the table rocked back and forth, dipping in all directions. I studied the faces of the others, seeing no telltale hints of a conspiracy. In fact, they all looked awed as the table continued its dance. Even Bertie seemed transfixed by what was taking place.

"Mrs. Pastor," Marybelle said, "do you know what killed you?"

More rocking ensued, with one side of the table dipping so low I thought it was going to topple over. It moved with such force that Marybelle had a hard time keeping her palms upon it while asking the next question.

"Did you die a natural death?"

The table suddenly came to a stop, giving those of us sitting at it a moment's rest. Glancing at the others, I saw that all concerned looked weary, save for Violet, who appeared to be utterly terrified.

"I don't like this," she murmured to no one in particular. "I think we should stop."

"Not now," Walter hissed. "We need to keep her talking."

Marybelle asked another question. "Mrs. Pastor, do you think you were murdered?"

If she had been at the séance, she would have known that her question was utterly outlandish. Mrs. Pastor's death was nothing but poor health and even worse timing. Murder had nothing to do with it.

Yet the table jerked back and forth with such fervor that I was forced to stand in order to keep my hands on it. Across the way, Bertie did the same, his chair tumbling backward. Soon, all five of us were on our feet, the table seeming to move with a mind of its own.

"Do you know for a fact that you were murdered?"

The table began to turn, right under our hands. The varnished wood slid beneath my palms, picking up speed until the table was practically spinning.

"Tell us, Mrs. Pastor!" Marybelle called out. "Do you know who killed you?"

To my astonishment, the table continued to spin, even after four of us removed our hands. The only stubborn one was Bertie, who looked to be trying to wrangle it into submission. But he could do only so much, especially when the table wrenched itself from his grasp and flew across the room.

The event was so surprising that it heightened my senses. I heard, for example, Marybelle shriek, the sound echoing off the ceiling. I felt Violet clutch at me, face buried against my shoulder as she whimpered softly. And I saw the table in midair, somersaulting its way through the room, coming to a stop only when it crashed against the opposite wall and broke into a dozen pieces.

V

Violet was so shaken by the table-tipping incident that I felt compelled to ride with her all the way back to the Willoughby residence. While it was a fair distance away from my own home on Locust Street, the state she was in prevented me from leaving her alone. The normal color in her cheeks — drained at Bertie Johnson's party — had yet to return, and she shivered uncontrollably although the weather was quite mild.

We sat in silence, listening to the quick and steady clopping of the horses' hooves as Winslow guided the brougham down Spring Garden Street. When the noise changed from hooves on earth to those on wood, I knew we had come upon the wire bridge that spanned the Schuylkill River. The bridge's quartet of stone pillars passed our windows, connected by thick cable that drooped in the middle like a Christmas garland.

Beneath us, the river was a black ribbon that cut through the city. On its bank sat the Fairmount Water Works, its many-columned building more resembling a compound in ancient Greece than a water distribution plant. Rising behind it like a half-height Mount Olympus was the hill that housed the Fairmount Reservoir.

It was an impressive view — one that Violet took no notice of. Instead, she stared at her lap, focused only on the events of that evening.

"I just don't understand, Edward," she said. "What we witnessed tonight . . . How was that possible?"

"It was Bertie and the others trying to frighten you," I assured her. "Nothing more."

Violet shook her head. "Bertie wouldn't do that. Not to me. I'm his oldest friend."

"It was pure foolishness, just like I told you it would be."

"The table *flew* across the room," Violet said. "I saw it happen. We all did."

"Which is exactly what Bertie wanted." I took her hand, patting it gently. "It was a cruel trick, and I would box his ears if I knew he meant any harm by it."

Violet seemed to believe me, although she had no reason to. We had both seen the exact same thing — that damned table flinging itself against the wall. While Bertie did have his hands on it before it took flight, he certainly didn't throw it. I only said that to calm Violet's nerves. In reality, I had no idea what had propelled that table. It certainly wasn't the great Bertie Johnson. He'd need better skills than Magellan Holmes to accomplish such an illusion.

"If it was Bertie playing a trick, then I'll never forgive him," Violet said. "Never, ever."

"You'll just have to play a trick on him then," I told her. "Something wicked."

A flicker of a smile crossed Violet's face as she no doubt envisioned just such a vengeance, but it quickly passed. "It's not ladylike to play pranks on others. Mother would be appalled that I spent even a moment thinking about it."

Our conversation seemed to have done a world of good, because by the time we arrived at her house, Violet was in much better spirits. I bid her a chaste good-bye on her doorstep, Winslow monitoring us from his perch atop the brougham. I promised Violet that I'd call on her the next evening before hopping back into the coach and letting Winslow drive me home.

Upon being dropped off at Locust Street, I found Barclay on my front stoop, smoking the corncob pipe he had purchased in Virginia during the war. I was there when he bought it at a dry goods store whose shopkeeper made no attempt to hide her contempt for

Yankee filth like us. But she was more than happy to take Barclay's money when he bought that silly pipe. It should have been falling apart by now, but Barclay treated it as if it were made from the finest ivory. He cherished the thing, for reasons unknown to me. I wanted nothing to remind me of that time and place.

"Edward," Barclay said when he saw me, the word pushing a puff of smoke from the pipe. "I was wondering when you'd return."

"And I'm wondering why you're waiting at my door," I replied, although I already knew the reason. He was there to talk about Lenora Grimes Pastor.

I invited Barclay into the house, but he insisted he was fine talking outside. "It might be better," he said, "considering what I have to tell you."

"It's bad news, then?"

"The coroner has concluded his autopsy on Mrs. Pastor. It is his belief that she was purposely killed. An official investigation into her death has now been opened."

This was stunning news, and most horrific. It was also, to my mind, extremely confounding.

"I don't understand," I said. "How did she die?"

"She was poisoned," Barclay said, puffing on his pipe as if that explained everything.

"But how is that possible?"

"During the autopsy, a small wound was discovered on her neck, a few inches below her left ear. It was a puncture wound. The skin was pierced, almost as if someone had pricked her with a sharp object of some kind."

"With the intent of stabbing her to death?"

"Not quite," Barclay said. "It was the kind of mark left by a vaccination."

Having received a fair number of vaccinations during the war, I knew exactly what he was describing. Those wretched needles as thick as a hay straw. I had been stabbed and prodded by so many, I'm surprised I didn't have nightmares about them.

"The coroner thinks, as do I, that the puncture mark on her neck was where someone used a needle and a syringe to administer a toxic substance," Barclay continued. "This poison caused her throat to swell and seize up, blocking the passage of air."

Despite my extreme tiredness, my reporter's instincts sprang to life. A sea of questions flooded my mind, each begging to be asked first. I settled on the most obvious one.

"What kind of poison was used?"

"That's an interesting question," Barclay said. "I wish I could provide an answer."

"You don't want it to appear in the *Bulletin,* I suppose."

Barclay puffed on his pipe, exhaling smoke as he replied, "Not particularly. Don't want to be giving other potential poisoners any ideas. But that isn't the reason I can't tell you. In truth, we don't know what kind of poison was used. The coroner has requested help from an expert on toxic substances in New York. He'll be arriving tomorrow morning."

"That's unusual," I said.

"It certainly is. But this was a most unusual murder."

"But it can't be murder," I said. "I assure you, no one laid a finger on Mrs. Pastor the entire time I was there. The first person to touch her was her husband, after the séance had come to its abrupt end."

"Are you positive of this?"

"Of course," I said, running through the events of the séance in my mind's eye. I once again saw Mrs. Pastor collapsed in her chair as the instruments floated about. I saw the wind, that startling and impossible breeze, rustling the skirts of her oversize dress. I saw the instruments fall around us like hailstones. Then Mr. Barnum's bloody head. Then the fire on the floor, springing to life. Then —

"I'm mistaken," I blurted out. "There *was* a moment when someone could have touched her."

I was referring to when I was trying to smother the fire. Although the room had been plunged into darkness, I saw someone approach Mrs. Pastor. I didn't see it for long. It was just the briefest of glimpses, forgotten in

214

all the activity that happened afterward.

Barclay leaned forward, eager to hear more. "Did you see who it was?"

"I couldn't," I said. "I was only able to see a darkened form. But the person went directly to Mrs. Pastor. I'm sure of that."

"For how long?"

"A few seconds at the most. It wasn't long before I put the fire out. Once I did, I saw Mrs. Pastor slumped in her chair. Dead, apparently, only we didn't know that yet."

A stream of guilt trickled into my heart as I realized that, other than her killer, I was in all likelihood the last person to see Mrs. Pastor alive. I even could have prevented her death, had I known someone intended to do her harm.

"Is it possible that someone could have crept into the room while it was dark and killed her?" Barclay asked.

"No," I answered. "The door was locked. Plus, we would have noticed it opening."

"Even with all that activity going on?"

"Especially with all that," I said. "The door would have let in light and let out the smoke. No, it was closed the entire time. I'm sure of it."

"So someone in that room is the culprit."

That seemed to be the case — a truth that unnerved me no end. I had been locked in a darkened room with a killer. A realization such as that would give the most stouthearted of men pause.

"Is there anyone under suspicion?"

"Several people, as a matter of fact." Barclay lowered his pipe and offered me a look of earnest sympathy. "I regret to inform you, Edward, that you're one of them."

So this was why he had come to my house. He wanted to tell me himself, instead of letting some low-ranking policeman do it. He had expected me to look utterly shocked, probably, although I was not. I was one of seven people in the room with Mrs. Pastor when she died. Of course I'd be considered a suspect.

Still, I wasn't pleased by the news. Not in the least.

"I see," I said, frowning.

Barclay placed a hand on my shoulder, offering cold comfort. "You know I don't really think you could do such a thing. You said yourself you were putting out a fire at the time. Others present confirmed your story."

"That right there should exonerate me, no?"

"And it will. Very soon. Just not at the moment. Someone at that séance committed the crime, and until I prove who it was, everyone present must be placed under suspicion."

"When will this investigation become public knowledge?" I asked.

"I'm afraid it already has," Barclay said. "There were a few reporters for the morning

216

papers idling about police headquarters. I'm sure they're writing about it as we speak."

I should have known that was a possibility. In fact, I should have been one of those very same reporters, hounding any policeman I saw for details. The news left me stunned. I stumbled backward, as if trying to stay upright in the face of a raging headwind. This would not only tarnish my reputation as a journalist, but also as a future member of the Willoughby family.

"Rest assured, Edward, that I will make every effort to clear your name immediately," Barclay said.

But that wouldn't matter to those at the *Public Ledger* or the *Times* or even those colleagues at the *Bulletin* who had regarded me with such envy that very morning. I was certain every effort would be made to associate me with Mrs. Pastor's murder for as long as possible. There was no riper target for other men of the press than a fellow reporter shamed.

"What am I supposed to do in the meantime?" I asked, wincing at how helpless I sounded.

"Just stay home and out of sight," Barclay instructed. "This will pass within a day or so."

"That's easy for you to say. You're not the one accused of murder."

Shifting his weight from one leg to the

other, Barclay popped the pipe back into his mouth before placing his hands on his hips. When he sighed, smoke snaked out with it. He resembled an agitated bull, huffing and puffing. I would have found it comical had I not been so angry with him.

"Edward, no one has accused you of anything. You're about as likely to commit murder as I am."

"Then announce my innocence at once," I demanded. "Find those reporters and forbid them from mentioning that I had anything to do with her death."

"You know I can't do that. For now, I need to treat you as I would any suspect."

In truth, I had expected more from Barclay, and not just because I had saved his life all those years ago. I thought our friendship would be enough to make him mount an immediate and strong defense of my character, to cause him to rally around me. That he hadn't disappointed me greatly. Even though I knew he was only doing his duty as a member of the nation's oldest police force, I couldn't help but feel betrayed.

Without saying another word, I went inside, leaving Barclay alone on the street. I slammed the door — the only retort I could muster — and climbed the stairs, feeling only exhaustion.

The depth of my anger should have kept me wide awake.

In truth, the opposite happened. I was so weighted with concerns that my entire body wound down, like a tin toy that needed cranking. My legs got heavier. Not even toothpicks would have kept my eyes open. For a moment, I wondered if I'd even make it up the steps, let alone into my room. I did, but barely. And when I reached the bed, I collapsed onto it facefirst, immediately plummeting into sleep.

VI

In the morning, I was awakened by sunlight yawning across my ceiling. I yawned right along with it, feeling more relaxed than I had in days. Tangled among my sheets, I enjoyed a blissful moment suspended between sleep and wakefulness. It didn't last long, of course. There's no way it could have. Before I knew it, all my thoughts and worries crashed over me like ice water thrown from a bucket. I sat up, recalling everything from the day before. The pale man with no nose. The flying table. The fact that I was a murder suspect.

But the thought at the forefront of my mind, the thing that concerned me most, was the newspaper. I needed to get to it before anyone else in the household did.

I sprang out of bed, heart palpitating. Since I had spent the entire night in my clothes, I traded one foul-smelling, wrinkled suit for a clean and pressed one before running downstairs. Lionel met me at the bottom.

"Good morning, Mr. Clark. Your breakfast is in the dining room. I took the liberty of pouring your coffee."

Food was the last thing on my mind, seeing how my stomach was knotted with worry.

"Where's the newspaper?" I asked.

"Which one?"

Like any journalist worth his salt, I read several newspapers, morning and evening editions. I paid a neighbor boy to bring them around twice a day.

"Any of them," I said, flustered. "Or all of them."

"Mrs. Patterson took the *Inquirer*," Lionel replied. "You know how she likes the —"

I didn't wait for him to finish, instead hurrying to the kitchen, where I found Mrs. Patterson slicing carrots to make a soup for lunch. A pot bubbled on the stovetop, and I felt exactly like the soup it contained — simmering with anxiety.

"The newspaper?"

Mrs. Patterson waved her knife in the direction of the small table where she and Lionel had their meals. "It's over there. But I haven't had time to read the —"

Again, I didn't listen. Instead, I ran to the table and grabbed the *Inquirer*, which had remained untouched. The front page contained the headline I was dreading to see:

MEDIUM WAS MURDERED.

Holding my breath, I scanned the article, stopping when I saw my name in print.

Chief among the suspects is Mr. Edward Clark, a writer for the *Philadelphia Evening Bulletin*. Just yesterday, Mr. Clark wrote grandly about having witnessed Mrs. Pastor's demise, never once mentioning that foul play was involved or that he would be implicated in this heinous deed.

Of course, I hadn't expected a rival newspaper to make an attempt to spare my reputation or give me the benefit of the doubt. Still, it made me furious. I stormed to the stove, opened it up, and tossed the newspaper inside, taking great satisfaction in watching it turn to ash.

"What in heaven's name are you doing?" Mrs. Patterson shouted. "I wanted to see the —"

I marched out of the kitchen and into the dining room, where two more newspapers sat on the table next to my untouched breakfast. Taking them in hand and returning to the kitchen, I threw those into the fire as well. Satisfied that every newspaper in the house had been destroyed, at least until the evening ones arrived, I departed for the offices of the *Bulletin*.

■ ■ ■ ■

Mr. Hamilton Gray, whose copy of the *Inquirer* I was unable to toss into the fire, of course had read the article that practically accused me of murdering Lenora Grimes Pastor. In a rare display of journalistic ethics, he announced it wouldn't be proper for me to continue writing about her death. He then suggested, much like Barclay had, for me to "hide under a bushel" until the police could uncover her real killer. I had no choice but to heed his advice. I was, at least for the time being, no longer employed at the *Evening Bulletin.*

I took my time walking home, shuffling over the sidewalk, a man shamed. In a single morning, I had gone from the toast of Philadelphia to the talk of it. It was humbling, to be sure.

During my walk, I made an attempt to ponder the bright side of the situation, which did exist, luckily. I knew that money wouldn't be an issue, no matter how long it took for this to blow over. The fortune amassed by my parents and inherited from my aunt sat safely inside Girard's Bank. Quite honestly, I didn't need to work another day in my life.

And that was the problem. I enjoyed work, toil, using my hands and my wits to make an honest living. I looked at men of the carriage class — men such as Bertram Johnson — and felt superior because I knew I was a cog in the machinery that kept Philadelphia running. There was value in that.

But now I didn't even have a job to call my own. Without it, I had no purpose. Days, perhaps even weeks, of boredom stretched before me, full of solitary dinners and evenings confined to my bedroom. I imagined becoming so bored that I'd seek employment from Violet's father, overseeing a squalid workroom of laborers constructing Willoughby hats — a dreadful prospect. Even death would have been preferable to such a fate.

By the time I reached home, lunch hour had arrived. Since I knew Lionel and Mrs. Patterson would be eating in the kitchen, I tiptoed through the front door and tried to make my way upstairs, too ashamed to face them. Their name was only as good as their employer's, and at that moment, he was being thoroughly dragged through the mud.

In the foyer, I passed a small table that contained a vase, a lamp, and a silver tray. Sitting on top of the tray was a white envelope. A calling card, addressed to me. Whoever it was from, I didn't want to see them or anyone else. Not for a very long time.

Sneaking to the main staircase, I got as far as the first step before overhearing Lionel, his voice rising from the kitchen. It was clear they already knew about Mrs. Pastor's death.

"It's a disgrace, no doubt about it," Lionel said. "Doesn't surprise me, the crowd he keeps company with. Those coppers coming by at all hours to take him to one corpse or another. I'll wager seeing all those murder victims pushed him off his rocker."

"He ain't been found guilty yet," Mrs. Patterson replied. "There's nothing for him to be ashamed of."

"If *I'm* ashamed then he better well be. I wanted to work in a respectable house, with respectable people. Now I find myself working for Edward Clark, the butcher of Locust Street."

Instead of continuing up the stairs, I pressed against the wall and inched closer to their conversation. Yes, I was blatantly eavesdropping, but not just because I was the topic of discussion. Their voices sounded strange in their informality — cocky, boisterous, unrefined. It made me wonder if Lionel and Mrs. Patterson often discussed me when I was gone and, if so, that this was how they always sounded.

"That Pastor woman was poisoned," Mrs. Patterson said. "Mrs. Brill, the new cook at the Douglas place, told me so this mornin'."

"So he's the *poisoner* of Locust Street. It still makes us look bad."

"I worry about Miss Willoughby. Such a lovely girl. This is going to be hard on her.

That engagement of theirs won't last much longer, I imagine."

"I could have told you that before this even happened," Lionel said. "What with that Collins woman now barging in here all the time."

My eyes widened at the mention of Lucy Collins, who to my knowledge had been here only once. Yet Mrs. Patterson's response — "What did she want this time?" — told me how wrong I was.

"She wouldn't say," Lionel said. "Just demanded to see Mr. Clark. After yesterday, I was ready for her. No way was I going to let her knock me down and search the house twice. I told her to leave a card, like a real lady would do."

I inched my way back toward the table in the foyer and removed the envelope from the silver tray. Taking great pains to open it as quietly as possible, I looked inside and saw a handwritten note.

I must see you. Christ Church Burial Ground. Two o'clock. Come alone. — Lucy

According to my watch, it was already one. Part of me knew I needed to stay home and ponder what I was going to tell Violet and her family later that evening. Yet another part of me insisted, quite rightly, that it would be torture to remain cooped up inside while the servants gossiped downstairs. Certain I wouldn't be able to stand hearing Lionel call

225

me the so-and-so of Locust Street one more time, I slipped out the front door, as silent and invisible as a ghost.

■ ■ ■ ■

BOOK FOUR:
THE MOST
RIDICULOUS NOTION
I HAD EVER HEARD

■ ■ ■ ■

I

Christ Church Burial Ground was a patch of land between Arch and Market streets, slightly northeast of the Pennsylvania State House. I passed that building, which in a few years would be renamed Independence Hall, on my way to the cemetery. As usual, it was a lively area, crowded with visitors lining up to touch the Liberty Bell, on display in the Declaration Chamber.

The cemetery was the complete opposite, as silent and still as the dead buried there. Mrs. Collins's coach was parked outside, with Thomas at the reins. While the horses shared a sack of oats, he occupied himself by puffing on a pipe as large as his fist.

I considered greeting the boy, but thought better of it. It wasn't inconceivable of him to dump the pipe's smoldering contents atop my head. So I hurried through the cemetery's wrought-iron gate, seeing Lucy standing before the grave of Dr. Benjamin Franklin. She wore a dress of black and white stripes, a black hat circled by white ribbon on her head. The dual colors made her look simultaneously festive and somber — a woman only partially in mourning.

The sight of her caused my heart to beat just a little bit faster. It was similar to the way any man's pulse quickened at the sight of a beautiful woman, yet also different. For while Lucy Collins was indeed a ray of light in the otherwise somber cemetery, I had a feeling the slight racing of my heart had more to do with anticipation. I didn't know what she wanted or what she was going to say, a fact that left me both eager and fearful.

Yet she smiled when she saw me. A good sign, I thought, considering our last conversation.

"You came," she said. "I wasn't certain you would."

"I wasn't certain I *should*," I said.

"Yet here you are."

"Indeed. Now, would you mind telling me *why* I'm here? It was my assumption we were never going to meet again."

"Our circumstances have changed, wouldn't you agree?"

Lucy took my arm and led me deeper into the cemetery. We traversed the path that bisected it, not stopping until we reached its end, near the back wall. Lucy only spoke once we traded the path for grass, the verdant blades swiping the hem of her skirts.

"Your friend the police inspector paid me a visit this morning," she said. "He told me that Mrs. Pastor was murdered."

"It's true. Poisoned."

"Inspector Barclay also told me, in no uncertain terms, that I am suspected of the crime. From the way he spoke, I get the sense that I'm his *only* suspect."

She said this with such indignation that it was clear she didn't see the logic of it. Yet how could she not? She was a fake medium who visited a competitor who later died. Now, knowing Lucy as I did, I couldn't put the idea of murder past her. Yet I also knew that at the moment of Mrs. Pastor's death, Lucy had been trying to stanch the flow of blood from P. T. Barnum's head. She was certainly not the figure I saw approaching Lenora Grimes Pastor in the darkness.

"Don't worry too much about that," I said. "I'm a suspect as well. So is everyone else who was with us in that room."

"I could care less about them. I'm concerned about myself." Lucy paused before swiftly adding, "And you, of course."

"I had assumed this wouldn't affect you very much."

"Your assumption was wrong," she said. "I'm a businesswoman, aren't I? My business lives or dies by my reputation. And with my reputation gone, there are far too many other mediums in this city who will take my lost business. Oh, if only the rest of them would drop dead as well!"

Being in her presence again reminded me of how vibrantly annoying she could be. Beneath her veneer of properness, she was as rough as sandpaper running against the grain. Take, for example, how she leaned against the nearest gravestone, insouciant as a schoolgirl.

"You're violating someone's final resting place," I told her.

"But he's dead," Lucy said, removing herself only long enough to read the name etched into the stone. "I doubt Commodore Thomas Truxton minds. If I were under there, I'd be all too happy to let the good commodore lean on my grave."

My patience, already worn thin, all but evaporated when Lucy resumed leaning on the gravestone and said, "I blame *you* for all this."

"Me? You're the one who wanted to visit Mrs. Pastor."

"We wouldn't have been there if you weren't determined to expose mediums in the first place."

At that moment, I'm certain there wasn't a beet in Philadelphia as red as my face. The nerve of that woman! I wanted to tell her that she certainly didn't need to blackmail me nor did she have to become a swindler in the first place, but I was too flustered. All that came out of my mouth was a single, unintelligible noise that sounded something like, *"Gah!"*

Lucy's eyes widened and her mouth formed a perfect, mirthful circle. She held a gloved hand to her mouth, trying to halt the torrent of laughter about to arrive. Instead, it only muffled the sound.

I couldn't help but laugh, too. It was either that or throttle her right there in the cemetery, and I was in enough hot water. So we both let our laughter rise in the burial ground until it echoed off its brick-walled border. When it subsided, Lucy pressed a hand against her flushed cheek and said, "Oh, Edward, what are we going to do?"

Despite my anger, I found myself softening upon hearing her use my first name. "There's nothing we can do but wait until our names are cleared."

"There has to be a better alternative than that. What if you wrote something in the *Bulletin* proclaiming our innocence?"

"As of this morning, I no longer write for the *Bulletin*," I said. "At least not until the matter of Mrs. Pastor's death is settled."

Rather than expressing sympathy, Lucy's response was a frustrated, "Well, we must do *something.*"

"We will be found innocent," I said. "It may take a day or two, but Inspector Barclay will discover who did this to Mrs. Pastor."

Lucy removed herself from Commodore

Truxton's headstone and resumed walking through the cemetery, aimless and anxious. "We can't simply wait and hope our names will be cleared. That could take weeks, perhaps years. I won't have a customer left if it takes that long. And think of your beloved Miss Willoughby. Eventually, she'll get tired of being engaged to a murder suspect and find someone more suitable to marry."

"What do you suggest we do?" I asked.

"We clear our names by ourselves."

"And how might we do that?"

"It's simple," Lucy said. "We combine our efforts and solve Mrs. Pastor's murder."

I replied with another outburst of laughter, one so loud and forceful I was certain it could be heard even by the dead who occupied that hallowed ground.

"It's not as ridiculous as all that," Lucy said.

But it was. The two of us playing detective! It was the most ridiculous notion I had ever heard. Neither of us knew the first thing about solving crime, especially one as heinous as murder. We'd be entirely out of our element.

"I think we should leave the police work to the actual police," I said. "Inspector Barclay will solve this particular puzzle. I'm certain of it."

"And what if he doesn't?" Lucy asked. "What if your inspector friend never identifies the culprit?"

Granted, I hadn't thought of that. But now that the idea was in my head, I couldn't rid myself of it. There were unsolved murders all the time in Philadelphia. On occasion, I'd heard Barclay moan about how he regretted never finding the person who had shot this man or strangled that woman. It was very possible Mrs. Pastor's death could end up like one of those — forever a mystery, a shadow of suspicion always hanging over us.

"All right. Let's for the moment pretend that I agree to this plan," I said. "How do you think we could go about it?"

"Well, you've reported on crimes such as murder," Lucy answered. "Surely you've learned something about how to solve them."

Her assumption was correct, although at that moment I wished I had paid more attention to the various crime scenes I'd visited. I had also learned a thing or two from Barclay, who enjoyed regaling me with stories of past crimes on nights when both of us had had slightly too much ale. I knew, for instance, that blood patterns on walls and floors could be studied to determine from which direction a bullet had been fired. That the angle and depth of a knife wound could show you what hand a culprit favored. And I learned that in cases of murder, an inspector's first instinct was often the correct one.

"But what skills do you bring?" I asked Lucy.

She gave a tiny shrug of her shoulders. "I don't have any. But I know plenty of people who do."

Of that, I had no doubt. She was, after all, the woman who'd persuaded Mathew Brady himself to show up at my doorstep and take my photograph.

"You're considering it," she said, watching me closely. "I can tell. You want the shadow of this crime to be gone from your life as much as I do."

I did, very much so, which was why I replied, "If we were to do this — and I'm not saying I will — how do you propose we start our investigation?"

"Clearly, someone in that room killed Mrs. Pastor. According to Inspector Barclay, the means was poison. But what about motive? I think we first need to uncover *why* Mrs. Pastor was killed. So I suggest we return to the scene of the crime, the Pastor residence, and talk to the person who knew Mrs. Pastor the best — her husband."

She had clearly given the matter a good deal of thought. Yet the more I considered it, the more it seemed like the wrong course of action. Robert Pastor was, after all, a suspect, just like us.

"I think we should speak to someone else," I said. "Someone who knew Mrs. Pastor almost as well as her husband, if not better."

"Such as?"

I thought back to an hour earlier, when I'd listened in on Lionel and Mrs. Patterson gossiping about me. They'd spoken with alarming candor, as if I were a scandalized neighbor and not the man paying their wages.

"The servants," I said decisively. "We need to question Mrs. Pastor's household staff. They know everything that went on in that house. And I have a feeling they'll be very willing to share it with us."

II

Shortly thereafter, Lucy and I stood outside the home of the late Lenora Grimes Pastor. While I hadn't officially agreed to her plan, she took my suggestion as an affirmative answer and whisked me to the scene of the crime. I was only going along with it on the chance that we might learn something important, which Barclay could then use to clear our names.

Normally, I would have felt wrong visiting a house in mourning so soon after a death. The rules of Philadelphia society dictated that only the closest of family members and friends could immediately call. Yet there were no signs that it truly was a house of mourning. No black crepe hung over the door or windows. Someone passing on the street, unaware of Mrs. Pastor's fate, would think it was an average day for the household.

The door was answered by the same mighty oak of a butler who had greeted us two nights earlier. Only the gentle, smiling face we saw then had been replaced by one that was deeply saddened.

"If you came round to pay your respects to Mister Pastor," he said, "he ain't home."

"Actually, we're here to see you," I said.

"And the servant girl," Lucy added. "And anyone else who might be in service to the Pastors."

The butler was rightfully suspicious. Doubt furrowed his brow as he said, "That don't make much sense, if y'all pardon me saying so."

He was right in that regard. It didn't make a lick of sense. Yet there we were on the doorstep, not knowing what to say next. A fine pair of detectives we were.

"We're sorry for disturbing you," I said. "It was wrong of us to come."

I made a move off the front steps, but Lucy grabbed me by the elbow and squeezed. She had a wicked grip, that woman, which held me in place as she stated our case to the butler.

"What's your name again?" she asked.

"Stokely, ma'am."

"Well, Stokely, this morning I was speaking to my own servants about Mrs. Pastor's passing. They spoke of how saddened they would be if a similar thing happened to me. 'Mrs.

Collins,' they told me, 'we'd be overwhelmed with grief if you ever died on us. We'd have nowhere to go and no one to talk to.' Hearing that, naturally, made me think of *you*."

It was the biggest lie I had ever heard. A cruder man than I would have correctly classified it as "horseshit." But it was a convincing one, aided by Lucy's sympathetic tone and the batting of her beautiful green eyes. I would have believed it myself if I hadn't known any better, so it was no surprise that the butler took it to be God's honest truth.

"That's right kind of you, ma'am," he said, widening the door. "Come in, but you can't be long. Mister Pastor will be comin' back any minute now."

We entered the humble foyer, seeing no signs of mourning there, either. Stokely's clothes, I noted, also gave no indication that someone had died. Usually, it was customary for servants to wear a black armband.

"You can sit a spell in here, if you'd like," Stokely said, gesturing to the very sitting room where Mrs. Pastor had died.

"Since Mr. Pastor will be home shortly," Lucy said, "and since we certainly don't want to bother him in this time of mourning, perhaps our visit will be made faster if I seek out the servant girl on my own."

"You mean Claudia?"

"Yes. I believe that was her name."

"She's upstairs," Stokely said. "But I'm tell-in' you now, she ain't gonna say nothin'."

Lucy, undeterred, offered him a wave of thanks before climbing the staircase just beyond the front door. I followed Stokely into the sitting room, which was only slightly less of a mess than two nights before. Instruments were still scattered everywhere, including the massive harp stuck in the floorboards. The chairs and tables had been set right, but the broken lamps were now in a pile of glass shards on the floor. Next to it was a streak of blackened wood. The site of the fire.

Stokely picked up a nearby brush and dustpan and began to sweep up the wreckage of the lamps, leading me to ask, "Is this where Mrs. Pastor will be lying in state?"

"No, sir. She's gonna be buried as soon as she comes home. That's the Quaker way, see. They live plain. They don't much care for them big funerals or all that mournin'. Missus Pastor once told me the best way to pay your respects is to live the way the one who passed lived. I'm gonna try. For her sake."

Stokely dumped the contents of the dustpan into the trash. When he returned for seconds, he said, "Now, you gonna tell me why you really came 'round? I know it ain't 'cause you're worried about the help."

Of course he hadn't believed us. It was foolish of me to ever think he had.

"We wanted to ask the two of you some questions," I admitted. "About the night Mrs.

Pastor died."

Stokely set the brush and dustpan aside to move on to the instruments. He placed the smaller ones on the tables and set the bigger ones upright while saying, "Why do you want to waste your time talkin' to us?"

"Because we're trying to find out who killed her."

"Accordin' to the papers, either of *you* might have done it."

I must have looked surprised, because Stokely let out an annoyed huff and said, "Yes'sir, I read the papers. Missus Pastor taught me how to read. First thing she done when I got here. Taught me readin'. Taught me some math. Tried to teach me writin', but I didn't take to it."

"How long did you work for her?"

"Eleven years."

"That's a very long time," I said, thinking about the three months Lionel had worked for me. Although a capable butler, I envisioned him leaving sooner rather than later. And after overhearing what he'd said about me, I had a feeling it would be very soon indeed.

"I met Missus Pastor in January 1858," Stokely said. "Knew from the minute I met her that she was different from most ladies. Right special, see? And kind. No one as kind as her."

"Were you always a servant?"

241

"No, sir," Stokely said, picking up Mrs. Pastor's tambourine and dropping it on the table. "I was a slave. And they are two very different things."

He moved to the harp, nudging it back and forth in an attempt to pry it from the floorboards. However, his sheer size proved no match for the heavy instrument. After watching him make a few more grunting tries, I jumped in to help. It took more effort than I expected, the harp being as stubborn and heavy as a hay-fattened mule. But together we managed to dislodge it from the floor and lift it to sturdier ground.

While the effort left me winded, it made Stokely, who had manned the heavier end of the harp, positively drenched with sweat. I offered him a handkerchief, which he used to mop his face.

"Much obliged," he said. "I don't know 'bout you, but that left me thirstin' for an iced tea. You want a glass?"

"If you're having one, then yes."

We left the sitting room and set off down the hall to a kitchen at the back of the house. It was a sunny room, warm and comforting. Hanging from the green-painted walls were a skillet, a calendar, and a rectangular slate with the words HOUSEHOLD NEEDS written on it in chalk. According to the slate, the Pastor household was in need of potatoes, flour, and a tin of Earl Grey tea. Just beyond the slate was a door leading to the cellar. Through the open doorway, I spotted a few crooked shelves, a patch of brick wall, and a single wooden step. Nearby was a stove that looked brand new; a sink with an indoor water pump; and a very large, very expensive icebox. For people who liked to live plain, the amenities in the Pastors' kitchen had cost quite a pretty penny.

Stokely led me to a woodblock table in the middle of the room. Already sitting out was a pitcher of iced tea.

"If you want, you can ask me a question or two," he said as he fetched a glass from the sink and filled it for me. "I'll try best as I can to answer."

"How did you come to work for Mrs. Pastor?" I asked.

"She didn't hire me so much as keep me 'round." While pouring his own glass of tea, Stokely nodded toward the cellar door. "I came up those cellar steps and never left."

"What were you doing in the cellar?"

"This here was a safe house."

"On the Underground Railroad?"

"That's what you folks call it," Stokely said. "The name don't make much sense to me, though. Makes it sound like there was a bunch of us ridin' the rails in high style. In truth, it was scary. Not knowin' who to trust. Not knowin' if the house you were walkin' into was truly safe. But I could tell this here house was safe. There's a tunnel down there, see. Runnin' from the river right to yon cellar."

"So this route was literally underground?"

"Yes'sir," Stokely said. "Word is Missus Pastor's daddy done had it built in secret for the sole purpose of helpin' folks like me. When he took ill, Missus Pastor kept it goin'. Back then she was Miss Grimes. In Virginia, every slave that was runnin' was told to go see Ole Maid Miss Grimes in Philadelphia. 'She'll help you,' they said. 'Go see her.' So that's what I done. I was in sore shape by then. I been runnin' for goin' on six months. All the way from Georgia. I was right sick. Fever so bad I was burnin' up and shiverin' cold at the same time. When I popped up from that cellar, the first person I met was Missus Pastor. She done took one look at me and sent me straight to bed. I healed quick, though. Soon I was helpin' out 'round the house. Tryin' to repay Missus Pastor, see. Soon, though, she started payin' *me.* The first wages I was ever paid. And I've been here ever since."

Stokely's tale was so fascinating that I momentarily forgot to ask another question. I was too busy thinking about the perseverance it took on his part to make the long and dangerous journey here. It wasn't until he said, "Is that all you're gonna ask?" that I remembered the true purpose of my visit.

"No," I said, taking a quick sip of tea to cover my distractedness. "I have plenty more. For instance, where were you and Claudia during the séance?"

"Right here, like usual. The séances always went the same. Folks show up, I open the door and tell 'em where to go, then I go wait right here in the kitchen with Claudia till it's done."

"The door was locked during the séance. Was that always the case?"

"Always," Stokely said.

"Who kept the key while the séances were taking place? You or Claudia?"

"Neither of us. It hangs right here in the kitchen, where both of us can grab it." Stokely pointed to a nail stuck into the wall near the kitchen door. Dangling from it was a small key that glinted in the afternoon sunlight. "It was still sittin' there when y'all called for help."

I remembered Stokely being the one to unlock the door after I realized Mrs. Pastor was dead. It was Robert Pastor who had pounded on our side, yelling to him for assistance.

"So no one could have used it to sneak inside the room?" I asked.

"No, sir. Me and Claudia would have seen them grab it."

"How often did Mrs. Pastor hold séances?"

"Every night 'cept Sunday," Stokely said.

"Lately, though, Missus Pastor started havin' séances on Saturday mornin', too. A one-on-one sittin', she called it. I was never s'posed to answer the door on Saturday mornin', on account of the missus's guests wantin' to keep the visits a secret."

"How long ago did these Saturday morning sittings start?"

"Six months, I s'pose."

"And did you ever get a glimpse of who came to them?"

Although Stokely answered with a prompt, "No, sir," I could tell he was lying. It made me wonder what else he was withholding. Still, since it was clear he didn't want to talk about it, I didn't press the issue.

"Did you notice anything unusual before the séance on Saturday night?"

"Nothin' I can think of other than you and that pretty Missus Collins showin' up."

"So everyone else present was a frequent customer of Mrs. Pastor?"

"Yes'sir," Stokely said. "Not Mister Barnum, though. Saturday night was only his second visit."

"When was his first?"

"I reckon it was a week ago. Maybe more. He showed up, bolt out of the blue like."

"Do you know why?"

"I s'pose he wanted to talk to the dead like the rest of 'em."

"Like Mrs. Pastor's regular clients?"

Stokely gave a firm nod. "Yes'sir."

"The others at the séance — Mrs. Mueller and Mr. and Mrs. Dutton — came quite often, did they not?"

"Yes'sir. They came by lots. Missus Mueller was here two, three times a week. The Duttons not so much, but enough for me to know their names and them to know mine. Mister Dutton always made sure to give me a hello when he came by."

"On Saturday mornings?"

Stokely, too sly to fall for such a trick, tilted his head and gave me the same look a schoolmarm would use only on her most troublesome pupil. "I seen him once on a Saturday mornin'. Whether he came again, I don't know. Not that seein' him surprised me none. Like you said, they was Missus Pastor's regular customers. Why, Missus Dutton came 'round just this past Friday mornin'."

"Did she often stop by during the daytime?"

"No, sir. This was the first time. She came 'round wantin' to see Mister Pastor. He weren't here, so I told her I'd pass along that she came by. She said, 'Don't you worry 'bout that, Mister Stokely.' And then she up and left."

More than anything else Stokely had said, this caught my attention. "Do you happen to know why Mrs. Dutton wanted to speak to Mr. Pastor?"

Stokely looked more exasperated than irritated. Just when I was getting on his good side, too.

"I can read the newspaper," he said. "But I can't read minds."

Taking that as a no, I gulped down some more tea before asking, "Other than the Duttons and Mrs. Mueller, did Mrs. Pastor have any other frequent visitors?"

"None that I can recall," Stokely replied. "People came and went 'round here. Some came every week for months then never came again. Others done come only once. Others came, then stayed gone a year, then came back. It didn't matter none to Missus Pastor. She just enjoyed helpin' folks."

"Do you think she truly helped them?"

"I think so. Folks came lookin' for comfort and that's what Missus Pastor done give 'em."

"Did you ever attend one of her séances? Perhaps to find comfort yourself?"

Stokely gave an emphatic shake of his head. "No, sir. Missus Pastor tried, though. Back when she was still Miss Grimes. She'd say, 'Stokely, come sit and we'll try to talk to your mama.' But I didn't want no part of it. I don't mess around with the dead. Some folks that passed, you don't want to meet again."

"When did Miss Grimes become Mrs. Pastor?"

Stokely took another long sip of iced tea and wiped his mouth with the back of his hand. "You sure do ask a lot of questions."

248

"I know," I said, well aware that I had already posed an absurd number of them. I blamed that on being a momentarily silenced journalist. "But your answers have me very curious. Now, about Mr. and Mrs. Pastor's marriage —"

"They got married about nine years ago or so," Stokely said with a sigh. "Mister Pastor came callin' in 1860. Spring, it was. Don't recall when they wed, but I think it was a month or so after that."

"Was Mrs. Pastor a medium back then?"

Stokely shrugged in response, his broad shoulders rising and falling. "I s'pose she was. Folks just knew she had the gift, so some came by on occasion. It didn't grow to nothin' till Mister Pastor came 'round and married her. Not too long after that, Missus Pastor was famous."

"So it was her husband who pushed Mrs. Pastor to become a full-fledged medium?"

I got another shrug from Stokely. "I guess. I s'pose he thought Missus Pastor could make good money talkin' to the dead like she could. But Missus Pastor refused to charge folks. Said it was wrong to make folks pay for somethin' God gave her for free."

"And what did Mr. Pastor think of this?"

"I suspect he wanted God's gift to start payin' the bills."

"To your knowledge, did Mr. and Mrs. Pastor often talk about finances? Did you ever overhear any arguments, for instance?"

Stokely raised an eyebrow. "You mean, was I eavesdroppin'?"

"Not necessarily," I said. "I was simply wondering if they ever discussed it in front of you."

"All the time Mister Pastor was askin' the missus to change her mind. He thought she was born to money, which is the truth. Her daddy's the one who done built that water-works in the park 'cross the way. Made a lot of money in the process. And when he died, Missus Pastor inherited it all. But she loved her charity work. Went and gave it all away. That plain livin' again, see. Finally, though, she told Mister Pastor she'd be willin' to take money if it went to her charities."

"What made her change her mind?"

"I reckon she got sick and tired of hearin' Mister Pastor harp about it so much," Stokely said. "Also, she had a lot of rich folks come sit with her. Some so rich, they could buy the whole city. I s'pose Missus Pastor thought if they was givin', she'd be takin' and helpin' others in the process."

It crossed my mind that Robert Pastor was just another of those unscrupulous rascals who found wealthy old maids to marry them. When I asked what Mr. Pastor did for work before he was married, Stokely said, "He was a salesman. That's how he and Missus Pastor met. He came 'round wantin' to sell her supplies."

"What kind of salesman and what kind of supplies?"

"Medical supplies. On account of her daddy bein' ill. His sickbed was upstairs instead of the hospital. That's also the Quaker way. They don't like no hospitals, see. But as soon as they was married, Mister Pastor stopped his sellin'."

The more Stokely talked, the more the puzzle pieces fell into place. I pictured a desperate Robert Pastor arriving in town, acquiring the only job he could find. He probably had contact with some of the city's doctors, finding out where he could sell his wares. It was easy to assume that a physician who knew Mr. Grimes was ill would also know that they — he and his unmarried daughter — were wealthy. Perhaps he was even informed about her gifts as a medium. This, of course, didn't mean Robert Pastor was the one who killed his wife. If he had, then he surely wouldn't have requested an examination of her corpse.

"I have a favor to ask you," I told Stokely. "A sizable one."

"Bigger than that harp?" Stokely asked, cracking a white-toothed smile for the first time that afternoon.

"Much bigger," I said.

"What is it?"

"I need to speak to Mr. Pastor. Alone. Without the presence of the police."

Stokely opened his mouth to protest, but I kept talking. "Someone killed Mrs. Pastor during that séance, and it certainly wasn't me, I swear to you. I believe the person who killed her did so for a specific purpose. They felt wronged by Mrs. Pastor somehow, or were angry enough to do her harm. It is also my belief that Mr. Pastor knew about this threat to her safety."

"Now what makes you think that?"

"He asked the police to perform an autopsy," I said. "You do know what that is, right?"

Stokely nodded. "Cuttin' open a body to see what done killed it."

"Exactly. I think he immediately suspected that Mrs. Pastor was murdered. I would like to know why."

"He ain't goin' to want to talk to you," Stokely said.

"I know that. This is where you come in. You could convince him to speak with me by telling him that you know I'm innocent."

"But I *don't* know you're innocent."

Still, from the way he lifted his chin slightly, I could tell Stokely was giving my request some thought. I studied his face, noticing how well the darkness of his skin hid the deep-set wrinkles around his eyes and mouth. Other than patches of gray at his temples, there was no immediate indication as to how old he really was. Someone seeing him for the first time could have pegged him as forty or eighty. My assumption was that his true age was somewhere in between.

"And you think talkin' to him could help you shed light on who killed Missus Pastor?" he asked.

"Possibly, yes."

"Let me stew it over," Stokely said. "I don't risk my neck for strangers, and you're a stranger, Mister Clark."

"Then do it for Mrs. Pastor," I told him. "Please."

We heard the sound of footsteps in the hallway. Light and quick, they echoed into the kitchen. A voice soon accompanied them.

"Edward? Where are you?"

It was Lucy, of course. I'd heard enough of her voice by that point to recognize its singularly determined tone.

"We're in the kitchen," I called back.

A moment later, Lucy appeared, practically dragging the poor servant girl behind her.

"Edward," she said. "We have a bit of a problem."

III

The problem, as far as I could tell, was that Claudia refused to speak. Sitting at the kitchen table, the thick braid of her hair

253

thrown over one shoulder, she gazed at Lucy and me with a wide-eyed mixture of innocence and fear. But she didn't make a sound.

"She's not talking," Lucy said. "I've asked a dozen different questions, but she refused to answer a single one."

Stokely, standing behind her, grumbled, "I warned you she ain't gonna tell you nothin'. Claudia can't talk."

"She's mute?" I asked, looking first to Stokely, then the girl, then back to Stokely again.

"Yes'sir. I ain't never heard her say one word since she got here."

"How long has she been here?" Lucy asked.

Although the question had been posed to Stokely, Claudia answered it by holding up an index finger.

"One year," Stokely said, clarifying.

"How does she communicate?" I asked him.

Stokely gave me yet another one of his shrugs. "She don't. We just tell her what needs done and she does it. Sometimes she nods, but not much."

"Well, this is wretched," Lucy said. "How can we possibly get her to answer any questions when all she can do is nod?"

Hanging on the wall directly behind her was the slate listing household needs. A piece of chalk, tied in a loop of twine, dangled from a corner of the frame. Hanging from the other corner was a small felt eraser. Quickly, I wiped away the reminder to buy potatoes, flour, and tea. Then I lifted the slate from the wall, pushed it into Claudia's hands and said, "Do you know how to write?"

The maid grabbed the chalk and scrawled three letters onto the slate's surface.

yes

"Very good," I said. "Do you think you'll be able to answer a few questions for us today?"

Claudia, unaccustomed to being the center of attention, appeared unsure of how to respond. It took an encouraging word from Stokely to get her to answer. When she did, it was by pointing to the word already on the slate.

yes

"How old are you, Claudia?"

She cleared the slate and wrote down *18.*

"Did you work for anyone else before coming into Mrs. Pastor's employ?"

Instead of using the slate, she shook her head.

"How did you come to work for Mrs. Pastor?"

Stokely answered for her, saying, "Same way as me, almost. I done found her beggin' outside last winter. Coldest, stormiest, snowiest day of the year. I brought her inside to get her warm. Missus Pastor told me to take her upstairs and give her a place to sleep for the night. The next mornin', I woke up and saw Claudia in the kitchen, cookin' and cleanin' away."

The more I learned about Lenora Grimes Pastor, the more I was convinced of her innate goodness. Only the most kindhearted of Christians would take in two complete strangers and give them employment.

"Why were you out begging in the middle of a storm?" I asked Claudia.

hungry

"Do you have any family?"

no

"Where were you living at the time?"

orphanage

"Where was this orphanage?"

On the slate, Claudia wiped away the identity of her home and replaced it with an equally expected location. *fishtown.* One of the poorest parts of the city.

This continued for the next several minutes, with me posing questions and Claudia writing her responses on the slate. For the most part, she gave one-word answers, such as writing *loved* when I asked how she felt about Mrs. Pastor. Other times, her responses were more expansive. After I asked what she thought about Robert Pastor, she took a while to write down *did not trust him.*

"Why not?" I asked. "Was he a mean man?"

no greedy

"Did you approve of the séances that took

place here?"

Claudia erased half of the slate, leaving only the word *no.*

"Why not?"

scared

"You were scared of the séances?" I asked.

"She don't like the noise," Stokely said. "All types of noise came from the sittin' room. Voices and music. I got used to it, but Claudia here never did."

"Stokely told me the other people here Saturday night had been here before," I said to Claudia. "Did you know them, too?"

The girl added a *yes* to the slate.

"Did you like any of them?"

mrs dutton. Claudia then erased the first word and replaced it with *mr.*

"So you like both of them?" I said, getting a nod in reply. "What about Mrs. Mueller?"

no

"You don't like her?"

Claudia tapped the slate twice and underlined the word for emphasis.

"Why not? Was she unkind to you?"

Claudia wiped away the answer and spent a few minutes with the slate held close to her chest, scribbling at length something the rest of us couldn't see. When she finally turned the slate around to show us, I saw she had written a full paragraph. The words, running together without punctuation, filled the entire surface of the slate.

she is a mean woman i heard her say mean things just cause i cant speak dont mean i cant hear

Lucy turned to Stokely. "Do you know what this is about?"

"Yep, I reckon I do," he said. "Missus Mueller came by one day last week to talk to Missus Pastor in private, see. Claudia here done served them some refreshments. I s'pose she heard Missus Mueller carryin' on 'bout somethin'. That woman ain't right, if you ask me."

"How so?"

"Touched in the head," Stokely said, tapping his own skull. "Flightier than a bird, that woman is."

"Can you write down some of what you heard?" I asked Claudia.

It took a moment for her to erase the epic response she had given earlier, all those words being wiped away slowly but steadily. By the time the slate was cleared, her hands had turned white with chalk dust. She seemed not to notice as she filled it again with new ones.

she asked mrs pastor why her husband never spoke said she paid good money to talk to him said she suspectin mrs pastor of stealin

"What day last week was this visit?"

"Thursday," Stokely said.

The household, it would seem, had been

very busy in the days before Mrs. Pastor's death. Mrs. Mueller stopped by on Thursday, followed by Mrs. Dutton on Friday. Mr. Dutton, presumably, was there Saturday morning.

"Did anyone else visit Mrs. Pastor recently?"

While Stokely shrugged one last time, Claudia cleared her slate and wrote down *yes a woman.*

"When did she visit?"

saturday morning

"Was Mr. Dutton here at the time?"

Claudia looked to Stokely, seeking guidance. He replied with, "You can go on an' tell them if you saw him here."

Soon after, the word *yes* appeared on the slate.

"Do you know the identity of this woman?"

Claudia nodded. Then, quite unexpectedly, she pointed right at Mrs. Lucy Collins.

IV

Ten minutes later, Lucy and I were in Fairmount Park, having retreated there for privacy's sake. I had been too angry with her to speak coherently in the Pastors' kitchen and didn't wish to get into an argument in front of their servants. But there, in the open air of the park, I could speak freely.

"It would have been nice of you to tell me

you paid Mrs. Pastor a visit on Saturday!" I all but shouted. "Or did the fact that you talked to her the morning of her murder simply slip your mind?"

"I knew this would make you angry," Lucy said. "Which is why I didn't tell you."

"Oh, is that the reason? I assumed it was because you didn't want to cast more suspicion on yourself."

Lucy feigned shock, something she had tried before with me. For all her abundant skills, that one needed practice. "*More* suspicion? It's not nearly as sinister as you're making it out to be."

"Then why the secrecy?"

"I wasn't being secretive," Lucy said. "I didn't think it was relevant."

"It is relevant!" I snapped at her.

We walked vigorously — some would even say angrily — down the path that led to the waterworks. To the right of the columned pump building was a wide promenade that jutted over the Schuylkill River. We crossed to the promenade's edge, where I gripped the railing and looked out at the water.

It was a lovely afternoon, warm and bright, with the faintest kiss of a breeze. To my left, the sound of steam engines and rushing water emanated from deep within the waterworks' marble walls. In front of me, the Schuylkill rushed over a small dam that stretched its width. The sun winked off the turbulent surface, as brilliant and clear as a crystal chandelier.

Yet despite all the lightness in the park, my mood was as dark as a winter's night. Learning about Lucy's earlier visit to the Pastor residence had left me feeling foolish and betrayed.

"Why did you go to see Mrs. Pastor?" I asked.

"It was simply a friendly visit, from one medium to another."

"Was this before or after you came to my house?"

"After," Lucy said. "I was in the process of choosing which medium to expose first."

"You were sizing up your competition."

"That's exactly what I was doing," Lucy said, adding the caveat: "In part."

A honeybee landed on my arm and began to crawl up my sleeve. I smacked at it, the insect alighting briefly before landing on my other sleeve. It was like Mrs. Collins in that regard — always coming back to pester you once you thought it had gone. With this comparison firmly in my thoughts, I took great pleasure in removing my hat and swatting the insect away.

As soon as I returned the hat to my head, the bee decided to take refuge there. Rolling my eyes upward, I saw it march along the brim on bristled legs, its wings vibrating.

"What's the other part?" I asked Lucy,

261

swatting at the bee a third time.

"For heaven's sake, stop that," she snapped.

"Would you prefer that it sting me?"

"If it means the end of this inquisition, then yes."

"This is far from over," I said.

It took one final swat to make the bee leap off my hat. It buzzed around my head a few times before retreating in the direction of the waterworks.

"As I was saying —" Lucy began.

"Saying or avoiding?" I asked. "Because it seems to me you were doing the latter."

Lucy, pretending not to hear me, continued. "I was there to make Mrs. Pastor an offer. My plan was to warn her about your newspaper's quest to expose the city's mediums in exchange for information from her."

I had no doubt what sort of information Lucy wanted. After being so easily and thoroughly exposed by me the previous night, Lucy had been in search of more tricks of the trade. And who better to get them from than the city's most famous medium?

"So Mrs. Pastor knew who you were and what you did for a living when we arrived at the séance," I said. "I assume she didn't agree to your plan."

"She refused to even consider my offer," Lucy said. "She answered the door herself and sent me away at once. That maid, Claudia, must have seen me out the window."

"Is that the moment you decided Mrs. Pastor would be the first medium to go?"

"Of course," Lucy said. "In my mind, she had it coming."

Her words prompted a chill to rattle down my spine. I couldn't tell if she meant that Lenora Grimes Pastor deserved exposure or death. Possibly, she intended both meanings. Either way, it served to remind me that no one had a greater motive for wanting Mrs. Pastor dead.

"I suppose we should pay a visit to both Mrs. Mueller and the Duttons," Lucy said, changing the subject. "I took the liberty of obtaining the home addresses of both parties."

"How on earth did you find out where they live?"

"I told you, Edward, I know some very helpful people." Lucy produced a scrap of paper from her silk purse and squinted at it. "The closest is Mrs. Mueller, who lives just north of the park. Thomas will take us there."

I, however, was still preoccupied with Lucy's earlier statement. Although I didn't truly think she had killed Mrs. Pastor, it wasn't the first time she had been associated with someone's murder.

"Who was Declan?" I asked.

"I know of no such person," Lucy answered, in what was clearly the least convincing lie she had ever told.

"He spoke to you during the séance," I said. "If I am to continue this investigation with you, then I need assurances that you can be trusted."

"You want to know my secrets, in other words," Lucy replied.

I nodded. "You certainly know plenty of mine."

My request prompted a moment of consideration on Lucy's part — I sensed the wheels turning in that scheming brain of hers as she compiled the pluses and minuses of such a confession. The positives must have outweighed the negatives, because she eventually said, "His name was Declan O'Malley. I knew him when I was very young."

"How young?"

"Fifteen," Lucy said, her voice dropping to a whisper.

"And what happened to him?"

"I find it ridiculous that we must even talk about this."

I let out a sigh that would have made Barclay proud. "Just answer the question."

"He was a mean brute of a man who took advantage of a young girl and then he died."

"How?"

"A stomach ailment," Lucy said. "Which, apparently, he has decided in the afterlife to blame on me. I don't care one way or the other. The important thing is that he's dead and I'll never have to see him again."

"Why did he call you Jenny?"

"Because that was my name when he knew me."

"Your real name?" I prodded.

"Yes," Lucy snapped. "Jenny Boyd. I grew up in Virginia, which is where Declan and I met."

"Why did you change your name?"

Lucy leveled her gaze at me, those emerald eyes of hers flaring with anger. "For the same reason you changed yours. Now, that's all you'll ever know about me, so I hope you're satisfied."

To be honest, I wasn't. My trust of Lucy Collins had, at that point, run out. Yet if I learned anything from our visit to the Pastor residence, it was that Lucy couldn't control what others said. If she was hiding more information from me, perhaps I'd find out from my fellow suspects. I knew I could question them just as easily without Lucy. But with her present, I would be able to gauge her reactions to what was being said and draw my own conclusions. For that reason alone, I chose to stick by Lucy's side.

"You said Mrs. Mueller lives the closest from our current location?" I asked.

"Yes," Lucy replied.

"Then by all means, let's talk to her."

V

A massive affair in view of the river, the home of Mrs. Elizabeth Mueller was the complete opposite of the Pastor residence. The difference wasn't just in size, although that was the most noticeable, seeing how the Pastor house could easily fit inside Mrs. Mueller's. There was also a contradiction in mood. While there were no signs of mourning at the former home of Lenora Grimes Pastor, they were in abundance at the Mueller place. From the mourning wreath on the front door to the black ribbons tied around the porch columns, the whole house seemed to be in a state of perpetual grief.

A sour-faced maid answered the door, wearing the same type of black armband that had been missing on Stokely and Claudia. After giving our names, we were allowed to enter the cold and quiet house. Our every footstep seemed to echo through the dwelling as the maid led us through a vast and empty entrance foyer. We bypassed a large staircase that wound its way to the second floor, stopping instead at two doors, one open, the other shut tight.

The maid ushered us through the open door, which turned out to be a parlor somber enough for a funeral. In fact, it appeared as if one had only recently taken place. The curtains were drawn, blocking out the afternoon sunlight. On one wall, a black cloth covered what was surely a gilt mirror. Nearby was a portrait, draped with black bunting, of a bulbous and mustachioed fellow. Mr. Gerald Mueller, I presumed.

"This place is certainly ghastly," Lucy whispered. "All that's missing is a corpse."

For that, I was grateful. Between the girl on the pier a few days ago and Mrs. Pastor, I had seen enough dead bodies for one week.

"Do you recall if Mrs. Mueller mentioned when her husband died?" I asked.

"I don't," Lucy said. "Although from the look of things, it might have been yesterday."

"It has been one year and two months since Gerald's death," answered a voice that arrived from the hallway, just outside the parlor.

I looked to the door, seeing Elizabeth Mueller pausing at the threshold. Once again she was dressed in black, although the hat and veil she had worn to Mrs. Pastor's séance were missing.

"Is that why you surprised me with this visit?" she said, stepping inside. "To ask when my dear husband died?"

"That and other matters."

I stood, remaining that way until Mrs. Mueller took a chair across from us. Just like at the Pastor residence, Lucy and I had arrived without any plan as to what, exactly, we would say to her.

Lucy, however, jumped right in.

"We're both still very shocked by Mrs. Pastor's death," she said, using the same lie that hadn't worked at all with Stokely. "We simply came by to see how you were holding up."

Unlike Stokely, Mrs. Mueller believed our ruse, confessing, "I'm not doing well at all. Lenora's death was horrible to witness. I thought she was the very picture of good health."

As we spent the next few minutes commiserating about the experience, two things became clear. The first was that Elizabeth Mueller had neither seen that morning's newspapers or been visited by Barclay, because it was obvious she didn't know Mrs. Pastor had been murdered. The second was that Mrs. Mueller looked to be on the verge of dropping dead herself. She seemed tired as we chatted, almost weak. Perhaps it was her mourning clothes, but she more resembled a corpse than a living soul. The skin stretched across her cheeks looked about as thin and pale as newspaper. When she rang to summon the maid, the wrist that poked from her frayed sleeve was no thicker than a skeleton's.

"Are you unwell?" I asked, fearing we had come at an inopportune time. "We won't continue to bother you if you are."

Mrs. Mueller offered a wan smile. "Not at all. It's nice to have company for a change, even if it is unexpected."

"I wouldn't be surprised if you were un-well," Lucy replied. "You seemed devastated by Mrs. Pastor's death. I assume the two of you were close."

"Not very," Mrs. Mueller said. "I consid-ered it more of a business relationship, although it turns out I got very little out of the bargain. That Quaker school of hers, on the other hand, gained a fair amount of my money."

"But you were so upset the other night," Lucy said.

The maid entered the parlor bearing three cups of tea and a plate of shortbread cookies wrapped in squares of paper. When I sipped the tea, it took all my willpower not to grimace. It tasted horrible — as if the water and tea leaves had barely come into contact with each other. For the sake of politeness, I continued to hold the cup, pretending to take a sip every so often.

"I was more upset about Gerald," Mrs. Mueller said, gulping down the tea like it was sweet nectar. "I've been trying to reach him for the longest time now. I'm quite at the end of my rope. Based on her reputation, Mrs. Pastor was my best hope of contacting him."

"So you've seen other mediums?" I asked.

"I have paid a visit to every medium in the city in an attempt to speak with him." Mrs. Mueller casually pointed to Lucy. "Including

269

you, on one occasion. I'm surprised you didn't recognize me during Mrs. Pastor's séance, Mrs. Collins. I certainly remember *you.*"

From the confused look on Lucy's face, it was clear she had no recollection of their earlier encounter. "I'm afraid I don't remember. I take it I wasn't able to contact Mr. Mueller."

"You contacted someone named Gerald," Elizabeth Mueller replied. "But either the spirit was an impostor or you are, for I did not receive the answer I was seeking."

"May I ask what you *are* seeking?" I said, feeling no reason to inform our hostess that Mrs. Collins was indeed a fraud. "Visiting every medium in Philadelphia —"

"And beyond," Mrs. Mueller interjected.

"And beyond," I added. "Well, that seems extreme."

I reached for a cookie, noticing that something had been printed on its paper wrapper. Closer inspection revealed the words to be the Lord's Prayer. Unwrapping one, I realized they were funeral biscuits, baked to be consumed in honor of someone who had recently passed away. I thought back to how Stokely had described Mrs. Mueller as *touched in the head.* Truer words, it seemed, had never been spoken.

Placing the cookie on my saucer — knowing what it was, I certainly couldn't eat the thing — I asked, "You say it's been more than a year since your husband's death?"

"You must think I'm quite strange," Mrs. Mueller said.

I'll admit that I did, especially when she dipped one of her husband's funeral biscuits into her cup of tea and devoured it in a single bite.

"But the circumstances of Gerald's death are also strange," she said after washing the cookie down with tea. "He was an importer. A very shrewd businessman. He knew what fashions and furnishings people overseas were enjoying and if they would be as equally enjoyed on these shores. It necessitated a lot of travel on his part, so he was gone for months at a time. His last voyage took him to the Orient."

Lucy took a cookie, read the verse on the paper, and, without a second thought, replaced it on the plate. "Did he go there often?"

"Yes," Mrs. Mueller said. "It was his fourth voyage."

According to his wife, Gerald Mueller's final trip was on a regular route of several cities in the Orient. Going from port to port, he planned to load an entire ship with silk, tea, and jade. He had made it to only one port before his ship sank somewhere in the Pacific Ocean, his body lost at sea.

"He never received a proper burial," Mrs.

Mueller said, consuming yet another morbid cookie. "It is my greatest hope that his body will be recovered one day and that he can finally be laid to rest. Until then, my house will remain in mourning."

"Is that why you visited Mrs. Pastor so often?" I asked. "You wanted Gerald to tell you where his remains were located?"

Lucy and I both fixed our gazes on Mrs. Mueller, watching as she unwrapped the last two cookies on the plate and consumed them one after the other. She took her time with the final swallow, either savoring the macabre treat or stalling her answer.

"Something of that nature, yes," she at last said.

"When did you first meet Mrs. Pastor?" I asked. "And how frequent were your visits?"

The answers Mrs. Mueller provided corresponded with what Stokely had told me. She had been visiting Lenora Grimes Pastor for a little more than a year, attending séances several times a week. She didn't, however, insinuate that Mrs. Pastor was a fraud or a thief, a concern that allegedly caused her to confront the medium a few days earlier. Which meant it was up to Lucy and myself to bring her around to that particular topic of conversation.

"I find it strange that Mrs. Pastor, for all her obvious gifts, never managed to contact your husband," I said.

Lucy caught on to my strategy right away, engaging me in conversation as if Mrs. Mueller wasn't even present. "She seemed so gifted in that regard. You don't suppose she was going out of her way to keep Mrs. Mueller and her husband apart, do you?"

I nodded. "It certainly sounds that way to me."

As impossible as she was to be around, Lucy and I apparently made a very shrewd team. We couldn't have baited that metaphorical trap any better had we been expert hunters. And like a hungry bear, Mrs. Mueller ran right into it.

"I was beginning to suspect that very thing," she said. "After all, Mrs. Pastor — may she rest in peace, of course — easily came into contact with other spirits."

"But why would she do such a thing?" I asked.

That prompted Lucy to say, "Perhaps Mrs. Pastor, sensing she had a generous patron in Mrs. Mueller, wanted to keep her coming back."

"Possibly," I replied. "But that runs counter to everything I've heard about Mrs. Pastor. Why, those are the actions of a petty thief."

Elizabeth Mueller jumped back into the conversation. "That's what I thought! In fact, I even confronted Mrs. Pastor about it on the Thursday before she died."

"Really?" I said, feigning surprise. "How

273

did Mrs. Pastor respond?"

"She denied it, naturally. She claimed that spirits can be fickle. Some don't want to be contacted, and there's nothing we can do in this realm to force them into it. I think she was simply making excuses."

"So you do believe she was stealing from you?" I said.

"I'm not certain of it. Even if she was, I can't blame her entirely. I'm certain Mr. Dutton had something to do with it."

"Eldridge Dutton?"

"The very one," Mrs. Mueller said.

I wanted to ask her to elaborate, but I was duly interrupted by a series of urgent knocks pummeling the front door. The maid rushed through the foyer to answer it, the knocks not ceasing until she opened the door. A moment later, she appeared in the parlor, looking more sour faced than ever.

"There's a policeman at the door, ma'am," she announced.

The teacup almost slipped from my hands, so surprised was I by this sudden development. "Policeman?"

"Yes, sir," the maid replied. "Says his name is Barclay."

"Barclay," Mrs. Mueller said. "I believe that's the inspector who arrived after Lenora died."

Of course it was. Barclay was here to inform Mrs. Mueller about the true nature of the death. And, knowing Barclay, he wouldn't take kindly to seeing Lucy and me chatting with her like old friends. In fact, I was certain it would make us look far more guilty than we truly were. Especially me.

"I suppose I should hear what he has to say," Mrs. Mueller told the maid. "Send him in."

I stood, searching for another way to exit the parlor. I saw nothing but the single doorway that led directly into the foyer — the same one that Barclay would be walking through at any moment.

"We really must take our leave," I said as I grabbed Lucy by the arm and hauled her to her feet. "I had no idea what time it was."

Mrs. Mueller, already confused by the presence of a police inspector at her door, now looked positively flummoxed. "Must you?"

"We must. And it's probably best if you don't tell the inspector we were here."

"Are you certain?" Mrs. Mueller said, a hand fluttering to her chest.

"Yes. Very." By that point I was well on my way to the door, pulling Lucy behind me. She waved to Mrs. Mueller over her shoulder and managed to utter, "Thank you for your hospitality!" before I yanked her out of the room.

Mrs. Mueller's maid was also in the foyer, hurrying again to the front door. I moved in the opposite direction, aiming for a small nook beneath the stairs. Lucy headed the other way, toward the door adjacent to the parlor, now wide open. We engaged in a frantic tussle — part tug of war, part whirling dervish — the two of us pulling and spinning in every direction as the maid opened the front door. Lucy released me and propelled herself to the hiding space under the stairs. I did the same, only into the now-open room.

I threw myself against the wall beside the gaping door and held my breath as Barclay stepped into the foyer.

"Forgive the intrusion," he told the maid, "but I must speak with Mrs. Mueller about what occurred the other night at Mrs. Pastor's home."

"Right this way, sir," the maid replied.

They approached the parlor, Barclay's familiar footsteps echoing through the foyer just as mine had done. Their shadows momentarily leapt into the room — twin spectres advancing through the doorway before retreating just as quickly. I turned away from them, surveying the room in which I was momentarily held prisoner. There was a bed there, its multiple blankets strewn across the mattress. A wardrobe sat to my left. A dresser was on the right. A silver-framed photograph of Gerald Mueller sat on the nightstand beside the bed, similar to the portrait that hung in the next room.

At last, Barclay reached the parlor. His

voice, muffled through the wall that divided the two rooms, greeted Mrs. Mueller. I took it as my cue to escape and crept back into the foyer. Lucy was there as well, tiptoeing past the parlor door as fast as she could without drawing Barclay's attention. We met at the front door and, taking great pains not to make a sound, slipped outside.

Thomas and the coach were waiting in front of the house, right where we had left them. Also idling out front was Barclay's official police coach and driver, a man who had whisked me to many a crime scene. It was only through sheer luck that he didn't see me exit Mrs. Mueller's house. He appeared to be resting — eyes closed and hands folded over his ample stomach — but I nonetheless tried to hide my face as we scurried toward Lucy's coach.

Before jumping in, Lucy thrust a slip of paper at her brother, saying, "Take us to this address as fast as you can."

Then we were off, Thomas lashing the pair of Cleveland Bays into full gallop. The coach creaked and rocked from the speed, tossing Lucy and me around like sailors in a storm at sea. There was even a spray of water through the window, courtesy of an enormous puddle that Thomas plowed right through.

"Where are we going?" I asked Lucy as I brushed the droplets from my shoulder.

"The Dutton residence, of course."

"You still plan on visiting them?" My heart beat wildly, unwilling to calm down after our close shave with Barclay. "We were almost found out back there."

Lucy dismissed my concern with a flick of her hand. "Since Inspector Barclay is speaking to Mrs. Mueller at this very moment, then he can't possibly be at the Dutton residence. Which makes it absolutely the most logical place for us to go."

While I didn't agree with her reasoning, I had no say in the matter, not with the carriage flying through the streets. The only way out of the situation was to fling open the door and leap, which meant risking injury or, even worse, death. So my only rational option was to remain where I was and try to stay upright as the coach bucked and jostled.

During the trip, I sorted through the information gleaned during our conversation with Mrs. Mueller. The visit, truncated as it was, had only served to raise more questions. For instance, why was the tea the maid served so wretched, considering that Mrs. Mueller's husband had presumably made a fortune importing tea, among other things? Then there was the house itself. Judging from how quiet and empty it felt, I assumed the only people present were the maid and Mrs. Mueller. A dwelling that large necessitated a household that numbered more than a single maid. Even I had Lionel and Mrs. Patterson, and my home was half the size. Then again, considering the way our footsteps echoed through the foyer, it wouldn't have surprised me to learn that the second level of the house was closed up — possibly for the winter, possibly forever. How else to explain the bedroom I had ducked into while escaping Barclay? Clearly it belonged to Mrs. Mueller, for her husband's photograph occupied the nightstand.

Unrelated to all of that was the question of just why — and what — Mrs. Mueller suspected Lenora Grimes Pastor of stealing. And where did Eldridge Dutton fit into all of this? There had to be some reason she thought Mr. Dutton was the man behind the alleged thefts. What that reason was, however, I couldn't begin to guess. Especially not with the coach careening through the streets.

Lucy Collins, for her part, swayed back and forth, riding every tilt as elegantly as one could. Obviously, she was more accustomed to her brother's breakneck driving. She even managed to pull a small tin of face powder from her purse, applying it to her cheeks in soft, unhurried dabs.

"I'm shocked you're able to do that," I commented. "I would have spilled that entire tin by now."

"Then it's lucky for you that you don't need face powder," Lucy said. "I, however, do. A woman must look her best at all times. Your

279

sex demands it of us."

I shook my head at this remark. "You underestimate my sex. The gap between what men want and what women *think* we want is staggering."

"Based on my experience, men want only one thing," Lucy said, lowering the powder tin to look at me. "Are you saying I've been wrong all this time?"

Her green eyes were agleam with mischief. Looking at them, coupled with the topic at hand, made me shift uncomfortably in my already rocking seat.

"N-no," I sputtered. "Men indeed want that."

"See?" Lucy said, resuming the powdering of her face. "I knew it."

"But we want more than that," I quickly added. "At least, some of us do."

"I'd say a very few."

"Gentlemen do," I said. "We long for engaging conversation, companionship, and comfort. To provide that, it's not necessary to smear your face with all those powders and colors."

"Does your dear Miss Willoughby powder her face and color her lips?"

"Sometimes. But Violet doesn't need to resort to such tricks to look beautiful. Neither do you, for that matter."

Lucy again lowered the powder tin to exclaim, "Why, Edward Clark, I do believe you just paid me a compliment!"

"I-I was —" I put a hand to my face, feeling a blossoming warmth on my cheeks. I was starting to blush. "I was merely stating a fact."

"No," Lucy said. "You're saying you find me attractive."

"For goodness' sake, I was just trying to be nice."

"There's nothing wrong with finding me attractive, Edward. Many men do."

"And you use that knowledge to manipulate them," I replied, regretting I had said anything at all.

"There are many weapons in my arsenal," Lucy said. "Beauty is one of them. And now that I know you find me beautiful —"

"I never said that!" I interjected.

"— I'll reserve that knowledge for later use."

I pressed a hand to my cheeks again. They were hotter than ever, although now it was more from frustration than embarrassment. I sorely wanted to change the subject from Lucy's beauty — which was undeniable — to something else.

Luckily for me, I didn't have to. For at that very moment, the carriage skidded to a stop. Lucy slipped the powder tin back into her purse, looked out the window and announced, "It appears we have arrived."

VI

If Mrs. Dutton and Mrs. Mueller had one thing in common, it was that both liked their parlors depressing. While not as funeral ready as the one in the Mueller home, the room in which Leslie Dutton greeted us was just as lifeless and dark. Curtains of heavy velvet covered the windows and a single lamp cast only the faintest glow on dark green walls. Adding to the gloom of the parlor were the hundreds of newspapers that covered almost every square inch of the room. Editions of the *Bulletin,* the *Public Ledger,* the *Inquirer,* and a half dozen others were either stacked on tables and chairs or strewn across the floor. They even covered the sofa-bound Mrs. Dutton herself, draping her lap like a wool blanket.

The single bit of gaiety and color in the room came from a pair of goldfinches flitting about in a gilded cage. They heralded our entrance with a series of jolly chirps that served as a bright counterpoint to their surroundings of darkness and newsprint.

"Those birds," Lucy whispered, "must shit like the dickens."

I could only nod in agreement, for indeed there were enough newspapers in that parlor to line the bottoms of a thousand cages.

Mrs. Dutton didn't apologize for the state of the room, nor did she appear ashamed by it. Rather, she simply sat up when we entered and brushed a few stray pages of newsprint from her crimson dress.

"Why, this is a pleasant surprise," she said. "A much-needed one, considering the horrible news about Mrs. Pastor's murder."

Unlike with Mrs. Mueller, I never wondered if Leslie Dutton knew about the poisoning. Headlines about it literally surrounded her. Despite the sea of newspapers in which she swam, her appearance was more than presentable. A handsome woman to begin with, her hair was pulled into an elegant upbraid, and her clothing was absurdly formal for an afternoon at home. With her blond hair and ivory skin, she was what I imagined my dear Violet would look like in ten years.

"I see you've been doing some reading about it," I said.

Mrs. Dutton eyed the newspapers at her feet. "While I have read every horrid word, I confess that my main goal has been to keep others from doing the same. I ordered my servants to buy up as many copies as they could. The fewer people who see such filth, the better."

While I knew her actions were futile, I understood her thinking. I was, after all, the man who had tossed my own morning papers into the fire.

"It's horrible to be associated with it," I

admitted. "And I'm speaking as a newspaper-man."

"Forgive me," Mrs. Dutton said, "but what are your names again? So much happened the other night that the simplest facts elude me."

"I'm Mrs. Collins and this is Mr. Clark," Lucy said.

"Clark." Leslie Dutton rolled the name around in her mouth like a taste she recalled but couldn't quite place. "You wrote that piece in the *Bulletin,* did you not?"

"Yes," I admitted.

"I've been meaning to call on you." Mrs. Dutton sorted through the pages surrounding her, stopping only when she found the previous edition of the *Bulletin.* She held up the front page so that I might see the article I had authored. "I wanted to thank you for your discretion. There were things said during the séance that I don't wish to become public. You exercised restraint, unlike those other spineless vipers who call themselves men of the press. Implying that my husband or I could be capable of murder. They should be hanged for such a thing."

"We're all passengers in that same boat," I said. "Adrift until Mrs. Pastor's killer is exposed."

"But that's the thing," Mrs. Dutton said. "I'm not entirely convinced Mrs. Pastor was killed to begin with. I can't imagine anyone being so brazen as to poison the woman while we were all there to witness it. As well, I can't think of anyone in that room who would have reason to do so. Mrs. Pastor was a gentle, kindhearted woman."

"Were the two of you close?" Lucy asked, echoing a similar question we had asked Mrs. Mueller. Already, we were falling into the same rhythm we had acquired there.

"Close, no," Mrs. Dutton replied. "But we were friendly."

It was my turn to ask the next question. "So you had no issues with her? No reason to suspect she was a fraud of some sort?"

"Heavens, no."

"What about your husband?" Lucy asked.

Leslie Dutton blinked before answering. It wasn't for very long, nor was it very noticeable, but it was enough for me to realize she was delaying her answer lest she give something away.

"Mr. Dutton admired Mrs. Pastor as much as I did."

"He seemed very disturbed by her death," I said. "It must have been a shock to you both."

The goldfinches, sensing another presence approaching the room, started to chirp again. Behind me, the parlor door swung open and a young woman of about eighteen swanned into the room. She slid toward Lucy and me, the skirt of her white dress brushing the floor. A silk ribbon held her flame red hair in place.

A darker shade of red circled her mouth. Lip paint, from the looks of it. One of the very things I told Lucy that women could do without.

"Oh, I didn't know we had guests," the girl said, her mock surprise indicating the exact opposite.

"Yes," Leslie Dutton said. "Mr. Clark and Mrs. Collins. This is Bettina, my daughter."

"Stepdaughter," the girl corrected.

Standing in front of us, she assessed first Lucy, then myself. Lucy, it must be said, barely received a second glance. Instead, young Bettina focused all of her attention on me.

"My mother died three years ago. Fortunately, I had a new mother not long after." She called over her shoulder, "Isn't that right, Mother? How long was it?"

Mrs. Dutton cleared her throat. "Six months, I believe."

"It was four," Bettina said, placing a hand on my arm. "How lucky for me. Wouldn't you agree, Mr. Clark?"

I took a step backward, repelled not only by the girl's brazen attitude, but by the cruel gleam in her eyes. It was similar to a look I had seen from Lucy Collins, only with more anger.

"Family is important," I replied. "You should consider yourself very fortunate."

The anger in Bettina's eyes darkened. She

was upset, I saw. Disappointed that I refused to play along. Finally, she turned away from me and took in the entire parlor.

"Really, Mother. All of these newspapers. What will our guests think?" She looked to me, making another attempt at engagement. "Mother is very concerned about appearances. What is it you always say, dear? Reputation is everything?"

Mrs. Dutton, too, surveyed the newspapers piled about the room. Only her expression more resembled shame than her stepdaughter's cruel amusement.

"Something of the sort, yes."

"You can imagine Mother's surprise," Bettina said, picking up the nearest newspaper, "when she saw *this.*"

She turned the front page toward me, revealing a copy of the *Inquirer* and its enormous headline declaring that Mrs. Pastor had been murdered.

"We're mixed up in that as well," I said. "It's nothing to make light of."

Bettina's eyes widened. Wickedly, I might add. "So, it's possible I could be sharing a room with a murderer. Perhaps I should summon the police."

"Really, Bettina." Mrs. Dutton stood, a newspaper slipping from her lap onto the floor. "Please, leave us in peace."

"Fine," Bettina said, shrugging. "I only came in to ask if you knew when Daddy would be home."

"His usual time, I should think," Mrs. Dutton replied.

Her stepdaughter gave an exaggerated curtsy before sweeping out of the room, conspicuously grabbing a few newspapers as she did so. Once she was gone, Mrs. Dutton dropped onto the sofa again, a hand pressed to her forehead.

"You must forgive Bettina. She only acts this way around strangers. I suppose it's her form of punishment."

I furrowed my brow. "Punishment?"

"Of me," Leslie Dutton said. "For marrying her father and replacing her mother. The odd thing is, we got along so well when her mother was alive."

Lucy, as intrigued as I was, removed a stack of newspapers from the nearest chair and sat down. "So you knew the first Mrs. Dutton?"

"Oh, yes," said the second. "I was a nurse, you see. I worked in a hospital during the war. Because of the commendations I had received, I was offered a position here. Eldridge's first wife was very ill, and I became her personal nurse. She was a very nice woman, and it was a shame when she passed."

"How long were you employed here?" I asked.

"About six months or so. Mr. Dutton asked me to stay on after his wife's death, becoming a sort of nanny for Bettina. He and I

288

became . . . very close during his time of grief. Soon after that, we were married. Eldridge is a wonderful man."

"Where is Mr. Dutton now, by the way?" Lucy said. "We were hoping to see how he was faring as well."

"At his law office," Mrs. Dutton replied. "I begged him not to go in today, but he said not going out in public would only make us look more suspicious. I suppose he's right, but I just don't have that kind of strength. Eldridge, though, is a workhorse. He even spends his Saturday mornings at the firm."

Hearing this, Lucy and I exchanged a brief, pointed look. It was clear Leslie Dutton had no idea where her husband had really been going on Saturdays. I wondered if she suspected even just a little bit that those mornings had, until recently, been spent at private séances with Lenora Grimes Pastor.

"So your sister was wrong about your husband?" I said.

Mrs. Dutton tilted her head. "Pardon?"

"During the séance, you spoke with your sister."

"Yes. Henrietta."

"Do you really believe it was her?" Lucy asked. "And not some trickery on the part of Mrs. Pastor?"

"It was Henrietta, believe me. She spoke of things only she could possibly know. Things I've never shared with anyone else."

"Getting back to my original question," I said, "she mentioned during the séance on Saturday not to trust your husband. Clearly, she was saying that in jest, because Mr. Dutton sounds like a most trustworthy gentleman."

If Mrs. Dutton was offended by our interrogation, she didn't show it. She even mustered up a smile as she said, "Dear Henrietta was melodramatic in life, so it's no surprise she's that way in death. She always fancied herself as a bit of an actress."

"Do you know what she could have been referring to?" I asked.

"I haven't the faintest idea."

Lucy and I tried to sound as casual as possible while posing more questions to Mrs. Dutton, who willingly answered them. Did she speak to her sister often during séances at Mrs. Pastor's house? (Yes.) How often did they go to the séances? (Once a week, usually.) Did they come into contact with any other spirit they knew? ("No," Mrs. Dutton quickly replied. "Only with my sister.")

Eventually, I asked, "Before Saturday night's séance, when was the last time you visited the Pastor residence?"

"The Saturday before."

Mrs. Dutton, as with all of her answers, said this without hesitation. Unlike the others, though, this response was a lie. I knew from Stokely that she had called upon Robert Pastor the day before his wife died.

"Very interesting," I said. "And your husband? When was his last visit?"

"Also the Saturday before."

"Are you certain?" Lucy asked.

The goldfinches, silent for so long, sang out again as they fluffed and fluttered in their gilded prison.

Footsteps sounded outside the parlor, both human and canine. A few sharp barks accompanied the growing symphony of boots and claws on the wooden floor. Eventually, a man's voice joined the fray. "Leslie? Bettina? Where in tarnation is everyone?"

"There's Mr. Dutton now," his wife announced. "You can ask him yourselves."

VII

Eldridge Dutton was a large man, in both height and stomach, with a full beard and an aura of self-satisfaction. He reminded me of Thornton Willoughby in that regard, making me notice just how much older he was than his wife. He probably had at least twenty years on Leslie Dutton.

Entering the parlor, he, too, seemed overwhelmed by the number of newspapers there. Stepping around first one stack and then another, he reached the sofa and gave his wife a dutiful kiss on the cheek. Surrounding him were three terriers, who wove between his

291

ankles and fought for attention by throwing themselves against his knees. The birds, either threatened or happy to see the dogs, darted around the cage in streaks of yellow.

"More newspapers, I see," Mr. Dutton remarked.

He pushed the dogs away. Rebuffed, they sniffed my way before moving on to Lucy then out of the parlor entirely.

"I can't abide this much longer, my dear. You need to stop trying to buy every damned newspaper in the city. That's like trying to sop up every drop in the ocean." Mr. Dutton turned to Lucy and me, chest puffed forward. "Don't you agree?"

He seemed neither surprised by nor concerned about our presence. In fact, he barely showed any acknowledgment that we were there, even when addressing us. For instance, instead of waiting for our reply, he pulled a gold watch from his vest pocket and checked the time. It was up to his wife to officially notify him of our presence.

"Eldridge, you remember Mr. Clark and Mrs. Collins. They were at Mrs. Pastor's final séance."

It was all too clear from his expression that Eldridge Dutton had no recollection of us. Still, he shook our hands while repeating, "Of course, of course."

"They, too, have been implicated by the police in her death," Mrs. Dutton said.

"Of course. Nasty bit of business."

Mr. Dutton returned his attention to his watch, first winding it and then buffing it against the wide lapel of his jacket. The watch was conspicuously new, bearing no noticeable nicks or scratches. It had the warm glow that only the best gold possessed and practically gleamed in Eldridge Dutton's hands. No wonder he was so smitten by it. I found it nearly impossible to take my eyes off it myself, especially when Mr. Dutton opened the hunter case to check the hour a second time.

"They wanted to know the last time you visited the Pastor residence," Mrs. Dutton said.

For the first time since his arrival, Eldridge Dutton took a long, hard look at us. I felt the heat of his appraising stare as he sized us up. He was wondering what our intentions were, probably. Wondering if we were trustworthy. I'm also certain he wondered if either Lucy or I had been the person responsible for killing Mrs. Pastor.

"Now why would you want to know that?" he asked.

"Mere curiosity," I said. "After the séance, we saw how bereaved Mrs. Pastor's death left you and wondered about your friendship with her."

"I wouldn't necessarily call it a friendship,"

Mrs. Dutton replied. "We were loyal customers."

"And you, Mr. Dutton? Is that how you would describe it?"

Eldridge Dutton snapped his watch shut, the sharp click startling those of us not in possession of it. "It's getting close to supper time."

"I suppose it is," his wife said.

"Did you invite" — Mr. Dutton tilted his head in our direction — "our guests to dine with us?"

"I hadn't thought of that."

"Then perhaps it's best they take their leave."

The parlor doors opened, admitting not only the terriers again but also the sulking form of Bettina Dutton, who no doubt had been outside eavesdropping. The finches greeted all of them with their usual series of cheeps and chirps.

"I'll show them out, Father," Bettina said.

I stood. "No need. We can see ourselves out."

"I insist," she said, hooking her arm through mine. "This house is so big, one can easily get lost."

Lucy and I barely had a chance to bid Mr. and Mrs. Dutton good-bye before their daughter whisked us away. Once we were out of the parlor, Bettina slowed considerably.

"How was your visit? Did the four of you

have a pleasant chat?"

"I suppose we did," I said, although I would have used a different word than "pleasant." "Curious," maybe. Or "perplexing." Similar to our conversation with Mrs. Mueller, it definitely wasn't as enlightening as I had hoped.

"And what did all of you discuss?"

"Lenora Grimes Pastor," Lucy answered. "Did you ever meet her?"

"Once," Bettina said. "She and her husband came for dinner. I found it duller than reading Shakespeare."

We were strolling through the foyer by that point, Bettina so close I could smell the perfume water she had splashed on herself. Up close, she looked younger than I had first thought. Perhaps fifteen at the most. All the tricks she used to make herself appear older seemed desperate when seen in close proximity. The lip paint had been sloppily smeared on, and loose strands of hair stood out from her head. She resembled a girl playing dress up, which, in a way, was exactly the case.

"Are you married, Mr. Clark?" she asked, pulling herself closer to my side.

"I'm engaged."

"Pity," Bettina said while giving a backward glance to Lucy. "Are you the lucky one who snagged him?"

Lucy rolled her eyes at such a thought. "Thankfully not."

"That surprises me," Bettina said. "You two make a fine-looking pair."

"Mrs. Collins and I are merely friends," I replied.

Behind me, Lucy said, "That's putting a gloss on things."

"I'm engaged to someone else," I continued, doing my best to ignore her.

"Does your fiancée have a name?" Bettina inquired.

By that point, I was beyond tired of the girl and her devilish games. Why she was playing them, I had no idea. But every word I said only seemed to encourage her, which is why I extracted my arm from hers and replied, "I highly doubt the two of you are acquainted."

Bettina's reddened lips formed a wicked grin as she once again turned to Lucy. "He doesn't talk much, does he?"

"He talks plenty when he feels like it," Lucy said.

"But he does like his secrets, though."

Lucy rolled her eyes a second time. "You have no idea."

"Tell me one of your secrets, Mr. Clark."

Bettina grasped my arm again and wouldn't let go, no matter how much I tried to shake her off. Her grip was so tight that it felt like my arm had been caught in the teeth of a ravenous badger.

"I'll tell you one of mine. Actually, it's my parents' secret. They tell people that going to see Mrs. Pastor was dear Leslie's suggestion. But it wasn't. Daddy is the one who wanted to go."

"Why?" I asked, suddenly very interested in what Bettina Dutton had to say.

"I haven't the faintest idea."

"Can you tell us anything else about your parents' relations with Mrs. Pastor?"

Bettina shook her head. "Not until you reveal the name of your fiancée."

I was torn. I had no desire to utter Violet's name in that house. Contrary to what I had said earlier, I had an inkling the Willoughbys and the Duttons *did* move in the same social circles, and I wanted to spare my dear Violet from whatever mischief Bettina had planned. Yet I was also desperate to know if her parents were hiding anything else. And at that moment, getting more information about the Duttons was of the utmost importance.

"It's —"

Lucy interrupted me. "Jenny. Her name is Jenny Boyd. She's my cousin, and they're quite happy together. Now, what else can you tell us about your parents?"

"Not very much," Bettina replied. "Only about Daddy's new watch. I'm certain he made sure you noticed it."

"We did," I said. "It's very impressive."

"Looks expensive, doesn't it?" Bettina said, slyness creeping into her voice.

Indeed it did. While I didn't get the chance

to view it up close, it had the kind of quality one could see from a distance. A watch like that must have cost a great deal of money.

"Daddy got it a few weeks ago," Bettina continued. "He won't tell me how, though. He merely said it was a gift. When I asked my new mother if she had been the one to give it to him, she pretended no such watch existed, the poor thing. Later that night, I overheard her and Daddy fighting about it. She demanded to know who it came from. He said it was none of her business."

"I think it's none of *our* business," I said, although it was exactly the sort of information we had been hoping to discover. Either Eldridge Dutton was lying and had purchased that watch himself or someone else *had* given it to him. In either case, Lenora Grimes Pastor was involved somehow. Otherwise, Bettina would never have mentioned it.

Still, it didn't make me like her any more, especially with her clinging flirtatiously to my arm like that. I sighed in relief when we finally reached the front door, forcing her to let go at last.

"It was a pleasure meeting you, Mr. Clark," she said, giving me a brazen wink. "Come around anytime you wish."

And with that, Lucy and I were out the door.

"Thank you," I said to Lucy once Bettina closed it behind us.

"For what?"

"For not telling that awful girl Violet's name. I really do appreciate it."

"You're quite welcome," Lucy said. "But Bettina is harmless. She's just a sad and lonely girl trying to get attention any way she can."

"I suppose you knew girls like that growing up."

"Knew them?" Lucy replied. "I was one of them."

"Did you start that early?"

"Oh, much earlier, Edward. And I was far better than Bettina. Her attempts to get you to notice her were downright embarrassing to watch."

"Is that jealousy I detect in your voice?" I asked, only half joking. Her voice *did* contain a strange tone, as if she was trying too hard to sound nonchalant. "Because it certainly sounds like it."

"Jealous?" Lucy replied, her eyes widening. "Of a mere girl? Don't be silly. If anything, she was jealous of *me.*"

"I didn't get that sense at all. She knew that you aren't my fiancée. In fact, you made it abundantly clear that you can't stand me. What could she possibly be jealous about?"

Lucy stopped and looked at me, head cocked. "Simple. She knew, unlike you, that I could have you wrapped around my little finger if I really wanted to."

And with that, she stepped off the front porch. I followed, blinking against the setting sun. The entire street basked in the sun's warm glow, with the trees, the neighboring homes, even the air itself tinted gold.

Using my hand to shield my eyes, I saw a familiar coach parked directly in front of the Dutton residence. Standing outside it, the sun casting a halo of light around the top of his hat, was none other than William Barclay.

Damn it all. He had found us at last.

VIII

Barclay wasn't happy, that much was certain. All his usual tics and habits were in full force as his coach rumbled toward the center of the city. He tilted his head to gaze at me in exasperation. He sighed like an idled steam engine. He tugged his mustache so frequently that I feared he was going to pull it clean off his upper lip.

"I'm disappointed in you, Edward," he said. "Incredibly disappointed."

"I've done nothing wrong," I replied.

We were alone in the carriage, having parted ways with Lucy Collins and her brother outside the Dutton residence. As roughly and recklessly as Thomas drove, I have to admit I would have preferred to be with them and not in that slow police coach, caught in Barclay's red-faced glare.

"Oh, but you have," he said as he rooted through his pockets, looking for his pipe. "You've only cast *more* suspicion on yourself, while I've been doing nothing but trying to clear your name."

"You had the opportunity to clear my name last night," I retorted. "You could have told those reporters that you were certain I had nothing to do with Mrs. Pastor's murder —"

"Edward, you know yourself it doesn't work that —"

I raised a hand to silence him. "Since you declined to do that, I have taken it upon myself to clear my own good name."

Barclay, still fumbling for his pipe, said, "But don't you see that questioning the other suspects just makes you look guilty?"

"I suppose Mrs. Mueller told you about our visit, then."

"She didn't need to. There were three teacups in her parlor yet she claimed to have been alone. It took just a small amount of cajoling to get her to admit the truth."

Barclay at last located his pipe. While stuffing that rotten cob with tobacco, he said, "It didn't take long to deduce that you and Mrs. Collins intended to visit the other members of Mrs. Pastor's final séance. Since the Duttons lived the closest, I tried there first. And there you were. Caught red-handed."

He lit the pipe, filling the coach with tobacco smoke. Despite having no interest in smoking myself, I enjoyed the scent. There was a sweetness to it that I found pleasing, especially when compared with my friend's sour mood.

"From the way you talk, Barclay, I think you're starting to have doubts about my innocence."

Barclay exhaled. "You know me better than that, Edward. I don't doubt you for a moment. I never could. But your new friend, Mrs. Collins? Well, that's another story. She's not exactly a paragon of virtue. Which is why I hate seeing you getting mixed up with her."

"She's not nearly as bad as you think."

If my words surprised Barclay, I can assure you that they surprised me even more. Had our conversation taken place immediately after Mrs. Pastor's death, I would have agreed with him completely about Lucy's personality.

Yet I had spent so much time with her since then that my opinion had somewhat softened. Clearly, I was aware of Lucy's many faults — chief among them being greed, selfishness, and general untrustworthiness. But she also possessed a keen mind and a sense of humor, both of which were admirable qualities. And as I thought about our afternoon of investigation, I realized that I had enjoyed myself far more than I expected.

Barclay's view of her, however, was more limited.

"I disagree," he said. "Honestly, Edward, what possessed you to align yourself with someone like her?"

Since I couldn't tell Barclay that simple blackmail was the prime reason, I had to come up with another excuse. "Because I know she didn't kill Mrs. Pastor."

Barclay lifted an eyebrow, which was barely visible through the undulating cloud of smoke coming from his pipe. "Are you certain of that?"

"Yes," I said. "Mrs. Collins may be many things, but she is not a murderer."

"How would you know? From what I've uncovered, Mrs. Lucy Collins didn't exist until a few years ago."

Barclay sounded scandalized that someone would purposefully try to escape their old life by forging a new identity. Little did he know that Edward Clark, his dear friend and former brother in arms, had done the very same thing. That irony wasn't lost on me as I replied, "I don't find that very unusual."

"I certainly do," Barclay said. "She doesn't seem to have had any life at all before she arrived in Philadelphia, wed to one Mr. Samuel Collins. No old friends of the man seem to know anything about her."

"Perhaps she lived a sheltered life before marrying him."

"Or," Barclay said, "she's hiding something."

The names Declan O'Malley and Jenny Boyd leapt into my thoughts. I knew little about Lucy's life under her birth name, and even less about this mysterious Mr. O'Malley. But I assumed that Lucy, like yours truly, had a very good reason to change her identity.

"It sounds like you think Lucy Collins is the killer."

"No," Barclay said. "To be quite honest, I have no idea who could have done it."

"That's disheartening."

"I'm sorry, Edward. But please understand that I am trying."

Barclay's apology didn't make an iota of difference to my situation. One more day of his not finding Mrs. Pastor's murderer meant another day spent under a cloud of suspicion.

"Do you know anything at all?" I said with a sigh that rivaled his greatest efforts.

Now it was Barclay's turn to avoid a question. He stuck his overturned pipe out the open window. With a few sharp taps, the still-smoldering tobacco left the cob and fluttered into the muddy street. Then, pipe cleaned, he shoved it back into his pocket. The whole display left me bristling with annoyance.

"I deserve to be told something," I snapped. "Especially if I might have to spend the rest of my life as a murder suspect."

"There's been a slight snag in our investigation."

"What sort of snag?"

"Remember me telling you about that poison expert from New York? Toxicologist — that's his official title. He arrived this morning and immediately went to work."

"That should be a good thing."

"It would be, if he could deduce what kind of poison killed Mrs. Pastor. He spent all day considering the most common ones. Arsenic. Thallium. Cyanide salts. Brucine. Even morphine. He's convinced none of them killed Mrs. Pastor. So now he's looking into poisonous plants. Thus far, all he knows is that it wasn't deadly nightshade or hemlock."

"Maybe she died of natural causes after all," I said.

"But she didn't." Barclay gave a sad shake of his head, immediately obliterating my naive hopefulness. "This toxicologist is certain she was poisoned. He's just not sure *how.* And until he learns that, well, it hinders the investigation."

Had I suspected that Barclay knew anything else, I would have pressed him. But the pale blankness of his face told me he did not.

"Thank you for being forthright with me," I told him.

"This will all pass quickly," my old friend replied. "I promise you it will."

"I hope you're right. My future depends on it."

We had, at that point, reached Locust Street, and it was time to take my leave. With a tip of my hat, I exited the coach. The sun had fully set by then, turning the sky a light purple that made the surrounding houses soft and hazy. The streetlamps were already lit, their glow casting long shadows across the sidewalk and into the street. One such shadow fell across the coach, darkening its interior so that Barclay was all but invisible. Even though I could no longer see him, I heard his voice as the coach began to pull away.

"This time, please heed my advice," he called to me. "Just lay low for a few days. And for the love of God, steer clear of Mrs. Collins."

IX

An hour later, I took the trolley west to dine at the Willoughby residence. The evening started off pleasantly, with a glass of spirits sipped on the front porch. We talked about the beautiful weather, the prognosis for this year's crops, and, of course, Violet and Mrs. Willoughby's new hats. Once we were at the dinner table, however, the conversation turned more serious. The first topic, discussed over cream of mushroom soup, was a recent bridge collapse in Ohio that killed scores of people. The next topic, served with a fish course of salted shad, was a series of grave robberies that had taken place across the river in Camden. When the entrée arrived — rare roast beef, maple-sugared carrots, and mashed potatoes — the conversation turned, unfortunately and inevitably, to the death of Lenora Grimes Pastor.

"I must admit, Edward," Thornton Willoughby said, "that I'm concerned about this whole mess you've gotten yourself mixed up in."

In addition to causing me immediate indigestion, the subject of Mrs. Pastor allowed me to witness the Willoughby family's round-robin way of communicating. For as soon as Mr. Willoughby was finished, Violet piped up with, "Father, I begged you not to mention that."

"I believe your father is right to broach the subject," Mrs. Willoughby said. "After all, it's been in all the newspapers."

Jasper Willoughby, looking as wan as ever, skipped his turn, electing to take a few extra sips of wine instead. He gave me an odd look over the rim of his glass, one that was both accusatory and conspiratorial. I was reminded once more that we shared a secret, a situation that didn't exactly put me at ease.

"As a gentleman of the press, I can tell you it's not wise to believe everything you read in the newspapers," I replied.

"Certainly not an account written by you." Mr. Willoughby pointed his fork at me. A chunk of beef was impaled on its tines, dripping blood. "Your article about Mrs. Pastor's death failed to mention murder. That looks mighty suspicious to my eyes."

Frustrated, Violet stomped the floor so hard the entire table shimmied. "Father, really! At the time, he didn't know it *was* murder. A subject, by the way, that isn't proper dinner table discussion."

"We're not talking about the murder, my dear," Mrs. Willoughby said. "We're merely discussing Mr. Clark's role in it."

Jasper at last weighed in, still giving me that strange look as he said, "Perhaps Edward has no role in it whatsoever. Maybe he was in the wrong place at the wrong time. He was just doing his job. Weren't you, Edward?"

Under the table, I clenched my fists, waiting for him to mention Lucy Collins. In my head, I was already devising an excuse to tell Violet and her family. Something that would easily explain my arrangement with Mrs. Collins without giving away the fact that I was really the son of a notorious killer. Yet, to my surprise, Jasper said no more. And while his words could have been an innocent statement, I took them to be a reminder that he knew more than he had let on to the others.

"But you *are* a suspect, are you not?" Mr. Willoughby asked me. "Surely the newspapers can't be lying about that."

"No, but they can exaggerate the truth," I said. "I am as much a suspect as everyone else who attended that séance."

"But it doesn't mean the police really think he killed someone," Violet added in my defense. "Why, Edward's very dear friend Inspector Barclay is the man investigating the crime. I'm certain he doesn't think Edward is guilty."

"No, he doesn't, as a matter of fact," I said.

"Is Mr. Barnum a suspect?" Mrs. Willoughby inquired. "After all, he was also there."

Her husband, completely bypassing Jasper's turn to speak, stabbed another chunk of beef while muttering, "If you ask me, *he's* the one who did it. Any man who seeks public attention as much as he does is capable of anything, including murder."

"Well," Violet said, "Mr. Barnum is of no concern to us. But Edward is. To me, at least. And if the rest of you care a whit about me, then you must care about Edward, too. That means believing deep in your heart that he is completely innocent."

"We do, my dear," Mrs. Willoughby replied. "It's just, well, we're concerned about —"

Her husband sputtered in exasperation. "Just come out with it, Marjorie. It's Edward's reputation that concerns us. And how his being embroiled in all of this will reflect not only on you, but on the entire family. Think of how it will look to others."

"Of course nothing can bring shame to the

Willoughby name. We certainly can't have that!" Violet leapt to her feet and tossed her fork onto her plate, where it clinked and clattered before falling to the floor in a spray of carrots and potatoes. "God forbid your daughter's happiness be more important than selling a few more stupid hats!"

With that, she removed her own Willoughby hat and whipped it across the dining room. Then she stormed away from the table, leaving me alone with her two stunned parents and one very amused younger brother.

"I'll try to calm her," I said, rising. "It's the least I can do, seeing that this is all my fault."

Thornton Willoughby stabbed at his steak as if it were my heart. "While you're at it," he said, "try to talk some sense into her."

I found Violet on the front porch, taking out her frustrations on a poor rocking chair. She swayed back and forth furiously, the chair groaning from the strain.

"My dear Violet," I said. "I'm so sorry I've put you and your family in this awful position."

"*You're* sorry?" she replied, the rocking chair creaking more as she increased her speed. "Edward, you have nothing to apologize for. I'm the one who's sorry. Sorry that I have such horrid, narrow-minded parents."

"They're only concerned about you."

"Don't you understand, Edward? They want me to break off our engagement."

310

"Did they tell you that explicitly?"

"Yes. Just this afternoon." Violet valiantly tried to hold back the tears pooling at the corners of her eyes. One slipped out anyway and rode the delicate curve of her cheek. "They say that if I marry you, it will be a black mark on the family name."

"They truly doubt my innocence, don't they?"

"Quite honestly, Edward, I don't think they care if you're innocent or not. Father only cares about what others will think. Mother only cares about what Father thinks. And it makes me sick. Utterly sick."

I rushed to her side and took her hands in mine. It was, I realized, a position similar to how I had proposed five months earlier. Only now the circumstances were far different.

"But what do *you* think?" I asked. "Do you believe I'm innocent?"

"Completely."

"And do you want to call off our engagement?"

"Of course not!" Violet cried out, the tears flowing freely now. "Nothing will keep me from marrying you. I just wish that my family would approve of you the way I do."

I was, for the moment, relieved. It's amazing how words of devotion from the woman you love can strengthen the heart. I stood, determined more than ever to clear my name. Certainly Violet deserved nothing less.

"They will," I promised. "Very soon."

This did little to ease Violet's tears. They kept up a steady stream as she said, "I'm so frightened, Edward."

"Don't fear, my darling. This will all end and, before you know it, we'll be married."

"Not about that," Violet said as she wiped her cheek.

"Then what are you afraid of?"

"I don't know how to explain it. It's silly, really. But I can't stop thinking about what happened the other night at Bertie's party. With the table."

"But I told you already. That was just a mean trick."

Violet gripped my hands, as fiercely as she had ever done. Her own hands, I noticed, were cold and trembling.

"It wasn't," she said. "It was Mrs. Pastor's spirit making that table move. She was trying to tell you that she was murdered."

"But everyone knows she was murdered."

"Not then, they didn't," Violet said. "That news didn't come until later."

She was right, of course. I didn't learn about Mrs. Pastor's murder until after I got home that night. Once Barclay had shared the bad news with me, the table-tipping incident fled from my thoughts. But now everything that happened that night came roaring back, crashing like a cold wave onto the shores of my brain. And the more I thought about it, the more it seemed possible that, other than Bertie Johnson playing the most elaborate prank ever devised, the only explanation for the table-tipping incident was that a spirit really had been in that room with us.

Yet I couldn't tell that to Violet. It would only have made her more fearful, and I wanted my beloved's mind to be free of such worries.

"You must be reading too many ghost stories," I said. "Because your imagination seems to be running wild."

"Edward, you know I'm right."

"You're scared," I replied. "Which is understandable. But it's also making you believe in things that didn't really happen. Why, for instance, would Mrs. Pastor want to communicate with us?"

"I don't know," Violet said. "Maybe she was trying to warn you somehow."

I didn't want to discuss the matter any further. For one, it pained me to contradict Violet when the possibility existed that she was correct. But more than anything, I didn't want her to sense my own fear, which had started to rise in me like the morning mist on an open field. None of what I had experienced in the previous days — speaking to my dead mother, the table tipping, Mrs. Pastor's death — made sense to me. The result of that utter incomprehension was a fear that more strange occurrences would come my way.

"It was all Bertie's doing," I told Violet. "You know that. Now, you should rejoin your parents inside. I think it's best if I take my leave. For now, I'm certain I've worn out my welcome here."

Before she protested, I hurried down the front walk, taking a moment to look backward and wave good-bye. Violet, a slender arm wrapped around one of the columns supporting the porch roof, could only sadly wave back.

X

The trolley ride back to my house took twice as long as usual, thanks to a pebble on the tracks and an overeager Clydesdale whose combined forces ultimately derailed us. Stuck motionless in the middle of Spring Garden Street, we men on board were forced to clamber out and help push the trolley back onto the tracks. We were a motley lot, consisting mostly of servants on their way home, factory workers heading to the night shift, and boisterous young men in search of drink. Yet there was enough muscle among us to eventually right the situation and continue our journey.

When we came to my stop, no one else disembarked, leaving me alone on the dark street. Several blocks lay between the trolley stop and my house, and as I began the lengthy trudge from one to the other, I cursed myself for not hiring a hack. Pushing the trolley had left me tired and, as a result, my progress was slow.

While I walked, I once again felt like I was being watched. There was no one around me — I constantly looked over my shoulder to make certain of that — yet the sensation persisted.

I chalked it up to still being slightly spooked about Violet's theory regarding Mrs. Pastor's spirit. If she really had tried to notify me of her murder once, then it was possible she could try a second time. An unnerving prospect.

Then there was the strange man with no nose I had seen on Sunday morning. I was certain he had been following me, although for the life of me I couldn't say why. And while I knew without a doubt that he hadn't trailed me home, his dark-eyed gaze continued to stay with me. That night, the feeling was particularly strong. So strong that I wouldn't have been surprised to see the noseless man lurch at me from out of the darkness.

Therefore, I tried to put all worrisome thoughts out of my mind. Instead, I thought of Violet and how soft her trembling hands felt in mine. When that didn't work, I thought of Barclay and his silly corncob pipe. Yet that also didn't shoo away the sensation that I was being watched.

What did work, much to my astonishment, were thoughts of Lucy Collins. I pictured her walking with me on that darkened street, chin thrust forward, emerald eyes challenging whatever lay before us. I knew that she, of all people, would show no fear. So I didn't, either. And by the time I reached my house, my mood had improved greatly and I no longer felt the presence of someone watching me.

That feeling, however, was short-lived. For even as I climbed the steps to my front door, a man emerged from the shadows along the side of the house. He lunged toward me, leaving me no choice but to yelp in panic.

It's the noseless man, after all! I thought. *He's been lying in wait!*

But when the figure stepped into the diffuse glow of the streetlamp on the corner, I saw that it was Stokely, the Pastors' butler.

"Didn't mean to startle you, Mister Clark," he said, although I could tell by his grin that he had found my yelp amusing.

"Stokely," I said, "what brings you around this evening?"

"I was thinkin' about what you said this afternoon. About helpin' Missus Pastor."

I had no idea how long he had been waiting for me. Probably a long time, for he looked cold and more than a little tired. I felt the same way.

"Come inside," I told him. "You need to get warmed up."

"I don't want to be no bother."

"This," I said, "is not a bother. Come in and stay as long as you need."

Inside the house, we found Lionel at the bottom of the main staircase, preparing to head upstairs for the night. Seeing Stokely at my side caused my butler to pause in mid-step, one well-polished shoe hovering inches above the green carpet of the stairs.

"Good evening, sir," he said, clearly surprised. "Is everything . . . all right?"

"Everything is fine. Why wouldn't it be?"

Lionel's gaze flicked to Stokely's intimidating form. Suspicion darkened his eyes, and for a moment it looked as if he intended to either flee upstairs or attempt to run outside and call the police. Nervousness radiated from his entire body.

"This is Mr. Stokely," I said in an attempt to put him at ease.

Stokely tipped his hat. "Evenin'."

Lionel ignored the gesture, turning to me and asking, "Is there anything you need before I retire for the night, sir?"

"I certainly could use a brandy. I'm sure Stokely is in need of one, too. Isn't that right, Stokely?"

"I'd be much obliged," he said. "If it ain't no bother."

Lionel certainly acted like it was. Moving away from the staircase, he let out a sigh before disappearing into the dining room. A second later, he was back in the foyer, bearing not our brandy but a curled finger beckoning me to join him.

"May I have a word with you, sir?" he asked. "In private."

"Excuse me, Stokely," I said, pointing out the parlor door. "Go make yourself at home. I won't be but a minute."

Stokely retired to the parlor while I headed to the dining room. Lionel was just inside the door, hands clasped behind his back and that dark look still in his eyes.

"Sir, if it's not a problem, I request to be excused from this task."

"Excused?" I replied incredulously. "All I want are two brandies."

"Which is one too many, if you ask me."

My chin dropped in shock. The nerve! While I had to tolerate the judgmental tone of Mr. Thornton Willoughby for Violet's sake, there was no way I was going to accept a similar tone from my butler.

"Well, I didn't ask," I snapped. "Do you have a problem with Stokely being here?"

Lionel straightened his back and lifted his chin. "I'll admit that I do."

"You shouldn't," I said. "He's a butler, just like you. You two are equals in my eyes."

"Equals, you say? I beg to differ. In fact, I

318

find it beneath me to serve —"

"One of my guests?"

"A *darkie*," Lionel replied, spitting out the word. "Being served by them is one thing. Serving them is quite another. As for drinking with one, well, that's just the lowest form of behavior."

In the past few days, I had certainly come to see my butler's true colors. Not only did he presume me to be a murderer — the poisoner of Locust Street, is how he had put it — but he was also prejudiced.

"The company I keep should be no concern of yours," I said.

"It wouldn't be," he replied, "if I didn't find your current and recent guests so objectionable."

"Objectionable, you say?"

"Yes," Lionel said. "This Stokely fellow, for one. That Collins woman is another."

"As far as I know, you are not a volunteer in this house," I told him. "I pay you for your services, do I not?"

Lionel lowered his head. "You do, sir."

"What I don't pay you for are your opinions. If you still want to work here, then you must keep those to yourself and treat every guest in this house with the respect they deserve. Do you understand?"

"I do, sir."

"Good," I said. "Now, I'm going to rejoin Stokely. If you bring us our brandy, I'll try

319

my best to ignore the fact that this conversation ever took place. If you don't, then consider yourself no longer in my employ."

Irritated beyond belief, I left Lionel and headed to the parlor. Stokely, who had taken a seat during my absence, tried to stand when I entered. I waved him back down.

"Please," I said. "There's no need for that."

"I didn't mean to cause a ruckus," Stokely said. "I got the feelin' your butler don't like me."

"That's his fault, not yours."

Before I could say anything more, Lionel stepped into the room with two snifters of brandy. Without a word, he placed one snifter in my hand. For Stokely, however, he slammed it down on the side table beside his chair.

"Thank you kindly," Stokely said.

Again, Lionel ignored him. Turning to me, he said, "I hope you don't require anything else, sir."

"No," I replied through gritted teeth. "That'll be all."

Unable to spend another second in Stokely's presence, Lionel practically stomped out of the room. Stokely, though, was too well mannered to comment on my butler's behavior. Instead, he swirled the copper-colored liquor in his snifter and inhaled its scent.

"This here's a nice house, Mister Clark," he said after taking a sip. "Your butler does a nice job."

I nodded my thanks, wanting only to ask if he had decided to help me. Still, courtesy dictated that I engage in small talk with the giant of a man filling the wing-backed chair across from me.

"He missed some cobwebs in the corners, though," Stokely informed me. "You need to look for those every day. Them spiders spin webs like a house a'fire."

"I'll be sure to tell him that."

"How long has he been with you?"

"Not very long," I said. "Three months."

Stokely chuckled to himself. "No wonder there's cobwebs in them corners. What's his name?"

"Lionel."

"Nice name."

"Your name is interesting as well," I told him. "Is that your surname?"

Stokely halted his snifter midsip. "My what?"

"Your last name. Or is it your first?"

"It's my only name. My mama didn't give me a proper last name, seein' how she and my daddy wasn't married. They been callin' me Stokely for as long as I can remember."

I leaned forward, my interest in Stokely's reason for paying me a visit momentarily eclipsed by another one of his personal stories. "Why is that?"

" 'Cause I was brought up in the kitchen,

stokin' the fire in the stove as soon as I could walk. When I was sent to the fields, the name went with me. Didn't matter none that I was pickin' cotton. They still called me Stokely."

He stopped, no doubt wondering if he should have shared that much with me. It's possible he thought he shouldn't be there at all. He was, after all, someone else's servant, relaxing in the parlor of a man who was practically a stranger. And while it wasn't my intention at all, it dawned on me that I had made him uncomfortable.

"I'm sorry," I said. "It seems that all I do is ask questions."

"You do," Stokely said, taking another sip of brandy. "But I think it's 'cause you have a curious mind. You like findin' things out."

"That I do."

"Which is why I decided to help you. I spoke with Mister Pastor. Told him you was a decent man. He said he'll talk to you."

The news left me overjoyed. I not only had the chance to get more information about who might have killed Mrs. Pastor, but Stokely's confidence in me signaled that yet another person was convinced of my innocence. Robert Pastor, after all, wouldn't have agreed to be in the same room with me if he thought I had killed his wife.

"I can't begin to tell you how grateful I am," I told Stokely. "When should I come by?"

322

"In the morning. I'll tell Mister Pastor you'll be there about eight."

Stokely finished his brandy in two mighty gulps. Thus fortified, he left the parlor, tipped his hat, and stepped once again into the chilly night.

I finished my own drink while thinking up questions to ask Mr. Pastor. Chief among them was why he had ordered an examination of his wife's body. But others came to mind, as well. Ones that I hoped wouldn't drift away during my slumber.

I needn't have worried, though, for I barely slept that night. My dreams were once more haunted by the ghostly images of old, departed friends. Davies, Cole, and Duncan were there again, along with a parade of others whose names I've forgotten but whose faces I'll remember forever.

All of them marched wearily through my bedroom, just as they had during their previous invasion of my dreams. This time, though, their presence was more pronounced. As they emerged one by one from the wall, it felt as if each of them had truly just stepped into the room.

They said not a word as they crossed in front of my bed. They merely marched, as if returning from a battle that had been sorely lost. As each of my friends passed, I called out their names in my sleep.

"Cole! It's me, Clark! Duncan! Do you hear

me, Duncan?"

They moved on — either unable or unwilling to address me — and finally slipped wordlessly through the wall to my left. Yet more arrived after them. Dozens more. One comrade, who died having his gangrenous foot amputated, moved with a pronounced limp, his left shoulder dipping low with each step. Another, killed when a cannonball landed mere yards away from him, retained only half his face. When he stared at me, it was with one piercing blue eye. The other was nothing but an empty socket.

When the last soldier made his retreat into the wall, I thought the nightmare had ended.

I was wrong.

For bringing up the rear of that gruesome parade was Lenora Grimes Pastor. Unlike the others, she paused for a moment at the foot of my bed, watching me with those intense eyes of hers.

Then she opened her mouth and a honeybee emerged from her pale, cracked lips.

■ ■ ■ ■ ■

BOOK FIVE:
UNINVITED GUESTS

■ ■ ■ ■ ■

I

Robert Pastor didn't appear to be a man in mourning.

Most people who lose a spouse look as if part of their soul has died as well. Gray faced and sickly, they gaze at you with deadened eyes while refusing to eat a bite.

By contrast, the rosy-cheeked and jovial Mr. Pastor seemed to be as healthy as a bull. As for his appetite, well, not even the death of his wife could dull it.

Because of the early hour, he suggested I have breakfast with him. Even though I had eaten at home before leaving, I agreed. What choice did I have? Only instead of the light meal I was accustomed to, breakfast at the Pastor residence was a stomach-busting feast. Biscuits with butter and jam. Eggs and bacon. Fried potatoes. Fried fish. Several slices of ham. Robert Pastor relished it all.

"I met Lenora nine years ago," he said before biting into a chunk of ham and washing it down with coffee. "A physician friend of mine told me about her father. I was a salesman, you see."

"Of medical supplies?"

"Yes. He thought Mr. Grimes might be in need of my wares."

Forgoing the dining room, we ate at the kitchen table as Stokely and the mute maid Claudia cooked and cleaned and made multiple trips to the cellar. Meanwhile, the food kept coming, even though I had barely touched what was already on my plate. I mostly partook of the coffee, which nonetheless did little to wake me up after my sleepless night.

"You're not eating, Mr. Clark," Mr. Pastor remarked after Claudia set a plate stacked high with bacon in front of me. "Aren't you hungry?"

"Not particularly," I replied. "Although this is quite a feast you've set out for us."

"The one thing we never skimp on around here is food. Even Quakers need to eat." Robert Pastor patted his ample stomach and laughed. "And it's rather obvious that I eat a lot."

"Were you always a Quaker, Mr. Pastor?"

"No, sir. I became a Quaker through marriage. Not a very good one, I might add. I prefer to have a few more creature comforts around me."

My gaze floated around the kitchen, taking in the new stove, the elaborate sink, the icebox that Claudia opened and closed as she gathered even more food to prepare.

"Such as this kitchen, I suppose."

"Oh yes," Mr. Pastor said, a noticeable twinkle in his eye. "I didn't care if the rest of the house was as plain as a post as long as we had a proper kitchen."

"It must have cost a pretty penny."

"It did, sir. Quite a lot. My wife, bless her soul, was against it, but I overruled her on this particular issue. We had the money for it, after all."

Because Mrs. Pastor's religion dictated that she live plainly, I wondered just how much money was in her name. Money that, now she was dead, would be passed to her husband. Robert Pastor was clearly a man with an appetite. If his desire for wealth was as strong as it was for food, I imagined he'd go to great lengths to get it. Maybe even murder.

"It must have been hard for you," I said. "Having all that money and not being able to use it."

"Not necessarily," Mr. Pastor replied, a glistening slice of bacon pinched between his thumb and forefinger. "It's not as if we were living like paupers. We spent that money well enough, I can assure you. Gave a lot of it to Lenora's favorite causes. That Quaker school was her latest project."

He bit into the bacon with a satisfied crunch.

"So you never argued about money?"

Stokely came to the table, giving me a quick shake of his head as he placed a bowl in front of Mr. Pastor. His message was clear — I was being too nosy.

"I'm afraid I've forgotten my manners. That's none of my business," I said, turning my attention to the bowl, which was heaped high with grits. A square of butter sat atop the pile, melting into yellow ooze. "I see you hail from the South."

"The grits gave it away, did they?" Mr. Pastor dug into them, not caring that he continued talking with his mouth full. "I can't help it. Reminds me of home."

"Where are your people from?"

"North Carolina. The coast. I plan on moving back there once all this business with Lenora's death is through."

I looked down at my still-full plate, suddenly reminded that, insatiable appetite aside, Robert Pastor had lost his spouse. She had been murdered, right before his eyes. Some acknowledgment of that fact had to be paid.

"Mr. Pastor, I hope you believe me when I say this. I swear I had nothing to do with your wife's death," I said. "By all accounts, she was a kind and caring woman, and her death is a tragedy."

My host scooped up another spoonful of grits, holding them before his mouth. "I appreciate you saying that. It's mighty kind.

And, no, sir, I do not believe you are the person responsible for Lenora's death."

"Then you must have an idea who is."

"An idea, yes. But not a certainty."

"Have you informed the police about this?"

"Of course," Mr. Pastor said.

His response caused me immediate bewilderment, which was quickly followed by anger at William Barclay. Despite being my best friend, Barclay had lied to me when he said the investigation was at a standstill. He knew all along the focus of Mr. Pastor's suspicions.

"I told them all about it when I requested that my poor wife's body be autopsied," Mr. Pastor added.

"I'm curious about that. Why *did* you request an examination?"

"Because, Mr. Clark, in the days before her death, my wife's life had been threatened."

I looked up from my plate, surprised. "By whom?"

"Unfortunately, I don't know."

"Then what makes you think a threat had been made?"

"Because I believe I witnessed it," Mr. Pastor said as he leaned back in his chair, mug of coffee resting on his ample gut. "Something strange happened a little more than a week ago. I remember that it was a Saturday morning, exactly a week before Lenora's death."

331

"What happened, and how was it strange?"
I asked.

"I usually spent my Saturday mornings strolling through Fairmount Park while my wife held a private séance."

Robert Pastor didn't tell me who the private séances were with, nor did he need to. I already knew about Eldridge Dutton's regularly scheduled appointment. Yet that isn't who Mr. Pastor saw when he arrived home.

"When I returned from my stroll," he said, "I found my wife in the sitting room with a gentleman dressed in black. Normally, I wouldn't have thought anything of it. Many old friends of Lenora's would come by to sit a spell and chat. But this was no friend. I could tell by the way they talked."

"Were they arguing?"

Mr. Pastor shook his head. "Their exchange was calm, but I detected tension. From what little I heard, of course. They stopped talking almost as soon as I stepped through the door. When I inquired if anything was wrong, Lenora told me that all was well. The man in black — I never did get his name — departed shortly thereafter. But Lenora was bothered by the visit for the rest of the day. She seemed lost in thought. Troubled, you know? Later that night, I again asked her about the man's identity. She told me he was a clergyman who, because of her apparent gifts as a medium, feared for her soul."

"It was a theological debate, then?" I asked.

"Apparently so," Mr. Pastor said. "But he was the most frightening-looking clergyman I've ever seen. Yet even more frightening was what happened the very next day. That's when Stokely found a letter left on our doorstep."

"What sort of letter?"

"A threatening one," replied Mr. Pastor. "It was brief — just a single sentence. 'Join us or pay the consequences.' Then later that week, on Friday, a similarly worded letter arrived. This time, however, it included a postscript: 'This is your final warning.' "

"How did your wife react to these messages?" I asked. "Was she fearful?"

"I didn't tell her about them. I know I should have. I just didn't want to cause her any undue worry. But now —"

Mr. Pastor set down his coffee cup and pushed away his plate. For the first time that morning, I saw a man wracked with grief.

"You wonder if you should have brought them to her attention," I offered.

"Yes," he said quietly. "Or to the attention of the police."

"And you think these threats came from the man you found speaking with your wife?"

"Clergyman or not," Mr. Pastor replied, "he looked like someone capable of doing harm. His face was horrifying."

"How so?"

A bud of unease formed in my chest, slowly blooming as Mr. Pastor described a man who had pale skin ("As white as chalk") and dark, cold eyes. The nervous bloom got worse when he told me how thin and angular the stranger's face was. By the time he got to the man's missing nose, which marred the center of his face like two bullet holes, the fear had blossomed fully, and I found myself trembling from the top of my head to the toes of my feet.

If I had closed my eyes, I could have seen his terrifying visage staring at me in the reflection of a shop window. His black eyes. His sneering mouth. His nose that was nothing more than two dark wells burrowing into the pale surface of his skin.

But I didn't close my eyes. Fearful of remembering that horrid face, I kept them open as I said, "I, too, have seen that man. I saw him this past Sunday morning. He seemed to be *following* me."

"Perhaps he knew you had attended my wife's final séance."

About that, I now had no doubt. The main question was *how* he knew I had been there. Yes, my name was on a widely read article about her death, but it was doubtful a stranger could pick me out of a crowd just from that alone. Besides, my encounter with the noseless man occurred before my words had been put to print.

334

"Let's say this man did indeed threaten your wife," I said. "Even if he had, he certainly didn't kill her. He wasn't at the séance."

"I have a theory about that," Mr. Pastor replied. "One I've told the police about, as well."

I leaned forward, eager to learn more. "Which is?"

"That this pale man was only working for someone," he said. "Someone who really *was* at the séance. Someone who then killed my dear Lenora."

"That doesn't leave too many suspects," I replied. "And it's doubtful any of us had a deformed henchman working for us."

"I can think of one person who might employ such a man."

Robert Pastor didn't need to say anything more. I knew he was referring to the one man at the séance known for hiring, and even exploiting, such people. The one man whose very name summoned up images of the freakish and the bizarre.

"Of course," I said, angry with myself for not thinking of it sooner. "P. T. Barnum."

In theory, it made perfect sense. It wasn't hard to imagine P. T. Barnum employing someone as strange as the noseless man. Nor was it too difficult to think Mr. Barnum would send such a malformed person to perform bits of dirty work, such as intimidating a medium. Since Barnum was present at the séance, it wasn't much of a leap to conclude that he was the one who had poisoned Lenora Grimes Pastor.

Yet two things cast doubt on Mr. Pastor's theory. The first was P.T. Barnum himself. Despite being known for unrivaled braggadocio and the uncanny ability to understand what entertained the common masses, he was, by all accounts, a devoted husband, a generous philanthropist, and a staunch abolitionist. In other words, not the type of man you'd think capable of murder.

The second seed of doubt was due to Mr. Barnum's location at the moment of Mrs. Pastor's death. Occupied at the time with putting out the fire on the floor, I hadn't kept track of his whereabouts. Yet someone else had. Before I dismissed Mr. Pastor's suspicions entirely, I needed to speak with that person.

And, despite Barclay's warning to steer clear of her, that meant another visit to the home of Lucy Collins.

II

I found Lucy in the room where she conducted her bogus séances. It looked the same as the last time I'd seen it — dim, sparsely decorated, a round table in the center, and a fraudulent spirit cabinet along the wall.

The only difference was that, instead of bells under glass, the table now held several musical instruments. I saw a small drum, a wooden flute, a pair of circular objects that resembled wooden clamshells and, in Lucy's hands, a bugle. A string, one end wound tight around the bugle's mouthpiece, stretched into the ceiling.

"Stealing a few ideas from Mrs. Pastor?"

"She doesn't need them anymore," Lucy said. "But once my name is cleared and customers return, I will."

"Or you could find a more honest profession," I replied. "Armed robbery, perhaps. At least then your victims know they're being swindled."

"The last thing I need from you, Edward, is another lecture." Lucy set the bugle on the table, bell side down, and turned to the spirit cabinet. "Try it now, Thomas."

The bugle rose into the air and hung limply a few feet off the table's surface. Instead of inspiring astonishment and awe, as the floating instruments at Mrs. Pastor's séance had done, this looked exactly like what it was — a horn on a string.

"Hmm. It's not very convincing, is it?" Lucy conceded.

"Not at all," I said.

Lucy stood beside me, scratching her head. "What do you think we should do?"

"We?" I said, my eyes bulging at her use of

337

the word. "There is no *we,* at least not involving this trickery of yours."

Sighing, Lucy crossed her arms and said, "Would you like to know what's absolutely maddening about you, Edward?"

"Not particularly."

"It's that you can be so judgmental. We both know you're skilled with illusions. It's in your blood. Just this once, I would appreciate it if you set your disapproval aside to help a friend in need."

"I'd hardly call us friends," I told her, chuckling. "As for need, I know you're not lacking money."

"Sometimes," Lucy said as she moved to the table, "it takes all the self-restraint I can muster to keep from slapping you."

"It pains me to say that the feeling is mutual."

"Well, then," Lucy replied, "we can either take turns flailing at each other like children or you can help me. Just this once."

Reluctantly, I joined her at the table, grabbed the dangling bugle, and untied the string from its mouthpiece.

"You're going to need a thinner string," I said. "What you have now is too visible, even when in dim light. Also, it needs more life and motion. Something to make it look as if a real spirit is carrying it."

I set about retying the string around the bugle's center. When that was finished, I went

338

to the cabinet and found Thomas crouched in his usual corner, the other end of the string in his hand. Above his head, a circle had been cut into the top of the cabinet. Beyond that was another hole in the ceiling, in which a pulley had been placed. There was, no doubt, another pulley located in the ceiling just above the table.

"You have to raise it slowly," I told the boy. "Don't be afraid to take your time with it. And don't hold the string so tight. It's not a kite. It won't fly away."

Thomas glared at me. "Why should I listen to you, you pile of manure?"

I looked away from the cabinet to address Lucy. "Must your brother always talk this way? And why doesn't he go to school?"

"Thomas talks the way he likes," Lucy replied with a detached shrug. "I've long ago given up trying to censor him. As for school, I tried to send him, but he kept running away."

"School is for girls and pantywaists," Thomas grumbled from inside the cabinet. "I got enough learnin'."

"Learn*ing*," I corrected him before turning back to Lucy. "Will you at least tell him to do as he's told?"

"Thomas," Lucy called to her brother, "do what Mr. Clark told you to."

"Why?"

"Because *I* told you to, as well."

"Fine," Thomas said before mumbling a series of words so profane I'm sure they would have caused hardened sailors to blush.

I returned to the table, where we gave it another go. This time, it worked beautifully. Thomas raised the bugle ever so slowly, giving the impression that it was being lifted by a pair of tentative, invisible hands. With the string tied at the bugle's midsection, both ends battled for dominance, making the instrument seesaw back and forth.

Lucy clapped her hands and exclaimed, "It's wonderful, Edward! You're a genius!"

"I wouldn't say that," I replied. "But perhaps a little of my father's skills rubbed off on me."

"Then you must help us with the others," Lucy said.

Apparently three more lengths of string were located just inside the ceiling. I was instructed to climb onto the table, retrieve the strings and work my magic on the other instruments in the room. Since I had already learned not to say no to Lucy Collins, I did as I was told.

"You know, I came here to do more than help you trick your customers," I said as I scaled first a chair, then the table. "I have information about Mrs. Pastor."

"Good news, I hope," Lucy said.

While I uneasily fished the strings out of the ceiling, I recalled not only my encounter with the noseless man on Sunday morning but my conversation with Mr. Pastor.

"He thinks this man without a nose was working for Mr. Barnum," I said, pulling the strings lower until they skimmed the tabletop. "Which makes Mr. Pastor think Barnum is the one who killed his wife."

Lucy set about knotting the strings around the other instruments. "Interesting, to be sure. But what does this have to do with me?"

"You were with Mr. Barnum at the end of the séance," I said as I hopped down from the table. "Did he leave your presence at any time between then and our discovery that Lenora Grimes Pastor was dead?"

"No," Lucy answered. "He was injured from that falling violin. I had a handkerchief to his head the entire time to stop his bleeding. I never left his side."

That was all the confirmation I needed to determine that Barnum was *not* Mrs. Pastor's murderer. I was certain her killer was the darkened figure who had approached her while I put out the fire. Since Barnum had an alibi, that left only four possible suspects: Mr. Pastor, Mrs. Mueller, and the Duttons.

"That doesn't mean Mr. Barnum is entirely innocent," Lucy said. "I'm intrigued by this noseless man you described."

Finished with tying string to the drum and the flute, she moved on to the small items that resembled wooden clamshells. There

341

were two pairs of them, each attached to one another with twine.

"What are those?"

"Castanets," Lucy said, holding a pair between her thumb and fingers and clicking them together. "They were a gift from a Spaniard who was trying to woo me a few years back."

"Was he successful?" I asked.

"It takes more than castanets to win the heart of Lucy Collins."

"What *does* it take, I wonder?" I said.

Lucy hesitated not a second before giving her response. "Money."

"Such an obvious answer," I said, shaking my head in mock disappointment. "I was hoping for something unexpected from you."

"An unexpected answer, you say?"

"Yes. Surprise me."

This time, Lucy gave it quite a bit of thought, standing for almost a minute with an index finger pressed to her lips.

"Acceptance," she eventually said. "Of who I am. Of *what* I am. And of what I want out of life. Did *that* surprise you?"

Indeed, it did. Only her answer, sincere though it might have been, wasn't the most surprising part. What truly took me off guard was *how* she responded — straightforward, sincerely, and without an iota of affectation. It was the first time her facade had cracked wide enough for me to glimpse the real person hidden behind it. I rather liked what I saw.

"In spades," I replied. "I can see how castanets wouldn't do the trick. Then or now."

"Now?" Lucy said, back to her old self again.

"Sorry to say, they'll never work properly for what you have in mind," I replied. "Replace them with one of your bells."

Lucy retreated to the spirit cabinet, where she tossed the castanets into a small box and retrieved an equally small bell. Tying the string around the bell's top, I said, "Back to the noseless man, I don't find him intriguing at all. Having seen him once, I don't want to lay eyes on him again."

"But let's assume Mr. Pastor is right and that he *is* working for P. T. Barnum," Lucy replied. "What reason would someone like Mr. Barnum have to threaten a medium?"

"We're not certain he wrote those threatening notes. It's just a theory."

"Well, it's one I think we should look into."

"And how do you propose we go about that?"

"I have it on good authority that Mr. Barnum is hosting a masquerade ball tonight at the Continental Hotel," Lucy said. "We simply need to show up and ask him about this gruesome man without a nose."

I finished attaching the string to the bell and set it on the table. Then I called to the cabinet one more time. "All right. Try all four of them now, Thomas."

All the instruments on the table started to rise. Not quickly, mind you, but slowly and eerily. Once they were in the air, the effect was now quite realistic, even with the strings visible. The bugle and the flute spun around each other while the drum rocked back and forth and the bell lightly rang.

"Splendid!" Lucy declared. "Simply splendid!"

"About this masked ball," I said. "You realize we haven't been invited, right?"

Lucy shook her head at me, disappointed by my apparent lack of imagination. "Honestly, Edward, you're more naive than I thought. An invitation isn't necessary. All we need is to arrive at the hotel tonight in costume. Which is exactly what we're going to do."

I wanted to protest, but decided against it. Even if I refused to go, I had no doubt that Lucy's coach would nonetheless arrive at my house that night. That's what Barclay, for all his advice, didn't know about Mrs. Collins. She was persistent beyond the point of annoyance. Faced with such determination, I could think of only one thing to say.

"But I don't own a costume."

"Well, Edward, you need to get one. And quickly."

III

Cobbling together a costume proved to be more difficult than I expected.

The mask was easy enough to acquire — I bought one in a shop on Market Street. Finding the proper outfit to wear with it was another matter. Normally, I would have ordered a costume from my tailor. But since the circumstances were anything but normal, I knew that not even the speedy Mr. Brooks would be able to stitch something together for me on such short notice.

Without any other option, I had to make do with a black morning coat, trousers, and a top hat pulled from my wardrobe. Still, even with the mask, it wasn't suitable enough for a masquerade ball hosted by P. T. Barnum. I needed something else — something that would turn my meager ensemble into a full-fledged costume.

So that evening, I again crept into the dusty attic on the fourth floor, once more looking for an object from my past.

I found it in a wooden trunk that had been shoved deep under the eaves. Its lid was darkened by dust, and when I swiped my hand across it, I saw words that had been branded into the wood.

THIS TRUNK AND THE CONTENTS WITHIN ARE THE SOLE PROPERTY OF MAGELLAN HOLMES.

Upon lifting the lid, I immediately saw what I was looking for.

A cape.

Made of black velvet and lined with red silk, it was the cape my father had worn during many of his performances. And despite a decade and a half spent languishing inside the trunk, it remained in excellent condition.

Removing the cape from the trunk, I shook off some dust and smoothed out a few wrinkles. Then I draped it over my shoulders, holding it in place with a diamond-encrusted pin. Thus dressed, I turned and studied my reflection in a mottled mirror that leaned against the wall.

What I saw astounded me.

I was the spitting image of my father.

Normally, I suspect, I bear only a faint resemblance to Magellan Holmes. Growing up, people always told me I looked more like my mother. Yet standing before the mirror, wearing my father's old cape, our resemblance was undeniable. So much so that, for a brief moment, I thought my father was in the attic with me. It was an improbable notion, to be sure, but that didn't stop me from spinning around, cape twirling, to look behind me.

Satisfied that the Amazing Magellan hadn't somehow escaped captivity, I turned back to the mirror, trembling slightly as I studied my reflection. I imagined I looked the very same way my father had when he was first starting out as a magician. Before "Amazing" became a permanent part of his name.

The realization didn't please me. I wanted to look like Magellan Holmes about as much as I did the noseless man. Yet there was no avoiding it. I was his son, as much as I hated that fact.

I hated it so much that I was inclined to tear off the cape, stuff it back into the trunk from whence it came, and never look at it again. The only thing stopping me was the fact that I still needed something to wear to the masked ball. Since time wasn't on my side, I swallowed both my pride and the dislike of my father and took the cape with me. It was better to have a costume I abhorred than no costume at all.

With my ensemble complete, I had nothing to do but wait for Lucy Collins to arrive.

Her coach stopped outside my house exactly at nine, a lit lantern swinging from the back and Thomas at the reins. Befitting the occasion, he wore a top hat, which made him look like a proper coachman in miniature.

Lucy was even more decked out, wearing a gown of emerald satin that brought out the green in her eyes. The bodice was cut low, revealing ample décolletage framed by a ribbon of scarlet silk. The gown then narrowed, hugging Lucy's tiny waist, before expanding again in a layered skirt so wide that it took up most of the coach's interior. A flock of red birds had been embroidered into the skirt — a touch of elegant whimsy. Her hair was piled atop her head in a riot of curls that were barely contained by an ivory comb inlaid with rubies. Her face, lightly powdered, had touches of pink at the cheeks.

"How do I look?" she asked.

"Quite nice," I said, in what might be the biggest understatement I have ever uttered. For Lucy, as a matter of truth, was stunning, and I felt inferior in every way as I climbed into the coach.

"You look very fine yourself," Lucy remarked as I sat down amid her rustling skirt. "Formal wear suits you. It feels like a handsome prince has just joined me in my coach."

I arched my brow. "*Handsome,* you say? Why, Lucy Collins, I do believe you just paid *me* a compliment."

"I was only being polite," she replied while straightening her skirt. "Seeing how you find me so beautiful, I felt it only right to return the favor."

"I never said beautiful. I believe the word was attractive."

"It's the same thing," Lucy was quick to add.

"But it's not," I said. "Trust the man who writes for a living. As for handsome, however, the meaning of that word is unmistakable."

"Which is why I take it back."

I gasped in mock surprise. "You can't retract a compliment."

"I most certainly can," Lucy said. "I've now decided that you look . . . presentable."

"I'll accept that," I replied. "I hope I'm presentable enough to allow us to enter. I still think this is a terrible idea."

Lucy gave me a small sigh. "Do try to have fun, Edward."

"This isn't about fun," I said. "We need to question Mr. Barnum and then take our leave."

"You've never been to a masked ball, have you?"

"I've never been invited to one," I said. "Come to think of it, I'm not invited to *this* one. I assume you've been to dozens, invited or not."

"No, not many," Lucy admitted. "But I've been to enough to know that they can be quite spectacular."

She was correct in that regard, for I was enchanted as soon as we arrived at the Continental Hotel. It appeared that Mr. Barnum had spared no expense. Lit torches had been placed outside, the leaping flames casting an orange glow onto the hotel's facade. A line of white-gloved footmen in top hats and tails greeted each arriving coach, helping guests disembark in their cumbersome finery.

When Thomas pulled our coach to a stop,

Lucy and I donned our masks. Mine was black, made of papier-mâché and tied in the back so that it covered the upper part of my face. The nose was elongated, tapering to a point, Cyrano-like, several inches from my face. Lucy's mask, the same emerald shade of her gown, was attached to a stick and bedecked with red feathers that matched the birds on her skirt.

Because of our outfits, Lucy and I both had trouble leaving the coach. Her skirt was too wide to fit through the door going forward, requiring her to exit sideways. My problem was my mask's nose, which insisted on knocking against the door frame several times. When I finally managed to step outside, my mask poked the eye of the footman who had hurried to help me.

"My sincerest apologies," I said as he backed away from me, hand over his face.

Lucy took my arm before I could do any more damage and guided me inside the hotel. There were more footmen in the lobby, standing before a wall of potted palms that led to the ballroom.

We joined the line of guests entering, fitting in quite nicely. Like Lucy, the ladies were dressed in all manner of silks and satins. The gentlemen wore coats and cloaks similar to my own. Every one of us was masked. We all paraded slowly through the lobby, passing more footmen, more potted plants, and crimson curtains made of silk.

Then it was into the ballroom itself, full of so much color and activity that it felt like stepping into a kaleidoscope. Banners of red, orange, and royal blue dripped from the ceiling and dangled in the corners. Large vases burst with flowers — roses; irises; lilies of every shape, size, and color. A full orchestra lined an entire wall of the ballroom, its musicians also masked. On the other side of the room was a large buffet containing oysters, roast lamb, a suckling pig, roast beef, and desserts so elaborately decorated they more resembled jewel boxes than something edible.

Situated between the food and the musicians, like a teeming sea that divided two continents, was the dance floor. So much activity was taking place there that I scarcely knew where to look first. The floor was a whirling dervish of color — crimson and periwinkle, emerald and gold, orange and purple. All those varied hues were constantly on the move. Reflected in the mirrored walls. Streaking across the dance floor. Shifting and blending and uniting in myriad combinations. There was noise, too, a joyous cacophony of music, laughter, and clinking champagne glasses.

And the costumes! I had never seen so many gathered in one place. It was an unceasing rotation of masks. Some were painted.

Others were bejeweled. Still others had been festooned with feathers — a flock of exotic birds. There were devils and demons and jesters and beasts.

Roaming among them were guests who required no costume to appear strange or fantastical. I saw one woman so tall that I at first thought she was walking on stilts. It wasn't until she passed right by me that I realized she truly was of such great height. In stark counterpoint, following her was a man shorter than Thomas. He was so small that the top of his hat barely reached my waist. Behind them was a rather sturdy woman in a bejeweled gown. She held a feathered mask to her face, and while it did a suitable job of covering her eyes and forehead, it did nothing to disguise the well-tended beard that dripped from her chin. And I can't forget to mention the twins who were joined at the hip. Dark skinned and exotic, they were attached at the rump, facing away from each other. They wore matching yellow gowns of crinoline and lace, the skirt wide enough to accommodate them both. Each had a different dance partner, the men circling them as the twins rotated in place.

"I told you it would be spectacular," Lucy said.

"It is," I replied. "But for what reason is Mr. Barnum throwing this party?"

Lucy shrugged. "He's P. T. Barnum. I doubt

he needs a reason to do anything."

Speaking of our host, he was naturally the center of attention, located on a platform that rose waist high above the far end of the dance floor. On top of the platform was a high-backed throne in which Barnum himself sat, hands moving along to the music. The greatest showman of our time looked far more at home there than he had at the Pastor residence. During the séance, he was a mere mortal — humble, lumpy, and quiet. But on that throne, visible to everyone in the ballroom, he was like a god.

Phineas Taylor Barnum, master of the spectacular and peddler of entertainment to the common man, lived an endless cycle of success and disgrace and success again. At the moment, though, he was in a slump and, according to recent reports, nearly broke again. His museums, though popular, had been too expensive to rebuild after being burned to the ground. His tours with Jenny Lind and Tom Thumb were distant memories. And while he had begun to take an interest in politics, social causes, and, ironically, the debunking of Spiritualism, I suspected this ball was his way of proving he could still put on a good show. In my opinion, he had succeeded admirably . . . so much so that the activity on the dance floor made it hard to reach him.

"How do we get to him?" I asked Lucy.

"Waltz, of course."

She stepped onto the crowded dance floor, forcing several couples to swirl around her or stop altogether. Lucy paid them no mind as she held out a hand. I paused on the edge of the dance floor, strangely and suddenly nervous.

Part of my hesitation was because I assumed that my dancing skills were somewhat lacking. But most of it stemmed from the way Lucy looked. Resplendent in her emerald gown, head tilted expectantly, she almost seemed like a complete stranger, one of those exotic and beautiful women who make grown men feel like knock-kneed youths.

I was completely out of my depth.

"Edward," she said, narrowing her eyes at me, "I'm beginning to feel like a fool out here all by myself."

I sighed, stepped onto the dance floor, and took her warm hand into my own.

We began to dance, trying to pick up mid-waltz. Lucy didn't miss a step. I, however, was rusty, and it took me a moment or two to ease into things. I stepped on Lucy's toes twice and, at one point, swatted her in the head with the nose of my mask.

"Relax," Lucy whispered. "You're too tense."

I truly was, moving stiff limbed around the floor. In the past year, I had never danced with someone other than Violet, and the foreignness of the situation left me feeling awkward and unmoored. Dancing with Lucy was different. She moved with effortless grace. Plus, she wasn't afraid to take the lead when necessary.

"You're too far away," she said after bearing another few moments of my fumbling. "Come closer."

She pulled me against her, tightening my left hand around her own. She then maneuvered my right hand until it was at the correct spot on her waist. We were so close that I could smell her perfume — a light lavender scent that filled my nose and allowed me to relax.

"That's *much* better," she said. "Now let's try moving to the music."

Lucy tugged me a bit, speeding up my steps until they were moving in time with the waltz. Soon we were gliding over the floor as if we danced together all the time.

"Fancy that," she remarked, eyebrows raised. "You're a better dancer than I thought you'd be."

"Thank you," I said. "Although I owe a great debt to my partner."

"When we first met, did you ever think we'd end up dancing together at a masked ball?"

"Not for a moment," I replied. "Our first meeting wasn't exactly . . . friendly."

"It most definitely was not," Lucy said, chuckling slightly at the memory. "Lord, did

355

I hate you."

"The feeling was mutual."

"And what do you think of me now, Edward?"

I paused a moment, trying to collect my thoughts into a suitable answer. It was difficult, what with Lucy looking so beautiful and the ball being so fantastical. It all left me feeling mildly intoxicated. Still, I was of sound enough mind to say, "That you're delightful company when you want to be."

"I can say the same about you," Lucy replied. "Miss Willoughby is a very lucky girl."

I frowned at the mention of Violet. Her name brought with it a strong sense of guilt. I hadn't thought of her at all during my time at Mr. Barnum's ball, even though I knew she would have been thrilled to attend. So the guilt washed over me as I imagined Violet gasping with delight as she took in the costumes, the dancers, the food. It felt wrong to be there without her. Dancing with another woman, no less.

"There's no need to feel bad," Lucy said, as if reading my thoughts. "I'm sure your dear Miss Willoughby won't mind that you're enjoying yourself without her for one night. At least, if she truly loves you, she shouldn't."

"She *does* love me," I replied, with perhaps a bit too much insistence. "And I love her."

"Then there's nothing to worry about."

"But how did you know that's what I was

thinking?"

"It was as plain as the nose on your face," Lucy answered, releasing my hand for a moment to tap the tip of my mask's elongated nose. "Besides, it's easy to tell what you're thinking. Your eyes and mouth betray your emotions. For instance, I could tell the first time I laid eyes on you that you had something sinister planned."

"Exposing frauds isn't sinister," I said. "It's a public service."

"Not to me, it's not," Lucy remarked. "But I knew right away you'd be a challenge. Just like I knew before you stepped onto this dance floor that you were worried about making a fool of yourself."

"I'm sure my hesitation also helped with that deduction."

"Well, yes, it did," Lucy said. "But it was more than that. I saw it in your eyes."

I looked into Lucy's eyes, trying to see if I could detect what *she* was thinking. Unlike mine, those twin emeralds gave no hint of her emotions or thoughts. Yet I continued to stare into them, hoping some hint of her mind-set would eventually peek through.

"You were right," I said. "I was worried about making a fool of myself in front of you."

"You needn't have worried," Lucy replied. "You're a fine dancer. Who taught you?"

"My mother. Many, many years ago."

"She taught you well."

I gave her a nod of thanks. "Where did you learn to dance?"

"Mrs. Day's Dance School in Baltimore. Her motto was that a proper lady *must* know how to dance."

"But you're no lady," I said with a gentle smile.

"I'm not," Lucy replied. "And you're far too much of a gentleman."

I was about to protest, but Lucy stopped me with a shake of her head. "Don't say anything else, Edward. It will only spoil things."

Heeding her words, I stayed silent, even as she pulled me closer. Pressed against her, breathing in her lavender scent, I felt more intoxicated than before. All my concerns drifted away. I forgot about Violet. And my father. And even why we had come to the ball in the first place. All I focused on was the swell of the music, the ease of our movements, the way the cool satin of Lucy's gown slid beneath my palm.

I quite likely could have remained that way for hours had it not been for a sight that yanked me back into reality.

I was spinning Lucy across the floor when someone standing near the orchestra caught my attention. It was a man wearing a cape similar to my own and a mask that covered everything but his eyes. The mask itself was featureless — a white blank that followed our progress across the floor. Behind it were eyes that studied us with distinct curiosity.

"I don't like the way that man is looking at us," I whispered to Lucy.

"Which one?"

"The man in the white mask," I said, twirling her around so she could get a look at him. "What if he knows we're not invited?"

"How on earth would he know that?"

"I don't know. Perhaps he's the noseless man. Maybe he's waiting for us."

"Nonsense," Lucy said. "Besides, it doesn't matter. We're near Mr. Barnum."

Indeed we were, having managed to swirl toward the platform. P. T. Barnum, maskless, still filled the throne. Standing next to him was the tiny man I had seen earlier, swaying with the music.

"Hello, Mr. Barnum!" Lucy called to him. "What a wonderful party you've put together. I'm having the time of my life! Thank you so very much."

Barnum acknowledged her gratitude with a nod. "You're quite welcome, my dear. Glad to see you're enjoying yourself."

"Oh, I am." Lucy gestured to the very short man standing next to Mr. Barnum. "Although apparently not as much as this little fellow."

"This is Commodore Nutt," Barnum said, extending his arm to the man by way of greeting. "One of my favorite performers."

I was only mildly familiar with the name.

Mr. Nutt was Barnum's replacement for Tom Thumb, who had struck out on his own after their contract ended. Although just as miniscule as the famous Mr. Thumb, I knew that the commodore couldn't match him in popularity. Still, he looked happy enough, bowing before me and trotting to the edge of the platform to kiss Lucy's hand.

"How do you do?" he said.

"Charmed," Lucy replied before turning again to our host. "Such delightful characters they are. Mr. Nutt, of course, and those twins and the lady with the beard. And that man with no nose."

Previously, Mr. Barnum had been looking past Lucy, interested more in the couples circling the dance floor. But now he gazed down at her with undivided attention. "I beg your pardon, my dear. What man?"

"Why, a very pale gentleman with no nose," Lucy said. "His face was quite alarming. I assumed he worked for you."

"I can assure you he does not," Mr. Barnum said. "And who, exactly, are *you*?"

Lucy lowered her mask and gestured for me to do the same. Mr. Barnum recognized us at once. Surprisingly, he looked happy to see us.

"Ah, Mrs. Collins and Mr. Clark! What a pleasure. It completely slipped my mind that I had invited the two of you."

At that moment, guilt got the better of me.

Perhaps it was because of how delighted Mr. Barnum was to see us, or maybe it was the extravagance of the ball itself, which must have cost a small fortune to host. Whatever the reason, I felt compelled to admit the truth.

"We weren't invited," I said. "We came because we needed to speak with you."

"About what?" Barnum asked, not surprised, but also not affronted.

"The death of Lenora Grimes Pastor."

Mr. Barnum leaned over the arm of his throne and whispered something into the ear of Commodore Nutt. Barnum then stood, gestured to an unobtrusive doorway in the corner of the room, and said, "Follow me."

With a boost from Mr. Barnum, the tiny commodore took his temporary place on the throne. Barnum then hopped off the platform and led Lucy and me through the doorway.

We found ourselves in the hotel's kitchen, an infernally hot cavern roughly the size of the ballroom itself and just as crowded. White-capped cooks stirred cauldrons of soup and basted sides of beef while waiters rushed by with trays both empty and arm-achingly full. Mouthwatering smells were everywhere. In just a few seconds, I detected fish, oranges, ripe cheese, roasted chicken, rendered pork fat. The scents rose to the ceiling, joining a cloud of smoke and steam that trapped the fragrant heat and made the room feel like one giant oven.

Mr. Barnum fanned himself as he asked, "So, what more do you know about Mrs. Pastor's death? Has there been any news?"

"Not much at all," I replied. "I know that she was threatened in the days before she was killed. Mr. Pastor seems to think it was the work of a man with a pale, deformed face."

"This man with no nose?" Barnum asked.

"Correct."

A waiter, burdened with a silver tray as large as a wagon wheel, pushed by us, forcing the three of us against the wall.

"And you assumed he works for me?" Barnum inquired.

"Mr. Pastor seems to think so, yes," I said. "But you say he doesn't."

"He most certainly does not." Beads of perspiration, due to the intense heat, had started to form on Mr. Barnum's wide brow. He removed a handkerchief from his pocket and dabbed his face with it. "I employ a wide variety of unusual specimens, to be sure, but no one missing a nose. And I certainly wouldn't send anyone off to threaten defenseless women."

"Our apologies," I said. "We meant no offense."

"No apology is necessary, my boy," Mr. Barnum replied. "I understand why Mr. Pastor would think the way he did. His wife's death was a terrible loss. Both personally and professionally."

"You knew her well?" Lucy asked him.

Mr. Barnum stuffed the handkerchief back into his pocket. "Oh, I wanted to, my dear. I wanted the *world* to know her well. I'm at a bit of a crossroads professionally, you see. My museums have become too expensive to maintain . . . seeing that they keep burning down. The authorities call the fires accidental, but I know they were set on purpose. Every one of them. Started either by my rivals or those who opposed my antislavery views. Whatever the cause, I now need a new business endeavor. Someone amazing. Someone who could enchant the world in the same manner Jenny Lind did."

"And you thought Mrs. Pastor was such a person?" I asked.

"I know she was," Barnum replied. "I had read a bit about her in the newspapers, but never paid much attention to it. Mediums, after all, are commonplace nowadays, and the majority of them are frauds."

I glanced at Lucy, eager to see her reaction. Born actress that she was, she offered none. Not even when Mr. Barnum said, "Those wretched crooks. They should all be tossed in jail for what they do. A whole lot of humbug is what it is."

I interjected before he could say anything more, "But you thought Mrs. Pastor was different?"

"Only after a lengthy period of time. I kept hearing from friends in this city about how amazing her séances could be, with floating instruments and invisible musicians and voices emerging from her small frame. Finally, I decided to go see for myself what all the fuss was about. I was left dumbstruck, and immediately I envisioned her doing the same thing in opera houses and music halls around the world. Imagine how glorious it would have been!"

"When was this first visit?" I asked.

"A little more than a week ago."

So far, this was in keeping with what Stokely had told me. Mr. Barnum had attended one séance the week before Saturday and then another on Saturday night.

"Between those two visits," Mr. Barnum continued, "I had reached out to Mrs. Pastor about possibly going on tour. She refused my offer outright. She said that although she didn't mind using her gifts to help others, she didn't want to profit from them. I told her that if she signed a two-year contract, I'd build ten of her precious Quaker schools. Even that failed to sway her. Yet I was determined to get her to change her mind, hence my visit to that sad, final séance."

"Do you know if Mrs. Pastor ever told her husband about your offer?" Lucy asked.

"I'm afraid I don't," Mr. Barnum replied. "I would assume she did."

"And did *you* mention the offer to anyone?"
I asked.

To that query, P. T. Barnum could only
laugh. "Of course not. I'm a businessman,
Mr. Clark. I never announce who I'm trying
to woo. That is, unless I want to burden my
rivals with a horrible act. Then I publicly announce my desire to sign that act and watch
my rivals fall all over themselves trying to
make a contract with what is surely a money-
losing prospect. I must admit, it's great fun."

Needless to say, such machinations left
Lucy more than a little impressed. "You are
truly an inspiration, my dear Mr. Barnum,"
she said.

"I've been in business a long time, Mrs.
Collins," he replied, "and I've learned many
lessons along the way. That particular one
came about after I announced my intent to
pursue an act I truly did want to work with.
When word got out, he decided to set out on
his own, and with great success, I might add.
I've stayed quiet ever since."

"Would we have heard of him?" Lucy asked.

"Perhaps. He was called the Amazing Magellan."

The name left me immediately and thoroughly breathless. I tried to appear calm, but
my heart was thrumming at a hundred beats
per second.

"You knew him?" I asked.

"We were quite close," Barnum said. "It

was a terrible thing, too, what happened to his wife. I don't know what possessed him to do it."

Behind him, one of the cooks tossed a hearty splash of wine onto the beef he was cooking, sending up a pillar of flames so bright that I had to close my eyes. When I opened them, I saw Mr. Barnum, head tilted, taking a long look at me.

"You know, Mr. Clark," he said. "You rather resemble the Amazing Magellan in a small way. Perhaps it's the way you're wearing that cape."

The damned cape! I knew it made me look too much like my father. Had I known that he was acquainted with P. T. Barnum, I never would have worn it. But Barnum had noticed our resemblance, and now I felt overheated, breathless, and downright ill. Not knowing how much longer I'd be able to remain standing, I reached out to the wall for support.

"Why, Mr. Clark," Barnum said, "you look like you're about to faint."

I nodded weakly, for that's exactly how I felt.

"It must be the heat," Lucy said, surely knowing that it wasn't. "It's hot as hellfire in here."

"Let's rejoin the festivities then," Mr. Barnum said. "Shall we?"

The two of them escorted me back to the main room, which was still a flurry of dancing even without Mr. Barnum's presence. After assuring him that I would be fine once I got some fresh air, I took my leave. Lucy followed me out.

"That must have been terrifying for you," she said as we reached the lobby. "Him bringing up your father's name like that."

"I don't want to talk about it," I murmured.

"Do you think he suspects who you truly are? He did notice the resemblance."

"I said I don't want to talk about it!" My reply was much louder that time, echoing through the lobby. "I need to go home."

At that moment, all I wanted was to flee the ball, lest someone else notice my resemblance to Magellan Holmes. I began to irrationally suspect that others had recognized me as well, and that my true name was now being whispered throughout the Continental Hotel.

Hurrying through the lobby, I unhooked the diamond pin at my throat and loosened the cape. It slipped from my shoulders and onto the floor, forcing Lucy to hop out of the way to avoid stepping on it.

"Edward, your cape!"

I continued walking. "I don't want it anymore."

"But it looks expensive," Lucy said.

"Leave it!" I barked. "Someone else can take it, for all I care."

By then we had reached the hotel's front

doors. Several guests in costume were arriving fashionably late to the ball, and each swing of the doors sent in a rush of cool air that perked me up considerably.

Just as I was starting to feel better, I noticed a streak of black on the edge of my vision. It was a man in a dark suit and cape, his footsteps echoing urgently off the marble floor as he moved from the ballroom into the lobby. At first, I thought it was Mr. Barnum, who had either suddenly remembered something he meant to tell us or else pieced together that I was really Magellan Holmes's son.

Instead, it was a man in a mask.

A white mask that covered his entire face.

And it was clear from his gait that he intended to catch up to me and Lucy before we could make our escape.

With the masked man fast approaching, I stepped behind Lucy and pushed her through the door. "Go quickly! We're being followed."

Lucy tried to look behind us. "By whom?"

"I don't know, nor do I care to find out."

We were outside by then, stumbling into a mass of carriages both arriving and departing. People streamed all around us — masked couples from the ball, coachmen running to and fro, hotel workers scurrying about.

As we sought out Thomas and our own coach, I glanced over my shoulder, seeing that the masked man had come outside as well. He paused in front of the hotel doors, urgently looking for us. Thanks to Lucy's expansive green gown, he caught sight of us easily enough and headed our way.

"Hurry!" I hissed to Lucy. "We must find Thomas."

"Maybe we should confront this man and ask him what he wants," Lucy suggested.

"Absolutely not."

It was a terrible idea, especially if I was correct about it being the noseless man behind that mask. And, yes, I feared he was up to no good, especially now that I knew he didn't work for Mr. Barnum.

Yet it was beginning to look as if Lucy and I would have no choice in the matter. With no Thomas in sight and the man fast approaching, it seemed a confrontation was inevitable. Frantically, I examined all the coaches in front of the hotel. None of them looked familiar nor did any have a top-hatted boy sitting at the reins.

"Thomas!" I called out. "Where are you? We're ready to leave!"

I looked behind us again. The man was closer still, his stride not slowing. As he walked, he took off his hat and began to remove his mask.

I braced myself for the inevitable sight of the noseless man's ghostlike face. But when the mask was fully off, I saw not flesh the same shade as chalk, but skin rosy from exertion. This face boasted a prominent nose, a creased brow, and a pair of curious eyes.

It was, quite shockingly, the face of Bertram Johnson.

IV

"Edward?" Bertie called out to me. "Edward, is that you?"

"Oh, no," I whispered.

"Is it the noseless man?" Lucy asked, too busy searching the street for her brother and her coach to look behind her.

"No," I said. "It's far worse."

Bertie continued moving in our direction, waving his mask frantically and saying, "It *is* you, isn't it?"

Faced with explaining to him why I was attending a masquerade ball with someone other than my fiancée, I did the most logical thing I could — I ran as if all the devils in hell were after me.

Grabbing Lucy by the hand, I set off into the street, our shoes sinking into the muck created by too many carriage wheels pulled by too many horses. We wound around coaches and dodged rearing steeds, the mud sticking to the cuffs of my trousers and splattering the red birds adorning Lucy's skirt.

"Edward, my dress!" she cried. "What are you doing? Are we in danger?"

"Not you," I said. "But I certainly could be."

I glanced back at the hotel, worried that Bertie had been foolish enough to follow us into the muddy street. But he had apparently returned indoors, because he — and his mask — were nowhere to be seen. Not that it mattered at that point. Thomas, either hearing my call or simply through provident timing, pulled the coach to a stop in front of me.

"Why in hell are you in the damn street?" he yelled down to us.

Lucy shook mud from her ruined dress while shooting me a look so cold it seemed capable of freezing fire. "I'd like to know the very same thing."

Although I scrambled into the coach, Lucy took her time, collecting her skirt before climbing inside. When I slammed the door shut, a good portion of her dress got caught in it. Thomas then lashed at the horses and we were off, departing the Continental Hotel at a breakneck pace. This time, I didn't mind the roughness of the ride. The faster I could get away, the better.

"Would you mind telling me what that was all about?" Lucy said as she tugged her skirt free of the door. "Who was that man?"

"It was a very good friend of Violet's."

"So?"

"So," I said, "he has now seen me in public with *you*. As has her brother."

Now it would be only a matter of time before one of them told Violet. There was no doubt in my mind that she was a patient person who trusted me completely. Mr. Thornton Willoughby, on the other hand, was a different story. Prior to my current troubles, the barest hint of impropriety would no doubt have made him force Violet to break off our engagement. But with my reputation now in jeopardy, I knew this would be the last straw.

"Perhaps instead of dragging me through a mud pit, you could have simply explained to him why we were there," Lucy said.

But it didn't work that way with Bertram Johnson. He wasn't known for discretion or silence when the situation called for it. He acted on emotion alone. And since I suspected he harbored romantic feelings for my beloved Violet, I envisioned him rushing to the Willoughby residence at that very moment.

Bouncing about inside the carriage, I regretted not heeding the advice of Barclay — yet another person who had seen me out and about with Mrs. Collins. None of this would have happened if I had kept my distance.

But now it was too late. Mr. Barnum suspected I was the spitting image of Magellan Holmes and Bertram Johnson saw me fleeing a masked ball with a beautiful woman.

My whole world had the potential to be upended.

I was certain the night couldn't get any worse.

How wrong I was.

Thomas had just turned us down an empty side street and was in the process of slowing the horses. Inside the coach, all was quiet. Outside, however, the sound of horses rose in the distance. It was light at first — like a rumble of distant thunder minutes before a summer storm. But it grew alarmingly loud. Soon all we could hear was the pounding of hooves in the mud as the horses drew near.

"What the devil is that?" Lucy asked.

As if in answer to her question, a massive brougham roared past us. Looking out the window, I was only able to catch a glimpse of two black steeds galloping by, nostrils flaring and foam flinging from their open mouths. The brougham they pulled was also black — a hulking one that rocked unsteadily. Guiding the horses was a beast of a man, all belly and beard, who couldn't even be bothered to glance our way as he passed.

"Well, they're in a hurry," Lucy said.

"I only hope Thomas doesn't try to keep pace with them."

"He might," Lucy replied. "Tell him to pull back on the reins a bit more."

I pushed open the door and poked my head out as far as I could without tumbling from the coach.

"Everything all right up there, Thomas?"

"Did you see that thing?" the boy said in awe. "It was like a bullet, it was so fast."

"About that," I replied. "Your sister doesn't want you to give chase."

I gazed up the street at the retreating brougham ahead of us. Unlike the coach we traveled in, there was no lantern hanging from the back to give any indication it was there. Instead, it almost blended into the distant darkness, as if disappearing into thin air. But just when it was about to vanish from view completely, it slowed down and — to my fearful astonishment — began to turn around.

"I . . . I don't like the looks of this," Thomas said.

"Neither do I."

Inside the coach, Lucy asked, "Like the looks of what?"

Up ahead, the black brougham had turned around fully and was now heading in our direction. The thunderous sound of hooves rose once again as the vehicle picked up speed. It appeared to be heading straight for us.

"Get the hell inside!" Thomas yelled down to me.

I ducked back into the coach, slamming the door shut and tightly gripping my seat.

"Brace yourself," I warned Lucy.

She said something in response, but it was impossible to hear her. Not with the pounding of hooves heading our way. Lucy's own pair of Cleveland Bays whinnied out their fear as the brougham continued to bear down on us. Our coach jerked to the right, Thomas managing to get us out of the way just as the black behemoth thundered past.

Out the window, I saw the horses again, as agitated as ever, then the bulk of the brougham itself. Peering out its window was a man's face. I glimpsed it for only a second — a streak of white standing in stark contrast with the darkness all around it — but it was enough for me to recognize who it was.

"It's the noseless man," I said, gasping.

"It can't be." Lucy rushed to the window, but it was too late. The brougham was now beyond us. "How is that possible?"

"I have no idea," I said. "Unless he followed us from the hotel."

If that was the case, then I assumed it meant he would continue to follow us. I opened the door again and looked behind us. Just as I thought, the brougham had slowed and was once again turning around.

"He's coming back for us!" I shouted to Thomas. "Go! Go as fast as you can!"

Thomas lashed at the horses, setting them off at a breakneck pace. Checking behind us, I saw that the brougham was again heading toward us, equally as fast.

"Damn," I muttered. "Damn, shit, damn."

Our coach crashed through a puddle, the muddy water splashing into my face. I tried to wipe it away, briefly letting go of the open door. It was, unfortunately, the exact same time Thomas decided to turn down another street, the sudden lurch of the coach sending me tumbling out the door.

Falling sideways, I managed to grasp the top of the door with one hand and its side with the other. My legs, however, dangled helplessly, the toes of my shoes sliding like a plow through the muck in the street.

Lucy lunged forward fast enough to grab me, her fingers curling around my shirt collar. Behind me, all I heard was the beating of hooves getting closer.

"Don't look behind you," Lucy warned as she tried to pull me back into the coach.

That was, thankfully, impossible. Yet I could still feel the rush of warm air from the horses' hooves as they approached.

"Just get me inside!" I yelped.

"I'm trying! Give me your arm!"

I loosened my grip on the top of the door and reached into the coach. Lucy grabbed my arm and gave a mighty tug. But Thomas took that moment to swerve the coach around another corner, and the motion propelled Lucy backward. I saw only a tumbling mass of satin and petticoats as her grip on me loosened.

I dropped away from the coach again, my left arm flailing, my right one clinging to the door for dear life. My feet continued to slide through the street, muck collecting on the top of my shoes.

During my struggle to keep hold of the door, my torso twisted, giving me a brief but terrifying glimpse of what was behind me.

The horses were practically on top of me, their necks outstretched, muscles straining to pull their burden faster, faster, faster. Their front hooves pounded against the ground mere inches from my dragging feet. One bit of slowness on Thomas's part — or one last push of speed from the other horses — meant I would be trampled to death. And if that didn't kill me, then the brougham's waist-high wheels would certainly finish me off.

Frantic, I twisted back into my original position as Lucy again reached out for me. I desperately swung my free arm, blindly trying to connect with her. It took a few tries, but Lucy finally latched onto my hand with both of hers and pulled once more. Feeling myself being jerked inside, I let go of the door, providing enough momentum for me to clutch at the seat and pull myself into the coach.

A second later, the brougham's horses overtook us. The steed closest to our coach barreled directly into the still-open door, wrenching it backward. The door slammed against the side of the coach, swinging back only after the horse passed. But then the brougham also smashed into it, this time tearing it clean off its hinges. The door fell into the street, the brougham rumbling over it.

"He's trying to kill us!" Lucy gasped.

I nodded in fear. "I believe he is."

"Edward, what should we do?"

"Slow down, let him pass, and hopefully get away from him."

Only, Thomas did the opposite, mightily lashing the horses until they increased their speed. We were now running side by side with the brougham, a mere six inches between us. We raced down the street that way, neither one slowing, not even when the mud was replaced by the clatter of wood. Out the window, I saw dark sky above and even darker water below.

Somehow, we had been chased onto Spring Garden Street and the wire bridge that spanned the Schuylkill River.

The horses of both vehicles, now unencumbered by street muck, raced over the bridge. First we pulled ahead, then our rival took the lead. Soon we were parallel again, which is when the brougham jerked to the left and slammed into the side of Lucy's coach.

The coach tilted briefly onto its two left wheels before rocking back onto all four. Lucy yelped and pressed herself against my side. I could do little to protect her, especially when the brougham rammed into us a second time. The only weapon I had was my voice, which shouted at full volume in the faint hope Thomas could hear me.

"Slow down, Thomas! For God's sake, slow down!"

I don't know if he heard me or if common sense at last took control, but Thomas yanked on the reins, slowing our horses considerably. The brougham continued onward, rumbling past us. As it did, I caught another glimpse of the noseless man in the window. He was, quite incredibly, smiling at us. He even waved — a gesture as surprising as it was infuriating.

Thankfully, Thomas brought the horses to a stop while the massive brougham continued to roll across the bridge.

"Are you all right?" I asked Lucy, who gave me a single, uncertain nod. "Good. I'll go check on Thomas."

Lucy nodded again, this time in gratitude. I slipped out the hole in the coach's side where the door had once been and called up to Thomas.

"How are you doing up there? Are you hurt?"

He gave no answer. Instead, he looked past the panting Cleveland Bays, toward the opposite end of the bridge. Following his gaze, I saw what concerned him.

The brougham had turned around on the

other side of the bridge and was coming toward us again. The two steeds pulling it — so black that they looked more like demons than horses — eagerly plunged forward, yanking their burden with astonishing speed.

Now stopped on the bridge, we had little chance of getting out of their way.

"Get these horses going as fast as they can," I told Thomas.

His response, half drowned out by the crack of his whip, was, "Don't let my sister get hurt!"

As I sprinted toward the coach's door, the bridge began to shimmy beneath my feet, warning me that the brougham was getting close. Our own coach lurched forward as the Cleveland Bays took off. I had no choice but to leap through the open door, push Lucy onto the floor, and shield her with my own body.

Outside, the sound of hooves got louder, no longer a distant thunder. The whole coach began to shake, the vibration quickening with each passing second.

The impact, when it arrived, was louder and more jarring than I ever imagined it could be. One of the black steeds hit us first, its shoulder sideswiping our coach and sending it rocking. Then came the massive brougham itself. It crashed into the back-left corner of Lucy's coach, ripping away wood and pushing the interior wall inward.

The coach, tilted to the right, skidded across the bridge on two wheels, dragging Lucy's terrified horses with it. It stopped only when it hit one of the swooping wire trusses that kept the bridge in place.

The impact of that collision, while not as strong as the previous one, was enough to throw us against the right wall of the coach. I hit it with my shoulder, pain instantly flaring.

Lucy, through sheer bad luck and poor body placement, sailed right through the unblocked doorway, a scrambling jumble of satin and lace heading over the side of the bridge.

I lunged for her, able to catch only the skirt of her dress as it slithered out the door.

Lucy hung there a moment — feet slipping atop the bridge railing, arms flailing, eyes terrified — as the dark chasm of the Schuylkill gaped beneath her.

"Edward," she wheezed, "don't let me go."

"I won't," I said. "I promise."

The words were scarcely out of my mouth when the fabric of her dress tore.

A sickening sound, it was followed by another rip.

Then another.

Before I knew it, the section of skirt I was gripping tore away from the rest of the dress, and Lucy, screaming the entire way, plummeted to the water below.

While the bridge wasn't too high off the

river, her descent seemed to last a full minute. Terrified, I took in every detail. Her dress catching the air and opening up like a blossom in spring. The features of her wide, fearful face blurring the closer she got to the water. Her cries piercing the night air until they were suddenly and completely cut off. The way the darkened river seemed like a hand reaching up to catch her before pulling her under.

Without thinking, I clambered onto the bridge railing and dove in after her.

Unlike Lucy's drop, mine felt like a shard of a second. I had no time to regret my action, for I was instantly in the water, thrashing about in the chilly river.

Although I was an able swimmer, the river — just south of the waterworks and the dam that fed it — moved too fast for me to navigate smoothly. Then there was the darkness, which only disoriented me further. Tumbling through the water, it was hard to tell the difference between sky, river, and horizon.

I didn't catch sight of Lucy until the current swept me beneath the bridge. The shadow of the span sliced across the river, allowing me to see the moonlit patch of water just ahead. In that faint bit of light, I saw Lucy struggling to stay afloat. She paddled desperately, arms tangled in the sodden mass of her dress. Her pale face bobbed in and out of the water a few times before disappearing altogether.

I quickened my strokes, using the current to my advantage. Soon I was out of the bridge's shadow and diving into the moonlit area where I had spotted Lucy. Visibility was worse under the water — a vast and inky blackness dotted with bubbles, algae, dirt. My eyes stinging, I spun around, desperately looking for some sign of Lucy. When my lungs began to ache, I rose to the surface and took a quick breath before plunging back under once more.

This time, I caught sight of Lucy, not ahead of me or behind me, but *beneath* me. Like an anchor, she had dropped to the river's bottom, unable to rise despite her frantic kicks. Diving downward, I scooped my arms under hers and tried to lift her. I wasn't able to, not with her sodden dress weighing her down.

I let go of Lucy and began to tear at her outfit. Tugging at the seams, I ripped away swaths of fabric. Buttons popped off and spun in the water. Silken strands floated away like kelp. Soon the dress was nothing but shreds and Lucy slipped out of it, finally free.

I swam to the surface, breathing the night air in deep, blessed gulps. Lucy, too winded to swim, wrapped her arms around my chest and rode on my back as I moved toward the riverbank. When the water was shallow enough for me to stand, I scooped Lucy up and carried her to shore.

Once on land, Lucy dropped to her knees, coughing and gasping. Through the ragged gasps, she managed to utter two words. "Can't . . . breathe."

"What's wrong?" I asked.

Lucy gasped out another word. "Corset."

She pointed to the lace-trimmed corset that squeezed her waist like a vise. It was so tight that I was surprised she had been able to breathe even out of the water. But her time in the drink had now left her with no breath at all.

I jumped behind her, only to see that the corset tied up the front. With Lucy still gasping helplessly, I scrambled in front of her.

It might come as no great shock when I say that, at that point in my life, I had never touched a corset. Inexperience caused my fingers to fumble with the garment's laces. Making matters worse was the panicked way Lucy stared at me.

"Hurry," she said, her voice no more than a squeak.

Having no luck loosening the corset the proper way, I grabbed the top of it, just beneath Lucy's bosom, and tried to pry it open. The laces barely budged as Lucy's ribs pressed against the garment, straining to break free. After two more grunting attempts, I managed to loosen the corset enough so that Lucy could catch her breath.

She inhaled, long and deep. At last able to utter a full sentence, she said, "Get me out of this damned thing."

We both began to tear at the corset's laces, our hands brushing and fingers entangling. Lucy's breath was hot on my neck as we worked, loosening the garment's laces row by row. With one final flourish, we tore the corset off and tossed it aside.

Thus freed of her constraints, Lucy collapsed against me, her head resting on my shoulder.

"Edward," she gasped out. "You . . . you saved —"

"Shh," I said. "Don't talk. Just breathe."

But Lucy insisted on trying to speak, her mouth opening and closing slightly as she struggled for the right words to say. Finally, she settled on, "Thank you."

She repeated those words several times, sighing them into my shoulder. I put my arms around her, noticing how she was soaked to the bone and freezing cold. She shivered uncontrollably, giving me no choice but to hold her tighter.

"We need to get you someplace dry and warm," I gently said. "You're going to catch your death from cold. We both will."

Lucy moved, but only far enough to face me. Looking into my eyes, she wore an expression I had never seen from her before. Curious and contemplative, it felt as if she were seeing me for the very first time. Her green eyes searched mine, desperately trying to communicate something she was unable — or unwilling — to say aloud.

Eventually, she settled on one last "Thank you."

Then she closed her eyes and, tilting her head back, lifted her face to mine. Her lips parted ever so slightly, like a rosebud opening up to the sun.

She was about to kiss me, and I wanted her to do so. I had, I realized, longed for it ever since climbing into her coach earlier that night. I even found myself leaning forward and bowing my head to meet her mouth halfway.

I would have continued, too, had good sense not chosen that moment to return. Violet, quite rightly, suddenly consumed my thoughts. No matter how beautiful Lucy was, I had pledged myself to Miss Willoughby. To kiss another woman — to give in to that temptation — would have been a betrayal on my part. One that would never allow me to forgive myself.

Pulling away from Lucy, I placed both hands on her shoulders and gently nudged her backward.

"We really need to get out of this chill," I told her.

Lucy's eyes snapped open, and her demeanor changed immediately. Her face, once soft in the moonlight, seemed to harden as her green eyes dimmed. She straightened her spine and backed away from me farther, suddenly conscious that she was now dressed only in a soaked petticoat.

"You're quite right." Her voice, much like her body, had become rigid and unwavering. "And a true gentleman would have already offered me his coat."

"Of course," I said, chagrined that I had failed to do so.

I started to remove my sopping wet coat, which was reluctant to unstick itself from my limbs. I finally wrangled out of it and handed it to Lucy. She wrung out the coat before draping it over her shoulders.

"If I didn't know you better, I'd say you planned this whole thing," she said, her voice now aiming for levity but falling far short of the mark.

"Why on earth would I do that?"

"Because you're still mad at me for seeing you in a state of undress after barging in on you and your tailor," she replied. "But rest assured, we are now even. For now we've both seen each other in our underclothes."

V

My coat did little good to warm Lucy. She huddled, still soaked and shivering, on one side of the coach, while I did the same on the other. Both of us remained silent. It was clear neither of us wanted to speak about my rescue of her or what happened on the riverbank after it.

According to Thomas, the brougham that tried to run us off the bridge departed as soon as Lucy fell into the water. Fearful of its return, he wisely steered the coach off the bridge and onto a dirt path that ran beside the Schuylkill. The coach had received a good amount of damage, but it still had four wheels and two tired but uninjured Cleveland Bays able to pull it.

Instead of returning to Lucy's house or having me dropped off at Locust Street, I gave Thomas the directions to the home of Inspector William Barclay. A crime of sorts had taken place, and we needed to report it to the proper authorities. And although my friendship with Barclay was currently strained, he was the best person to tell.

Barclay answered the door in rumpled bedclothes and wild hair. Lord only knows what went through his mind when he spied me dripping wet on his doorstep. I'm sure he was baffled, as any right-minded person would have been. Yet the only thing he could utter was, "What the devil happened to you?"

"We were almost run down," I told him.

Lucy pushed out of the coach, urgency overcoming any modesty she might have had about standing in the street in only a damp petticoat and my equally wet coat. "By the very man who had threatened Mrs. Pastor days before her death!"

Barclay, eyes as wide as wagon wheels, said, "Get inside at once! All of you. Before you catch your death from cold and I become the scandal of the neighborhood."

We moved indoors, retreating to Barclay's sitting room. Thomas curled up on a divan and promptly fell asleep. Lucy traded my coat for a few wool blankets. I warmed myself by the fire while Barclay lit a pipe, his hands shaking. After a hurried puff, he said, "I see you've spoken to Robert Pastor about the man without a nose."

"I have," I said. "I've also seen this man in person. Twice now. And, considering what just happened to us, I don't relish seeing him a third time."

"What reason would this man have to kill you?" Barclay asked.

"You don't believe that it happened?" Lucy asked as she angrily tightened the blankets around her shoulders.

"I see no reason to doubt your story," Barclay said. "I'm just curious as to what could have prompted this man to want you dead."

"We obviously know too much," I declared. "I haven't a clue as to what that information might be. But this man had something to do with the murder of Lenora Grimes Pastor and now he's targeting us."

Barclay, as was his wont, sighed in my direction. "I suppose this means you've been continuing your ill-advised investigation?"

"We certainly have," Lucy retorted. "And it's only ill-advised if you're not the one being blamed for murder."

"But don't you suppose it would be wiser to let me, as the official investigator, do that? Especially seeing that your efforts have now apparently put you in danger."

I didn't, and I told Barclay as much. While I was fearful of the noseless man, his actions indicated that Lucy and I were on the right path. A dangerous path, to be sure, but one that could possibly lead to our exoneration.

Barclay stroked his mustache for a moment, no doubt thinking about the best way to handle the situation. He then surprised me by saying, "Perhaps it's best if we shared information. You tell me what you have learned, and I'll do the same."

While he smoked his pipe, I told him everything Lucy and I had discovered in our two days of sleuthing, from that first chat with Stokely to what Mr. Barnum had told us in the kitchen of the Continental Hotel. Barclay seemed to know many of the same things we did, such as Barnum's failed efforts to convince Mrs. Pastor to tour the country. Other tidbits, like Mr. Dutton's private Saturday séances, were a surprise to him.

"This is all very interesting," he said when I had finished. "The two of you are tenacious, to say the least."

"Thank you," Lucy replied. "Unlike you, our situation demands it."

"Now I suppose it's my turn," Barclay said. "And the biggest bit of news is that the toxicologist has discovered what substance led to Mrs. Pastor's death."

"What was it?" Lucy asked.

"Apitoxin."

"Apitoxin? I've never heard of it," I said. "Is that some new form of poison?"

"I thought the same thing," Barclay admitted. "I had never heard of it, either. But the toxicologist told me it's very common. I've been poisoned by it, as, most likely, have the two of you."

"I don't follow," I said. "How have we all been poisoned?"

Barclay gave me a coy smile, pleased that he at last had more information than we did. "You've been stung by a bee, haven't you?"

"Of course," Lucy said.

"Well, that's what apitoxin is. Bee venom."

I scratched my head, confounded by this news. "Bee venom? You mean Mrs. Pastor was killed by a bee sting?"

"Not quite," Barclay said. "She was still poisoned. It's simply that bee venom was the method. It's a natural neurotoxin, you see. In large doses, it causes paralysis of the body and its organs. Everything inside her simply seized up."

"Are you certain it wasn't a bee sting?" I asked, naively holding out hope. "Perhaps Mrs. Pastor had an allergy to them."

"She didn't," Barclay said. "The toxicologist discovered far more apitoxin in Mrs. Pastor's body than what is possible from a single sting. And the puncture wound in her neck was far larger than one left by an average sting."

"But how can someone be poisoned by bee venom without being stung by one?" Lucy asked.

"By using the venom of many bees," Barclay said.

"You're telling us that someone collected bee venom?" I then asked. "How is that possible?"

"I haven't the foggiest idea," Barclay replied. "But that's what happened. And one of the seven people in that room is responsible for it."

Lucy leaned back in her chair, seemingly relieved by the news. "Well, it certainly wasn't me. I don't know the first thing about bees."

"Neither do I," I said. "In fact, I can't recall ever being stung by one."

Yet at that moment, I *did* recall something else. What I remembered was Mrs. Pastor's surprise appearance during my nightmare and the way a single bee had flown from her mouth. At first I had thought it strange, but only in the way that dreams are, with long-forgotten faces suddenly popping up and doing unexpected deeds. Had it been any other person, I would have chalked up her nightmarish appearance and what Barclay was telling us as mere coincidence. But since it was Lenora Grimes Pastor we were dealing with, I began to suspect that coincidence had nothing to do with it. Just like the table-tipping incident on Sunday, it was possible that her presence in my dream had been real and on purpose. As ridiculous as it seemed, I was starting to think that Mrs. Pastor had been trying to tell me how she had been murdered.

Even more startling was the fact that she wasn't the first nightmarish apparition to involve a bee. A similar incident had occurred only a day before her death.

"Sophie Kruger," I blurted out.

Lucy and Barclay both looked at me as if I were mad, which I was starting to think I was.

"The girl who drowned the other day," I reminded Barclay.

"I remember her," he said. "But why bring her up now?"

"Because it is my belief that she was *also* killed by bee venom."

It took a good deal of explaining on my part. I must have spent at least ten minutes describing Mrs. Pastor's visit in my dream before reminding Barclay how Margarethe Kruger witnessed her daughter Sophie make a similar appearance the morning she drowned.

"Mrs. Kruger said Sophie was in the room with her and a bee flew out of her mouth," I said. "The same thing happened to me last night, only it was Mrs. Pastor."

Lucy reached out to me, concerned. "Edward, when you jumped off the bridge, did you hit your head?"

"No," I said, swatting her hand away. "I'm quite right in the head at the moment. Enough to think that Lenora Grimes Pastor and Sophie Kruger were both killed in the same manner, most likely by the same person."

"But that's impossible," Barclay said. "I doubt the two of them had ever met. Then there's the fact that the Kruger girl drowned in the Delaware River."

"We don't know for certain that she drowned," I quickly replied. "If you recall, I questioned her cause of death that morning on the pier. And I doubt the coroner did an examination of her body."

Barclay released another sigh. "He did not."

"So we have no idea why Sophie Kruger died."

"Edward," Barclay said with as much patience as he could muster, "you realize what you're saying is preposterous."

Preposterous it was. But a small, stubborn kernel of certainty rested in my gut, telling me I was right. I just needed to find a way to prove it.

"Is that toxicologist from New York still in the city?" I asked.

"Yes," Barclay said. "He's scheduled to depart in the morning."

"Then he must examine the girl's body before he leaves. It's the only way to know for certain."

Barclay scoffed at the idea, saying, "That's impossible. The girl was buried days ago."

"Then you must exhume her. Right away."

This time, I thought Barclay was going to faint dead away from disbelief. His jaw dropped, followed by the pipe that had been lodged between his lips. Then he stammered, unable to form actual words. Finally, he laughed, hoping I was joking.

"You're . . . you're not serious, are you?"

"As serious as I've ever been," I replied. "I understand your doubts. If I were in your position, I'd likely feel the same way. But the worst that could happen is that we learn Sophie Kruger really did drown. *Or* we could learn that she died in the same manner as Mrs. Pastor and that their deaths are indeed related."

I could tell from the way Barclay tugged on his mustache that he was actually considering it. I'm certain Lucy swayed him further when she said, "If you don't do it, I'll grab a shovel and go do it myself."

"Don't think she's bluffing," I told Barclay. "I've seen her do far worse."

My old friend looked first to me, then to Lucy. Seeing that neither of us had any intention of giving in, he said, "I don't know why I'm about to agree to this."

"Because you believe me," I replied.

"Possibly," Barclay said. "But that's not much of an excuse to offer when I cart in the corpse of a girl who has just been buried."

Knowing that Barclay had faith in me made my heart swell. After our friendship had been strained to the snapping point, we were once again on the same side and working together.

"Tell whoever asks," I said, "that you're helping the man who once saved your life."

VI

If this was a work of Gothic fiction, and not a true account of my experiences, I'd feel compelled to embellish the details of the cemetery into which we crept that night. I'd write about the elaborate tombs we encountered and how a mist as thick as cotton swirled around them. But, since my goal is honesty, I must admit that no such frights awaited us.

The truth is that Sophie Kruger was buried

in an unnamed cemetery on Front Street. Barely a step above a potter's field, it was a vast meadow of wooden crosses caught in the light of our lanterns, their shadows stretching and bending across the trampled grass. Because the souls resting there had been poor in life, there were no proper family plots or spaces reserved for loved ones. The dead were buried in the order in which they died, the graves filled in one after the other like bricks in a wall.

When we reached Sophie Kruger's grave, I saw there were already six fresh ones beyond it — which said a great deal about the city's mortality rate. Even at that late hour, two gravediggers were busy digging more.

"Who's that one for?" Thomas asked them.

"Don't know yet," one of the dirt-smeared men said.

"But it'll be filled in the morning by someone," the other added. "Mark my words."

Meanwhile, over at the grave of the Kruger girl, three policemen were performing the opposite job — unearthing a hole that had just been filled in. The trio of policemen, taken off the streets to do Barclay's bidding, muttered as they stuck shovels into the ground, disgruntled by their task.

"Can I dig, too?" Thomas asked any adult who would listen. Wide awake now, he circled the grave eagerly, dodging the shovelfuls of dirt being thrown his way.

"Back away, Thomas," Lucy told him.

She was wearing a shirt and trousers borrowed from Barclay. Somehow, she had managed to make even menswear look fetching, as if she wore it all the time.

Again, I thought about what had transpired between us on the bank of the Schuylkill River. The events between then and now had clouded my perception a bit, and I wondered if perhaps I had misinterpreted Lucy's intentions. After an ordeal such as the one we had experienced, it was only natural for emotions to be high.

Either way, it didn't matter. I had kept my pledge to Violet and Lucy seemed to be back to her old self. What had happened earlier that night was now in the past.

"Thomas!" Lucy said again. "I told you to leave those men alone. You're being a pest."

Barclay stood next to her, pretending to watch the gravediggers but secretly eyeing her instead.

"So, Mrs. Collins," he said, "how is business?"

"Not very well, thanks to you."

"I'm simply doing my job."

"And I would like to do mine."

"Don't worry," Barclay told her. "Business will be back to normal once your name is cleared. In fact, I suspect the notoriety will only benefit you in the end. That is, *if* your name is cleared."

Lucy huffed with indignation. "I assure you, Inspector, it will be."

While I knew no good could come from letting the two of them converse, I was too exhausted to intervene. Still trying to recover from one sleepless night, I found myself in the midst of another. By that point, I was so tired I could have lain atop a grave and instantly fallen asleep, not caring if the grave-diggers mistook me for a new resident there. Yet I remained standing, trying to keep my eyes open as the policemen emptied the grave and Barclay continued to pepper Lucy with questions.

"Were you in the Spiritualism business before you came to Philadelphia?"

"No," Lucy said. "It wasn't until Mr. Collins passed away."

"And where did you meet Mr. Collins?"

Lucy laughed — a nervous, birdlike chirp. "It was so long ago, I scarcely remember."

Thomas, still circling the grave, looked up at his sister and said, "You remember, Lucy. It was in Baltimore."

"Of course," Lucy said through gritted teeth. "Baltimore."

"Is that where you hail from?" Barclay asked.

"No," Thomas called out again. "We come from Richmond."

Barclay gave the boy a grateful nod. "Son, you have a better memory than your sister, it would seem."

Thomas, however, wasn't listening, for the goings-on in the grave at his feet had consumed his attention. It seemed the three policemen had finally reached Sophie Kruger's coffin.

"I see the lid!" Thomas yelped, hopping up and down at the lip of the grave. "Can I be the one to open it?"

"For the last time, Thomas, get away from them," Lucy snapped.

"Can't I even look inside?"

"No," Lucy said. "As you get older, you're going to see plenty of corpses, and not a one will be pleasant."

She was right. I had no desire to see one that night, but it couldn't be avoided. So while Thomas retreated from the grave, Barclay and I moved in. The policemen used the edges of their shovels to sweep dirt away from the top of the plain coffin. When it was cleared, they hopped out of the hole, content to let Barclay and me do the real dirty work.

Because lifting the entire coffin from the ground in which it had been interred was difficult, Barclay suggested we move Sophie Kruger's body to a new coffin waiting on a nearby wagon. While a logical plan, it required lifting the corpse from its pine box and placing it on a length of canvas spread at the foot of the grave. Unlike the digging, that task belonged to Barclay and me.

The coffin lid had been nailed shut at all four corners and once in the middle of each side. Using the tip of a shovel as a crowbar, we easily pried the nails loose.

In hindsight, I wish I had prepared myself for what awaited us inside that coffin. Taken a few breaths to clean my lungs, perhaps, or held a handkerchief to my nose. For as I crouched at the edge of the grave, I was confronted by a wretched stench that instantly turned my stomach. It smelled like rotting meat mixed with traces of urine and excrement. The odor burst out from beneath the coffin lid and filled the entire area. Behind us, I heard Lucy cough in disgust while one of the policemen rushed off to discreetly vomit in some nearby weeds.

Cold sweat formed on my forehead and at the back of my neck, and for a moment I, too, thought I was going to be sick.

"Don't you dare faint on me, Edward," Barclay said, his face taking on a greenish hue. "This was your idea, remember?"

"I know," I replied. "I hope it's worth it."

"It better be," Barclay said.

With that, we lifted the lid, revealing the sorry corpse of Sophie Kruger. Although only in the ground a few days, the change was horrifying. She was no longer the pretty girl I had seen lying peacefully on Pier 49. Now her skin had a purple tint to it, like a light bruise. Her eyes, closed for burial and covered with copper pennies, had bulged open again, one penny now stuck to her cheek, the other somewhere in the coffin's depths. Her tongue poked out, sluglike, from between darkened lips. The dress she wore was similar to the one she had been found in. Darkened by stains, it already lay loose on her shrinking form.

"One of us should take the arms," Barclay said. "The other the feet. Do you have any preference?"

I gazed down at the emaciated and rotting corpse. "I imagine both are equally unpleasant."

"Then I'll take the hands, if you don't mind," Barclay said.

We got into our positions and, holding our breath against the foul smell, grasped Sophie Kruger's limbs. Despite the skin around her ankles moving like wet clay beneath my fingers, she was easy to lift.

The hard part was the stench, which was so overpowering it made my eyes water and my head dizzy. Still, Barclay and I managed to lift the corpse out of the coffin and to the canvas on the ground.

"Well," Barclay said, "the hard part is finished. Now to the wagon."

We prepared to lift her again, this time holding the corners of the canvas instead of the girl's limbs. As I bent to pick her up, I noticed that the sleeve of her dress had been pushed upward. The fabric was now bunched at her elbow, revealing a slender forearm the same color as a ripening eggplant.

"Barclay, take a look at this."

Barclay bent down on one knee and held the girl's arm in his hands. He turned it slightly so it could catch the lantern light, finally seeing what I had noticed.

"I'll be damned," he muttered. "It looks like you were right after all."

As Barclay continued to study Sophie Kruger's arm, the light from the lamp illuminated the skin just beneath the crook of her arm. And in the center of that patch of flesh was a small puncture wound that could only have come from a vaccination needle.

VII

That night I slept, if you'll pardon the expression, like the dead. After such an eventful and shocking evening, I think even the most stolid insomniac would have found sleep. If I dreamt of corpses and ghosts, I didn't remember it, and for the first time in days, I woke refreshed and energetic.

Sadly, that lasted no longer than a minute.

For as soon as I left my bed, I heard agitated voices coming from downstairs. One belonged to Lionel. The other was Mrs. Patterson. Neither seemed to be in high spirits.

I rushed down the spiral staircase to the kitchen, finding the two of them locked in heated conversation. For a moment, I stayed pressed against the wall just outside the kitchen, eavesdropping on my servants yet again. Peering into the kitchen, I saw Mrs. Patterson with her back to the stove, wagging a wooden spoon in Lionel's direction. He, meanwhile, had a pair of suitcases on the floor at his feet.

"I'm fully capable of deciding what's best for me," Mrs. Patterson said, spoon slicing the air. "You can keep your opinions to yourself."

"Fine by me," Lionel replied. "But don't say I didn't warn you. Mr. Clark's reputation has taken a turn for the worse, and I refuse to be here when it crumbles completely."

"Then by all means, go. But I'm staying right here. Mr. Clark is a good man."

"Good?" Lionel said. "You should hear what people are saying about him."

"The only person I've heard speak ill of him is *you*," Mrs. Patterson said with a huff.

"Well, you won't hear me much longer, that I can assure you."

I chose that moment to finally peel myself from the wall and step into the kitchen. Upon seeing me, Mrs. Patterson lowered her wooden spoon. Lionel, however, lifted the suitcases.

"Going somewhere?" I asked him.

"Ah, Mr. Clark," he said. "Awake at last after another one of your late-night adventures. Did you bring more shame to your name and this house?"

"Not as much shame as you're bringing on yourself," I replied. "Am I to assume that you're leaving my employ?"

"Indeed I am, sir."

From the stove, Mrs. Patterson piped up with a hearty, "Then good riddance!"

Lionel sneered in her direction before heading toward me, bags in tow. I jumped out of his way before following him down the hall.

"Serving Stokely a single brandy distressed you that much, did it?"

"While a low point of my career, it's not just that," Lionel said. "It's your insistence on ignoring acceptable behavior. First, you let that Collins woman barge in while you're indecent. Then you become accused of murder."

"No one's accused me of anything," I interjected. "At least, not outright."

"This morning I heard from Inspector Barclay's butler that you and Mrs. Collins showed up at his house unannounced and soaking wet. With Mrs. Collins in nothing but a petticoat, no less!"

"It's not as scandalous as you think."

"It's scandalous enough," Lionel said with a haughty sniff. "Enough that I don't want to

405

be associated with you or this household any longer."

He was at the front door by then, reaching for the handle while juggling his suitcases. I stepped around him and opened it for him, all too eager to show him the door.

To the surprise of us both, Lucy was on the other side. Wearing a lavender dress and matching hat, she stood on the front stoop, just about to ring the doorbell.

"Speak of the devil," Lionel said. "Emphasis on devil."

Lucy's eyes widened. "I beg your pardon?"

"You'll get no pardon from me, miss." Lionel gave one last look in my direction. "And neither will *you.* Good luck, Mr. Clark. I feel you're going to need it."

He pushed out the door, brushing Lucy aside as he passed. Then he hopped down the stoop and onto the sidewalk, hurrying as fast as his legs and suitcases would allow.

"What was that about?" Lucy asked.

"He just up and quit," I replied. "I can't say I'm sad to see him go. I didn't much care for him. But now I have to find a new butler. Not a pleasant way to start the morning."

"Your morning is just starting?" Lucy said. "I've been awake for hours. I've been very busy. Didn't get a wink of sleep."

I arched an eyebrow. "No rest for the wicked?"

"More like no rest for people suspected of

murder."

Much to my relief, there was no unspoken tension between us about the kiss that may or may not have almost occurred on the riverbank. From the way she moved, chin thrust forward and green eyes afire, it was clear Lucy was there solely on business matters.

"I got my coach fixed during the night," she continued, "thanks to an admirer of mine who specializes in such things. It's not pretty, but we need the coach to pay someone a visit this morning."

"Who are we visiting? Not Mr. Barnum again, I hope."

"A bee expert," Lucy said. "A devoted customer of mine put me in touch with an entomologist at the University of Pennsylvania."

"A what?" I said.

"Entomologist. He studies insects. He's agreed to see us this morning."

"Why would we need to do that?"

"Because, while Inspector Barclay is waiting to find out what poisoned the Kruger girl, we can find out how a person might collect enough bee venom to kill someone. Knowing that should make it easier for us to pinpoint who gave Mrs. Pastor the fatal dose."

I heartily agreed. Just because we were sharing information with Barclay didn't mean we still shouldn't investigate on our own. After all, we had more to lose than he did. Much more.

That is why, five minutes later, I found myself once again thundering through the streets of Philadelphia in Lucy's coach.

The missing door had been replaced with a new, mismatched one. ("I told you it wasn't pretty," Lucy said.) The wheels were also new, which allowed Thomas to ride rough-shod over seemingly every groove and puddle between Locust Street and the University of Pennsylvania.

At one point, we hit a hole in the road so roughly that both Lucy and I were lifted out of our seats. We careened into each other, me flopping across the seat and Lucy landing right on top of me.

Uncomfortably stacked like that, we both tried to twist away from each other as quickly as possible. That only made things worse, for we kept moving in the same direction, our bodies rubbing together. I finally had the good sense to remain still and let Lucy crawl off me. She was all elbows and knees, how-ever, nudging me in the chest, the stomach, the groin.

"Sorry," she said, face flushing.

"Of course," I replied, at last sliding out from under her.

We spent a moment in awkward silence, smoothing out our clothes and avoiding eye contact. I aimed my gaze at the floor of the coach, seeing that our altercation had caused something to drop from the folds of Lucy's skirt.

I caught only a glimpse of it, but a single glance was all I needed to know what it was — a pistol.

Seeing the gun, Lucy grabbed for it, but I was faster. Scooping the weapon into my hands, I saw it had a squat barrel and a handle inlaid with ivory. Clearly, it was designed for a woman's hand, although I wasn't sure I wanted the one sitting across from me to have it.

"Where did you get this?" I asked.

Lucy sniffed her response. "It's no concern of yours."

"Let me rephrase my question then. *Why* did you get this?"

She held out her hand, silently imploring me to give her the pistol. I refused. Eventually, she crossed her arms and said, "It's for protection. In case we run into that noseless man again. Next time, just let him try to run us off a bridge."

I stared at the gun in my hands, amazed at how light and tiny it was. Something so small seemed incapable of causing harm, yet it could. I knew that very well.

"I don't want you carrying this around," I said.

"You're in no position to tell me what I may or may not carry."

"I've seen up close what a pistol can do to a man," I said. "I don't want any part of it. Neither should you."

"I promise I shall only use it if the situation warrants it."

Lucy held out her hand again. Reluctantly, I gave her the pistol, which she once more hid in the ever-resourceful folds of her skirt. After that, we rode in silence, bouncing around inside the coach until we were in front of the University of Pennsylvania.

The university was composed of twin buildings that sat, wide and imposing, on Ninth Street. One was for medical education, the other for general learning. Between them was a narrow grass lawn filled with studious young men rushing to and fro, all weighed down by books the size of butchers' blocks.

"What's this professor's name?" I asked Lucy once we were out of the coach. "And where is he located?"

"Sherman Abernathy. His office is on the third floor of the College Building."

We followed a stream of undergraduates into the building, which was as crowded and musty as I expected a hall of higher learning to be. Women, apparently, were an uncommon sight at the university, because the undergraduates present treated Lucy as if she were a rare peacock that had wandered inside. Some youths tipped their hats grandly as she passed. Others simply stopped to gawk.

410

The reactions of the students created a small flame of possessiveness that smoldered in my chest. From their well-polished shoes to the hats tilted jauntily on their heads, I didn't like the looks of them. I especially didn't like their wide smiles, which brought to mind a pack of wolves licking their chops. To discourage their stares, I put an arm around Lucy's waist and guided her to a grand staircase just beyond the entrance.

"Now who's the jealous one?" she commented as we began our climb to the third floor.

"It's not jealousy. It's protection."

"You of all people know I don't need protecting," Lucy replied. "Or have you forgotten that there's now a gun hidden in my dress?"

"I remember," I said.

"And I'm not afraid to use it."

I nodded. "I know. Which is why I'm protecting all these young men from *you.*"

This, I'm pleased to say, delighted Lucy. She let out a hearty laugh that began when we reached the third floor and continued as we traversed the long hallway to Professor Abernathy's door.

When I rapped on it, a voice on the other side called out, "You may enter!"

The first thing I noticed about Professor Abernathy's office was the décor. The walls were either obscured by bookcases or covered with specimens encased in glass and framed like portraits. Every insect imaginable was held within those frames, from beetles with turquoise shells to butterflies boasting foot-long wingspans. And bees, of course. So many varieties of bees it took three separate frames to display them.

Surrounded by all of those bugs was Professor Abernathy himself, a thin man with crinkled skin and a tuft of white hair. He wore a pair of spectacles that contained not two lenses, but several, all attached to tiny hinges that allowed them to be pushed into or out of place as needed. At that moment, the professor had one lens over his left eye and two covering his right. When he looked up at us, they distorted the size of his eyes, making them appear huge and, quite appropriately, buglike.

"How may I assist you?" he said.

Lucy did the introductions, prompting the professor to say, "Of course. I've been expecting you. How may I be of assistance?"

"We were told you could answer a few questions for us," Lucy said.

"If it's about the insect world, then I most likely can. And if it's about the Goliath bird-eater, then this is quite a fortuitous occasion, because I just received the most fascinating specimen."

The desk at which the professor sat had been positioned to catch the direct light from the room's lone window. On top of the desk, basking in the sun, was a spider the size of my hand.

"Good God!" I shouted, practically leaping to the door and dragging Lucy with me.

Professor Abernathy gave a good-natured laugh. "Fear not, Mr. Clark. This specimen will cause you no harm. It is most definitely dead."

That didn't make me feel a whit better. Dead or not, I wasn't keen on being in the same room with such a creature.

"Could you shove it in a drawer or something?" I asked. "Just until we're gone?"

"Skittish around spiders, are you, Mr. Clark?" the professor said as he opened the top drawer of his desk and gently plopped the spider inside.

"Yes," I admitted.

It was silly, I suppose, for a grown man to still be afraid of spiders, but certain fears run deep. For me, that was arachnids, which manifested itself after I tumbled into a nest of wood spiders when I was at the impressionable age of four. Thrown into a frenzy by my sudden presence, they had crawled all over me. Arms, face, hair. Some clung to me even after I had fled the nest, forcing me to shake them off as I screamed and cried my way home. The memory haunts me still, almost as much as the horrible sights I witnessed during the war. To this day, out of all of God's creatures, spiders are the ones I detest the most.

The professor chuckled again. "Most are quite harmless."

"We're here to discuss bees," Lucy said. "Honeybees, to be precise."

Apis mellifera," the professor said. "Fascinating creatures. What about them would you like to know?"

"Their venom," I answered.

"Ah, yes," Abernathy said. "Apitoxin."

"Can you kill someone with it?"

Professor Abernathy adjusted the lenses of his spectacles, moving them around until he was looking through only regular glass. The other, magnifying lenses surrounded his eyes, making them resemble the petals of a glass flower.

"It's possible," he said. "Apitoxin is potent enough, I suppose. But it's rare for someone to die from it unless they have an allergy of some sort."

"This woman wasn't allergic," I replied. "She was injected with it. In her neck."

"And another girl might have received an injection in her arm," Lucy added.

"Fascinating," the professor said. "I suppose you're wondering how much bee venom was needed to complete such a heinous act."

I gave him a nod. "We are."

"Honeybees are quite interesting, because even though a single colony might contain thousands of them, they work as a single entity with a single purpose — to ensure that the colony survives."

The professor crossed the room and removed a frame of bee specimens from the wall. He brought it to me and Lucy, letting us see how the bees behind the glass had been pinned to a square of white silk. The professor pointed out three in the center of the display.

"There are three types of honeybee in each colony — a queen, worker bees, and drones."

He pointed to the insect in the middle. The longest of the three, it had a narrow body and a lengthy, tapered hind section.

"That is the queen. She's the ruler of the colony and the reason all the other bees do what they do."

"There's only one queen?" Lucy asked.

"That's correct," Professor Abernathy said. "But there are thousands of drones."

He pointed to the shortest of the three, which was thicker and heartier than the others.

"Drones are the males of the colony. They do all the hard work and serve the queen."

"Are those the ones that sting?" I asked.

The professor tapped the glass above the third bee, which sat meekly beside the queen, nothing but stubby wings and black and yellow stripes.

"Those would be the worker bees. These

are the ones you see flitting from flower to flower." He tilted the frame so we could get a better view of the specimens. "See that thin rod on the back of the worker bee? That's the ovipositor."

"A what?" I said, brow creasing.

"Ovipositor. The stinger. It's attached to a small venom sac that can inject apitoxin into its prey."

"How much apitoxin?" Lucy asked.

"Oh, just a drop or two."

"Is it possible for someone to collect bee venom?"

"Quite possible," Abernathy replied. "One could find a worker bee, remove the ovipositor and squeeze a small amount of fluid from the venom sac. Another way is to get the bees to sting something flat and impermeable, such as the glass in this frame. When the bee flies away, the drop of venom remains. Once dry, bee venom becomes a yellowish powder that can easily be scraped up. I suppose one could collect it, dissolve it, and use it like arsenic or any other poison."

In the case of Lenora Grimes Pastor and, most likely, Sophie Kruger, someone had combined the bee venom with a liquid and injected it into their bodies. Yet one question remained, which I posed to Professor Abernathy.

"Can you estimate how much bee venom it would take to kill someone?"

The professor mulled it over while hanging the framed specimens back on the wall. "That depends on the person's size, weight, and, of course, tolerance for bee stings. But I'd say the venom from several hundred, perhaps even a thousand, bees would be necessary."

"But where can one find that many bees?" Lucy asked.

"Well," the professor said, "it's easy to find that amount in nature, if one knows the location of a rather large colony. But harvesting venom would be difficult in an outdoor setting. The bees could easily escape, even start a new hive elsewhere if the queen chose to do so."

"So the best way for a person to collect enough bee venom is from an *indoor* colony?" Lucy said.

"Quite right," Professor Abernathy replied. "Where the bees can be contained. Do you know of such a place?"

Unfortunately, I did. I had stumbled upon it only days earlier — and promptly forgotten about it. But standing in Professor Abernathy's office, surrounded by a thousand dead insects, I was reminded of it once more.

"I do," I said. "I know exactly such a place."

VIII

Less than a half hour later, Lucy and I were on Broad Street, standing in front of the former home of the Willoughby family. The place looked exactly the same as the last time I had been there — silent, empty, abandoned.

"This is where you and Miss Willoughby intend to settle down?" Lucy asked.

"Once we marry, yes."

"It's quite big."

"Indeed it is."

Lucy tilted her head, examining the house from a slightly different angle. "I don't think it suits you."

"How would you know what suits me?" I asked, irritated that she presumed to know me so well.

"Because I've been inside your home," Lucy said. "And it's clear to me *that* place suits you."

"Well," I replied, shrugging, "perhaps this will, too."

"And you say there are bees inside?"

I set off up the flagstone walk. "An entire legion of them."

Once we reached the front porch, as creaky as ever, I moved to the shutter where Violet had shown me the hidden key. When I pulled it away from the wall, however, all I saw was a single nail where the key should have been hanging. Lucy, meanwhile, had gone straight for the door, which opened with no effort.

"It isn't locked," she said.

"Winslow must be here."

"Who's that?"

"The Willoughby coachman," I said. "He checks in on the house from time to time."

It occurred to me that it wasn't the best idea to enter Willoughby property with a beautiful young woman who was not Violet. Winslow was practically a stranger to me, after all, and I had no idea how discreet he would be. Judging from the way my former butler spoke when he thought I wasn't around, I assumed Winslow was the same way. In other words, no discretion in the least.

"You should go back to your coach," I told Lucy. "Tell Thomas to take it around the block."

I instantly thought better of that plan, considering that Bertram Johnson lived just around the corner. Since he had laid eyes on Lucy the night before, seeing me with her again — in his neighborhood, no less — could raise even more suspicion on his part.

"On second thought, don't do that," I said. "Just have Thomas take you home."

Lucy, her patience wearing thin, tapped the toe of her boot against the porch floor. "Edward, you're not making a lick of sense. You're the one who suggested we come here."

"You can't be seen with me," I said. "At least not by Winslow."

"Then I shall wait in the coach," Lucy replied. "But Thomas and I aren't going anywhere until you finish whatever you intend to do here."

I waited to enter the house until she had crossed the lawn and climbed back into the coach. Once inside, I stood just beyond the door and called out, "Hello? Winslow?"

There was no response. The house seemed as quiet and unoccupied as when Violet and I had first set foot into it. After a few more moments of waiting, I crept up the main staircase.

My destination was the old nursery, and my goal was to gauge just how many bees had taken up residence there. If it was as many as I remembered, then it meant there were also enough to obtain a fatal dose of venom. And that, unfortunately, would confirm a new, heretofore unknown suspect in the death of Lenora Grimes Pastor.

On the second floor, I listened again for signs of Winslow. Hearing nothing, I began to make my way down the hallway.

Guilt burrowed into my conscience as I sneaked through the house that belonged to my future father-in-law. It felt wrong somehow, despite knowing the home would one day be mine. Careful of my pace and mindful of every creak and bump, I felt more like a common thief than the future master of the house. Still, I kept moving until I reached the end of the hall and the narrow set of steps that led to the third-floor nursery. Just beyond the staircase was the faint but distinct sound of buzzing.

The bees were still there.

The noise grew louder as I climbed first one step, then another. Just as I touched a third, the hum of bees was joined by another sound.

Coming from behind me in the second-floor hall, it began as a few bumps before changing into the sound of glass bottles clattering together.

A door flew open and someone burst into the hall. Soon all I heard were footsteps, frantic and fast on the floorboards. Someone was running, the noise so loud it drowned out the bees humming above me.

Bursting back into the hallway, I caught sight of the stranger heading toward the staircase at the other end of the house. He wore a black cloak, the hood pulled over his head. I gave chase, flying down the hallway in a flash. I reached the top of the stairs just as the mystery man was nearing the bottom. He ran toward the front door.

"Stop!" I called as I rushed down the stairs. "I know the police!"

My threat, meager as it was, did nothing to slow the trespasser. He threw open the front door and ran outside. I followed once I reached the ground floor, although I feared he was too far ahead of me to catch. Especially now that he was outside, where there were any number of directions in which to run.

Bursting onto the front porch, however, I saw the intruder had taken the flagstone walkway that led to the street and Lucy Collins's coach. Thomas, I noticed, still sat at the reins, enjoying a bit of tobacco.

"Thomas!" I yelled across the lawn. "Stop him!"

Spitting out a splash of tobacco juice, Thomas leapt from the top of the coach directly onto the black-cloaked trespasser. Both of them dropped to the ground in a writhing, rolling mass. Soon the man was on his stomach, face mashed into the grass. Thomas sat on top of him and uttered a stream of obscenities while pummeling the man's head.

Lucy had hopped out of the coach by the time I reached it, and stood over the man. She had fished the pistol from her skirt and now held it at arm's length, aiming it at the intruder's head. Running in front of her, I barked, "Put that away at once!"

I then turned my attention to Thomas, who was still pounding on the stranger. I was forced to grab both of the boy's arms to keep him from beating the man to a pulp. Then, while Lucy dragged her brother away, I crouched down and grasped the intruder by the shoulders.

"Who are you, and what were you doing in the Willoughby home?" I demanded.

The man, still facedown in the grass, gave a

muffled reply. "I could ask the same of you."

He rolled over, the hood slipping from his head.

And looking up at me, just as I feared, was the battered face of Jasper Willoughby.

■ ■ ■ ■

Book Six:
In Which the
Plot Thickens

■ ■ ■ ■

I

Not wanting to create any more of a scene, I sent Lucy and Thomas home in their coach. I then hailed a hansom cab for Jasper and me, intent on escorting him back to West Philadelphia. Sitting side by side in the open carriage, it occurred to me that it was the first time we had ever been alone together. Knowing this fact made what I was about to say all the more awkward.

"I want to apologize for what happened back there," I began. "You must forgive young Mr. Collins. He only attacked you because we thought you were an intruder."

Jasper reclined in the seat, arms crossed. A small bruise marred the side of his face, made all the more noticeable by the paleness of his skin.

"Clearly, I was not," he said.

"But you must admit, you have some explaining to do."

"Me?" Jasper replied. "What about you? You're the one who broke into a house that

isn't yours."

"Violet showed me where the key was hidden. Besides, the house will one day be mine."

Jasper let out a bitter laugh. "Not if my father has any say in the matter."

I tried my best to ignore the jab, but it stung nonetheless.

"I had good reason for being there. What was yours?"

"I go there when I need to think," Jasper said. "Not that I need a reason to enter my own family's property."

"Did you say think or *drink*?" I asked. "Because I suspect it's the latter."

I had been tipped off by the sound of clanking glass when Jasper fled the bedroom. I had a feeling that, had I gone in there, I would have discovered several half-empty bottles. Yet the telltale indicator was Jasper's breath, for every word he spoke produced a puff of whiskey-scented air.

"That's no concern of yours," he said.

"No, but it is your parents' concern."

"I suppose you plan on telling them now. Maybe in an attempt to get into my father's good graces. Do so, if that's what you'd like. I don't care. I truly don't."

"I'm worried about you," I said. "So is Violet."

"Worried? About *me*? Pray tell, why?"

"For one thing" — I paused to check my pocket watch — "eleven o'clock in the morning is a little early to be hitting the rotgut, don't you think? But most of all, you're now as much of a suspect in the death of Lenora Grimes Pastor as I am. Probably even more so."

I spent the next five minutes laying out all the reasons. The first, of course, was the massive colony of bees located in the nursery, which was able to produce more than enough venom needed to kill someone.

The second reason was the footprints I had noticed in Jasper's childhood bedroom a few days earlier. It was clear they had been made by Jasper himself. They looked fresh, which meant he had been in that house, with those bees, in the days before Mrs. Pastor's death.

Then there was the fact that Lucy and I had encountered Jasper outside the Pastor residence just before the séance in which she had died. At the time, I didn't think it was anything more than coincidence, but now I wasn't so certain. While Jasper hadn't been in the locked room with us when Mrs. Pastor died, he certainly could have provided the venom that killed her. Perhaps he had met one of the attendees before the séance began, giving the murderer the fatal dose.

Finally, there was the matter of Sophie Kruger. When I lunched with the entire Willoughby family on Friday afternoon, Violet had mentioned Jasper's late return home the night before. The very same night the Kruger girl was killed.

Jasper, of course, greeted my theory with nothing but disbelief.

"You should quit being a reporter and take up novel writing," he said. "For that is the grandest piece of fiction I think I've ever heard."

"I'm not saying that's what actually happened," I said. "It's not even what I *think* happened."

Truth be told, I had no idea if Jasper had something to do with the murders. But if I could come up with such a scenario, then so could Barclay and his fellow policemen.

"You must admit," I added, "it's plausible. Every bit of it."

"But it isn't," Jasper replied. "Other than you and Mrs. Collins, I've never met any of the people who were at that séance. So it would have been impossible for me to provide them with the bee venom. Also, I know nothing about bees or how to extract their venom. And what reason would I have to kill a medium?"

"I don't know, Jasper. What reason did you have for being outside Mrs. Pastor's door last Saturday night?"

If I were a betting man, I'd wager Jasper, at that moment, wished he had possessed facial hair as robust as his father's. A grand beard or an elaborate mustache would have better masked his emotions. Without them, his pale face gave away everything he was thinking and feeling — a palpable combination of sadness and fear.

"Fine, Edward. Since you want the truth, I'll give it to you," he said. "I was going to attend the séance that night. I won't lie to you about that. I went to that house with every intention of sitting with Mrs. Pastor. But when I saw you and Mrs. Collins about to do the very same thing, I realized I couldn't. Not with you present."

Jasper's revelation wasn't as shocking as he made it out to be. We had, after all, discussed the city's mediums at length during lunch the day before. But I also recalled Jasper agreeing with his father that they were all crooks, making it odd that he later intended to visit one.

"Was that your first visit to Mrs. Pastor?"

Jasper merely shook his head.

"So you had sat with her before?"

This time, he nodded.

"How many times before?"

"Once."

"And when was this?"

"A week or so ago," Jasper said.

"What reason did you have for seeing Mrs. Pastor?"

"Does one need a reason to visit a medium?"

"Most times they do," I said. "They want to contact a lost loved one. Is that why you went? To contact someone who died?"

Jasper uncrossed his slender arms and crossed them again the other way. "I . . . can't tell you."

"Can't?" I said. "Or won't?"

"Let's just please change the subject."

I had no intention of doing that. Not if there was still information to pry out of the reluctant Jasper Willoughby. I continued to press him, saying, "I don't understand why you can't just provide a simple reason for why you intended to go to the séance."

"Because no good will come of it," Jasper said. "None at all."

"But you can trust me."

"Oh, can I?" Jasper asked. "Can I really trust you, Edward? Even more, can *Violet*? Every night, I'm forced to witness the same dinnertime arguments. My parents tell Violet that, while they don't think you murdered Mrs. Pastor, the fact that you're one of those suspected of it doesn't bode well for your character. They don't like how you run around to murder scenes and write up the grisly details for all to read. They distrust you, unlike Violet. She spends all her time trying to convince them you're a kind and honorable man. I say nothing, but my heart breaks for her, knowing you've been roaming the city with Mrs. Collins. Who knows what else the two of you have been up to. So tell me, Edward — what reason do I have to trust you?"

His words were so pointed and cruel that each one felt like a physical blow. By the time he was through, my entire body ached. This was what my future brother-in-law truly thought of me, and it felt horrible to hear. Even worse was the ring of truth contained in what he said. My actions between Friday night and that moment did look incredibly suspicious. It was easy to understand how an outsider might misinterpret everything I had been doing.

"Mrs. Collins and I are simply trying to clear our names by discovering who really killed Mrs. Pastor," I said, my voice shaky.

"That's very odd," Jasper replied. "Because I saw the two of you together *before* Mrs. Pastor was killed."

We had reached the wire bridge on Spring Garden Street, rolling over it at a leisurely pace. Still, my heartbeat quickened as I recalled the pure fear I had felt there the night before. When we came to the location where Lucy had fallen, I couldn't help but look down at the Schuylkill below. In the late-morning sunlight, the river's surface seemed far away — alarmingly so. It was shocking to me that Lucy and I had both survived our drops into the water.

"I understand how it appears," I said. "But we are simply allies joined in a common goal.

You must believe me."

The words sounded false even to my ears. That was because I could clearly see the spot on the riverbank where I had pulled Lucy ashore. The very same spot where both of us had almost let our emotions get the better of us. With that on my mind, it's no surprise I didn't sound convincing.

Jasper shifted in the seat, the movement causing his hair to fall over his eyes. Peering at me from between the golden strands, he said, "I honestly don't know what to believe. Are you truly in love with Violet?"

"Of course!"

This time, the conviction in my voice was unmistakable. For I did love Violet with all my heart. The fact that I had come close to kissing Lucy Collins didn't change that. The only difference now was the guilt I felt because of it.

"I adore your sister," I told him, "despite what your parents say and what you assume. And I still intend to marry her."

"That will make us brothers-in-law," Jasper said. "If that means anything to you, then I beg of you, please give me the benefit of the doubt. I understand that I appear suspicious. But, in my case, the facts are different from appearances."

"As it is with me."

"Then let's make a promise, as future brothers, not to tell anyone — not my sister, or my parents, or the police — what we know about each other. If not for our sakes, then for Violet's sake."

I reluctantly agreed to this truce. The two of us then shook hands, bound by mutual distrust. While I didn't necessarily think Jasper had a role in Mrs. Pastor's death, I also didn't want to remain silent about the possibility. Yet I felt as if I had no choice in the matter. Not if I wished to stay in Violet's good graces. This entire attempt to clear my name, after all, was more for her benefit than mine. I couldn't risk letting her drunken brother ruin it all. Nor could I risk bringing further shame upon the Willoughby name, which would certainly happen if outside suspicion fell on Jasper. So I decided to not tell a soul about his potential link to Mrs. Pastor's death. At least not until I had further proof that he was somehow involved. For better or worse, I *needed* to give him the benefit of the doubt.

When we reached the Willoughby residence, Jasper climbed out of the carriage without saying another word. I was preparing to give the driver directions to my own home when Violet stepped outside. Seeing me, she ran to the open carriage.

"Edward!" she said, reaching inside to clasp my hands. "What a pleasant surprise!"

I made myself appear glad to see her, when in truth it was the opposite. After what had almost happened the night before, I felt unworthy to be in her presence. Adding to my shame was her obvious joy upon seeing me.

"Hello, Violet." I kissed her on the cheek, hoping she wouldn't notice how dry and tentative it was. "I was running some errands in the city when I saw Jasper here taking a stroll. I thought I'd take him home and save him a walk."

"How very nice of you," Violet said. "Were the two of you able to get better acquainted?"

"Yes," Jasper replied as he made his way to the porch. "Very."

The direction in which he moved allowed Violet to see the bruise on his face, prompting her to gasp, "Gracious! Jasper, what happened to you?"

Jasper's hand flew to his cheek. The bruise hadn't faded much at all, remaining a pink blotch on his otherwise pale face.

"I fell," he said. "Tripped over my own two feet right in the middle of the sidewalk."

"You need to be more careful," Violet replied before turning to me. "And you, Edward, must join us for lunch."

I looked to the cab's driver, who was doing a bad job of pretending not to hear our conversation. It made me wonder what else he had heard on the journey there. Probably every word. He gave me an impatient stare, waiting to know if he needed to find another fare.

"I'm afraid I can't," I told Violet. "I have a very busy afternoon ahead."

"Oh, I wish you'd stay," she said. "It would be so much fun. Like an impromptu party, what with Bertie here and all."

"Bertie? He's *here*?"

"Yes. He stopped by for lunch, too."

Looking toward the house, my heart dropped into my stomach as Bertie Johnson stepped onto the porch. Now instead of just guilt, I also felt panic, which manifested itself in a series of heart palpitations.

"Bertram," I said, my tongue sticking to the roof of my suddenly dry mouth. "How have you been?"

"Fine, fine," Bertie replied. "And what have you been up to lately?"

"Just trying to keep busy."

Violet tugged on my arm. "You two can catch up inside. Please, let's all go in and eat."

"I really can't." I took Violet's hand one last time, hoping she couldn't notice how much my hands were trembling. "I'm sorry, my darling. I must be off."

Before she could argue, I tapped the driver's shoulder and the carriage jerked to a start. I turned around and waved good-bye, watching the figures of Jasper, Violet, and Bertie Johnson recede in the distance.

Leaving them did nothing to quell my panicked thoughts. I didn't know for certain why Bertie had called on Violet. I didn't even know if he had clearly seen me the night before, outside Mr. Barnum's party. But just like my run-in with Jasper, Bertie's presence at the Willoughby home was an ominous turn of events. No matter how much I tried to remain discreet, my secret activities were catching up with me.

Yet when the cab reached Locust Street, all thoughts of Bertie Johnson and Jasper Willoughby vanished. That's because Barclay's police coach was parked in front of my house. My nervousness was immediately replaced by hopeful anticipation that he had come upon some useful information. My hopes got even higher when I saw Barclay leave my house and head down the front steps. I paid the driver and jumped out of the cab, intercepting Barclay before he got into his coach.

"You're here with good news, I hope."

"News, yes," Barclay said. "But I can't say it's good, Edward."

"What have you learned?"

Barclay opened the door to his coach and gestured for me to climb inside.

"The toxicologist finished his tests on the Kruger girl's corpse. You were right, Edward. She was indeed poisoned. With bee venom."

II

The Fishtown section of Philadelphia was as gritty and hard-scrabble as its name implied. Stone buildings and wooden shacks lined its narrow streets, pressed as tightly together as sardines in a tin. Wash lines, stretching from window to window, crisscrossed overhead, each one drooping with shirts, frayed trousers, and plain dresses. Stoop-shouldered residents lumbered to and from the docks, the women wearing kerchiefs, the men in fishermen's caps. And rising from everywhere — the river, the streets, the houses themselves — was the pungent smell of fish. The air was thick with it, an all-encompassing stench that filled my nostrils and coated the back of my throat.

The odor was especially strong outside the Kruger residence, thanks in no small part to the hovel next door that sold fried shad. Inside the home was no different, although the smell there was tempered by the scents of other foods — boiling cabbage, frying potatoes, Wienerschnitzel.

Margarethe Kruger stood at the stove, dealing with the intrusion of Barclay and me by not dealing with us at all. Her remaining daughter, Louisa, sat with us at a small wooden table, trying her best to get her mother to talk. Following a brief and tense exchange in German, Louisa turned to us and said, "My mother doesn't want to discuss Sophie with you. She's dead. That's all that matters to her."

"But your sister was very likely murdered," Barclay said. "Doesn't she want justice?"

Louisa and her mother exchanged more tense words in German. When they were finished, Louisa told us, "She only wants peace."

I looked to the stove, where Mrs. Kruger, stone-faced, tended to her cooking. Our presence made her uncomfortable, that much was clear, and I longed to retreat with Louisa to another room where we wouldn't be a bother. Only there was no other place to retreat to. Upstairs was their sleeping quarters, off-limits to two grown men who weren't members of the family. The ground level was just a single, cramped space — part kitchen, part keeping room. Other than the table and stove, the furniture was sparse. I spotted a few more wooden chairs in the corner, a side table with uneven legs, and a tall cabinet. With such a lack of storage, much of the family's belongings dangled from the rafters. Shoes and satchels hung next to clusters of herbs, frying pans beside cured meats. Above the door was a rusted horseshoe, which had done little to bring this family luck.

"What about you?" I asked Louisa. "Don't you want to see your sister's killer brought to justice?"

"I do," the girl said. "But not at the risk of displeasing my mother. I must respect her wishes."

From the stove, Margarethe Kruger said something to her daughter.

"What did she say?" Barclay asked.

"She asked me when the two policemen planned to leave," Louisa said.

"I'm not a policeman," I replied. "And we're not leaving until one of you answers our questions."

"I have a question of my own." Louisa stared at us from across the table, her face calm but her eyes fiery and inquisitive. "Why do you say Sophie was murdered? It was our understanding that she drowned."

Barclay fielded that question, explaining how we had found the needle mark on Sophie's arm. Mention of a needle prompted Louisa to push up the sleeve of her dress until it was bunched past her elbow. In the crook of her arm was a mark similar to the one found on her sister.

"See? I have one as well. Last week, both of us were —" She struggled to find the right word in English, using her thumb and two fingers to mime receiving an injection in her arm.

"Inoculated?" I offered.

Louisa nodded. "Yes. That. Against smallpox."

Her mother, hearing an English word she

441

recognized, waved a spoon at us and said, "Smallpox. *Es wurde viel krankheit hier.*"

"She said that there has been a lot of illness in the neighborhood," Louisa told us. "She didn't want either of us to get sick as well."

"That might account for the injection mark on your sister's arm," Barclay said. "But it doesn't explain the poison found in her system."

Louisa looked more confused than ever. "What poison?"

"Someone had dosed her with bee venom," Barclay said. "Much more than what could be achieved by a single sting."

I could tell young Louisa believed us, for tears began to leak from her eyes. My heart ached for her. It was bad enough that a girl her age should be forced to speak about her sister's death. The fact that murder was involved made it all the more heartbreaking.

"I'm sorry for your loss," I said.

"Danke."

Louisa used a sleeve to wipe away the tears, leaving a streak of moisture on her cheek. Then she went to the stove and broke the terrible news to her mother. Margarethe Kruger's reaction consisted of a few nods and little else.

"My mother thanks you for bringing us that news," Louisa said.

"We would like to ask our questions," Barclay replied. "If we may."

Mrs. Kruger approached the table and placed plates of food in front of us. It was the Wienerschnitzel, potatoes, and cabbage, piping hot and smelling delectable.

"Bitte iss," she instructed.

Then she took a seat, staring at Barclay and me through sad, tired eyes. *"Warum sind sie nicht essen?"* she asked her daughter.

"My mother asks why you aren't eating," Louisa informed us.

I wasn't hungry. Neither was Barclay, from the looks of it. But we both dug into our plates, knowing that appealing to a cook's pride was the likeliest way to get Mrs. Kruger to talk.

"It's delicious," I said.

"Outstanding," Barclay added.

Louisa smiled at her mother. *"Kostlich."*

"Sie kann mehr fragen stellen."

"What did she say?" I asked.

"That you may ask more questions," Louisa said.

Barclay did just that, posing several to Mrs. Kruger, with Louisa serving as the interpreter between them.

"Did Sophie attend school?"

"No."

"What did she do?"

"She was a washerwoman, like my mother," Louisa said. "Sometimes she'd earn extra money at the docks mending torn fishing nets."

"Did she meet any unsavory characters at the docks? Anyone who might wish to harm her?"

"No."

"Did your sister have any close friends?"

"She was friends with a girl in the neighborhood," Louisa said. "I do not know her name."

"That's all?" Barclay asked. "No gentlemen friends? No sweethearts?"

Louisa shrugged, unable to help us. "If there were, I did not know them."

In an effort to appease Margarethe Kruger, I had continued taking intermittent bites of food as they conversed. But Barclay's last question reminded me of something Louisa had said the morning her sister's body was found.

"You said Sophie often slipped away at odd hours of the night," I said. "For what reason?"

"I already told you, sir, I do not know."

"Did this happen frequently?" Barclay inquired.

"I believe so," Louisa said. "It wasn't unusual for people to come to the door asking for Sophie."

"And your mother let her go with them?"

"Yes, sir."

Barclay pushed his plate away and leaned forward, elbows on the table. "Were these callers mostly men?"

While an awful question, it needed to be

asked. I had seen prostitutes younger than Sophie roaming the city's streets. If she had been among their ranks, we had to know about it.

Louisa, sensing the unspoken accusation in Barclay's question, began to cry again. "I do not know."

"Does your mother know?" Barclay asked.

Louisa asked her mother something in German. Mrs. Kruger shook her head and said, *"Nein."*

"I apologize for what I'm about to say next," Barclay said. "But it sounds to me that your sister was also earning money as a prostitute. It also appears that your mother knew about it. Did she?"

Louisa, though visibly scandalized, handled the words well. "Please, sir. I cannot ask my mother such a question."

"Louisa, your sister might have been murdered because of her actions," Barclay said. "We won't leave until we get an answer."

Louisa faced her mother. She took Mrs. Kruger's hands in hers and asked, *"Mutter, war Sophie eine prostituierte?"*

Margarethe Kruger released a hand and held it to her open mouth. *"Gott in Himmel! Nein!"*

"See," Louisa told us. "She wasn't."

"Then why did she leave at all hours of the night?" Barclay angrily asked. "What else could she possibly have been doing?"

Louisa posed the question to her mother, who lowered her head in shame.

"Sie konnte mit den toten sprechen," Margarethe Kruger said.

A gasp caught midway in Louisa's throat — a hiccup of shock. "Is this true?"

Mrs. Kruger gave a solemn nod. *"Jah."*

"What is she saying?" I asked. "What is it that your sister did?"

"My mother," Louisa replied, "said that Sophie could speak to the dead."

III

Barclay and I heard the full story, first in German from Mrs. Kruger, then translated by Louisa.

Apparently, Sophie began communicating with the dead at a very early age. Mrs. Kruger said she first noticed it not long after her husband died, when Sophie was six. The girl had invented an imaginary friend, whom she chattered with constantly for days. When Margarethe Kruger finally inquired about the name of this invisible friend, Sophie replied, *"Ich bin mit Vater reden."*

I'm talking to Father.

At first, the recent widow assumed it was nonsense, simply her daughter's way of coping with her grief. Sophie missed her father, after all, so it was natural she would pretend

446

he was still with them. But when the girl started telling her things only Mr. Kruger could have known, Margarethe began to suspect something unusual was taking place. She posed a series of questions to Sophie, ones in which the answer could only be provided by her late husband. Sophie gave a correct response to all of them.

That was when Margarethe Kruger realized the truth — her daughter really was conversing with her deceased husband.

Over the years, Sophie continued to communicate with the dead. Not just her late father anymore, but others who had shuffled off this mortal coil. Some were familiar to Mrs. Kruger — distant relatives or long-lost friends — but many were strangers. When a few neighbors got word of Sophie's gift, they asked the girl to contact their own loved ones from the Great Beyond. Soon the news of Sophie's abilities spread beyond the neighborhood, and strangers sometimes arrived at their doorstep at all hours, begging the girl to reach loved ones.

At first, Mrs. Kruger refused to allow her daughter to perform such acts, reconsidering only after the strangers began to offer money. Still, she drew the line at letting Sophie talk to the dead in their own home, fearing it would bring nothing but bad luck. So the girl was whisked to the customers' homes or a nearby inn to play medium between them and their loved ones.

"An der Nacht Sophie hat verschwunden, hatte jemand an die Tür kommen, und suchen ihre dienste," Mrs. Kruger said.

"On the night Sophie vanished," Louisa told us in translation, "someone had come to the door, seeking her services."

"Did your mother see who it was?" Barclay asked.

"Or where they were going?" I added.

"No," Louisa replied. "Sophie answered the door herself and woke my mother up long enough to tell her that she would be leaving for a while. She never came home."

After that, there was little left to be said. Barclay certainly tried to get more information, asking Louisa a few more questions about friends or enemies her sister might have had. The answers were all the same — Louisa Kruger didn't know of any.

Having exhausted all possibilities for questions, Barclay and I took our leave. I thanked Mrs. Kruger for the delicious meal, receiving a respectful nod of appreciation in return. Then it was out of the cramped house and back into the crowded streets of Fishtown.

"First Sophie Kruger and then Lenora Grimes Pastor," I said to Barclay as soon as we were outside. "Could someone be trying to kill the city's mediums?"

"It certainly seems that way," Barclay replied. "Which should cause you alarm, considering your ill-advised friendship with Mrs. Collins."

"I'm not worried. Lucy — I mean, Mrs. Collins — isn't a real medium."

"I hope you don't expect me to be surprised by that," Barclay said, quickening his pace as we headed toward the police coach. "I always assumed she could contact the dead about as well as you or I can."

"But some people can," I said. "Some, such as Mrs. Pastor and Miss Kruger, possess powers we can't begin to understand."

"So, you really believe in all that now?" Barclay asked. "Spiritualism and the super-natural?"

In all honesty, I didn't want to. I was far happier during my skeptical days. Yet all that I had seen and heard that week forced me to think differently. I had heard the dead speak to the living and seen tables fly into walls of their own accord. After that, how could I not be a believer? These things were real, I now knew, but I was damned if I understood what any of it meant.

"My eyes have been opened," I told Barclay. "It might seem like hokum to you —"

"It does —"

"— but I believe that something strange is occurring here. And now two mediums are dead because of it. The key to finding out who killed them, I think, is learning which member of Mrs. Pastor's final séance had also

449

been to see Sophie Kruger. Which means we must interview them again. All of them."

We had just reached the police coach when Barclay raised a hand to silence me. "That won't be necessary, Edward."

"Why not?"

"Because," he said, "I have a very good idea who is responsible for both of these murders. And now, I must see if I'm right."

This was unexpectedly exciting news. So exciting that my face began to grow warm in happy anticipation.

"Where are we going?" I asked.

"I'm afraid it's only me who can go."

Barclay climbed into the coach, closing the door before I had the chance to get in as well. Left out on the street, I could only shout my protestations.

"You're just going to leave me here?"

"I'm sorry, Edward!" Barclay yelled out the window as the coach pulled away. "This is a matter of some urgency! You can find your way home, can't you?"

I started walking faster, trying to keep pace with the quickening coach. "I suppose so, yes. But aren't you going to tell me who you suspect?"

"I can't at the moment!" The coach had sped up to the point where I could no longer keep pace with it. As it rumbled down the street, Barclay poked his head out the window to look back at me. "I'll call on you tonight to tell you everything!"

With Barclay gone, I was forced to leave Fishtown on foot, locating a hack only once I had reached Front Street. I told him to take me northwest, to the home of Mrs. Collins. Common sense dictated that I should just return home, wait for Barclay to visit, and hear who he thought had killed both Lenora Grimes Pastor and Sophie Kruger. Yet a stubborn part of me resisted common sense. I was still a suspect, and would remain so until the real killer was identified. Barclay's hunch aside, I could only rely on myself to do that.

With some help, of course.

Once I arrived at Lucy's house, I found her and Thomas again tinkering with the instruments and pulleys in the séance room. All four instruments — the bugle, drum, flute, and bell — hovered over the table.

"What do you think?" Lucy asked me. "Is this better?"

It was, truth be told, much better. She had taken my advice and used thinner string from which to hang the instruments. Now they floated in a manner that was suitably ghostly. In spite of my disapproval about what Lucy did for a living, I couldn't help but feel a twinge of pride.

"I'm impressed," I said, "but that isn't why I came."

"I assumed not." Lucy stood next to the table, the instruments floating in the air at the same height as her shoulder. "How was your talk with young Mr. Willoughby? Do you think he's our murderer?"

"I don't know what to think," I said. "The situation is now slightly more complicated."

I explained what had happened after she and Thomas departed the Willoughbys' old home, from Jasper's claims of innocence to the fact that Sophie Kruger had also been killed by bee venom.

"So we now have a double murder on our hands?" Lucy asked.

"We do indeed."

"This does complicate things." She used a finger to push one of the hanging instruments — the bugle — making it spin around and around on its string. "Or maybe it doesn't."

"I don't follow you."

"Let's look at the suspects," Lucy said. "Among them, which one do we know has gone to see other mediums?"

"Not Mr. Pastor, of course. He was married to one."

Lucy nodded. "I expect the same of Mr. Barnum. He was interested in exploiting Mrs. Pastor's gifts for profit."

"That just leaves the Duttons and Mrs. Mueller," I said. "And the man without a nose, of course."

I was certain he was directly involved, although I didn't know how. While he wasn't at the séance when Mrs. Pastor died, he

452

certainly could have been the person to call upon Sophie Kruger in the middle of the night.

Then, of course, was the fact that he had tried to kill us the night before.

"You still believe he's working with one of them?" Lucy asked.

"I can't shake that notion. Robert Pastor assumed he had threatened his wife on behalf of P. T. Barnum. Since we now know that wasn't the case, it's safe to assume he was employed by someone else."

"And that someone would be either Eldridge Dutton, Leslie Dutton, or Elizabeth Mueller." Lucy reached out and grabbed the bugle, halting its rotation. "Which of them should we suspect the most?"

The answer was simple — the one who had admitted to seeing every medium in the city.

IV

It was clear that Mrs. Elizabeth Mueller was deeply unhappy to see us. Standing beneath the oil painting of her late husband, she sniffed and said, "The two of you shouldn't be here."

"We're sorry about the intrusion," I said, removing my hat. "Again."

Mrs. Mueller wore the same black dress I had seen her in twice before. This time, it was augmented with a lace shawl, which she tightened against her shoulders as she said, "The police inspector was quite upset when he learned the two of you were here."

"Then perhaps you shouldn't have told him about our visit," Lucy replied.

"I only confirmed it." Mrs. Mueller retreated to the sofa, looking just as tired and weak as during our previous visit. "He had already figured it out for himself."

"What did you tell Inspector Barclay when he came around?" I asked. "I assume he questioned you about Mrs. Pastor's death."

"He did," Mrs. Mueller said. "And I relayed to him exactly what I had told the two of you."

"You told him everything?" I asked. "Including how you have seen every medium in Philadelphia?"

"That might have slipped my mind," Mrs. Mueller admitted.

"Interesting," Lucy said. "Is that because you didn't want him to know about some of the mediums you have called upon?"

"Of course not."

Without being invited to, Lucy took a seat opposite Mrs. Mueller. I remained standing, positioned behind Lucy's chair. Directly across from us, the dour portrait of dearly departed Gerald Mueller stared at us with oil-painted eyes.

"Was one of those mediums a young girl by the name of Sophie Kruger?" I asked.

"I can't remember the names of all of them."

"But you recalled visiting me," Lucy said.

"I remembered because I was most unimpressed by your performance."

"Then you should have no trouble remembering the mediums who *were* impressive," I said. "That is, ones who were legitimate, which Mrs. Collins here is not."

Lucy opened her mouth to protest, but thought better of it. Even she realized this was not the time to defend her dubious line of work. Instead, she looked at Mrs. Mueller and said, "By all accounts, this Sophie Kruger was the real thing. A medium so skilled that she could rival Lenora Grimes Pastor."

Mrs. Mueller adjusted her shawl for a moment, undoubtedly stalling. Eventually, she said, "Was she the German girl near the river?"

"Indeed she was," I said.

"Then yes. I paid her a visit on one occasion."

The maid entered the parlor, bearing a tray of tea and more of those ghoulish funeral biscuits. Placing the tray on the table next to Mrs. Mueller, she offered us tea. Remembering how terrible it was during our previous visit, we declined.

"Only one visit?" I asked Mrs. Mueller once the maid had gone. "She wasn't able to help you?"

Elizabeth Mueller shook her head. "She was able to contact an old school friend. But not the person I was hoping to reach."

I looked past her to the portrait of Gerald Mueller. It was a bit disturbing, the way he seemed to be watching the room. The artist had captured a stare that wasn't so much soothing as it was probing. The dead man's face seemed constantly on guard.

"Why do you want to speak to your husband so badly?" I asked.

"You're not married, are you, Mr. Clark?"

"Not yet. But soon."

"When you do marry, you will understand the comfort a spouse's voice can bring." Mrs. Mueller turned to Lucy. "Don't you agree, Mrs. Collins?"

Lucy's eyes darted briefly to Mr. Mueller's portrait. No doubt she was thinking about the painting of Mr. Collins, which hung in her parlor with a spy hole in his heart.

"Not particularly," she said.

"Do you miss your husband?" I asked Mrs. Mueller. "Or do you miss his money more?"

A pale, veined hand flew to her chest. "How dare you imply such a thing!"

"You are penniless, though, aren't you?"

It was clear to me that she was. All signs — from the closed-up house to the single servant to the tea weakened to the point of nothingness — pointed to the fact that Mrs. Mueller was in dire financial straits.

"Yes," Mrs. Mueller answered after a moment's hesitation. "Unfortunately, I am."

"But you told us your husband had amassed a fortune," Lucy said.

"He did. Only now it's nowhere to be found."

The truth, as is often the case, seemed to set Elizabeth Mueller free. Standing, she suddenly threw the shawl from her shoulders and approached her husband's portrait.

"Gerald was a horrible man, to be quite honest," she said. "As cold and cruel as the longest winters. Suspicious, too. He thought everyone was only after his wealth, including his own wife. Me, of all people! He kept shifting it from bank to bank, hiding it in places only he knew. When he died, there was no last will and testament drawn up. No indication, even, of where he had placed all of his money. It's out there somewhere. I just need to find it."

"Have you looked for it?" I asked.

"Of course," Mrs. Mueller spat out. "First, I inquired at every bank in the city. When that turned up nothing, I widened my search to other cities — New York, Boston, Baltimore. I hired attorneys and private investigators, at great cost, to assist in the search. When that yielded nothing, I —"

"Turned to mediums," I said.

Mrs. Mueller offered me a firm nod. "It's silly, I know. But I thought that if I could

457

contact Gerald from beyond the grave, he would tell me where the money was. I even went so far as to spend my life in mourning, just in case he . . . he could see me somehow and know I was sincere."

"The money might still turn up one day," Lucy said.

"Perhaps," Mrs. Mueller replied. "But I fear it's too late for that. My suspicion is that it's already gone."

"Gone?" I said. "That's not possible if no one knows where it is."

"I suspect that someone does know. Two people, actually. I also suspect they heard the location from Gerald himself."

"And who might that be?" I asked.

"Come now, Mr. Clark," Mrs. Mueller said with a wry smile. "Who do we all know that had access to the dead?"

The realization struck me harder than one of Thomas Collins's kicks to the shins.

"Lenora Grimes Pastor."

"And don't forget," Mrs. Mueller said, "about Eldridge Dutton. Several months ago, I confided in him about my true reason for attending the séances. He was sympathetic to my situation and offered a confidence of his own."

"That he had started to visit Mrs. Pastor in private on Saturday mornings," I said.

Mrs. Mueller nodded eagerly. "Those sessions, he claimed, dealt with matters in his own life. Matters that he said his wife would find distressing."

"Did he say what they were?" Lucy asked.

"No, but he offered to spend some of that time contacting Gerald on my behalf. At first, it seemed like a generous offer. But then several weeks passed without him addressing the matter. Finally, I approached him after a séance and inquired as to whether he had heard from Gerald. He told me he hadn't.

"But," she continued, "I noticed something out of the ordinary. He was carrying a new gold watch. Quite expensive from the looks of it. And as he talked, he seemed to be caressing it."

That's exactly what Mr. Dutton had been doing the afternoon Lucy and I were in his home. I, too, had assumed the watch to be expensive. Even Bettina, his daughter, had thought to mention it.

"And how do you think Mr. Dutton came to own this watch?" I asked.

"I assume he bought it," Mrs. Mueller said. "Using money he located with the help of my late husband."

I had to sit down after hearing that one. It's not easy to remain standing when faced with the prospect of a dead man helping a living one to steal from him. What Mrs. Mueller implied was strange, to be sure, but the more I thought about it, the more it seemed possible. While Mrs. Pastor hadn't been able to contact the spirit of Gerald Mueller during her nightly séances, that didn't mean she couldn't reach him at other times. Once you got past the improbable notion of speaking to the dead in the first place, it was easy to imagine that ability being used for bad as well as good.

"Did you confront anyone about your suspicions?" I asked Mrs. Mueller. "Mr. Dutton himself? Or perhaps Mrs. Pastor?"

"I intended to tell Lenora," she said. "I went to her house last week."

That was the visit Stokely and Claudia had mentioned, the one in which Elizabeth Mueller accused Mrs. Pastor of stealing.

"I was terribly angry," Mrs. Mueller said. "Crazed, actually. And the more I spoke, the more ridiculous I sounded. Other than seeing Mr. Dutton's watch, I had no proof. And even while I was hinting that Lenora was stealing from me, I realized it was quite possible she had no idea it was taking place."

I hadn't considered that possibility. With Mrs. Pastor in a trance, it was unlikely she could have known what was happening. I pictured Eldridge Dutton and Lenora Grimes Pastor seated alone in her séance room. While Mrs. Pastor was in her trance, the voice of Gerald Mueller emanating from her lips, Mr. Dutton scribbled down everything he was told. It could all have been his doing, which went a long way in explaining why not even his wife knew of his Saturday morning visits to the Pastor residence.

I stood again, grabbing Lucy's arm until she was on her feet.

"Thank you for your honesty," I told Mrs. Mueller. "We both sincerely appreciate it."

"You're welcome," she said. "Although I doubt it will help anything."

Ah, but the opposite was true. Thanks to her, Mr. Dutton was, in my mind, now our prime suspect.

V

Back in Lucy's coach, I instructed Thomas to drive as fast as he could to the Dutton residence. He obeyed me without argument, whipping the Cleveland Bays to a speed reminiscent of our harrowing chase the night before.

"Would you mind telling me why you now think Mr. Dutton murdered Lenora Grimes Pastor?" Lucy said as the coach rattled through the streets. "It doesn't make sense."

"But it does," I replied. "Perhaps Mrs. Pastor had somehow come to suspect what Mr. Dutton was doing. Maybe she confronted him about it and he killed her in order to keep his secret. The same scenario is also a possibility with Sophie Kruger, who, too, might have unwittingly helped Mr. Dutton contact Gerald Mueller."

"That's all well and good," Lucy said, "but what do you intend to do when we get to his house? Barge in and accuse him of killing two mediums?"

"Something like that, yes."

"Then what will stop him from killing the both of us?"

I straightened my spine, trying to make myself look more imposing. "I'm an able-bodied man and a war veteran. I can defend myself."

"Men," Lucy said, rolling her eyes. "You all forget that when times are desperate, it's the women who make the best fighters."

"Of course," I replied. "You have your gun. If the need arises, I suppose you can just shoot Mr. Dutton."

"I'll shoot *you* if you don't stop hounding me about it."

As it turned out, everything said in the coach turned out to be a moot point. For when we arrived at the Dutton residence, we were informed that the master of the house wasn't home. The person who disclosed this was none other than Bettina Dutton, she of the lip paint and brazen manner. Both were on display as she leaned against the door frame to say, "Father's at the office."

"Where is that?"

"Walnut Street."

"What about your stepmother? Is she home?"

"She's resting," Bettina said. "Not to be disturbed. Is there something *I* can help you with, Mr. Clark?"

"I'm sure you'd like to help Mr. Clark with a great many things," Lucy remarked. "But we were hoping to speak to one of your parents."

"Or both of them together," I added.

"They're rarely together," Bettina said. "At least, not recently."

The last time we spoke, Miss Dutton mentioned hearing her parents arguing over the pocket watch. I wasn't above accepting secondhand information, even if it forced me to do one of the things I loathed the most — gossip.

"Still fighting about that watch, are they?"

"I can't reveal family secrets," Bettina replied as she put a hand to her hair and twirled a lock around her index finger. "At least not without something in return."

By that point, my patience with her was worn so thin it barely existed. Still, we needed information, and it was apparent that playing parlor games with a schoolgirl was the only way we were going to get it.

"Violet Willoughby," I said.

Bettina's brow crinkled. "Pardon?"

"That's the real name of my fiancée. Violet Willoughby. Not Jenny Boyd."

"Violet?" Bettina said. "I know of her. She's a charming girl. You're very lucky, Mr. Clark."

463

She smiled again — a ruby-lipped grin of deviousness that made me regret what I had just told her. It was hard to gauge if Bettina really did know Violet or if she was merely bluffing to agitate me. Either way, I hoped my revelation wouldn't cause trouble in the future.

"I offered you a secret," I said. "Now it's time you do the same. Why were your parents arguing over your father's watch?"

"I don't know for certain. I didn't hear everything that was said. I was next door in my sitting room, you see, writing a letter to one of my many suitors." Bettina paused, hoping for a reaction from me. I didn't give one. "I heard them arguing. Quite loudly, which was odd. This house is usually so quiet you can hear a mouse drop a pin."

"And you heard Mrs. Dutton mention the watch?"

"I did," Bettina said. "She repeatedly asked my father who it was from. Then there was too much door slamming and stomping around for me to hear much else. But I did catch one word Mother said."

"Which was?"

My heart sank a bit when Bettina smiled yet again. It was time for another round of games.

"Oh, I *could* tell you," she said, "but there's no fun in that, is there?"

Having neither the time nor the inclination

to participate in whatever she was planning, I asked, "What do you want this time?"

"A kiss," Bettina replied. "I'm sure your dear Violet won't mind."

Suddenly, I felt myself being shoved aside by Lucy. Stumbling across the porch, I watched her push Bettina Dutton against the door frame. The girl tried to squirm out of Lucy's grip, to no avail. She was pinned there just like one of Professor Abernathy's glass-encased bugs.

"Listen to me and listen well," Lucy said, her voice a growl of exasperation. "This performance might work when punishing your stepmother or getting your father's attention, but it doesn't work on *me*. I've seen girls like you. I know what will happen. You'll fall out of favor with your family. You'll have no friends to help you in times of need. You'll take up with a man who neither deserves you nor treats you well. When he leaves, you'll be forced to find another. You'll be penniless, desperate, alone. I know your future because it was *my* past. And the only way you can change it is to wipe that whore's paint off your face, respect your elders, and show some common courtesy."

She released her grip and walked away. Not just from the door, mind you, but off the porch entirely and into her coach. Bettina remained against the door frame, as if Lucy still had hold of her. There were tears in her eyes and, for the first time since meeting her, I felt a pang of sympathy for the girl.

"I'm very sorry," I said. "That was unnecessarily harsh."

"But not unwarranted," Bettina replied with a shake of her head.

"Why do you despise your stepmother so much? She seems like a perfectly kind woman."

"That's what she wants you to think," Bettina said. "But she can scheme with the best of them. I'm certain she tricked Father into marrying her."

"Which is why you're angry with both of them."

Bettina let out a laugh startling in its bitterness. "Of course I'm angry. Mother was barely dead before they started carrying on. It's as if she never existed."

"I imagine losing your mother was very hard on you."

"I miss her," Bettina said. "Sometimes so much that I can scarcely breathe. I suppose that sounds odd."

But it didn't at all. In the years after my mother's death, I was surprised by all the unexpected things that reminded me of her. The scent of lilacs, for example, or the soft coo of mourning doves. The memories would overwhelm me, making me feel cold and empty.

"I can't promise you it will go away," I said.

466

"But, in time, you'll learn how to live with it. At least that was my experience when my own mother died."

If Bettina was surprised by my admission, she didn't show it. She simply offered a nod of understanding while drying her eyes with the sleeve of her dress. To make the task a little easier, I offered my handkerchief.

" 'Engraved,' " she said while dabbing her eyes. "That's the word my stepmother said during their fight."

"Engraved? That's unexpected."

"It surprised me, as well. I can only think she was still referring to Father's watch."

That was all the information I required. No matter what Eldridge Dutton had been up to — or was guilty of — I suspected the key to it all was that gold watch he cherished so much. It was necessary to see it for myself.

I thanked Bettina before rushing from the porch to Lucy's coach. Before climbing inside, I glanced back at the Dutton residence. Bettina was still in the doorway, using my handkerchief to wipe the paint from her lips.

VI

It was late afternoon by the time we reached Mr. Dutton's office, and Walnut Street was teeming with gentlemen leaving their vocations for the day. They crowded the sidewalk

467

in a well-mannered pack — a surging tide of top hats, morning coats, and walking canes. Tucked among them were a few well-dressed women, no doubt late with their shopping, along with the usual assortment of vendors, beggars, and street urchins.

Standing on the corner, Lucy and I watched one particular delinquent as he elbowed through the crowd. While outfitted in attire that was cleaner than an average miscreant's clothes, Thomas Collins had the attitude down pat. He strutted against the tide of businessmen, chin thrust forward, occasionally tipping his cap. Once he reached the door to Mr. Dutton's office, he stopped and waited.

"Are you sure he's capable of doing this?" I asked Lucy.

"Of course," she said. "He's quite gifted, actually."

"I just don't want anything to go wrong."

"It won't, Edward. Calm yourself."

That wasn't possible. I was about to witness my first pickpocketing. While I mostly frowned upon such a crime, in this instance I knew it was the only way to get our hands on Eldridge Dutton's watch. Our entire investigation depended on Thomas's skills.

"I don't mean practicing in your parlor," I said. "Has he done it for real?"

Lucy sighed. It sounded so similar to Barclay's that, for a moment, I thought he had somehow sneaked up behind us.

"You'll see soon enough."

Indeed I did, for that was the moment Eldridge Dutton left his office. Because of his size and facial hair, he was hard to miss, resembling a well-tailored grizzly bear as he stepped into the street. Thomas swooped in immediately, heading straight toward Mr. Dutton, his cap pulled low. He didn't stop walking until he smacked into our target's considerable midsection.

"Pardon me, mister," Thomas muttered. "Should watch where I'm going."

"You certainly should," Mr. Dutton sniffed before continuing down the street.

Thomas began to run in the opposite direction, directly toward Lucy and me. As he moved, I caught a glimpse of gold clutched in his hand. He had managed to snag the watch, proving Lucy right. He truly was gifted.

Unfortunately, he wasn't so good that Mr. Dutton didn't catch on to the theft. Stopping in the middle of the sidewalk, he felt around in his pockets, finding them empty of his precious timepiece. When he turned around and saw Thomas's retreat, he knew what had happened.

"You! Stop right there, boy!" he yelled. "Give me back my watch!"

Thomas continued running, stopping only until he reached the corner where Lucy and I waited. Rounding the edge of the building, he held up the watch so that we both could see.

"Here you go," he said, handing it to me. "One gold watch, as requested."

Knowing Eldridge Dutton was on the way, I gave the watch a quick examination. It was heavier than my own, and far more elaborate. Like mine, it had a hunter case, with a hinged lid that protected the watch face inside. An ornate pattern had been engraved on the lid — a circle of swoops and curlicues accented with small rubies. Opening it, I saw more rubies on the watch face itself, one marking each hour. What interested me more than that impressive display, however, were the words engraved on the inside of the lid.

To E, All my love — L

Clearly, the watch had been a gift from someone whose name began with an L, and it wasn't his wife, Leslie. That left only one other possibility, which leapt into my head the same moment Mr. Dutton rounded the corner. He stopped when he saw us and took an unsteady step backward, as if buffeted by a strong wind.

"We borrowed this," I said, offering him the watch. "It's so magnificent, I had to get a better look at it."

Dutton clutched the timepiece against his

chest. "By stealing it? How dare you!"

"Borrowing," I reminded him. "Someone has given you a very thoughtful gift. L, whoever she is, must think very highly of you."

"That would be my wife," Mr. Dutton said. "Leslie."

"Come now, sir," I replied. "We both know that's not the truth. Your daughter told us as much."

"You spoke to Bettina?"

"We have," Lucy said. "So who really gave you the watch?"

"That's none of your business," Mr. Dutton snapped.

"I think it was Lenora Grimes Pastor," I said. "Judging from the heartfelt inscription, I take it the two of you were engaged in, say, more than séances?"

The eyes of Eldridge Dutton widened ever so slightly as he said, "Are you implying, sir, that I had an improper relationship with Mrs. Pastor?"

It was exactly what I was implying, although I couldn't picture it myself. While both were roughly the same age, physically Eldridge Dutton and Lenora Grimes Pastor were complete opposites. And even though the old adage claims that opposites attract, I wondered what these two could have seen in each other.

"He's referring to your Saturday séances," Lucy said.

471

"I know what he's referring to," Mr. Dutton snapped. "And he couldn't be more wrong."

"So your watch wasn't a gift from Mrs. Pastor?" I asked.

"It was a gift, yes. But not from her."

"Then who was it from?"

"It was a gift from my late wife." Mr. Dutton shifted from one foot to the other, the watch still held to his heart. Color rushed into his cheeks — the unmistakable pink blush of shame. "Her name was Laura. She gave it to me three weeks ago."

VII

Eldridge Dutton elaborated a few minutes later when Lucy and I sat in his law office. Thomas was sent to wait with the coach and all of Mr. Dutton's partners and clerks had left for the day, leaving the building largely silent. The only sounds I heard were the gentle ticking of a grandfather clock in the corner and, of course, Mr. Dutton's voice.

His tale was a lengthy one, which trickled out in fits and starts. Sometimes he repeated himself or, suddenly recalling another detail, went backward in his story and started again. There were plenty of pauses — long, nervous ones that allowed many ticks of that corner clock to pass uninterrupted.

To spare you, dear reader, I have chosen to

simply narrate the story. It is an interesting one, to be sure, with many similarities to my own tale. But it is better doled out in one large piece instead of the halting manner in which I had received it. Still, I must begin with a direct quote from Mr. Dutton, which sets everything up nicely.

"We do a bit of investigative work at this firm," he said. "Tracking down heirs, for instance, or finding witnesses if one of our clientele has been accused of a crime. Because I have proven myself adept at such investigations in the past, a strange request came my way."

That request, made by one of the firm's new clients, was for Mr. Dutton to go on a series of visits to mediums throughout Philadelphia. Because he was seen as a sensible man, the client wanted him to find out if there were any legitimate mediums in the city, ones who didn't rely on illusions or trickery.

In short, the client requested of Mr. Dutton what my editor Hamilton Gray had requested of me. In his case, however, he was offered a tidy sum for his task, and his job was not to unmask false mediums but to discover real ones.

He agreed and enlisted the help of his second wife, who had a vague interest in Spiritualism. In the beginning, they were amused by the ways in which the city's charlatans tried to fool them. They were even more astonished by the many people they met who believed such trickery.

"They say a fool and his money are soon parted," Mr. Dutton said. "I saw plenty of fools parted from their money by common thieves."

Upon hearing this, I made sure to keep an eye on Lucy. While she never said a word in her defense, I saw her flinch several times. It made me wonder if, like with Mrs. Mueller, she and the Duttons had crossed paths before.

Mr. Dutton was preparing to tell his client that every medium in Philadelphia was a fake when he and Leslie attended their first séance at the home of Lenora Grimes Pastor. They realized that night that Mrs. Pastor was the real thing — a true communicator with the dead. It was during that séance that Leslie Dutton first spoke with her long-dead sister, Henrietta. Mr. Dutton also heard the voice of a person from his past.

"It was Laura," he told us. "My first wife."

So surprised was he by her presence that he couldn't respond. Hearing her voice again after several years left him frozen, unable to speak or even think.

It was, I imagine, similar to the feelings I had experienced upon hearing my mother. Shock, sadness, and regret had rendered me numb. So it was with Eldridge Dutton. While

I had managed to break through the shock and respond to my mother, Dutton could do no such thing with his wife.

Laura's voice soon vanished, replaced by someone else's. Yet when the séance was over, he vowed to return and speak to her again, should she reappear. Leslie, who had been equally thrilled by the brief conversation with her sister, also wanted to return. So began their weekly Saturday night engagements at the Pastor home.

Weeks went by. While Leslie Dutton heard from Henrietta often, Eldridge heard not another word from his late wife. It occurred to him that it was possible the presence of the second Mrs. Dutton prevented hearing from the first. The two women had known each other, after all, having been patient and nurse. Mr. Dutton's theory was that Laura's spirit detected the presence of Leslie, and therefore remained silent. If he wanted to hear from her again, he realized he needed to do so without the new Mrs. Dutton around.

So he took the liberty of calling on Lenora Grimes Pastor one Saturday morning, requesting a séance in which it was just the two of them present. Mrs. Pastor was reluctant at first, agreeing only after Mr. Dutton offered a generous contribution to her Quaker school. They immediately retired to the séance room, where Mrs. Pastor fell into her trance. In mere minutes, the voice of Laura Dutton emerged.

"It filled my heart with joy to hear her again," Mr. Dutton said. "To talk to her. To tell her how much I had missed her. And to apologize."

It was here that I interrupted his tale. "What did you have to apologize for?"

Eldridge Dutton cast his eyes downward and said, "It's shameful to admit, but my relationship with Leslie began while my Laura was still alive."

According to Mr. Dutton, his first wife's illness had left her in so much pain that morphine was her only relief. She spent her final weeks glassy-eyed and numb, unable to speak to her husband or daughter. ("It was as if she was already dead," he told us.) Lonely and grieving, he was comforted by the pretty young nurse who shared their home.

"She was so kind," he said of Leslie. "So warm and understanding. She was the only thing that made life bearable for me."

"What about your daughter?" I said, thinking of Bettina and her anger at both her father and stepmother. Not only did I now understand it, but thought it wholly justified.

"She did comfort me," Dutton said. "But a daughter can do only so much. A man needs other comforts as well."

"Men!" Lucy said, huffing with disdain. "I declare, that's all you think about."

Mr. Dutton's face reddened again. "I make no excuse for my conduct, Mrs. Collins. It was wrong of me. Yet I found myself in love with Leslie, even while poor Laura suffered."

Her suffering didn't last much longer. A few weeks after his affair with the nurse began, Laura Dutton died quietly in the middle of the night. Leslie stayed with the family, mostly because Dutton said he couldn't bear to let her go. They eventually made their love known to all and married. Yet the guilt stayed with him.

Once his first solo séance with Mrs. Pastor had ended, he immediately scheduled another for the following Saturday morning. When that one proved to be equally as successful, he decided to make a standing engagement with Mrs. Pastor. On Saturday mornings he would arrive alone to laugh and reminisce with the spirit of his first wife, returning later that night with his second wife. He never told Leslie about his communications with Laura. Nor did he mention it to Bettina, even though Laura Dutton had begged him to bring her to one of the Saturday morning séances. And if another form of guilt began to nip at the edges of Mr. Dutton's conscience, he managed to brush it aside.

Then, one recent Saturday morning, Laura asked him what he thought of the gold watch she had given him. She had ordered it the day before her illness overtook her, as a token of her love. Dutton told her he had received no such watch and suggested that perhaps she was mistaken. Laura insisted it existed, even providing the name of the shop in which it had been purchased.

Dutton went to the shop that afternoon and inquired about the order. It turned out that although the watch had been paid for, no one had come by to retrieve it. And so it had stayed in the shop, collecting dust in the hope that someone would eventually come to claim it.

"But now it is in my possession," Dutton said, patting the jacket pocket in which it rested. "And I shall cherish it always."

The watch, precious though it was, complicated his situation. The time he spent with the spirit of Laura now had a physical representation, reminding him of how much he missed her and how he longed to have her back. He held the watch as much as he could — polishing the case, winding the hands, watching the rubies on the face glint in the light. And he began to live only for those Saturday mornings, counting down the days, hours, and minutes until he could speak with her again.

"Outside, you implied that I was being unfaithful to Leslie," he said. "Although wrong about the object of my affection, you were quite correct about my unfaithfulness. It was through Mrs. Pastor that I rekindled a love affair with Laura. But now they are both gone. And unless I somehow find another true medium, I shall never hear from Laura again."

His tale finished at last, Eldridge Dutton began to weep. It was a sorry sight, watching him cry so extravagantly, holding a hand over his face in a failed effort to shield our eyes from his tears. Lucy and I comforted him as best we could, knowing it would make little difference. The man had lost his first wife twice now — once upon her death and again upon Mrs. Pastor's.

"Please forgive me," he said amid the sobs. "This has been very hard."

"I'm sure it has," I replied. "Being present for Mrs. Pastor's death must have distressed you greatly."

Dutton dried his eyes and nodded. "It did. Only I couldn't express it. Not in front of Leslie."

"Do you think she knew about your" — I struggled with the right wording to describe what, exactly, Mr. Dutton had been engaged in — "affair from the Great Beyond?"

"Not at all," was his reply. "I told her I came to this office on Saturday mornings. She noticed the watch, though, and demanded to know where it came from. I had no choice but to admit it was a gift from Laura that had only recently been delivered. That was at least some version of the truth."

And Lucy and I now knew everything. No, Mr. Dutton hadn't been stealing from Elizabeth Mueller, nor had he even talked to the spirit of her husband. He and Mrs. Pastor hadn't been engaged in a torrid affair and there was no motive I could think of for wanting her dead. In fact, other than Robert Pastor, Mr. Dutton had the biggest reason to keep her alive. Yet doubt nagged at me. Not about Mr. Dutton, mind you, but about the person who had hired him.

"I'd like to know more about your client," I said. "This man who hired you to seek out true mediums."

"Mr. Black?"

"Is that his name?" Lucy inquired.

"Yes. Corinthian Black."

"Odd name," I said.

"Quite," said Mr. Dutton. "But appropriate considering he is an odd man. Ghastly looking."

"How so?"

I doubt many of you will be surprised to learn he described a pale man with a ghastly face that was missing a nose. I can't say I was, either.

In fact, it was my suspicion that the man who hired him was the same one who had threatened Lenora Grimes Pastor and attempted to run down Lucy and me.

The revelation, while not a shock, did prompt a flurry of questions from us. "Did you discover any other true mediums in the city?" she asked. At the same time, I said, "Did he say why he sought them out?"

Faced with two questions at once, Mr. Dutton tackled the first. "I came upon one other medium in the city who seemed to be legitimate. Instead of voices emanating from her, as was the case with Mrs. Pastor, she conversed with spirits as if they were sitting right there in the room with us. Amazing to witness, especially in one so young. Her name was —"

"Sophie," I said. "Sophie Kruger."

Dutton looked perplexed. "How did you know that?"

"Because her talent brought her to the attention of several people," I answered. "Including someone who killed her in the same fashion that caused Mrs. Pastor's death."

The embarrassed flush in Mr. Dutton's cheeks, which had flared even brighter during his crying spell, vanished in an instant. His face quickly took on the same color of the sky just before a snowfall — gray and burdened with an unknowable weight.

"That can't be," he said. "Tell me, Mr. Clark, that you are simply being cruel."

"I'm afraid not. She was found dead the day before Mrs. Pastor's murder."

Mr. Dutton rocked sideways in his chair, swooning first left, then right. When it became apparent that he was going to topple right out of it, I ran to his side and propped him up.

"This was my fault!" he moaned. "All my fault! I located them and now they're dead."

For the second time that week, I longed for the smelling salts still lodged in my old desk at the *Evening Bulletin* offices. Luckily, Lucy had some stored in that surprising bag of tricks she called a dress. Waving them beneath Mr. Dutton's nose, she said, "Breathe deeply."

The smelling salts did their job. Eldridge Dutton righted himself again and said, "This is terrible. I never thought that is what they wanted."

"They?" I said. "I thought it was just Corinthian Black who hired you."

"He did," said Mr. Dutton. "But he made it clear it was on the behalf of an organization."

"I don't suppose he mentioned doing mediums harm?"

Mr. Dutton shook his head. "Of course not. If he had, I would never have agreed to the job. He said he represented men of science researching Spiritualism."

"Did he give the name of this organization?" I asked.

"Yes. Only once, in passing. But I remembered it, because it, too, was a strange name."

"What was it?"

"Something Latin," Mr. Dutton said. "Praediti, I think it was."

Hearing the word left me stunned. I couldn't have been more surprised had the earth decided to stop turning. In fact, for a moment it felt like it had. Everything ceased to exist. No more Lucy Collins or Eldridge Dutton. No more quiet office and ticking clock. No more Philadelphia, with its bustle and smells and teeming streets. For a brief time, it was just nothing but that word, so loud in my skull that I felt it reverberate throughout my entire body.

Only instead of Mr. Dutton's voice, I heard it spoken by my mother, just as she had done right before Mrs. Pastor died.

Praediti.

In truth, the word had become half forgotten in the days following Mrs. Pastor's death. I had been too busy trying to clear my name to really ponder its meaning or why it had been so important for my mother to say it.

Now, however, it was all I could think about, even as the rest of the world came into focus once more. I again heard carriages in the street outside the office and the ticking of the clock inside. I saw Lucy and Mr. Dutton both eye me with concern.

"Edward?" Lucy said. "What's wrong? You look as if you've seen a ghost."

Seen? No. But heard? Most definitely.

The ghost in question was my mother, and I was suddenly haunted by the instructions she had given me during Mrs. Pastor's final séance. Instructions I now felt compelled to follow.

"I must leave," I said. "There's somewhere I need to be."

Lucy widened her eyes in confusion. "Right now?"

"Yes. You must excuse me."

With that, I left the office, stumbling through it as though the floor was slanted. Things didn't right themselves once I stepped onto Walnut Street. The buildings there appeared tilted, as did the street itself and everything on it. Horses looked to be pulling carriages up ridiculously steep inclines, while passersby seemed to defy gravity.

I set off into this new, lurching world, no doubt looking like a drunkard as I made my way northwest. As I walked — or, more accurately, stumbled — the word Praediti echoed through my head, still in my mother's voice.

She had known its meaning. She had understood its importance. And even though she had never spoken it to me in life, she had found a way to pass it along to me in death.

That, improbable as it might have been, was easy to understand. What left me utterly baffled was *why* she had felt the need to say it to me. My best guess was that, through ways that defied logic, she had somehow predicted my current troubles, and uttering that word was her way of trying to help me.

So I continued my dizzying trek across the city, the echo of my mother's voice guiding me all the way to Eastern State Penitentiary. Standing outside the prison, my head still spinning and my heart pounding, it was clear that I was meant to be there. My mother had wanted it this way.

It was never my intention to obey her instructions. Yet now I had no choice in the matter. If the Praediti were involved in Mrs. Pastor's death, then I needed to know who they were and what they wanted.

My mother had, in essence, provided the key to understanding all the strange things that were happening to me.

It was now up to me to use it.

Only that required speaking to the person on this earth I hated the most. It meant that, for the first time in fifteen years, I needed to see my father.

VIII

Eastern State Penitentiary stood, fortresslike, on Fairmount Avenue, its eleven acres bordered by a stone wall thirty feet tall. The entrance gate, embellished with turrets and towers, rose even higher. From the outside, the prison resembled a foreboding castle, plunked down in a northeastern patch of the city.

Because of its size and initial expense, the prison was very likely the most famous in the country. Everyone from presidents to Charles Dickens had walked its cell blocks. Tourists, for reasons that eluded me, flocked there. I had been asked many times over the years if I wanted to see this architectural marvel, declining on every occasion. I had no desire to set foot inside the place.

Now, however, I had no choice. If I wanted to understand who the Praediti were and what they were up to, I needed to speak with Magellan Holmes.

Despite that fact, I wasn't quick about it. I don't know how long I stood outside the prison. Long enough for the sky to darken from the onset of evening and an approaching late-spring storm. When I at last moved, it was only because I spotted a guard shooing a well-dressed couple through the front gate. The last of the day's tourists, no doubt.

"Wait!" I yelled as the guard began to close the wrought-iron barricade. "I need to speak with one of your prisoners."

The guard — a man as thick and impenetrable as the prison's walls — continued his task. "Personal visitation is only on Sundays."

"This is an urgent matter."

"Whatever it is, it can wait till Sunday."

"I'm a man of the press," I said, pleading. "I write for the *Evening Bulletin*."

Yes, it was a lie. But a small one, which I

saw as forgivable. Plus, it finally caught the interest of the guard, who halted the gate before it closed completely.

"Who do you need to see?"

"Magellan Holmes."

The guard cocked an eyebrow. "The wife killer? What do you need to see him for?"

"An article I'm writing," I said, lying again.

"You ain't tryin' to get him freed, are ya?"

Although it was a good-natured joke, I was able to answer that question honestly. "Not at all. I have no desire to see that man free."

The guard contemplated me through the gate's bars, sizing me up and determining my trustworthiness. Standing stock still before him, I wondered just how much I really looked like my father. It was enough for P. T. Barnum to notice a resemblance, and as I underwent the guard's inspection, I became convinced that he had spotted it, too.

Imagine my surprise, then, when he nodded and told me to enter. Yet I felt a great deal of disappointment as well. Slipping through the gate, I realized I actually wanted to be turned away just as much as I wanted to be let in.

Those emotions continued to tug at me as I followed the guard deeper onto the prison grounds and down the middle of a triangular-shaped courtyard. Two sides of the triangle were made up of long, low-slung cell blocks that reached to the wall behind us. Another entrance gate was positioned at the triangle's tip. Rising over it, outlined against the darkening sky, was a rotunda.

"This is as far as I go," the guard said as we reached the second gate. "Callahan will help you from here on out."

This Callahan on the other side of the gate was as thin as the other guard was wide. The two men had a brief, whispered exchange before the first guard left and Callahan took over. Opening the second gate, he said, "Welcome to Eastern State, Mr. —"

"Clark," I said, stepping inside. "Edward Clark."

"We get a lot of newspapermen here," Callahan said. "We're very popular with the press."

I was inside the prison proper now, standing directly beneath the rotunda. Cell blocks stretched in every direction, like the spokes on a wheel. Another guard stood in the center, slowly rotating so he could keep an eye on every long block. Callahan greeted him with a nod before veering into one of the blocks.

"Mr. Holmes is in Cell Block seven," Callahan said.

It would be incorrect to call the long hallway I found myself facing a block. To my eyes, it looked more like a tunnel, with a rounded ceiling that stretched as far as the eye could see. Damp-walled and dim, there was definitely something subterranean about the place. Not even a few windows in the ceiling, letting in the last breaths of daylight, could help brighten the place.

"You ever visited us before, Mr. Clark?" Callahan asked.

"No," I said.

"We're a model prison. Solitary confinement, that's what it's all about here. One man per cell. Little fraternization. We want them to reflect on their misdeeds."

I pictured my father alone in a cell with nothing to do but think about how he had killed my mother. I wondered if, while staring at the cold, stone walls, he ever regretted it. I wondered if thinking about it tortured him. I hoped to God it did.

"Mr. Holmes is in the last cell on the right," Callahan said. "I'll guide you there and leave you alone for a few minutes to talk."

We began the long journey down the cell block, my trepidation growing with each step. I was still torn by the desire to either move faster or run in the opposite direction, each emotion compounded by the sights along the way. Evenly spaced cells sat on both sides of the hall, each one equipped with a narrow window in the roof that let in a slit of fading light. Instead of bars or wood, these doors consisted of flattened strips of iron, welded together in a gridlike pattern. In the center of the door, at eye level, was a rectangle big enough to pass through a plate of food.

The design of the cell doors did little to hide the men inside. Passing cell after cell, I caught sight of shadowy figures lying on cots, sitting on commodes, standing up while simply watching the wall. Some approached their doors and reached out to us. Hands both white and black emerged from the rectangular slats, fingers curling and uncurling. A man inside one cell we passed, standing with his trousers around his ankles, shoved his manhood through the iron slats of the door and flapped it at us, grinning. I looked away, toward the cell across the hall. Inside that one was an inmate lying on the floor, loudly weeping.

Accompanying all of these sights was a chorus of voices, some whispering, some shouting. They taunted us, pleaded with us, asked for money, lawyers, food, tobacco. Floating above them, like a lullaby on a breeze, was the sound of a hymn being sung with regretful sincerity. Someone who had adequately reflected on his misdeeds, I presumed.

Callahan ignored all of this, walking with his narrow chin thrust forward. He was accustomed to such things. He saw — and heard — these men every day. I, however, did not, and the sights and sounds reduced my already-conflicted resolve.

I didn't belong in that place, not even as a

visitor, and every forward step we took further tilted my emotional balance toward fleeing. I would have, too, if my legs had allowed it. But they were too weakened by nervousness to do any running. By the time we neared the end of the cell block, I thought they would buckle and collapse beneath me.

"Holmes is just up ahead," Callahan announced.

We were at the second-to-last cell, where an inmate lay snoring on his cot. Then it was on to the last cell.

My father's cell.

I stopped before I could reach the door, my heart pounding loudly in my ears. Sweat had broken out on my brow and my legs wobbled. I was certain I was going to faint. I hoped for it, in fact. I wanted to tumble to the floor, unconscious, and not wake up until I had been dragged all the way back to the street outside.

But then I again thought about my mother. I thought of her voice during Mrs. Pastor's final séance, gently instructing me to see my father. And, of course, I thought of her final word to me, the one I needed to ask my father about.

Praediti.

I needed to know what it meant. So I wiped my brow, took a deep breath of rancid prison air, and stepped in front of the cell.

Just like his neighbor, my father also lay on

a cot, only he was awake. He was reading a book, taking advantage of the last few minutes of light coming from above. The book — a Victor Hugo novel — covered his face, leaving me with only a glimpse of thin legs in gray wool trousers and a pair of hands I no longer recognized.

Once upon a time, those had been among the most famous hands in the world. People truly believed that magic sprang from those fingertips, that a whole other world was contained in those delicately creased palms. Now they were veined and spotted. The hands of an old man. If any magic had truly existed in them, it was long gone.

"Holmes," Callahan said. "Someone's here to see you."

My father didn't look up from his book. "Who is it?"

His voice. Unlike my mother's, I had forgotten how it sounded. For a moment, I didn't even recognize it. It seemed too strange, too foreign to be my father's. Unfamiliar though it was, it unlocked hundreds of memories — ones that had eluded me for years. I recalled him bidding me good night, reading me stories, telling me how much he loved me.

"A reporter from the *Evening Bulletin*," said Callahan. "He wants to interview you."

My father turned a page of his book. "I don't wish to be interviewed."

"Well, he's here now. Might as well talk to

him." Callahan turned to me, his smile an apology. "I'll leave you two alone. If, after a few minutes, he doesn't talk, hurry back and I'll show you out."

Then he was gone, leaving me alone with the Amazing Magellan.

I remember very little about those first few seconds with him. My emotions were too unruly to pick up many details or preserve thoughts. I recall my throat being dry, so much so that I wasn't sure I could talk. And I remember my right leg twitching — a nervous tic I had no control over.

But mostly I recall desperately wanting to see my father's face. I wanted to gaze upon the Amazing Magellan to see what had changed and what was the same. I wanted him to see me, as well. I needed him to lay eyes on me and see that I was still standing, that his unthinkable act all those years ago hadn't broken me.

I cleared my throat and spoke.

"Father."

The book, lowered slowly, revealed my father's face in small increments. First was the thinning patch of hair, not so much gray as it was colorless. Next came the wrinkled forehead, followed by his eyes. Those eyes, at once friendly and unknowable, had long ago left crowds mesmerized. Now they stared at me, recognition flickering deep within them.

"Columbus?"

It felt intensely strange to be addressed by my given name. It had been so long since I'd answered to it. Still, I said, "Yes. It's me."

The book dropped to the floor. My father sprang off his cot and rushed to the cell door, gripping the iron slats while peering at me from between them. He studied my features, seeking out similarities to the boy he had once known. He nodded at each one. Nose. Eyes. Mouth. Convinced I was really his son, Magellan Holmes did something that surprised me.

He began to weep.

"Thank God," he said. "Thank you, sweet merciful God. They told me you were dead. That you died in the war. I thought you were truly gone. I thought I had lost you forever."

The tears poured from his eyes, raining down his cheeks and dampening his shirt. I felt tears of my own pushing at the corners of my eyes, begging to be released. I held them back. I refused to cry in front of my father. I refused to cry *for* him.

"Columbus Holmes *is* dead," I said. "I go by Edward Clark now."

"But you're alive," my father said. "The name is unimportant. What matters is that you're here. Oh, Columbus, you can't know how much I've dreamt of this moment! My boy. My sweet, sweet boy."

He smiled at me, even as the tears continued. The smile was, unlike the rest of him, something I recognized. Neither time nor prison had been kind to him. He was far too thin and his skin had the pallor of a corpse. But his smile was still the same.

That recognition, strangely, created more anger than comfort. It made me think of the man standing onstage fifteen years earlier. The one who had disappeared behind a red velvet curtain and changed my life forever. So my rage took hold, momentarily eclipsing the true purpose of my visit. Fifteen years of resentment woke inside me, flooding my heart with blackness. Fifteen years of questions followed — a veritable storm of them swirling inside my skull. Only the most important one was strong enough to make its way from my brain to my tongue.

"Why did you do it?"

My father's expression changed instantly, going blank. It was as if yet another velvet curtain had been drawn shut in front of him, blocking everything out.

Despite not receiving an answer, I continued to speak. Now that my initial question had been uttered, all those other words that had accumulated over the years poured out in a seething torrent.

"She loved you," I hissed. "She couldn't have been a threat to you. If you wanted to be rid of her so badly, why didn't you just leave? You could have left us both. We would have been fine without you. You didn't have to take her from me. You didn't have to kill her."

I had started to cry, despite my best efforts. In contrast, my father's tears dried quickly, his damp collar the only remnant of them.

"There are things you can't understand, Columbus," he said. "Things you can never know."

Deep down, I was hoping that he'd somehow be able to explain everything. To lay out, step by step, the reasons for what he had done. Even if the rationale was nothing but pure hatred of my mother, it would have been better than uncertainty. Better than not knowing why he felt she had to die. But Magellan Holmes was unwilling to give me even that, and I despised him for it.

"You owe me an explanation," I said. "After the hell you put me through, I deserve something."

"I have nothing to give," my father replied, backing away from the cell door.

I moved *toward* it, gripping the slats just as he had done earlier. I wanted to get as close to him as possible, so that he might see my face, my hurt, my hatred. I wanted it to haunt him.

"May you rot here, you bastard," I said, my voice wavering between anger and pain. "May you live a long, long life, with nothing but this cell for comfort. May you suffer within these walls. And when it's your time to die, may your last thoughts be of my mother and what you did to her and how despicable you are."

I released the door, my fingers white knuckled and numb, and stumbled away from it, spent. I felt empty then. Hollow.

My father, meanwhile, had retreated to the gloomy rear of his cell. I could only make out his silhouette against the cell's gray walls. Although I couldn't see his face, I heard him weeping again.

"Is this why you came here after all this time?" he asked, his sob-choked voice emerging from the shadows. "To say that?"

After my speech through the door, I wasn't sure I had any words left in me. It certainly felt that way. Yet I was able to answer, "No. I was told to see you."

"By whom?"

"That's not your concern."

I couldn't tell him the truth. Even if he believed me, I didn't want him to know I had communicated with my mother. I didn't want to tarnish that memory.

"And why do you need to see me?"

"I was told a word," I said. "A word only you can explain to me."

"What is it?"

"Praediti."

My father burst out of the darkness, flying to the door with a speed as frightening as it was unexpected. His eyes, wide and tear

497

stained, darted about a moment before locking on to my own. His hands, I noticed, trembled.

"Where did you hear that?"

"I told you, it's not your concern."

"Nor is it *yours*!" he said. "You must promise me, Columbus —"

"It's Edward."

"Fine. Edward, you must promise never to utter that word again. Forget you ever heard it. And if you somehow hear it again, you run. Run as far away as you can. Do you understand?"

I didn't. Not in the least. Still, I said, "Yes."

"Promise you'll do what I say!"

"I . . . I promise."

My father, looking slightly relieved yet far from calm, turned his back to me and began to move deeper into his cell once more.

"Aren't you going to tell me what it means?" I asked.

He shook his head. "I can't. Don't ever ask me that again."

"But it has to be something important. It's something I need to know."

As Magellan Holmes retreated into the darkness again, he seemed to merge with the shadows, making it impossible to see him. One final illusion.

"So that's all you're going to say?" I asked.

My voice, plaintive and pleading, echoed around the cell, almost as if it were suddenly empty. Only through the sound of his voice did I know that my father was still there.

"You shouldn't have come here," he said. "Leave now, and don't ever return. You should stay dead, Columbus Holmes. It's better for both of us that way."

IX

It was raining when I left the prison. One of those chilly, late-spring showers that felt inescapable, as if the dampness has seeped into your very marrow. I trudged through it, ignoring the growing puddles and streams of rainwater that flowed to the gutters.

Seeing my father again had left me tired more than anything else. Yes, rage and grief were still present, simmering like a fever. But it was a deep, shoulder-slumping exhaustion that made me not even care when the rain suddenly picked up, leaving me exposed in an outright downpour a few blocks from home. Instead of sprinting, I slowed down, removed my hat, and tilted my face to the sky. The drops that hit my cheeks were cold and jarring — each one a tiny slap. My hope was that the rain would either wake me from my stupor or wash me away entirely.

Unfortunately, it did neither. By the time I reached Locust Street, I was a soggy mess, made even more fatigued by the long walk in inclement weather. All I wanted was to retire to my bed and sleep for days, not seeing or speaking to anyone. I finally wanted to do what Barclay had advised all along — withdraw from the world until this particular storm passed.

But that plan, like many a previous one, was laid to waste when I noticed a brougham sitting in front of my house. As I got closer, I recognized Winslow in the driver's seat, hunched, collar up, against the rain.

One of the Willoughbys had decided to pay me a visit.

The door swung open when I reached the brougham. Inside was Violet, staving off the chill with a wool blanket and one of the hats that had made her family's fortune.

"Violet?" I said. "Have you been waiting long?"

"An hour or so."

"For heaven's sake, why didn't the two of you go inside? Winslow looks like a drowned rat up there."

"Quite honestly, Edward, I don't want to enter your home."

Although Violet was looking in my general direction, her eyes refused to meet mine. Instead, her gaze settled somewhere on my chest and remained there, not budging until I entered the coach and sat beside her. Then her focus shifted to the window.

"Why would you say such a thing?" I asked, fumbling beneath the blanket until I found her hand. Violet pulled it away as soon as I touched it.

"Bertie told me everything, Edward," she said. "How he saw you at Mr. Barnum's party. How you ignored him and ran away."

In hindsight, I should have known this conversation was coming. Yet Bertie and even Violet had been forgotten during the course of the day, eclipsed by bees and secrets and the pale, gaunt face of my father.

"Yes," I said. "It was quite a coincidence."

"He said you were with someone. A woman."

"I was," I replied. "Her name is Mrs. Lucy Collins."

"The same Mrs. Collins suspected of Mrs. Pastor's murder?"

"Like me, she's one of the suspects, yes," I said. "But I have no doubt about her innocence, nor does she about mine. Which is why we have been working together to prove it."

"Is that what you were doing at Mr. Barnum's ball?" Violet asked. "Trying to prove your innocence?"

"As a matter of fact, we were. We had questions to ask of Mr. Barnum."

"I suspect you didn't get the answers you were seeking," Violet said. "Bertie told me it appeared as if the two of you were arguing as you left the hotel."

"He was mistaken," I said.

Violet edged away from me. Not by much, but enough for me to notice the slight space that widened between us.

"He also said you ran when he spotted you."

"I did," I admitted. "It was foolish of me. It was my assumption that if Bertie spotted me with Mrs. Collins, he would assume the worst. And so he has. I should have simply introduced the two of them and avoided all this trouble."

Yet there was more to it than that. Bertram Johnson had seen Lucy dancing in my arms. He had seen me lost in her company. I wasn't certain if he had mentioned *that* to Violet, but it was my suspicion that he had.

"How badly do you want to marry me, Edward?" Violet suddenly asked. "Do you truly love me?"

"Of course I do," I said. "How can you even question that?"

Sadly, I already knew the answer. Violet doubted my devotion because I had given her good reason to. Flitting about the city with Lucy. Dancing with her. Coming perilously close to kissing her. Looking back on my actions, Violet had every reason to question what was in my heart.

Yet I was certain that I loved her. I had loved her ever since that first bite of cake at that silly veterans' dance. Only lately, that love had become more complicated, thanks to the presence of Lucy Collins in my life.

I certainly had no intention of pursuing a dalliance with Lucy, nor did I expect us to remain friends once our names were cleared. Yet my feelings for her had undoubtedly evolved since our first meeting — a fact that caused much guilt where Violet was concerned.

"I don't question it," Violet replied. "But everyone else *does*."

"I don't give a damn what everyone else thinks."

"Neither do I," Violet said. "I've said the same thing to Bertie and to my parents. But I don't like secrets, Edward. Everything you have done could be forgiven if you had simply told me about it."

"I've told you all along that I'm attempting to clear my name."

"But you didn't say *how*," Violet replied. "You could have told me that you struck up a friendship with this Mrs. Collins and were investigating the crime together. You could have told me of your intentions to attend Mr. Barnum's masked ball. I, of all people, would have understood. But for some reason, you felt you couldn't trust me. You refused to share your plans with the woman who wants to be your wife. That is the part I can't forgive."

It suddenly became clear what was happening. So clear, in fact, that I felt stupid for not seeing it sooner. Violet hadn't come here to ask me about Lucy Collins. The purpose of her visit was far worse.

"You're breaking off our engagement, aren't you?"

"I am," Violet said, her tone heartbreaking in its finality.

She finally faced me, revealing how much she had changed since we first met. She was no longer the bright young thing marching after me as I left that soldiers' ball. No longer the pretty girl concerned only with frocks and hats and the gossip of her friends. Now heartache pinched her delicate features and pain filled her blue eyes. Sorrow weighed on her, and it was all my doing. In my effort to shield her from harmful information, I had only caused more damage.

Yet there were many things I didn't dare confide to her, no matter how much she wanted me to. My mother, for example, and how she had spoken to me from beyond the grave. Or my father and the crime that he had committed. Then, of course, there was my biggest, most shameful lie — that the name everyone but Lucy knew me by wasn't truly my own.

Sitting in that brougham, listening to the rain pounding on the roof, I realized our entire courtship and engagement had been a folly. How stupid I was for thinking none of that would eventually affect Violet. How utterly crazed I was for believing it possible I could marry into one of the city's richest families without my past coming back to muck it all up.

But now I knew the truth. There was no escaping my past. At least not where Violet Willoughby was concerned. I should have known that it would snake its way back into my life somehow and tear the two of us apart.

"You're right," I said quietly. "I was wrong not to trust you. And I accept your decision."

"I'm truly sorry." Tears had formed in Violet's eyes, brimming over and threatening to spill down her porcelain cheeks. "Perhaps we can be friends at some point."

"I hope so," I replied. "For I wish you nothing but happiness."

After that, there was nothing left to do but part ways. I gave Violet one final kiss on the cheek before easing out of the brougham and letting the rain once again surround me. I remained standing in the downpour until the brougham departed, its wheels sloshing through the growing puddles in the street. Only when it was out of sight did I turn and go inside.

I entered a dark and empty house, Mrs. Patterson having gone home to her husband hours earlier. Instead of making noise or trying to brighten the place, I welcomed the pitch-black stillness. In the parlor, I dropped into the first chair I could find, staring at the darkened walls and waiting until my head was clear of painful thoughts.

I don't know how long I stayed there. Not being able to see the clock on the mantel, time passed in a hazy, unpredictable way. It could have been an hour or five minutes. I probably would have remained there the entire night had it not been for a sudden pounding on my door, which forced me to get up and light a lamp.

Opening the door, I found Barclay standing on the other side, rain dripping from the brim of his hat. His presence wasn't a surprise, seeing how he had said he was going to stop by later. Still, I asked, "What are you doing here?"

Barclay took one look at me and knew something was amiss. "What's wrong? Has something bad happened?"

"Violet just broke off our engagement," I said.

Barclay's mouth dropped open. "Oh, Edward, I'm so sorry. Was it because —"

I raised a hand, effectively stopping him. "Not entirely, no."

"You don't know what I planned to say."

He was correct. I didn't know, really. But whatever cause he was going to suggest, I knew it wasn't the sole reason for the loss of my fiancée. There were many factors for why Violet was now out of my life. The biggest one, incidentally, was me.

"I assume you're here to fulfill the promise you made to me earlier," I said, having no desire to speak any more of Violet.

"I'm sorry I left you in the lurch like that," Barclay replied. "What the Krugers told us led me to believe I knew the identity of Mrs. Pastor's killer. I needed to do one more bit of investigating before I could be sure."

"And are you now sure?"

"Positive." Barclay, still standing in the doorway, gave a few quick glances both indoors and out. "Do you mind if we talk about it inside?"

I led him to the parlor, where I poured us both a brandy. Barclay, as was his habit, pulled out his pipe and stuffed it with tobacco.

"So you know without a doubt who killed Mrs. Pastor?" I asked dully.

"And Sophie Kruger," Barclay added.

"Do you feel like sharing the name of the killer?"

"I do," Barclay said, lighting his pipe. "It was Lucy Collins."

I at first assumed he was making a joke in an attempt to cheer me up. But as I searched his features through the haze of his pipe smoke, I saw that he couldn't have been more serious.

"That's ridiculous," I said. "She was right next to me the whole time when Mrs. Pastor died."

"How can you know for certain? You said yourself there was a moment of darkness. And as for Sophie Kruger, Mrs. Collins could have easily paid her a visit in the middle of the night."

"But why would she do such a thing?"

"The motive is plainly clear," Barclay said. "She wanted to get rid of her competition."

Although it angered Barclay, I couldn't help but laugh. The notion that Lucy was the killer was preposterous. Barclay didn't know what I knew. About ways of collecting bee venom or the noseless Corinthian Black. He hadn't seen Lucy tirelessly try to clear her name. Most of all, Barclay didn't know about the Praediti.

"Has Mrs. Collins told you about Declan O'Malley?" he asked.

The name caused my laughter to immediately cease. When I replied, it was with a cautious, "She has, yes."

"So you know all about her previous life as Jenny Boyd?"

"Not everything," I said. "Just that it was part of her past."

"And you didn't think to tell me about this?"

"I didn't know it was important."

Barclay, disappointed, shook his head. "Well, as it turns out, it *was,* Edward. When Mrs. Collins's brother told me last night that they hailed from Richmond, I took the liberty of contacting a policeman friend who works there. He told me a young woman who fit Mrs. Collins's description vanished with her baby brother almost a decade ago. Her name was Jenny Boyd, and there were rumors she had married and gone north."

"That's not so strange," I said. "She got married and moved away."

"Edward, she lied," Barclay said. "Not only that, but she changed her name entirely. Newly wedded wives don't do that unless they have something to hide."

Or else they're ashamed of their family, I thought. That was certainly my excuse. Perhaps it was also true of the woman now known as Lucy Collins.

"What does this have to do with Declan O'Malley?" I asked.

"He was Jenny Boyd's husband. Although there's no proof that they actually were married, they lived together as man and wife. He was a laborer. She stayed home to mind her infant brother."

"So they might have been living in sin," I said. "That doesn't mean she's a murderer."

"Then she probably mentioned how Mr. O'Malley died."

I nodded. "It was a stomach ailment."

"I suppose you could call eating beef stew laced with arsenic a stomach ailment," Barclay said. "Most people, though, call it poisoning. The police weren't able to prove it was her, but they knew she was behind it. They kept an eye on her for weeks afterward, hoping she'd do something to give herself away. Before long, she was gone, having slipped away in the night."

By that point my heart was in my throat, beating so quickly it made me cough. I spent a moment or two hacking like a man dying of consumption while my thoughts raced. And going through my mind was the distinct possibility that Lucy really had killed Declan. Knowing this made me doubt everything else she had ever told me.

The more I thought about it, the less certain I was that she hadn't killed Lenora Grimes Pastor as well. I thought she was near me the whole time, but it would still have been possible for her to dash to Mrs. Pastor in the dark and plunge a needle into her neck. As for Sophie Kruger, I had no inkling of Lucy's whereabouts the night she died. She had no alibi for when the poor girl was killed.

More and more, it was starting to look like Barclay was right.

Earlier that week, outside the Dutton residence, Lucy had joked that she could have had me wrapped around her little finger if she wanted to. Looking back on it, I realized that I already was. I had gone along with nearly everything she had suggested, from teaming up to investigate the crime to showing up at Mr. Barnum's ball. I had been so quick to presume her innocent, when, in fact, I should have doubted her all along.

My coughing died down but my heart continued to race and desperate thoughts still galloped through my head. Was Lucy Collins really a killer? Had all of her words and actions — the kindnesses, flirtations, even her attempted kiss — merely been a way to fool me into thinking she was innocent?

Marching among all these questions was one louder and more urgent than the rest: By helping her, what, exactly, had I gotten myself into?

"Do you plan on arresting her?" I asked Barclay.

"Not yet," he said. "If Mrs. Pastor and Miss Kruger had been killed by arsenic, Mrs. Collins would already be in chains. But right now, I can only do what the police in Richmond did — wait."

I, on the other hand, could not wait. If I had been fooled by Lucy, I wanted confirmation of that fact immediately. But I couldn't do it with Barclay sniffing around. For all I knew, he planned on hauling Lucy to jail the next morning. I needed to take him off the scent. Just for a day or so until I could confront her myself.

"You might have to wait," I told him.

"What do you mean?"

"Mrs. Collins . . . has gone to . . . New York. For a few days . . . at least."

The lie was so blatant that I had trouble saying it. The words came out haltingly, so much so that I was certain Barclay didn't believe a word of it. Yet to my surprise, he sat up and said, "Are you sure?"

"Positive. I put her and her brother on the train myself."

"Did she say why she was going?"

"Family business," I replied, the lie expanding by the second. "Something to do with her late husband's sister. It was all very sudden."

"When will she be back?"

"I'm not sure. I believe she said the day after next."

"Will you notify me if you learn of her return?"

"Of course," I said. "She's a murderer. She must be brought to justice."

Barclay, pipe in mouth, eyed me through the smoke. Perhaps I hadn't been so convincing after all. I sensed that, for the first time in our friendship, he quite rightly doubted what I was telling him.

"Well then," he said, standing, "I suppose I should go home and get a good night's sleep. You should, too. Nothing heals heartache better than rest and the passage of time."

I saw Barclay to the door, wishing him a good night and assuring him that I'd contact him if I heard from Lucy Collins.

Two minutes after he was gone, I prepared

to leave as well. Steeling myself with a gulp of brandy, I grabbed my hat and coat and rushed back outside, right into the heart of the storm.

X

I must have pounded on Lucy's door for a good five minutes before someone answered it.

When it finally opened, Lucy herself was on the other side, dressed in a cotton nightgown and carrying an oil lamp. Her hair, twisted into a braid, hung over one shoulder. Her other shoulder was fully exposed, the fabric of the loose-fitting nightgown having slid down her arm. When she saw me, surprise shot through her sleep-clouded eyes.

"Edward? What are you doing here?"

Lucy's surprise increased once I pushed through the door and, gripping both of her shoulders, backed her against the wall.

"Is it true?" I asked, my body shaking with rage and disbelief. "Did you kill Declan O'Malley?"

"How dare you come here and utter that name!" Lucy hissed. "Go home, Edward. Go home and don't come back until you've calmed down."

Using an outstretched foot, I slammed the door shut. "I'm not going anywhere."

I remained in the foyer, pressed so close

against Lucy that I could feel the wild thrumming of her heart beneath the thin cotton of her nightgown. I was soaked to the skin, the water rolling off my clothes to form a miniature rainstorm indoors. The coldness of the water combined with the warmth of the house to produce small tendrils of steam that rose around us.

"Edward, you're scaring me."

"I need to know what happened to him," I said.

"We already went over that."

"Yes. Only you left out the part about the arsenic," I replied. "So now I want the truth — did you kill him or not?"

Lucy couldn't bear to face me. "That was years ago. I don't see how it matters now one way or another."

"It matters because I trusted you!" I shouted. "I believed every damn lie you've ever told me!"

A floorboard creaking on the second floor alerted us to the presence of someone else. Lucy shoved me away as we both looked to the staircase. Thomas was there, standing on the top step, barely visible in the darkness.

"What's going on?" he asked, voice thick with sleep.

Lucy raised her lamp, casting a circular glow on the foyer walls. In the middle of it, like characters in a pantomime, loomed our two shadows.

"Nothing," she told Thomas. "Mr. Clark came by unannounced to discuss a few things."

"Do you need me to take care of him for you?"

Lucy's voice turned warm. "No, Thomas. Everything is fine."

She shot me a quick look, fearful yet bossy. She wanted me to say something as well.

"Nothing's wrong, Thomas," I called. "I'm sorry. I didn't mean to wake you."

We heard the boy's feet pad away from the stairs, followed by a sleepy, "Good night, then." When he was gone, Lucy grabbed my arm and dragged me into the séance room. She set the lamp on the table and shoved me into a chair before taking one opposite me. It was exactly like our first argument — just the two of us facing off in an empty room. Fitting, really, for what I assumed would be our final disagreement.

Once again, a palpable tension filled the room, although it was heavier than the initial animosity that had run between us. Most of it stemmed from our appearances. Beads of water continued to drip from my rumpled clothes and pool around my feet. Lucy remained in nothing but her nightgown, modesty the furthest thing from her mind.

Yet there was more to it than that. We now had a shared history — of conversations, of bickering, of peril. There was an understanding between us, and the frisson it created sizzled through the air like heat lightning.

"Would you mind telling me," Lucy said, "what the hell has gotten into you?"

"I came to my senses," I replied. "Now answer the question. Did you kill Declan O'Malley?"

Lucy leaned forward, palms pressed together, as if she were in prayer. Her breath came out in ragged gasps.

"Before I say anything, I want to thank you, Edward. For your friendship and your trust in me. And I assure you that I didn't kill Mrs. Pastor or that Kruger girl. You must believe me about that."

"I'll consider it only if you tell me the truth about Declan."

Lucy clapped a hand to her mouth, clearly torn. Her eyes darted nervously as her palm pressed further against her lips. It gave the impression that she was physically trying to halt the words about to come out of her mouth. But then she pulled her hand away and let them be released.

"I met him when I was fourteen," she said. "He worked on my father's farm. A big man. Rough. But I was drawn to him. Drawn in that intense way only young girls can be. Girls like Bettina Dutton, who think they know everything when in fact they know nothing."

"Did your parents approve?" I asked.

"Of course not. But I didn't care. They told

516

me to end things with him or leave their house. I chose to leave. So Declan and I went to Richmond. We scraped by for a while. He was a laborer. I did wash from time to time. We lived in a rented room above a dry goods store, telling the landlord that we were man and wife. I insisted that we get married, and Declan promised me we would, just as soon as he saved enough money. But there never was any money. He drank it all away. And when times got leaner, he drank even more."

"But did you kill him?"

Lucy reached into the bodice of her nightgown, removing a strand of beads around her neck. Her rosary. Hanging from it was a wooden cross. Fingering the cross absently, she closed her eyes and took a deep breath.

"Yes, Edward. I killed Declan O'Malley." She huffed lightly — a surprised exhalation at her confession. "I've never said those words aloud before. I didn't think they'd sound so —"

"Guilty?" I suggested.

Lucy shook her head. "Liberating."

"But you don't regret it?" I asked. "You killed a man."

"I did. A wretched, horrible man. A man who did *this*."

Taking her hands way from the cross around her neck, Lucy pushed up the sleeve of her nightgown until her left forearm was visible. There, situated between wrist and elbow, was a patch of dark red skin. I had seen enough similar marks during the war to know it was a healed burn wound.

"He did that with a scalding-hot iron," Lucy said. "Because I was trying to earn money doing someone else's wash instead of making his dinner."

She stuck out her right leg, lifting the nightgown's hem until I could see a crimson line just above her knee.

"That was from a hot fireplace poker. As were these."

She stood and turned around, lowering the collar of her nightgown further until all of her left shoulder and part of her upper back were exposed. I saw three more slashes of red. Three more places where the poker had seared her flesh.

"I'm sorry," I said. "I had no idea."

"Of course you didn't." Lucy pulled the nightgown back into place. "Men never know what some women go through. They never know the beating and the cussing and the brutal humiliation."

"No woman should have to endure that."

Lucy stared at me, lips pursed, eyes fiery. "But they do, Edward. All the time. Everywhere."

"Then those women should leave. Run away, as you should have done."

"It's not that easy."

"Why?" I asked. "If Declan treated you so

518

badly, why didn't you just leave him?"

"Because," Lucy said, "I was carrying his child."

All at once, I understood. It was a revelation so sudden and so forceful that, had I been standing, it would have knocked me to the floor. Even seated, I needed to grab the table to steady myself.

"Thomas," I said, gasping. "He's not your brother."

Lucy lunged toward me, hand outstretched. She pushed an open palm against my mouth and hissed into my ear. *"Never* say that again. Understand me? *Never."*

Unable to speak, I attempted a nod. Although the gesture caused Lucy to pull her hand away, she remained on top of me, her breath hot against my face.

"Promise me," she demanded.

I wiped my mouth, trying to erase the feeling of her hand crushing my lips. "I promise."

"He doesn't know. He will never know."

"I won't tell a soul," I assured her. "Truly."

Finally convinced of my sincerity, Lucy slowly backed away and collapsed into her chair. Slumped and askew, her arms dangling from the chair's sides, she looked utterly exhausted.

"Now do you see why I stayed?" she said. "I couldn't run off while I was with child. I would have been disgraced, scandalized, most likely punished. My parents made it clear I was dead to them, so I couldn't return home. My only choice was to stay with Declan."

"Did he know about the baby?"

"He knew," Lucy said. "And, oh, was he furious about it. He said I had tricked him. Said I must have been carrying on with another man and was just using him as cover. But when he knocked me down and started kicking me in the stomach, well, that was the last straw. I could take the beatings. I was used to them. But an unborn child? He had no way to defend himself. I was his only protection."

Lucy looked past me, as if just behind my head she could see her past being acted out like a shadow play on the wall. Her features were devoid of emotion — a mask of calm. But I could tell she was recalling everything, experiencing that part of her life all over again.

"I knew that once the baby was born, Declan would treat him the same way he treated me," she said. "And I couldn't have that happen. So I started taking in extra wash, hoping he wouldn't notice. I hid the money in a tin behind the stove, working and saving for months."

"By the time the baby was born, did you have enough money for the two of you to get away?" I asked.

Lucy broke her reverie, the corners of her mouth lifting into a half smile. "Yes. With enough left over to buy some rat poison."

As she told me the rest of her story, Declan O'Malley's death seemed inevitable — a series of preordained events clicking into place. When the baby was a month old, Lucy fled, taking shelter in the next town over. Declan found her within a day, dragging her and the screaming infant back to their rented room before beating her senseless. That's when Lucy knew that no matter how far she ran, no matter where she hid, Declan would surely find her. There was only one way she could ever truly escape.

She waited another week — enough time to let her bruises heal — before cooking his favorite beef stew, adding the arsenicladen rat poison for good measure. Declan gobbled it down, not noticing that Lucy hadn't taken a single bite.

"He was dead within five minutes," she told me. "I threw out the remainder of the stew and summoned the police."

When a policeman arrived, she told them Declan had brought the stew home with him, from where she didn't know. She said the baby was her newborn brother, placed into her care after her mother died in childbirth and her father killed himself in a fit of grief. The lie, she figured, would make the police more sympathetic to her plight.

They believed her, at first. But when the storekeeper downstairs told the police he had overheard fighting, doubts crept in. They examined Declan's body, finding traces of arsenic. Once that happened, they began to question Lucy mercilessly. As the weeks passed, it was clear the police knew what she had done. So she did the only thing she could do — she fled, taking infant Thomas with her to Baltimore.

There, she changed her name to Lucy Smith. It wasn't very creative, but no one seemed to care. She kept up the ruse about being Thomas's older sister. That way no one judged her unfairly. In fact, people admired her for taking on such a burden.

Within a month, she met Mr. Collins, a man thirty years her senior. They wed a month after that and moved to Philadelphia.

"Mr. Collins was also a wretched man," Lucy said. "But at least he never hit me. And he tolerated Thomas. When he died — quite naturally, I might add — I became the person I am now."

And I understood why she had been so eager to clear her name after Lenora Grimes Pastor died. The longer the investigation went on, the more time someone like Barclay would have to look into her past.

"Thank you for being honest with me," I told her. "My mind has changed. I don't think you killed Mrs. Pastor and Sophie Kruger."

"I didn't, Edward," Lucy said. "I swear to you."

"But Inspector Barclay thinks otherwise."

Lucy brought a hand to her mouth again, this time in shock. "My God. That means he knows about Declan."

"He does," I said. "But his concern is those murdered here in Philadelphia. We must prove you innocent of those as soon as we can. After that, you must tell Barclay the truth about Declan. Tell him everything you just told me. He's a good man, Lucy. He'll understand. But you'll need to show that you regret your actions."

"But I don't have any regrets," Lucy admitted. "I could say I regret taking up with Declan in the first place, but that would mean I'd never have had Thomas. I know he's rough around the edges, but deep down, he's a good boy."

"So you're *glad* you killed Declan?"

"I'm happy to have gotten away from him, yes," she said. "If I had stayed, I'm certain he would have killed me. Thomas as well, most likely. I wish it could have been different. I wish he would have let me go."

"And from what we heard during the séance, he still holds a grudge."

Lucy shuddered. "Hearing him was awful. I didn't think such a thing was truly possible. And now . . . now I fear that someday I'll hear him again."

"I highly doubt that," I said.

"But how can we know for certain?" Lucy asked, green eyes wide and plaintive. "What if his spirit seeks me out again?"

"Then you won't be as shocked by it. You've already heard his spirit once."

"You can't imagine the terror I felt when I heard that voice," Lucy said. "It was as if no time had passed. Like he was right there beside me, that iron poker raised. I was so shaken that I was prepared to confess everything, just to get that damned voice to stop."

Her words took a moment to sink in. They trickled into my brain like ice water, slowly filling it, freezing into something solid, something tangible.

An idea.

I thought about our situation and how things had gone terribly wrong for both of us. I was a murder suspect, a fact that had caused the loss of my job. The effort to clear my name resulted in the end of my engagement. Lucy's situation was more dire. Because of her past deeds — and despite our best efforts — she had emerged as the prime suspect.

Yes, it was easy to see why Barclay would think Lucy was guilty. She had a true motive for wanting Mrs. Pastor and Sophie Kruger dead. There was also the fact that she had killed before, although under extremely different circumstances. But Barclay didn't know about Corinthian Black and the Prae-diti.

My theory was that Mr. Black had had a hand in both deaths. There was a strong possibility he had killed Sophie Kruger himself. As for Mrs. Pastor, he wasn't in the room with us when she died and therefore couldn't be the guilty party. But someone present was, perhaps working on orders from Mr. Black himself.

Eldridge Dutton, having been the only one to admit meeting him, was the most obvious culprit. But I doubted his guilt, for he knew that killing Mrs. Pastor would sever the final link to his late wife, Laura.

That left only four other people who could have done it. Lucy and I had spoken to all of them. We had learned their secrets. Yet we still weren't any closer to identifying which one of them was the culprit.

Time, unfortunately, was running out. My lie to Barclay had only bought us a day or so. But soon he was going to realize the ruse and arrest Lucy for two murders. Because of our investigation, I would be forever associated with her. My job at the *Evening Bulletin* would still be lost. Violet would continue to want nothing to do with me. Even Barclay, my old friend, would rightfully put distance between us.

It was a desperate time indeed. We needed to take desperate measures.

"Do you really mean that?" I asked Lucy. "Being so tormented that you almost confessed to what you had done?"

"Of course," she said. "Why?"

"Because it wouldn't surprise me if others were to have the same reaction."

I looked around the dim room, my attention settling on the nearby table. There were still instruments scattered on top of it, lying dormant. My gaze shifted to the so-called spirit cabinet against the wall and I thought about the sham of a séance I had witnessed in that room. What Lucy and Thomas had devised weren't bad illusions. While they had failed to trick me, the bells on the table and the "ghost" in the cabinet had managed to fool others. Perhaps they could again.

"You need to hold a séance," I told Lucy. "You need to contact Lenora Grimes Pastor."

She responded with a confused laugh. "You, of all people, should know I'm not capable of that."

"I know," I replied. "But I don't mean for real. We gather everyone who was in the room with us when Mrs. Pastor died. We bring them here and hold a séance. If the mood is right and the illusions convincing, the person who killed her —"

Lucy, suddenly catching on, gasped and said, "— might confess to her murder."

■ ■ ■ ■ ■

BOOK SEVEN:
THINGS HALF
IN SHADOW

■ ■ ■ ■ ■

I

We worked nonstop through the night, preparing the room for what we hoped would be a convincing séance. It wasn't easy. There were plenty of small problems to solve and, I hate to admit, much arguing involved. But by the time dawn spread its misty wings across the sky, we were finished.

"Do you really think this will work?" Lucy asked.

She was slumped in a chair, seemingly on the cusp of sleep. I lay on the floor, trying to stave off exhaustion. Until she spoke, I had been taking a series of seconds-long naps, my eyes flying open and my body shuddering each time I woke.

"It needs to work. We have no other option."

Lucy looked around the room through heavily lidded eyes. "I have to admit, it's impressive. Your father taught you well."

"I'd rather not speak of him," I said.

I hadn't told Lucy about my prison visit,

529

nor did I intend to. Despite toiling all night, I knew a large part of my exhaustion stemmed from my earlier encounter with Magellan Holmes. Memories of seeing him were still too raw to be able to hear his name. It was like a hangover in that regard.

"I'm sorry," Lucy said. "So now that the room is ready, what next?"

Forcing myself to sit up, I outlined the rest of our day. In order for our plan to work, we needed every member of Mrs. Pastor's final séance present. That meant rounding them all up and inviting them to Lucy's house. If they resisted, then we needed to coerce them into coming. I wasn't above using blackmail, if necessary, vowing to expose all of their secrets. And if that failed to work, then I was prepared to get Barclay involved. They would have no choice but to come if the police ordered them to.

With the understanding that the task was too great to complete together, Lucy and I divided the list of suspects. She agreed to reach out to P. T. Barnum and Elizabeth Mueller. I assigned myself Mr. and Mrs. Dutton and Robert Pastor. With our tasks set, we parted ways until later that evening.

Once home, weary and unkempt, I got as much sleep as time would allow. It wasn't much, a few hours at most, but it left me far more alert than if I hadn't slept at all. Still, the unkempt part needed to be taken care of.

Without Lionel around, that proved to be more difficult than I expected. Carting buckets of water upstairs for my bath wasn't easy work, and by the time I had bathed and shaved, I was again exhausted. Once the whole business of Mrs. Pastor's murder was over — if it would *ever* be over — my next order of business had to be finding a new butler.

I then ate a quick lunch under the watchful eye of Mrs. Patterson, told her I wouldn't be needing her for the rest of the day, and set off for the home of Eldridge and Leslie Dutton.

My plan for the Duttons was to force their attendance by vowing to reveal the two things they didn't want exposed. For Mr. Dutton, that was the otherworldly affair with his late wife. For Mrs. Dutton, I simply needed to mention how I could get something about her role in the Pastor murder written up in the *Bulletin* at a moment's notice. It turned out I didn't need to do either, for it was Bettina Dutton who answered the door.

"Mr. Clark," she said, surprised but pleasantly so. "What brings you here?"

Her face had been scrubbed clean of that awful paint, leaving her looking almost like a stranger to me. She was prettier that way — a fresh, young woman who would have no trouble eventually finding a beau.

"I came by to invite your parents to a séance this evening," I said, offering her a card with Lucy's address. "It begins at seven o'clock sharp."

"After what happened last time, I doubt they're too eager to attend another séance."

"They must come," I told her. "I'm surè you'll be able to convince them. It would mean the world to me."

"I'll try," Bettina said. "Will your fiancée, Miss Willoughby, be there?"

I lowered my head. "I'm afraid Miss Willoughby and I are no longer engaged."

It still hurt to say it out loud, like my heart was being squeezed in a vise. But I said it for a reason, getting just the reaction I had intended. Bettina, while aiming for a somber expression, nonetheless couldn't hide being overjoyed at the news.

"They'll be there," she said quickly. "I promise you."

With that task easily accomplished, I next headed to the Pastor residence. I knew convincing Robert Pastor was going to be more difficult than the Duttons. Out of everyone involved, he had lost the most when Mrs. Pastor died, and I doubted he would agree to a séance in which the surface goal was to contact her. Therefore I was happy to see Stokely answer the door.

"You here with more questions?" he asked, more amused than annoyed, although I detected both in his voice.

"I am," I said. "Chief among them is how you're holding up. When we spoke a few days ago, you were quite broken up about Mrs. Pastor's death."

"I'm still mournin', but I'll be right as rain sure enough."

"I'm sure you will," I said. "By the way, I never got the chance to thank you for helping me. It was very kind of you to convince Mr. Pastor to speak with me. Under the circumstances, I wouldn't have blamed you for refusing."

"I told you before, Mister Clark, I think you're innocent," Stokely said. "I only hope it helps you find out who really killed Missus Pastor."

"It hasn't yet. Hopefully soon, though. But that requires more help from you."

Stokely eyed me with suspicion. "How much help?"

I told him everything. He would have figured it out himself even if I hadn't. But because he trusted me, and because I wanted to retain that trust, I truthfully laid out our entire plan. I urged him to tell Mr. Pastor only that we'd be trying to contact his wife's spirit at a séance. It wouldn't work if any of those suspected knew our real goal.

"That don't sound like much of a plan," Stokely said once I had finished.

"It's not," I admitted. "But we're desperate. And we need Mr. Pastor to be there."

"My allegiance is to Missus Pastor. Not her husband."

"Then you'll help me?"

"He'll be there," Stokely promised. "If it'll help bring justice for poor Missus Pastor, then I'll make sure he's there, even if I have to drag him my own self."

I thanked Stokely as profusely as one could without embarrassing himself, and departed.

While it might have appeared that my task was complete, I knew it wasn't. There was still one more person I needed to bring to the séance. He, unfortunately, lived in the last place that I wanted to visit. Still, I went, catching the trolley at Spring Garden Street and taking it across the river to West Philadelphia. Soon I was at the home of Mr. Thornton Willoughby and his family.

The maid who came to the door looked downright flummoxed to see me, an indication that everyone in the houschold already knew of the broken engagement. Before I could speak, she retreated into the house, fetching none other than Violet herself.

Wearing a pink dress, with her hair pinned up, she looked as pretty as the day we'd met. But there was a noticeable change to her, as well. The kindness that had once radiated from her was gone, replaced by a weary sadness. My sweet Violet's light had been dimmed.

"Hello, Mr. Clark," she said in a tone so

cold it could have frozen Hades. "Why are you here? I thought I had made my intentions quite clear last night."

"I'm afraid there's been a mistake," I told her. "I'm actually here to see Jasper. I apologize for the confusion."

Violet seemed to dim even further, darkening right before my eyes. Seeing it broke my heart all over again. I wanted to kiss her, badly. I wanted to hold her hand and apologize for every stupid thing I had ever done. But more than anything I wanted to assure her that all of my actions had been for her and that, hopefully soon, my name would be cleared.

Instead, I said nothing as Violet left the door to fetch her brother.

Jasper emerged from the house five minutes later, looking worse than I had ever seen him. His hair was uncombed, his shirt was untucked, and his trousers were so wrinkled they resembled an accordion. His face was alarmingly pale, save for his eyes, beneath which hung dark purple circles.

"You went back to your old house again, I see."

Jasper simultaneously winced and nodded. "I had to finish off those bottles. Couldn't let Winslow find them."

"I wish you'd tell me what's troubling you."

"Maybe," Jasper said, "I'm just a drunk."

But it was more than that. He was haunted

535

by something. A recently lost love, perhaps, just like I was. Or maybe it was simply guilt, gnawing at him after some misdeed. If so, I wondered about the nature of his crime, and if it involved Lenora Grimes Pastor or Sophie Kruger.

"Well, you can't drink today," I told him. "At least not until after seven."

"What's at seven?"

I handed him the card with Lucy's address. "A séance. You're coming to it."

"Mrs. Collins again," Jasper said. "You really don't learn, do you, Edward?"

I ignored the jab, unwilling to give him the satisfaction of getting a rise out of me. "Just be there."

"What if I'm not?"

"Then I'll notify your entire family about that whiskey habit of yours. I'm shocked they haven't noticed it already."

"I'm certain they have their suspicions," Jasper said wearily.

"Then imagine how your father will react," I said with a tip of my hat, "when I confirm it for them."

II

People began arriving at Lucy's house shortly before seven. Elizabeth Mueller was the first, followed by P. T. Barnum. Lucy had done her job well. Soon after that came Robert Pastor

536

and, just behind him, Mr. and Mrs. Dutton, with Bettina in tow. Jasper Willoughby was the last to arrive, in much better shape than earlier in the day.

We all convened in the parlor before making our way to the séance room, where Lucy was already seated at the round table. A single tambourine sat in front of her, the other instruments having been relegated to side tables scattered about the room. There were at least a dozen of them, ranging from the smallest of bells to a dusty violin I had found in a corner of my attic. Joining them on the side tables were several candles, their collective flames casting a flickering glow on the ceiling.

Just for show, I picked up one of the instruments — the bugle — and turned it this way and that, proving to anyone who might be watching that it wasn't attached to anything. Some of the other attendees did a similar examination of the remaining instruments. Mrs. Dutton, for instance, touched one of the bells and gave it a single ring.

The spirit cabinet, no longer against the wall, now straddled one of the room's corners, so everyone seated at the table might have a better view of it. Because the curtains had been drawn tight over the windows, the only light in the room came from the candles and a single lamp situated behind Lucy.

"Thank you all for coming," she said.

"Please take a seat. Anywhere you'd like."

Thanks to the hole in the portrait of the late Mr. Collins, she had been able to see the number of guests and place a corresponding number of chairs around the table. I took the seat to her right, knowing it would help when her prosthetic arm came out of hiding. Mr. Barnum sat to her left, which was nothing but luck. Being a showman himself, I doubted he'd alert the others if he caught Lucy in the midst of one of her tricks.

The rest of the table, starting at Barnum's left, was arranged in this manner: Mr. Pastor, Mrs. Mueller, Jasper Willoughby, Mrs. Dutton, and Mr. Dutton. Bettina, unsurprisingly, squeezed in between her father and me.

Once all of us were seated, Lucy said, "Before we begin, are there any questions?"

"Yes," Mr. Pastor said. "Why, exactly, are we all here?"

Lucy, radiating patience, replied, "As you may know, I am also a medium of some renown. Considering what recently happened to Mrs. Pastor, may she rest in peace, I thought it would be fitting to hold a séance in her honor. Perhaps we might even be able to contact her and bid her a fond good-bye."

That prospect caused a stir around the table as people whispered to their neighbors or shifted in their chairs. Jasper, I noticed, glared at me for having forced him into attendance.

"My gifts aren't as great as Mrs. Pastor's

were," Lucy continued, "so I took it upon myself to try some of her ways of contacting the dead in addition to those that I employ. Hopefully the result will be a successful, meaningful séance for all of us."

She next instructed everyone to hold hands. When I took Bettina's, she gave it an extra squeeze and whispered, "This is exciting."

"Yes," I whispered back. "It certainly will be."

To my left, Lucy began her usual act, telling me and Barnum, "I trust you both will be honest gentlemen. If you feel my hands or arms move, pipe up. It's important that no one present thinks there's any trickery involved in this séance."

A sharp laugh rose in my throat, for I knew that everything about to happen involved tricks of some sort. With no small amount of force, I swallowed it down.

"Has everyone linked hands?" Lucy asked. "I ask that this human chain not be broken during the séance, no matter what transpires. In my experience, spirits who speak through me prefer silence, stillness, and near darkness."

Her hand wriggled beneath my own in the exact same way it had during my first séance there. "You must pardon me, gentlemen. I need to lower this lamp."

Barnum and I released her hands, allowing her to dim the lamp behind her. Now the room was lit just by candlelight. The open flames leaped and twisted, giving movement to the shadows in the recesses of the room, almost as if they were alive. I could only faintly make out the others seated around the table. The darkness obscured their faces, leaving only silhouettes against the candles' glow.

Lucy turned back to the table and I felt the prosthetic arm slide across the tablecloth toward me. I happily clasped it, knowing what was about to happen next.

"Is everyone comfortable and ready?" she asked.

The others responded with a couple of nods and a few murmurs that they were.

"Good," Lucy said. "Let's begin."

She closed her eyes and gave a single, extravagant sigh.

"I sense something. A presence. One not of this earth." Her head tilted upward, and she spoke to the air above us. "I feel you, presence. Hovering just beyond this room. Do not hesitate. We are all friends here."

Lucy then addressed those of us at the table. "This is a familiar presence. A comforting one. A woman . . . now entering. I feel her."

At that moment, someone really was entering the room. Two people, actually. They were Lucy's old cohorts, Pierce and Millicent Rowland, who emerged from behind the spirit cabinet. Dressed all in black, they crawled along the floor, invisible to those of us at the table.

"Spirit," Lucy intoned, "if you will, please make your presence known to the others."

Everyone seated at the table waited for a response. Everyone, that is, but Lucy and me. Since we knew what was about to happen next, neither of us was surprised when one of the candles rose from a nearby side table. The candle hovered in the darkness, high enough so that everyone seated could see it. Next to me, I heard a sharp intake of air from Bettina. A logical reaction, I assumed, if one didn't know the bottom of the candle had been affixed to a wooden stick being manipulated by Pierce Rowland.

"Thank you, spirit," Lucy said. "Your presence is welcome here. Are you, by chance, named White Sparrow? Extinguish the flame if you are."

The candle, still floating, suddenly went out.

"White Sparrow!" Lucy exclaimed. "How good it is to be in your presence once again. Are you well?"

This time, the candle leapt into flame again, causing Bettina to give a startled yelp. That pleased me no end, for the trick was my handiwork. The candle was really a thin, hollow rod of wood that had been dipped in wax. Inside it was a lit wick that rose and fell while being pushed or pulled from the bottom by

Mr. Rowland. A push of the wick made the candle appear to light itself. A single pull yanked the flame inside the hollow rod, making it look as if the candle had been snuffed out. Such a simple illusion, but highly effective.

"I'm detecting an additional presence in the room," Lucy announced. "White Sparrow, have you brought more spirits with you?"

When the candle went out again, she asked, "May I speak directly to them?"

The flame popped into view again.

"Thank you, White Sparrow." Lucy closed her eyes again. "Spirits of the Great Beyond, I beseech you, honor us with your presence. We have gathered together in the spirit of curiosity and respect to communicate with you. If you wish to join us, please enter this solemn room."

When she spoke, I felt two taps on my right foot. They were from Millicent Rowland, on the floor behind me — a signal that the second phase of our grand illusion was ready. I, in turn, reached out with my left foot and tapped twice atop Lucy's toes.

Prompted by the cue, she said, "Now, kind spirits, please make your presence known to us. Show us that you are here."

That was Thomas's cue to raise the instruments scattered about the room. While Mr. Rowland had been manipulating the trick candle, his wife had set about attaching the instruments to strings that descended from the pulleys in the ceiling. Now all of them rose, pulled by Thomas from inside the spirit cabinet. The bugle I had handled earlier twirled convincingly. The bell Mrs. Dutton had touched now swung gently back and forth.

Yet I hadn't been content to let the instruments simply float about. Some of them also began to play themselves. At least, that's how it appeared. The invisible hand that tapped out a steady beat on a hovering drum was actually Pierce Rowland, beating a twin instrument in the darkness just below it. It was the same trick for the bells, which Millicent Rowland was manning. The bugle was actually being played by Thomas, who tooted on one inside the spirit cabinet.

And what about the thrumming strings of the violin that floated a few feet behind me? That was yours truly, plucking a beaten-up banjo — also found in my attic — that sat on the floor between Lucy and me. The whole illusion provided the desired response, for gasps of awe rose from around the table.

"Thank you, spirits," Lucy said once our guests had been suitably impressed. "Are any of you familiar with someone seated at this table? Rap once for no, twice for yes."

Mr. Rowland rapped on the drum two times.

"Do you know *more* than one person present?"

Two taps again.

"Spirit, have you only recently entered the Great Beyond?"

Another two taps.

"Spirit, I thank you and welcome you back to the earthly realm," Lucy said. "May I ask, are you the famous Mrs. Lenora Grimes Pastor?"

This time, the two beats of the drum arrived slowly, with Mr. Rowland pausing between them to draw out the tension. When the second tap arrived, it caused a noticeable tension at the table. I felt it zip through our clasped hands, the frisson of fear and excitement being passed from palm to palm.

"If you are indeed Mrs. Pastor, kind spirit, then please find some way to prove that it is you."

The tambourine in front of Lucy, untouched since the séance began, started to tremble. It rattled across the tablecloth in front of her for a moment before leaping into the air. That, of course, was also the work of Thomas, pulling the string Lucy had attached to it while the rest of us were watching the other instruments. Still, it prompted Robert Pastor to cry out, "It's *her*! Only Lenora would choose the tambourine!"

Some of the others nodded their agreement

as the tambourine continued to bob up and down.

"Welcome, Mrs. Pastor. You honor us with your presence." Lucy flinched, as if she had just been insulted. "No, you're wrong. We *do* welcome you."

A confused murmur rose from the table, lifting and falling in the same manner as the tambourine. Lucy, meanwhile, continued her one-sided argument. She had rehearsed it several times during the night, and by that point it was utterly convincing.

"Not all of us wish you ill. Some of us miss you. We long to see you again, to speak to you again."

The tambourine shot upward, slamming into the ceiling. The impact, coupled with a mighty tug from Thomas, separated the instrument from its string. It dropped to the table with a rattling crash, now lifeless.

Mr. Pastor cried out, "Lenora, no!"

"She's angry," Lucy warned us. "After all, one of us killed her."

The other instruments, which had been floating quietly the entire time, began to sway and spin. The violin, just like the tambourine before it, flew to the ceiling before crashing to the floor. That set off a shriek from Mrs. Dutton, who repeated it when the bugle followed the same course. Next was the drum. Then the bell. One by one, all the instruments hurled themselves toward the ceiling before raining onto the floor.

Leslie Dutton continued to shriek, now joined by Mrs. Mueller. Their screams ended once the last instrument fell, only to start up again when the table began to shift beneath our hands.

"What's happening?" Bettina asked in the darkness.

"It's Mrs. Pastor," I said. "She's seeking to disrupt the séance."

In truth, it was Lucy, using the lift she had devised to make the table shimmy and shake.

"Please, Mrs. Pastor," she begged. "Let us speak with you!"

The table rose, prompting surprised yelps from everyone seated there. Bettina's grip tightened around my right hand as the table rose and fell. Someone was crying, although darkness made it difficult to tell who it was. Soon the sound was completely drowned out by Lucy's voice.

"She knows!" she exclaimed. "She knows which one of us killed her!"

Under the table, she tapped my knee. It was my cue.

"Who did it?" I asked, trying my best to feign frightened curiosity.

Unlike Lucy, I hadn't had the luxury of much rehearsal. But whatever flaws there were in my performance, they were covered by Mrs. Collins, who ominously said, "She won't say. She refuses to say. Instead —"

She paused to give a gasp of horror so well rendered it belonged on the stage.

"No, Mrs. Pastor! Please, not that!"

"What is she saying?" I asked.

Lucy stuttered for dramatic effect. "S-S-She says she wants revenge!"

By this point, Pierce Rowland was hurrying around the table, using a fire puffer to shoot bursts of air at us. The table, meanwhile, bucked and swayed as Lucy continued her frenzied speech.

"Mrs. Pastor plans to manifest herself," she said. "She wants to appear to us once again. And when she does, she intends to bring harm to the person who killed her. She intends to commit murder, just as *she* had been murdered!"

A strong gust of air pushed into the room, snuffing out the candles. The wind swirled around the table, circling us. All of the scattered instruments sounded out in the breeze — a chaotic symphony of drumbeats, horn blasts, and discordant plucks. One of the instruments — a bell, from the sound of it — flew across the room and clanged against the wall.

Bettina released my hand. Everyone, in fact, had let go, breaking the circle entirely. In the dimness, I saw people cover their ears, their eyes, their heads. The only hand that remained clasped was my own, gripping the fake one Lucy had laid on the table. When the fingers wriggled beneath my own, I realized she had, at some point unnoticed by me, taken my hand for real.

"What's happening?" she whispered fearfully. "This isn't what we planned."

No, it wasn't at all. Inside the spirit cabinet, tucked in tight with Thomas, was the painted-white figure for the Pepper's ghost illusion. We had planned an additional trick, one in which the ghostly figure flew from the cabinet, riding a wire stretched along the ceiling. But when Thomas pushed it through the cabinet door, the figure merely caught on the wind and flew away. It, too, hit the wall — a crumbling bundle of wood, leather, and lace — before joining the bell on the floor.

I was the only one who noticed it. Everyone else was too busy shrieking or cowering. Mr. and Mrs. Dutton clung to each other, her face buried in his shoulder. Mrs. Mueller covered her eyes, peeking now and again through her fingers. Robert Pastor, half standing, looked to the ceiling, the wind whipping his hair.

"Lenora, stop!" he shouted into the breeze. "Stop this at once!"

Shockingly, it did. The wind ceased. The instruments stopped their clamor. The table dropped back to the floor, a slight wobbling the only sign it had been airborne at all.

Something rose from the center of the table, passing easily through the wood and tablecloth. Not quite a figure, not quite a shadow, I can only describe it as a black fog that stretched upward and then outward. It reminded me of a bat unfurling its wings, opening up, revealing a human figure hidden inside.

Soon the fog faded entirely, leaving behind the shape of a woman. Not much taller than a child, she stood on the table, shifting and shimmering. Features began to appear. Rounded cheeks first, then a slight curve of chin. A small nose bumped outward before eyes appeared. Keen, sparkling eyes that stared directly at me.

I could only stare back, dumbfounded and convinced without a doubt that I was looking at the ghost of Lenora Grimes Pastor.

III

"Hello, Mr. Clark," Mrs. Pastor said.

I stood, my chair tipping over. I almost went with it, stumbling backward until I was against the wall. Mrs. Pastor remained at the table. While not exactly floating, she wasn't standing on top of it, either. She was simply present, as if the table didn't matter at all.

"You're frightened," she told me. *"I understand. I was frightened, too, in the beginning. But you'll soon get the hang of it. The fear won't last."*

I scanned the room, waiting for a reaction

from everyone else, confused when none came. Certainly others saw and heard what I was experiencing. But no one looked to the center of the table where Mrs. Pastor held sway.

Instead, everyone looked only at *me.*

"Edward," Lucy said. "What on earth is wrong?"

She had brightened the lamp behind her, filling the room with light. There was debris everywhere — the scattered remains of our illusions. Thomas had emerged from the spirit cabinet, while the Rowlands hugged each other near the door.

"I need to say a few words," Mrs. Pastor told me. *"I hope you don't mind."*

Across from me, Robert Pastor's hand fluttered to his heart as he said, "It's her! It's Lenora's voice."

Relief flooded my body. At last, someone else had heard her. I wasn't imagining things or, worse, going insane. That sense of relief, sadly, vanished when I noticed that Mr. Pastor had yet to look at the table. His eyes were fixed only on me.

"Yes, Robert," Mrs. Pastor said. *"It is I, your Lenora."*

My mouth moved as she said it, jaw lowering, tongue curling. When she spoke again, I felt the words forming inside my mouth before being pushed from my lips. But it wasn't my voice I heard.

It belonged to Lenora Grimes Pastor.

She was speaking through me.

"This is likely the last time I'll talk to you," she and I both said to Mr. Pastor. *"This is the last time I'll talk to most of you."*

I tried to say something of my own. A protest of some sort. But I had no control over my voice, no way of stopping what was taking place. I attempted to cough or clear my throat, without success.

I put a hand to my mouth, my fingertips scraping my lips. I couldn't stop myself from speaking. My voice belonged only to Mrs. Pastor.

"I know you married me for my wealth, Robert," we told Robert Pastor. *"I also know that you eventually grew to love me, as I did you. Thank you for your companionship over the years. I wish you only happiness in the future."*

Although my voice was gone, my mind functioned normally. It was filled with panicked thoughts, ones I wasn't capable of expressing. I looked to Mrs. Pastor, my thoughts pleading with her to stop. She merely shook her head.

"Not yet, Mr. Clark."

This time, her voice was only in my head, loud inside my skull. I felt weak, overcome by both dizziness and fear. I reached out, hoping to steady myself with something.

Lucy guided me to the nearest chair. I collapsed into it, my body spent. The longer this strange phenomenon lasted, the less energy I had.

"Mrs. Collins," I said in Mrs. Pastor's voice. *"You must be careful. Declan is still furious about what you've done. He's not through with you yet. Protect yourself and take care of Thomas."*

Lucy stepped away from me, stunned betrayal clouding her face. I longed to tell her I was sorry. In my thoughts, I certainly did, offering a hundred apologies for saying something I had no control over. My eyes pleaded for forgiveness, trying to wordlessly tell her none of this was my fault.

Her expression continued to shift, moving from betrayal to fear as Mrs. Pastor's warning at last sank in. Her shoulders drooped a bit, and she knitted her hands in worry. Yet I detected a defiant gleam in those bright green eyes of hers. Deep down, I knew that Lucy would be prepared for Declan O'Malley, if and when he confronted her again.

"Thank you for the warning, Mrs. Pastor," she said. "I will do my best."

"Now we come to Mr. Barnum," Lenora and I announced. *"I'm sorry I couldn't agree to your plans for me. But you will have continued success, I'm sure. Something big is coming just around the bend."*

P. T. Barnum gave a solemn nod. "Then I

552

shall be on the lookout for it."

Next, it was on to Mrs. Mueller, who perked up when her name emerged from my lips.

"Yes?" she said.

"Your husband's fortune is being held at Girard's Bank, registered under a name not his own. He wrote this to you in a letter he intended to post as soon as his ship reached port. That letter, much like your husband and his ship, is now at the bottom of the sea."

Mrs. Mueller trembled, on the verge of tears. "Do you know the name he used?"

"Eliot Anderson. That should be all you need to find the money. Goodness knows, you have suffered long enough."

"Thank you," Elizabeth Mueller said, the large, happy tears bursting forth. "Thank you so very much."

Jasper Willoughby, who had been standing alone by the wall, approached me. Of all the people in that room, his presence was the one that humiliated me the most. I could only imagine what he would say to Violet or their parents, how he would describe seeing me in such a state. He peered at me as he got closer, more fascinated than fearful.

"What about me?" he asked urgently. "You must tell me. *What about me?*"

I closed my eyes when Mrs. Pastor's voice began to answer. I didn't dare look him in the eye as she spoke. Not to the man whose opinion of me — whose family's opinion of me — mattered the most. It would have been too degrading.

"Ah, yes. You're Mr. Willoughby, if my memory serves. I'm afraid I can't assist you. If only we had been given more time together. Sadly, your trouble will persist. I am sorry, young man."

When I opened my eyes, I saw that Jasper had already retreated. He looked to be on the verge of collapse, grasping at the wall for support. Whatever trouble he was experiencing, it had certainly taken its toll. I saw in his sunken eyes the desperate need for a drink. Had I been able, I would have sought out the nearest whiskey bottle in the hope that it could console him.

But I couldn't move. Not for whiskey. Not for anything. I was still in the grip of Mrs. Pastor's spirit when it by then had moved on to the Duttons. Eldridge Dutton was flanked by his second wife and his daughter, a protective arm around each of them. Bettina seemed almost embarrassed to look at me, while Mrs. Dutton held her silk purse in front of her with both hands, as if it could shield her from whatever harm Lenora and I might bring.

"Eldridge," we said, *"Laura wants you to know that she cherished every moment in your company these past few months. She only wishes she could have talked to Bettina, as*

well. She adores you both and would love to hear from you in the future, if that is possible. But for now, it's time for her to go. Let her rest in peace."

"I understand," Mr. Dutton said as he pulled his daughter close. "Thank you, Mrs. Pastor."

"As for you, Leslie," we said, "I forgive you."

Mrs. Dutton clutched her purse tighter. "Forgive me? What is it that I have done?"

"The time for truth has arrived," Mrs. Pastor and I announced. "It's time everyone here knows that it was you who killed me."

The words were scarcely out of my mouth when Mrs. Dutton lunged for me, screaming.

"Stop talking! Stop, you wretched bitch!"

Her hand was in her purse, fumbling about. When she removed it, I saw a glass syringe attached to a stubby needle. She raised the syringe, a single drop of liquid quivering on the needle's tip.

Lucy leapt in front of me before ramming directly into Mrs. Dutton. The blow knocked Leslie backward, the needle and syringe dropping from her hand. Lucy continued to shove, propelling Mrs. Dutton into the arms of her husband, which closed around her like a bear trap.

"What must I do to keep you quiet?" Leslie cried out to me. "I already killed you! What more does it take?"

She struggled in her husband's grip, writhing and kicking. The other men surrounded her, in case their assistance was required. All the while, Leslie kept on shouting at me, although in reality I had nothing to do with it.

"I didn't want to hurt you. I only wanted to get rid of *her*!"

On the table, the spirit of Lenora Grimes Pastor began to change again, growing hazy and translucent. Her features faded, the nose retreating, her chin slipping away.

"I'm afraid this isn't the last you'll be seeing of me." Her voice was again in my head only. I heard it over the sound of Mr. and Mrs. Dutton arguing. *"When we do, I suspect you'll be better prepared for how this works. It's strange, I know. But we'll soon get the hang of it, Mr. Clark."*

Her transformation continued, turning her back into that undulating pillar of black fog. It wrapped itself around her again, like a cocoon, until only those keen eyes of hers were showing.

"Or," she said, *"should I refer to you as Mr. Holmes?"*

Mrs. Pastor winked at me — a hint of conspiratorial mischief. Then her eyes vanished, turning like the rest of her into a bit of smoke that quickly withered into nothingness.

Only when she was entirely gone did I get my true voice back. I felt it instantly, as if someone clutching my vocal cords had simply released them. I cleared my throat, relieved to hear the noise it produced.

Still, my heart pounded as quickly as my thoughts churned. Myriad questions pinged around in my skull. *What just happened? What does it mean?* Even though I again had control of my voice, I didn't dare speak them. Saying them aloud would have been admitting that something strange and incomprehensible had occurred, and I wasn't ready for that. Not just yet.

Besides, no one would have heard me. Across the room, the Duttons continued to confront each other. Leslie Dutton now stood alone, facing her husband and stepdaughter. Too weak and addled to join the other bystanders, I could only sit and listen.

"But why?" Mr. Dutton asked his wife. "Why would you want her dead?"

"Good God, Eldridge, don't you see? It wasn't Mrs. Pastor I wanted dead. It was *Laura.*"

The name of his first wife sent Mr. Dutton backward a step, as if he had just been shoved. That was followed by a plaintive, *"Why?"*

"Did you really think I was that stupid? That blind?" Leslie asked. "I knew all about your precious watch. I knew where you went all those Saturday mornings. You were talking to her. With Mrs. Pastor's help, you were again falling in love with her."

"That's what this is about? You . . . you were jealous? Of a dead woman?"

"Not jealous, no," Leslie Dutton said. "Afraid."

"Afraid of what?"

"That she'd tell you —" Leslie clamped a hand over her mouth, swaying unsteadily.

"Tell me *what*?" Eldridge said, his voice firm.

His wife shook her head. She put her free hand atop the one already covering her mouth — a second barrier against her emerging confession.

"Tell me, Leslie!" Eldridge gripped her by the shoulders and shook her, as if that would make her words tumble free. "You must tell me!"

"I was scared Laura would tell you the truth about her death!" Leslie blurted out. "That she would tell you how I killed her!"

Mr. Dutton's mouth dropped open and a strange noise came out of it — a cry of despair, only partially choked out. Behind him, Bettina's eyes rolled back in her head, a sure sign she was about to faint.

Jasper rushed forward and caught her, pulling her to a nearby chair. Lucy then swooped in, smelling salts in hand.

A few feet away, Eldridge Dutton looked

like he, too, was going to pass out. His skin had turned an ashen shade while huge, tearless sobs shook his entire body.

"You killed her?" he moaned. "You killed my Laura?"

"No, no, no. I helped her. That's what I did." Mrs. Dutton, standing alone once again, began to lower herself to the ground. Her descent was slow, skirt spreading across the floor, as if she were deflating under the weight of her guilt. "She was as good as dead. You knew that. We all did. I just helped her along. Put her out of her misery."

"No, you murdered her!"

Eldridge Dutton fell to his hands and knees, joining his wife on the floor. Leslie reached out to him, fingers straining to make contact.

"I did it for you, my love," she said. "For *us*. And we were so happy."

When her husband swatted her hand away, Leslie looked to the rest of us, begging for something. Confirmation, I suppose. Or approval.

"We were," she told us. "So happy. And I couldn't have Mrs. Pastor ruin it. Not after all this time. I had to keep my secret."

"So you killed my wife," Robert Pastor said.

His voice was flat, as colorless as his face. I suspect it was utter shock that kept him so calm. Either that or an unfathomably deep reserve of self-restraint. Had I been in his place, I'm afraid my reaction would have been quite different.

"Yes," Leslie said, covering her face in shame. "I did. During the séance, when my sister told me not to trust Eldridge, I knew that causing her death was my only option."

Mr. Pastor turned away from her, tears leaking from his eyes and hands trembling with barely controlled rage.

"Because my wife has already forgiven you," he said quietly, "I must do the same. May God have mercy on your wretched soul."

He retreated to a corner, caught in the comforting embrace of both Mrs. Mueller and P. T. Barnum. Lucy took his place in the center of the room, staring down at Leslie Dutton.

"How did you do it?" she asked, holding out the needle and syringe for all to see. "Was it with this?"

The initial catharsis of her confession over, Mrs. Dutton recited the rest in a defeated monotone. "Yes. When the lamps went out during the séance, I pulled it from my purse and stabbed it into her neck. I didn't know if it was enough to kill her. I didn't even know if the needle had broken the skin. I wasn't thinking clearly. I . . . . I just wanted her silenced."

"And the first Mrs. Dutton?" Lucy asked. "How did you kill her?"

"The same way," Leslie said. "A needle and

some morphine. A large enough dose to put her to sleep for good."

"Morphine?" I said.

Everyone turned to me, surprised by the sound of my voice.

"Is that what you used to kill Mrs. Pastor?"

"Yes," Leslie said. "There was plenty left over from when the first Mrs. Dutton was alive."

Perhaps some of Mrs. Pastor's spirit was still present, guiding my thoughts. Or maybe, after thinking about it for days, a new insight had occurred on its own. Either way, the situation became clear. It was as if someone had wiped grime away from a window, finally allowing me to see through the glass.

"You didn't kill Mrs. Pastor," I told Leslie Dutton. "No one in this room did."

"But she confessed," Robert Pastor said. "She admitted plunging that needle into my wife's neck."

"And so she did," I said, "leaving a needle mark to prove it. But your wife was poisoned with bee venom. Not morphine. Which means your wife was already dead when Mrs. Dutton got to her."

I turned to Lucy, who appeared just as dumbfounded as everyone else. "Send Thomas out to summon Inspector Barclay and the police. Don't let anyone leave until they arrive."

I then hurried out of the room. Lucy followed me, barely able to keep up as I headed to the front door.

"How am I going to do that?"

"You'll find a way," I said. "Use your gun, if necessary."

"What should I do when the police get here?" Lucy asked.

"Tell them that Mrs. Dutton killed her predecessor," I replied. "Then send Barclay to the Pastor residence."

"Why there?"

I flung open the door and stepped outside. "Because it's where he'll find the person who really did kill Lenora Grimes Pastor."

IV

I ran from Lucy's house, heading westward. No doubt I looked like a madman as I dodged pedestrians and flew past lamplighters brightening the city flame by flame. When the sidewalks got too crowded, I veered into the street, mud sucking at my shoes and carriages brushing my elbows. None of it slowed me.

Common sense told me that I should have gone straight to Barclay. Or at least grabbed the nearest policeman for help. Yet I forced myself to ignore common sense's nagging voice.

I had spent the week in a fog of suspicion. My fiancée was lost, as was my job. The only thing I had of any worth was my good name, and even that was fake. I needed to immediately uncover the truth about Mrs. Pastor's death.

Within ten minutes, I had reached my destination. I longed to pause, just for a second, to catch my breath. My body, still shaken from whatever it was that had happened at Lucy's house, begged for rest. Pain hummed in my legs. My chest heaved. Yet I pressed on, running up the front steps and bursting into the former home of Lenora Grimes Pastor.

"Stokely!" My shout ricocheted off the bare walls. "Where are you?"

I peeked into the séance room to the left. Seeing that it was empty, I pushed farther down the hallway. "Stokely?"

This time, there was an answer. "Is that you, Mister Clark?"

It came from the kitchen, exactly where I was headed. Reaching it, I found Stokely near the door that led to the cellar, standing straight backed and unsmiling, arms at his sides.

"Did you tell Claudia about our plans for the séance?"

"Yes'sir," he said slowly. "I reckon I did."

"And where is she?"

Instead of giving an answer, Stokely winced in pain.

I stepped deeper into the room, moving

slightly to the side. Just behind Stokely, almost hidden by his massive frame, was Claudia. A knife was in her hand, the tip pressed against the small of his back.

"You're one of them, aren't you?" I asked her. "One of the Praediti?"

Claudia didn't move. She simply peered out from behind Stokely, eyes as wide as saucers. The knife, I noticed, poked farther into his back, the tip all but vanishing into the fabric of his shirt.

"You killed Mrs. Pastor and Sophie Kruger because they wouldn't join you," I said.

She had been Sophie's friend, the one Louisa Kruger knew about but had never seen. I knew that because Claudia had made the mistake of writing down that she hailed from Fishtown, the same place the Krugers lived. The Praediti had likely told her to befriend the girl, to gain her confidence. I suspected Claudia knew what Sophie had been capable of, was aware of the power she possessed.

With Mrs. Pastor, she pretended to be in need, knowing she would be taken in. That way Claudia could get closer to her, to assess her skills, and, if necessary, kill her.

"Did you kill Sophie the same way you killed Mrs. Pastor? With a glass of poisoned lemonade?"

Claudia spoke, just as I suspected she could. Her voice, bearing a slight German accent, was hoarse and uncertain, no doubt the result of being forced to remain silent for such a long time.

"Yes," she said.

Not that I needed an answer. It was now clear to me that Mrs. Pastor's poisoning had begun before the door to the séance room was locked. It had started when Claudia brought in cups of lemonade. She had let most of us choose which cup to drink from. Mrs. Pastor was the only person handed a cup directly. When she drank from it, her death was all but inevitable. It happened slowly, unnoticed as the séance progressed. I had an inkling the conversation with my mother ended so abruptly because Mrs. Pastor's death had at last been complete.

"Someone put you up to it, didn't they?" I asked. "You were ordered to kill them both."

"Yes," Claudia said again.

This was no surprise. The girl was nothing more than a worker bee. One of the many who protected the hive.

"Was it Corinthian Black?"

This time, Claudia shook her head. "You'll never understand. We serve a higher purpose."

"What did you get for killing them?" I asked. "Money? A reward?"

"Glory," she said. "That is my reward."

"And now that they're dead, what will you do?"

Claudia blinked once. "I shall claim it."

Stokely remained motionless as we spoke, eyes forward, head held high. But his right hand, I noticed, had lifted slightly, fingers curling into a fist. He suddenly lurched forward and, in a flash, spun around to face Claudia, fist flying.

Claudia, lightning quick herself, dodged the blow. With a sneer, she thrust her knife forward, plunging it deep into Stokely's stomach.

He stumbled backward, pulling himself off the blade. Blood poured from the wound — a crimson flow that wouldn't stop, not even when he placed both hands against it. Then he dropped to the floor. At the same moment, Claudia let go of the knife and rushed into the cellar.

I flew to Stokely's side, grabbing a towel sitting by the sink and pressing it to his stomach. The white cloth turned red in an instant.

"I'm going to get help," I told him. "Just keep still."

"No," Stokely said, a wet gurgle accompanying his words. "Catch Claudia."

I looked to the cellar door. Claudia was down there, yes, but trapped.

"She's not going anywhere," I said. "There's no way out."

Stokely shook his head. The motion pushed another tide of blood from his stomach that bubbled from beneath the towel.

"The . . . tunnel." Each word pained him. I could tell by the way he paused between them. "Rail . . . road."

Of course. I had forgotten all about the Underground Railroad tunnel that ran directly beneath the house. It was how Stokely had come to stay at the Pastor residence, following it all the way to the basement. Reminded once again, I realized that if there was a way into the cellar, then there was also a way out. Claudia, I was certain, realized it, too.

"Let her escape," I said. "I won't leave you."

"Go." Stokely gulped, the pain obviously unbearable.

"I'm staying. Help is on the way."

At least, I hoped it would be. I had no idea how long it would take Thomas to fetch the police, nor did I know how soon Barclay would get there. Meanwhile, Claudia was somewhere underground, making her escape.

Stokely sensed this, because he said, "Go. Do it . . . for Missus . . . Pastor."

I didn't want his last words to be wasted pleading with me. So I pressed the towel firmly against his stomach. I placed his hands on top of it, telling him to try to put as much pressure on the wound as possible and that help would be there soon. Then I was up, running across the blood-streaked floor and hurrying through the cellar door.

I found myself at the top of a narrow set of

steps that descended into inky darkness. I went down them as fast as possible, feeling my way along the stone walls. The darkness was leavened somewhat by the light trickling in from the kitchen, and by the time I reached bottom, my eyes had adjusted to the gloom. I could make out support beams overhead, a few barrels in the corner, and, directly across from me, several shelves lined with jars of preserved vegetables.

One of the shelves had been moved, its contents now on the floor in a heap of broken glass. Behind it was a wooden door no higher than my waist. That, too, had been opened to reveal a dirt tunnel.

The hole resembled a large rabbit burrow dug into the wall. I dropped to my knees and poked my head inside, unable to see more than a few inches in front of me. Although wooden boards had been placed along the sides, with additional planks crisscrossed overhead for support, the tunnel didn't come close to appearing safe. The thought of squeezing into it filled me with dread. I didn't want to get halfway through the tunnel only to have it collapse around me.

But then I thought of Claudia, already worming her way through it. I couldn't let her escape. Stokely was right. I had to go.

I crawled forward, the darkness overtaking me. For a moment, I froze, overwhelmed by the sudden absence of most of my senses.

There was no light. There was no sound. Scent was useless to me, what with my nose filled with nothing but the odor of earth.

That left only my sense of touch, which was aflame with alertness. As I resumed crawling, I felt the damp ground slicking my bare hands and seeping into the fabric of my trousers. One of my shoulders pressed against the tunnel's walls — a series of wood, then dirt, then wood again, like a rib cage.

And so it went for what seemed like fifteen minutes. Possibly longer. The farther I traveled, the more my other senses slowly came to life again. Sight, naturally, was impossible. Down there, I was as blind as Homer. But my nostrils started to detect more than wet earth. I could also smell my fearful sweat and, from somewhere far ahead of me, water. I heard it, too, a rushing sound in the distance. And, just beneath that, strained breathing.

It was Claudia, still working her way through the tunnel.

I picked up the pace, crawling as fast as my hands and knees would allow. Beneath me, the ground grew soft, almost muddy. This was a blessing, because it allowed me to move even faster as I slid along the slick bottom of the tunnel.

The rushing noise ahead of me got louder, as did the sound of breathing. Not only was I getting closer to Claudia, but both of us were nearing the exit. Yet there was no gentle receding of the darkness. Light, it seemed, was not at the end of this tunnel.

But there *was* mud. Plenty of it. The tunnel's walls and ceiling were by that point completely wood — the only way to hold back the softened earth. The hole also descended sharply, turning from relative flatness to a steep decline.

The angle, coupled with the mud, caused me to slide. It was smooth, at first, a welcome acceleration. Soon, though, I couldn't stop myself, my arms struggling to keep up. I started hurtling forward on my stomach, sliding faster.

The tunnel's end point came quickly — a gaping mouth made of wood that spit me out into more darkness. I tumbled through the gloom, limbs flailing, my fall broken by a shallow pool of water.

Unharmed, I was able to quickly get to my feet and collect my bearings. While still dark, I could see slightly better than in the tunnel. I was in a channel of some sort, narrow but with high ceilings. The walls were stone, as was the floor.

Ahead of me, a square had been cut into the wall to let water pass through. Just beyond that, unseen but most definitely heard, was what sounded like rushing water, grinding gears, and the pressurized hiss of a steam engine.

The tunnel had taken me from the Pastor

home all the way to the Fairmount Water Works.

I waded forward, water sloshing at my knees, and ducked through the opening in the wall. There was light on the other side, courtesy of oil lamps hanging from the walls. I could see clearly at last.

Spread out before me like a giant mechanical beast was the heart of the waterworks. Turbines moved iron arms, which connected to turning wheels twice my height. Spinning around them were gears and pulleys and more arms and wheels. Coursing through it all was water pulled in from the Schuylkill River, flowing and trickling and rising and falling. Steam floated around and through the heaving contraption.

No sign of life was evident as I surveyed my surroundings. No workers. No Claudia.

The only indication that I wasn't alone was the sound of hurried footfalls coming from somewhere above me.

Tearing my gaze from the machinery, I noticed a ladder to my immediate right. I climbed it, finding myself on a wooden catwalk that ran between two of the turbines. One direction led to more churning equipment. The other moved inward, skirting the wall of the channel I had just emerged from.

In that direction, I caught a flash of soaked skirt disappearing around a corner.

At last, I had located Claudia.

I gave chase, hurrying around the corner. Claudia was just ahead of me, now climbing another, higher ladder. I caught the ladder a few rungs below her, arms straining to grasp one of her feet and yank her downward. But she eluded my grip, lifting herself effortlessly to another rung just out of reach.

The ladder led to another catwalk, higher and narrower than the first. Claudia scrambled onto it and turned left without hesitation. She easily knew her way around this place.

I could only try to keep up, heaving myself onto the catwalk. We were near the top of the waterworks by that point, with most of the machinery far below. It was still loud, though, and still fogged with steam. Ahead of me, Claudia burst through a wall of it, momentarily vanishing. I followed, catching sight of her again as she climbed yet another ladder.

This was a shorter one, leading to a nook nestled at the very top of the building. Claudia reached it in no time at all. I climbed it slightly more slowly, my whole body aching. Above me was the sound of more machinery, humming away. I also heard Claudia talking to herself, chanting something in Latin.

"Gloria enim Praediti. Gloria enim Praediti."

Reaching the top of the ladder, I peered into the room. It was larger than I expected, stretching a good twenty feet in width. A hole in the roof revealed a patch of night sky and winking stars. The walls of the room weren't visible, thanks to stacks of small wooden boxes that rose from floor to ceiling. What I didn't see was any more machinery. Odd, considering how loud it was in there.

Claudia continued her chant as she grabbed one of the wooden boxes and smashed it to the floor.

A black cloud burst out of it, rising for a moment before breaking away into smaller pieces.

Bees.

Hundreds of them poured out of the box and scattered everywhere. They crawled along the walls, flitted off the ceiling, flew like wind-whipped leaves.

"Gloria enim Praediti," Claudia continued to chant. *"Gloria enim Praediti."*

She smashed another box. Then another. More clouds of bees swarmed the room. Some of them flew away through the hole in the roof. Others swooped down toward me on the ladder.

Mostly, they crawled all over Claudia. Dozens were in her hair, burying themselves in its strands. More gathered along her shoulder, her neck, her face.

"Gloria enim Praediti. Gloria enim Praediti."

Two more boxes hit the floor, the wood splintering, the bees joining their brethren. Instead of fighting them off, Claudia wel-

573

comed them, opening her arms as if to embrace them. Bees had covered one side of her face — a writhing mask of yellow and black. Claudia urged them forward, pushing them toward her mouth and nose. Some crawled inside her nostrils. Others entered her mouth, buzzing in and out of her open lips.

The room had become so thick with bees that I was forced to retreat down the ladder. I swatted them with one hand while clinging to the rungs with the other. Just as I ducked out of the room, I spied Claudia holding one more box. The bees had mostly covered her, leaving only her hands and a bit of forehead untouched.

She raised the box over her head, the bees inside it trickling onto her scalp.

She gave one final cry, *"Gloria enim Praediti!"*

Then she threw the box to the floor, letting the bees that poured out of it fully engulf her.

V

It took no time at all for the bees to reach me as well. I was halfway down the ladder when they swarmed around my head and crawled over my arms. I tried to shake them off, instead losing my grip on the ladder and tumbling the rest of the way down.

I landed hard on my back, the catwalk beneath me shimmying from the full and sudden force of my weight. Despite the pain that now pulsed up my spine, I continued to move, crawling backward as fast as I could. Part of my haste was to get away from the bees, which stubbornly insisted on following me. The other reason was to get off that catwalk, which continued to buck and sway.

When I reached the curtain of steam I had passed through earlier, the bees at last retreated. That gave me the opportunity to stand, although my fall had left me sore and weary. On my feet again, I hurried through the slip of steam to the ladder on the other side of the catwalk.

I descended the ladder to a lower, more stable walkway. This was the one that overlooked the channel from which I had entered, the water below quiet and still. I continued back into the heart of the waterworks. The machinery there still moved at full speed — an army of gears and pumps and turbines working with ceaseless purpose. Water sloshed in all directions as jets of steam shot across the walkway.

One such column of steam contained a silhouette of a man crossing the walkway in the opposite direction, the mist holding his shadow a moment. The darkened form shimmered slightly before being released as the man finally emerged.

I sucked in a deep, horrified breath, finding myself face-to-noseless-face with Corinthian Black.

He halted just beyond the curtain of steam, one hand in his pocket. His other hand was outstretched, palm forward, as if he was trying to prevent me from coming closer, although I had no intention of doing so.

"Claudia is dead, I suppose," Mr. Black said.

His voice contained neither accent nor nuance. It was a flat plain of a voice, and all the more frightening for it.

"I think so," I replied. "I can't tell if you're happy or sad about that."

"I am . . . indifferent."

"How did you know we were here?"

"I was waiting in my carriage outside the Pastor residence. I saw you enter. When neither you nor Claudia emerged, I knew where to find you. This is where I told her to go in the event she was discovered."

"Did you also instruct her to kill herself?" I asked. "For that's what she did."

Mr. Black's lips twisted into a cruel smile. "She knew what she was getting herself into."

"And what is that, exactly? Surely, you had her kill Mrs. Pastor and Sophie Kruger for a reason."

Corinthian Black, hand still in his pocket, took a step forward. Alarmed, I looked for a place to escape, finding few satisfying options. The path behind me led only to the ladder and unsteady catwalk above. To each side of me were watery pools filled with hissing machinery.

I was trapped.

"They died because they were stubborn," Mr. Black said. "They died because they refused to acknowledge the full power of the Praediti."

"Who are they? Are you their leader?"

Mr. Black barked a slithering, mocking laugh that caused the skin surrounding his gaping nostrils to quiver. "I merely serve a higher power, Mr. Clark. As do my brethren."

Fear stabbed at my gut, sharp and frigid. "How many more are there?"

"Scores of us," Mr. Black replied. "With many more joining us all the time. Those who refuse are dealt with in the same way as Mrs. Pastor and the Kruger girl."

"But what about me and Mrs. Collins? Why did you try to kill us?"

"Quite simply, Mr. Clark, because you know too much."

"But I don't know anything," I said. "I'm as ignorant as the day Mrs. Pastor was killed."

"You know enough," Mr. Black replied. "Enough to make you a threat to our cause."

At last, he removed the hand from his coat pocket, revealing the knife that had been hidden there. He lifted it close to his face, as if trying to study his reflection in the flat of the blade.

"I acquired this knife many years ago," he said. "From someone else who knew too much. In fact, he's the one responsible for *this.*"

He gestured to the gaping nostrils on his face, his breath still hissing out of them.

"He thought cutting it off would deter me. It did, for a time. But I returned. And I killed him, using the very same knife that removed my nose. This knife right here."

Without wasting another second, he rushed toward me, blade aiming for my stomach.

I leapt out of his path, jumping off the walkway and into the pool of churning machinery. A turbine was right in front of me, with long, steel arms that pulled water deeper into the building. The turbine's movements formed waves that almost made me lose my balance. It was only through the grace of God that I remained standing and, with one unsteady leap, cleared the turbine's arms.

A second turbine lay in front of me, moving at the same speed as the first. Behind me, I heard a splash as Corinthian Black entered the water. I allowed myself a quick glance over my shoulder, seeing him confronting the turbine I had just cleared. The knife remained clenched in his fist.

I tried to jump over the sloshing arms of

the second turbine. This time, I wasn't so lucky. My right boot caught on one of the moving arms, which sent me flailing over the machinery.

I fell facefirst into the pool, mere inches from a massive wooden waterwheel that stretched to the ceiling. It rumbled just beyond my head, and for a moment I thought I was going to be either crushed beneath it or scooped up and carried skyward. I only managed to avoid those fates by twisting my body under the water and rolling away from the rotating monstrosity.

Pushing off the floor, I managed to get to my feet again. Looking behind me, I saw that Mr. Black had cleared the first turbine and was now attempting to do the same with the second. All that separated us was a single turbine wheel and its iron arms pushing back and forth through the water.

Behind me, the twenty-foot-tall waterwheel continued to roll, blocking me. My first instinct was to try to duck through it to the other side. But the waterwheel — a wide and heavy thing — had too many support spokes to do so. Not that it mattered much, for beyond it was nothing but a stone wall.

I spun around again, seeing Corinthian Black leap over the turbine's arms. He landed in the water a few feet to my right, lunging toward me with his knife raised.

Helpless, I pivoted and grabbed the edge of

the waterwheel. My hands slipped an inch or so before my fingers caught one of the wheel's blades. I gripped it with all my strength, a slave to its powerful roll as it lifted me off my feet.

I continued to be swept upward as Mr. Black surged ahead, the knife slicing thin air. The blade struck the outer rim of the waterwheel, right near my knees. The tip sank into the wood, the motion of the wheel jerking it upward and away before Mr. Black had a chance to pry it out again.

While he leapt against the waterwheel in a vain attempt to retrieve the knife, I let go and dropped to the water a yard or so away from him. My goal was to escape the same way I had come, jumping over both turbines and back to the walkway. Mr. Black, however, was too quick and determined to let me do that. He turned away from the waterwheel and slammed into me, sending us both tumbling sideways into the drink.

I thrashed in the water, trying to kick him off me, but he was too strong. Shockingly so. I found myself helpless in his grip.

He scrambled on top of me, hands grasping my throat. His face pressed close to mine. Hot, stinking breath hissed through the twin holes where his nose should have been. His eyes locked on my own, angry, fierce, and confused.

As he stared at me, emotion flickered over

his deformed face. Recognition. A dawning realization on his part that I couldn't begin to understand.

"Columbus Holmes?" he said in an awed, surprised voice.

His fingers were still tight around my neck and it took all the breath I had left to ask, "How do you know who I am?"

"How are you still alive?" he asked. "All of us thought you were dead."

"Why would my fate be any concern of yours?"

Corinthian Black smiled again — a rictus grin that struck fear into my very soul.

"I don't think I'm allowed to answer that," he said. "You'll have to ask your mother."

In one swift and startling motion, he shoved my head underwater as his grip tightened around my throat. I struggled beneath him, thrashing my legs and swinging my fists. Yet the more I fought, the weaker I became. Mr. Black was too heavy, too strong.

Inches above my face, the water's surface was an undulating veil through which I could only see his narrowed eyes, open mouth, and wide, flaring nostrils.

All the while, the breath was being squeezed out of me. Gurgling sounds erupted from my constricted throat. My heart, beating wildly not a minute earlier, had started to slow. A bubble of pain formed in my chest, growing and expanding until I thought it would break right through my rib cage.

By then, all the fight had left my body. My legs went still, ignoring my desperate desire to keep them moving. My arms dropped to my sides. In that moment, I knew I was going to die. The life was going to be choked right out of me in a pool of water, just like my mother.

I thought of Annalise Holmes just then. As my body weakened further and the pain in my chest grew, I wondered if this was how she had felt right before her death. Did she fight for her life, as I had tried doing? Did her limbs grow numb with the same ferocious speed? And, most of all, did she think of me in her final moments, as I did of her?

Not wanting to end my life gazing up at the noseless face of Corinthian Black, I was about to close my eyes. My sight had already dimmed. Darkness was approaching from all sides.

Then I heard a sound. Sharp and quick, it was muffled by the water in my ears and the hum of the machinery. But there was no mistaking what it was.

A gunshot.

Drops of blood fell into the water around me, blooming into crimson clouds. Above me, Corinthian Black's expression changed once more. His eyes widened and his mouth opened with a surprised howl. His once-tight grip loosened around my neck as he slumped sideways, knocking against the waterwheel before being pulled beneath it.

I sat up, gulping in air while shaking the water from my face.

Standing in front of me was Lucy Collins. Her drenched hair had come loose and now hung over her shoulders in soaked tendrils. The tunnel from the Pastor residence to the waterworks had left streaks of mud on her skirt. And in her hand was the pistol that she had promised to use only in the event of an emergency.

VI

I'm afraid I can't adequately describe how I felt upon seeing Lucy. I've now spent countless hours trying to summon the right words to express the relief, disbelief, and utter joy I experienced. But, in this case, words have failed me.

Instead, I can only tell you my actions following Lucy's surprise rescue.

I stood, my legs wobbly, and stumbled toward her. Lucy rushed to help me, the skirt of her dress swirling in the water around her. When we reached each other, I fell against her, overcome with gratitude.

"Thank God," I whispered. "Thank God you were here."

"Actually," Lucy said, "it's *me* you should be thank—"

She didn't have time to finish her sentence. I wouldn't let her. Cupping her flushed cheeks in my still-trembling hands, I silenced her with a kiss.

Her lips were as soft as I expected them to be, and her kiss was both tender and forceful. And the longer it lasted, the more I became lost in it. I didn't exactly know why I was kissing her. Nor did I care if we would ever kiss again. All I knew was, in that moment, it felt like exactly the right thing to do.

The regret came later, once we broke away from each other, both of us short of breath and me quite dizzy.

"I'm so sorry," I quickly said.

Lucy looked at me, head tilted in a way that left me wondering if she was either confused or disappointed. "You're *sorry*?"

"I have no idea why I just did that."

"You don't?"

"Well, I —"

My mind, churning as fast as the machinery all around us, struggled to come up with an excuse. In truth, there wasn't one. I had kissed Lucy. Whether it was out of gratitude or desire, I truly didn't know. Not then. Not even now.

Fortunately, I didn't need to explain any further. For at that moment, Inspector William Barclay and a dozen policemen swarmed the waterworks.

They seemed to come from all directions,

splashing through the water and running across the catwalks over it. When I caught sight of Barclay, he was at the very same spot where I had come face-to-face with Corinthian Black.

Peering down at Lucy and me, he said, "Are either of you hurt?"

"No," I replied. "What about Stokely?"

"Mrs. Pastor's butler? He's badly hurt, but alive," Barclay said. "A doctor is stitching him up as we speak."

I exhaled a long sigh of relief. If Stokely had perished, I never would have forgiven myself for leaving his side.

"I'd like to see him, if I could," I said.

"Later," Barclay replied. "First, could one of you please tell me what in tarnation happened here?"

Explaining the situation to Barclay was easier said than done, although Lucy and I certainly tried. I started off by giving him a tour of the waterworks and the two corpses that rested within.

Corinthian Black was first, found wedged between the waterwheel and the stone wall behind it. Lucy's single shot had struck him in the back of the neck, killing him within seconds.

I felt no remorse about his death. He had ordered the murders of two people and tried to kill me, as well. His ultimate punishment was justified. If I felt anything while staring at his lifeless body, it was regret that I would never know how he was familiar with both me and my mother. Corinthian Black's secrets died with him.

Next on our morbid tour was the bee colony hidden in the upper reaches of the waterworks. More insects had made their escape through the hole in the roof, although quite a few still crawled over Claudia's corpse. Enough of her flesh was exposed to reveal the full extent of her wounds. Her entire body was pockmarked with stings.

As we left that strange and secret hive, I took one last look at Claudia's corpse. I doubted she had found the glory she was expecting. In fact, I doubted it ever existed in the first place.

I didn't tell Barclay much about why Claudia and Corinthian Black wanted both Sophie Kruger and Lenora Grimes Pastor dead. Since it was hard enough for me to fathom, I didn't think it wise to try to explain it to him. I simply told him the basic truth — that Claudia had confessed to both murders, stabbed Stokely then brought about her own death via the bees. As for Mr. Black, I told Barclay that he had confessed to coercing Claudia into committing the murders. I left out any mention of the Praediti, my opinion being that the less Barclay knew about them, the better off he would be.

After that, it was back to Lucy's house,

where we found Leslie Dutton in police custody and her husband and stepdaughter consoling each other. Everyone was still present, from P. T. Barnum to Mrs. Mueller to Jasper Willoughby.

"What in heaven happened to you?" he asked, clearly surprised by my sorry state. "You look half dead."

I looked down at my clothes, seeing them stained by water, mud, and blood. When I ran a hand through my hair, I felt a wild patch of wet and untamed locks. Dirt was still streaked across my face and Stokely's blood continued to color my hands.

"That's better than fully dead," I said. "Which is what almost happened."

Before I could elaborate, a policeman pulled Jasper away to be questioned with the others about what had occurred during the séance at Lucy's house. As everyone who had been present — Lucy included — was ushered into another room, I couldn't help but notice the queer looks they sent my way.

No doubt, they were as confused by the events of the séance as I was. Not only had Mrs. Pastor spoken from beyond the grave, but the speaking had been done through *me.* I didn't know why or how, but it left me with a worried feeling that everyone's strange expressions only amplified. Watching them leave the room, I feared that whatever had happened in Lucy's séance room would happen again. If it did, I'd have yet another secret to suppress.

I would have continued to dwell on that fact had Barclay not grabbed my arm and led me from the room. At first, I thought he was taking me to join the others for a thorough questioning. Instead, he guided me out of Lucy's house entirely and into a waiting police coach.

"Where are we going?" I asked as the coach started to roll.

"I'm taking you home. Your day has been long enough."

"But what about Stokely?" I asked. "And Mrs. Collins?"

I longed to speak to them both, but especially Lucy. My actions in the waterworks required at least some form of explanation, even though I still hadn't come up with one.

Yet it wasn't to be. At least not on that night.

"They'll be there in the morning. Besides, I have something I need to tell you."

"Which is?"

From the way Barclay shifted uncomfortably, I knew an attempt at an apology would soon follow.

"I just want you to know," he said, "that I understand how difficult this past week was for you. While I never for a second doubted your innocence, I didn't make it any easier for you. I'm truly sorry about that, and I hope you can forgive me."

I looked out the coach window at the city gliding by. It was a clear night, the stars bright and glistening. Below them, Philadelphia was hushed and calm, rare for a place so bustling and crowded during the day. It was a city of people colliding with one another, arguing with one another, killing one another. So many inhabitants, and yet I considered very few of them my friends. Barclay, for all his annoying habits, was one of them. The knowledge of that put me in a generous mood.

"You're forgiven," I said. "You were only doing your job."

Barclay harrumphed. "Not very well, seeing that you're the one who found out who killed Mrs. Pastor and Sophie Kruger. You even exposed a murder I didn't know existed."

"In a strange way," I said, "I suppose we owe a debt to Mrs. Dutton."

It was clear that, despite her malfeasance, Leslie Dutton had been of valuable service. Her attempt to kill the already-dead Mrs. Pastor had left behind the puncture wound that pointed to murder in the first place. Without it, no one might ever have known that Lenora Grimes Pastor was poisoned with bee venom. She ended up unwittingly exposing two murders when it would have appeared there were none.

"She's still a murderess," Barclay said.

"And she will be punished as such."

Bettina Dutton entered my thoughts just then. The poor girl, still coping with the loss of her mother, now had to deal with the fact that it had actually been murder. It would be hard for her. I knew that from experience. But I hoped, unlike my situation, it would bring her and her father closer. Judging from the way they had been embracing at Lucy's house, I suspect it already had.

"That must have been quite a performance you put on during that fake séance of yours," Barclay said. "You had everyone in the room convinced it was real."

Again, that was another thing he was better off knowing little about. Not that I could explain it with any coherence. Besides, I was all too happy to pretend it was a grand ruse, expertly performed.

"Perhaps there's a bit of showman in me," I said. "But it wasn't just all my doing. I had a good deal of help from Mrs. Collins."

"Now that this is all over, do you still plan on associating with her?" Barclay asked.

Alas, that was a question for which I had no answer. Lucy saving my life and my subsequent reaction to it certainly complicated matters. Complication — that seemed to be her specialty. I thought about how uncomplicated my life had been before we met. Less than a week later, everything about my world was now askew. And while some of it was undeniably enjoyable, I was also eager to settle back into my old, run-of-the-mill existence.

"I suppose I must," I said, choosing my words carefully. "She did save my life, after all. I owe her some form of thanks. I think I'll start by trying to convince you that she didn't kill Declan O'Malley."

Barclay gave me a quizzical look. "How much do you really know about all that?"

"Nothing," I lied.

My old friend didn't believe me, as evidenced by the irritated sigh that followed my response. Still, he said, "I suppose it's no concern of mine. The police in Richmond can do what they want. As for me, I consider that particular case to be closed."

"I think," I said, "that's the best course of action."

It was past midnight by the time we reached Locust Street. Despite the late hour, I invited Barclay inside for a drink. I wanted to raise a toast to celebrate the solving of Mrs. Pastor's murder. But when the coach stopped in front of my house, I saw another one waiting there.

Inside was Mr. Hamilton Gray, who yelled at me from the coach window, "Well done, Clark! Very well done!"

Seeing my former editor, Barclay said, "It seems you have company."

"Yes," I replied. "Unwanted company."

I left Barclay's coach and stood beside Mr.

Gray's. He leaned out the coach window, so excited that I detected traces of pink in his usually colorless cheeks.

"You've made our newspaper proud, Mr. Clark," he said.

"I thought I was no longer a respected employee of the *Evening Bulletin.*"

"After what happened tonight," Mr. Gray said, "consider yourself our most respected employee."

"How do you already know about tonight's events?"

"I have my ways," Mr. Gray replied. "One of which is paying a policeman a small sum to inform me if something exciting happens. He told me all about your adventure this evening. Now you must write the whole thing down. Get in and I'll discuss it with you."

Reluctantly I climbed into the coach, Mr. Gray not caring that I was dirt covered and damp. He was too busy presenting his grand plan to notice how mussed and weary I truly was.

"Much like the article you wrote after Mrs. Pastor's death, we would like you to write a first-hand account about how you solved her murder," he said. "It's quite a story, I'm sure. Our rivals will be positively sick with jealousy."

So, after practically firing me, the *Bulletin* now wanted me back, all because I had solved a few murders. It made me so angry I had

half a mind to tell Mr. Gray to take his carriage and drive it straight into the Delaware.
Yet one of the things I had missed terribly
during my time under suspicion was being a
reporter. I knew I could have gone to the
Public Ledger or the *Times,* but that wouldn't
have been nearly as much fun. At the *Bulletin,*
I now had leverage.

"I'll do it," I said, "on one condition."

"Anything," Mr. Gray replied.

"When this is finished, I want to go back to
my old job, writing about crimes in the city."

Mr. Gray heartily agreed and instructed me
to report to the *Bulletin* office bright and early
the next morning.

I did as I was told, returning to that dim
tomb on Chestnut Street for what felt like
the first time in ages. I took great pleasure in
sitting down at my desk and writing how,
after witnessing it, I had come to solve the
death of Lenora Grimes Pastor.

It wasn't the truth, of course. Few things
you read in a newspaper ever are. Unlike this
tome, it was mostly fiction, with a few bits of
truth scattered about to make it seem legitimate.

Still, it was enough to satisfy Mr. Gray and
the bloodthirsty readers of Philadelphia. And
when it was printed the next evening, I found
myself in fashion once again. In the days that
followed, my home was inundated with well-
wishers.

The most impressive of the lot was P. T. Barnum, who came around before departing the city. Sitting in my parlor, sipping tea presented to him by an awestruck Mrs. Patterson, he addressed an issue that had been bothering me since the séance at Lucy's house.

"You've probably been curious, good man, about what myself and the others told the police," he said in typically grand fashion.

"I have," I admitted.

"And I suppose you were nervous about what we revealed regarding your . . . gifts."

"Quite nervous."

"There's no need to be," Mr. Barnum replied. "We lied. Every single one of us. It was all Mrs. Collins's idea, of course, but the rest of us agreed. While you appeared to be as fine a medium as Mrs. Pastor herself, it was clear to all of us that you had no control over what was taking place."

"I didn't," I said. "I'm still not sure how it happened."

"Which is why, dear boy, we told the policeman questioning us that it was all an elaborate trick. If we had told the truth — if the public knew you truly could contact the dead — you'd be overrun with people begging for your services. It was obvious that's the last thing you desire."

"It is," I said. "The absolute last thing."

At this, Mr. Barnum shook his head. "I

must admit, I find that an utter shame."

"A shame, sir?"

"Why, if I had the faintest inkling that you were interested, I'd draw up a contract and take you on tour. Imagine the crowds you'd draw. Even better, Mr. Clark, imagine all the money we'd make."

While Mr. Barnum's eyes were aglow as he spoke, the very thought of being a touring medium repulsed me. I had already spent enough time living out of a suitcase and following my parents from city to city. It had ended badly for all of us, and no amount of money or persuasion on P. T. Barnum's part could make me return to that life.

"Your suggestion, while flattering, isn't something I'm interested in."

"But if you change your mind —"

"I won't," I assured him. "I'm quite happy where I am."

Mr. Barnum stood and shook my hand. "Then I wish you the best, Mr. Clark. As for me, I must keep on looking for that new venture Mrs. Pastor hinted at. I hope I find it soon, and when I do, I hope it's something grand and spectacular. This world needs a bit more spectacle. Don't you agree?"

"I do," I replied. "Very much."

Strangely, P. T. Barnum wasn't the most important visitor to my house that day. Two more came by later that evening, arriving separately but remaining inextricably entwined in my thoughts.

The first was Violet Willoughby, who rang the bell shortly after dinner. Still without a butler, I answered the door myself. Seeing Violet, looking as pretty as ever, made my heart skip with happiness.

"I won't blame you," she said, "if you slam that door right in my face."

"I could never do that," I replied. "Not in a million years."

Violet then rushed to embrace me, enveloping me in a flurry of kisses and an equal number of apologies. "I was such a fool, Edward. An utter, dithering fool. Jasper told me everything."

I pushed her away for a moment, holding her at arm's length. *"Everything?"*

"About the fake séance," Violet said. "He told me that you and Mrs. Collins had planned it so thoroughly. No wonder the two of you had been spending so much time together."

I blinked in grateful disbelief. "That's what he told you?"

"Of course. When I asked him why you had requested his presence, he told me it was because you wanted him to witness it and report back to me about how hard you had been working. Now I understand why you couldn't tell me everything about your investigation. In order for the séance to be a success, you needed to keep the entire thing secret."

I let her envelop me again, well aware that I owed all those embraces and kisses to Jasper Willoughby. I felt bad about doubting his innocence, especially based on something as tangential as a hive of bees. But I also got the sense Jasper had lied to his sister for reasons that had nothing to do with our happiness. He wanted me to remain silent, just as he had done.

"Will you accept my apology?" Violet asked. "Will you forgive my foolishness?"

There was no question about that. I had forgiven Violet the moment I saw her at the door. Yet my thoughts turned to Lucy. Honestly, how could they not? I had held her in my arms and pressed my lips upon hers. A part of me longed to do both again. Yet I also hated myself for thinking that way, causing guilt to settle over me like a woolen blanket — heavy and suffocating.

"Will you, Edward?" Violet asked again. "Can we be engaged once more?"

My emotions consisted of two equal parts — assent and hesitation. I desperately wanted to spend the rest of my life with Violet. And yet . . . I didn't. Those opposing feelings made it almost impossible to give her a definitive answer.

"Well, I —"

Because she excelled at creating complications, Lucy Collins chose that precise moment to also come to my house. Unlike Violet, she ignored the doorbell and burst right in, a flush on her cheeks and fire in her eyes.

"Edward, we must talk about —"

Lucy halted when she saw us. Her demeanor immediately changed, just as it had done on the riverbank days earlier. Fast and startling, it brought to mind a storm cloud darkening a bright summer day. Her green eyes dimmed, her spine straightened, and the rosy hue in her cheeks faded.

"I'm sorry," she quickly said. "I didn't know you had a guest."

Violet released me and spent a moment sizing up Lucy.

"Are you Mrs. Collins?" she asked.

Lucy nodded. "Miss Willoughby, I presume?"

Violet, to my great consternation, rushed to Lucy and enfolded her in an embrace almost as tight as the one she had given me.

"By all means, call me Violet," she said brightly. "It's a joy to meet you at last!"

"It's lovely to meet you, too," Lucy replied, with far less enthusiasm.

She looked at me over Violet's shoulder, her expression unreadable. Like a character from myth gazing directly at Medusa, Lucy's face had turned to stone.

Violet noticed none of this, not even when

she broke the embrace to say, "I think what you and Edward did was wonderful. So inventive of you both. And then to save his life after that! Why, Lucy — May I call you that? Lucy?"

"Of course."

"Why, Lucy, I owe you all the thanks in the world!"

"It was nothing," Lucy said, her voice still a dull murmur. "Mr. Clark would have done the same for me. In fact . . . he already has."

"Still, thanks is due," I said. I, too, tried to keep emotion out of my voice, lest either one of them catch on to my true, conflicted feelings. "And it's nice to see you again, Mrs. Collins. Have you been well since we last saw each other?"

"Quite well," Lucy answered, shooting a sidelong glance at Violet. "I see you're also doing fine."

"You said you came by to discuss something with Edward?" Violet said. "Don't let my presence bother you."

Lucy opened her mouth, then closed it again without making a sound. It was one of the very few times I had seen her at a loss for words. When she did find her voice, it was to say, "I stopped by to thank you, Mr. Clark. For writing such a fine article in the *Bulletin*."

"That's all?" I asked.

"Of course," Lucy said. "Unless *you* have something you wish to discuss."

"I don't."

"Then I wish you both a good night."

Lucy accepted another of Violet's enthusiastic embraces, gave me a cold nod, then left just as quickly as she had arrived. I should have let her depart without another word. It certainly would have been the easy thing to do. Yet there was something about her stony demeanor that demanded I go after her.

"I'll be right back," I told Violet before rushing outside.

Lucy must have been walking as fast as her feet could carry her, for when I reached her, she was already at her coach, preparing to open the mismatched door.

"Lucy, wait!"

"I'm a very busy woman, Mr. Clark," she said as she gathered her skirts to climb inside the coach. "And I'm certain Miss Willoughby doesn't want to be kept waiting."

I grabbed her elbow, pulling her away from the door. Thomas, sitting at the reins, yelled a few obscenities my way, but Lucy silenced him with a raised hand.

"What do you want, Edward?" she said with a sigh.

"Are you certain there's nothing else you want to talk about?"

"Yes," Lucy answered. "Quite certain."

"It's just that . . . after what happened between us —"

"Nothing happened," Lucy said in a clipped

voice. "At least, nothing of consequence."

"Nothing of consequence," I repeated. "That's right. I just wanted to be clear about that."

"Of course it's clear," Lucy said. "We simply let our emotions get the better of us. I'm sure it will never happen again."

"It won't. There's Violet, for one thing. We were apart for a time, yes, but now it seems like we'll —"

"Be reuniting?"

"Exactly," I said. "I have my job back. And my good name."

"I'm happy for you," Lucy replied with nary a trace of happiness in her voice. "Are *you* happy?"

"Yes. I suppose I'm back to being the man I was before we met."

Lucy placed a hand against my cheek. The silk of her glove was cool and smooth against my skin, like a balm. I closed my eyes, just for a moment, to bask in the sensation. When I opened them, I saw Lucy staring at me, disappointment in her green eyes.

"Oh, Edward," she said, removing her hand. "I'm afraid I misunderstood you. Remember how I once told you we were very much alike?"

"Of course," I replied.

"I was wrong. We're not alike at all."

"Why do you say that?"

"Because," Lucy said, "I at least know what

I want out of life."

She turned and, without a single glance backward, climbed into her coach. Thomas then set the horses in motion and they rumbled out of sight.

With Lucy gone, a sense of finality pierced my heart. It was a strange sensation — part loss, part regret — that made me want to run after the coach and stop its retreat. It was possible, I knew. I still heard the faint churn of the coach's wheels and the dull clop of the Cleveland Bays' hooves. Catching up to it would be easy. And when I did, I could take back all the things I had said and tell Lucy what I really thought and how I truly felt.

Yet I stayed where I was, wondering when — or if — I would ever see her again. And if I never did lay eyes on her in the future, I wondered how much I would ultimately come to regret it.

Lucy, you see, was right about me. No, I didn't know what I wanted out of life. But I knew what I *needed* — an existence far different from the way in which I was brought up. One free of endless travel and illusions and shame. One exactly like what I had created for myself before I ever met Mrs. Lucy Collins.

A life such as that required a wife who was calm and trusting and kind. Someone from a proper family who behaved in a proper manner. Someone who worried about nothing more than pretty frocks and hats and the importance of having a bite of cake.

Violet Willoughby was the kind of woman I needed to spend the rest of my life with. And if my heart also possibly desired someone else, it would be my duty to deny it. Violet, after all, deserved my full affection, and I was prepared to give it to her.

Without wasting another moment, I marched back into the house. Violet remained in the foyer, hands folded demurely in front of her.

"I wasn't expecting you to be gone so long," she said. "Is something wrong?"

I kissed her on the cheek and pulled her into the tightest embrace I'd ever given her. "Nothing's wrong at all."

"So you forgive me?"

"Of course," I said. "Now, would you do me the honor of once again agreeing to be my wife?"

Violet rested her head on my shoulder. "Of course, silly. All I ask is that, no matter what trouble might occur in the future, you tell me about it. No more secrets."

"I promise," I said. "No more secrets."

VII

But of course there were secrets. With me, there always would be. Because no matter how much Violet loved and trusted me, there was one thing I couldn't share with her. Not then. Not ever.

There was, in fact, only one person with whom I could speak freely about my past. So when Sunday arrived, I returned to Eastern State Penitentiary.

The guard, Callahan, was again there to greet me, using the long walk down Cell Block 7 to tell me how much he had enjoyed my article in the *Evening Bulletin.*

"It seems you've had quite an adventure, Mr. Clark," he said. "Now I know why you were so eager to visit Magellan Holmes the other night."

I stopped so fast that my boots squeaked on the cell block floor. "You do?"

"You can't fool me," Callahan said. "No, sir. I know exactly what you were up to."

"And what" — I cleared my throat, hoping my utter fear of being exposed didn't shine through — "do you assume we were talking about?"

"Magic, naturally," the guard replied. "In regards to that séance you pulled off. I'd wager that such an elaborate trick required expert planning, so you came here to ask the world's greatest magician for advice."

"You're right about that, Mr. Callahan," I said, relief filling me from head to foot. "I can't fool you. That's exactly what Mr. Holmes and I talked about."

"Did he tell you anything useful?"

"If he hadn't, then I wouldn't have come back here to thank him."

Callahan, his curiosity sated, allowed me to walk the rest of the way by myself. Soon I was standing before the cell of Magellan Holmes, alone with him once again.

This time, my father stood in the center of his cell. The window sliced into the ceiling cast a narrow sliver of sunlight over him, illuminating his hair and his drawn, pale face. He wasn't pleased to see me, nor did I expect him to be.

"I told you to stay away," he said. "You should learn to take my advice, Mr. Clark."

I gripped the door of his cell, in no mood for his disdain. "Corinthian Black is dead. He tried to kill me, but someone else got to him before he could finish the deed."

My father did a poor job of hiding his surprise. Sudden concern for my well-being was etched across his face. "Why are you telling me this?"

"Because you know who he is," I said. "And I know he was a member of the Praediti."

My father rushed to the door, just as I'd expected he would. "You promised to never say that word again!"

"Things have changed, Father," I said. "And I require answers. Now tell me, who are they?"

"Trust me, Columbus. You need to leave them alone."

"I no longer have a choice." I thought about Corinthian Black, so surprised to realize my true identity, and his ominous warning about there being many more members of the Praediti. If he knew who I was, then others might as well. "You need to tell me everything."

Clearly, that was the last thing my father wanted to do. He paced his cell like a caged animal, tormented by the decision he faced. Eventually, he returned to the door, curling his fingers around the slats of woven iron.

"What do you need to know?" he quietly asked.

"The meaning of the name, for starters."

"Praediti," my father said. "It means 'the gifted ones.' "

Claudia's voice shimmered in my memory, echoing that strange chant. *Gloria enim Praediti.* Now I knew what it meant.

For the glory of the gifted ones.

"Who are they and how are they gifted?"

The once-amazing Magellan backed away from the door. He sat down on his cot, hands on his knees, unable to face me. "Do you believe in ghosts, Columbus?"

A week earlier, I would have said no. But by then I knew better. I had seen them. I had spoken to them. Even more, one had spoken through *me.*

"Yes."

"That's good," my father said. "Because they exist. They roam this earth as surely as you or I do. Few can see them, which is as it should be. They are things half in shadow, glimpsed briefly and not fully understood. The Praediti consist of people who know these spirits exist, people capable of contacting the dead."

"Mediums?"

"Oh, they're more than that. Not only can they communicate with the dead, but they can call upon them to do their bidding."

"I don't understand," I said. "What could a ghost possibly do?"

"Plenty," my father replied. "Let's say you want to drive someone out of a home. If you possess this gift, you can summon a spirit who might agree to haunt the home for you. They're also very strong. Gather enough spirits together and they could lift an entire house if you wanted them to. But those are rather innocent examples."

"Are they capable of doing harm?"

"If they wanted to, yes. It all depends on the spirit. Just like those still living, some spirits are good and some are evil. How a person behaved in life usually determines how they'll be in the spirit realm. Fortunately, for centuries, the people with this gift mostly used it to entertain. So-called wizards and witches and conjurers. They were simply among the few who could cooperate with spirits."

"And some mediums," I said, thinking of

the instruments that had floated around Mrs. Pastor's séance room.

"And magicians," my father added.

He looked at me then, curious to see my reaction. I'm afraid I disappointed him, because I was too stunned to react much at all. Perhaps I blinked a few times, or gulped in surprise. But for the most part, I remained still, gripping the iron of the door like my life was at stake.

"You?" I said, dumbfounded. "You possess this gift?"

It all made sense then. The Amazing Magellan, after all, had gained world renown by floating over theater audiences and causing giant beasts to levitate. Yes, he created some illusions the old-fashioned way. Those tricks and sleights of hand were something I had seen and picked up over time. But the bigger illusions, the ones he practiced in secrecy, hadn't been illusions at all.

They were the work of the spirit world.

"Many of the Amazing Magellan's greatest tricks were helped by spirits in my employ," my father confessed. "I had several of them, mostly beloved family members who had passed on long ago. But you're wrong about one thing. I have *never* had the power to communicate with the dead."

He didn't need to say any more. In that moment, I understood everything.

"Mother did," I said.

My father nodded gravely.

"I was called the Amazing Magellan, but *she* was the amazing one. It was all her, Columbus. She summoned the spirits and told them what to do. I simply made it look like magic."

"But how did she get this power?"

"She was born with it," my father said. "Some think it's hereditary, so one of her parents most likely possessed it as well. I suspect they never even knew it."

"Hereditary," I repeated, my voice made dull from shock.

My father noticed the tone and stood. He approached the cell door slowly, his eyes aflame with worry.

"Please, Columbus," he said quietly. "Please tell me you didn't inherit it from her. I beg of you, Son. Tell me you don't have the same gift your mother had."

I longed to tell him exactly what he wanted to hear. He looked so concerned about me, his entire body coiled with fear, that I considered lying just to spare him from the truth. But I feared it would only silence him, and I needed to know more. Not just about my mother's powers, but about my own.

"I can't," I said.

"What have you noticed? What have you seen?"

I told him everything then, from speaking with my mother to visions of long-dead friends roaming my bedroom. I talked of the table-tipping incident in which Lenora Grimes Pastor informed me of her murder and of the bee that had flown from her mouth, leading me back to Sophie Kruger. Finally, I described the séance at Lucy's house, where Mrs. Pastor spoke through me, her voice becoming my own.

"This is terrible," my father said once I had finished. "You have no idea how much danger you're in."

"But why?"

"Because of the Praediti, of course!" he snapped. "Because of what they have planned."

I was plunged again into a pool of confusion. Every time my father began to make sense, he would suddenly veer off into nonsense.

"What do they plan?"

"Earlier, you asked if a spirit could cause harm," my father said. "They can, if the spirit has enough ill will toward the living. Now, imagine if many people with this power summoned the most evil spirits they could find. Think of the damage they could cause."

"*That's* what the Praediti want to do?" I asked. "What could causing damage possibly bring?"

"Power," my father said, unblinking. "Unbridled power, the likes of which man has never seen."

"But you said most people were like you and Mother, using it for tricks or conjuring."

"Which is all true," he said. "Not everyone who shares the Praediti's gifts shares their mind-set. There were many out there like your mother, content to use their gifts for innocent purposes. Some were eventually recruited by the Praediti through nefarious means. Those who refused to join were killed."

Of course. *Join us or pay the consequences.* Mrs. Pastor and Sophie Kruger had done just that.

"How long have the Praediti been doing this?"

"Quite some time. The first murder was fifteen years ago." My father's eyes rose to meet mine. "When they killed your mother."

His words entered me like a poison, forcing my blood into stillness.

"That . . . that can't be," I said. "*You* killed her. *You* confessed to it."

"Yes," my father said. "But only to protect you. The Praediti had been trying for years to recruit your mother. She refused to even consider the idea. To get away from them, we decided to tour the world. But they followed us. Then came the threats against your mother. When that didn't work, they threatened me. After that, the Praediti threatened to go after what we loved the most — you. So we returned to Philadelphia to plan our escape, not just from them, but from the stage entirely. Our homecoming performance would also be our final one. After that, we were going to try to disappear, for real this time, and for good. Yet the Praediti learned about our plan."

"And they killed Mother."

My father, the once-amazing Magellan Holmes, nodded. A lifetime of sadness rested in that rise and fall of his head. My father was completely innocent. He loved my mother to the very end. Just like mine, his world had collapsed around him that long-ago Independence Day.

Words can't describe the sense of relief that washed over me. It was like a baptism, leaving me light and unblemished. Although I had begun to cry, releasing tears held back for fifteen years, it was from joy, not sorrow.

"I'm so sorry," I sobbed. "I hated you for so long, Father. All those years, I despised you for something you didn't do."

"You have nothing to apologize for," my father quietly said. "It was for the best."

I wiped my face, my knuckles damp and salty. "Why did you take the blame? You've been here for so many years."

"Because I knew it would make things safer for you. With your mother gone and me in prison, I hoped the Praediti would simply leave you alone. That's why you must continue the ruse you've already started. You *must* remain Edward Clark. You're safe as long as they believe Columbus Holmes is dead."

His words might have made sense to him, but not to me. Now that I knew he was innocent, I wanted Magellan Holmes to be my father again, not a stranger rotting in a prison cell.

"Tell me where to find them," I said. "I'm friends with important people. We can bring the Praediti to justice."

My father managed a sad smile. "It's not that simple, Columbus. There are too many of them."

"Then what about the person solely responsible for killing Mother? Do you know who did it? Was it Corinthian Black?"

"No, although you are correct in one regard. We did know each other. We moved in the same circles, Corinthian and I. But we chose different paths."

"But did he kill Mother?" I asked, this time with more urgency.

"I don't know!" Magellan Holmes averted his eyes, too ashamed to look at me. "I never saw who did it. All I saw was your mother, already dead and floating in that godforsaken glass tank. Then I caught sight of someone running out of the theater. I ran, too, intent on catching them. But it was of no use. Your mother's killer was too fast. I only got a few blocks before I realized what had really happened, and what I had to do. And that was to take the blame in order to protect you."

"So Mother's killer could still be out there."

My father turned his back to me, unwilling to let me see his fear, his grief, his shame. "Most likely, yes."

"Then there's still a chance we can catch him and prove your innocence," I said. "You must tell me everything you remember about that night."

Thoughts tumbled through my mind as I already began to plan this great undertaking. I would recount to Barclay what my father had told me, and he would properly investigate. I would help, of course, using my resources at the *Evening Bulletin* and doing everything in my power to secure my father's release.

Yet the plan vanished when I looked into my father's eyes. There was no spark there, no sign of hope.

"I know what you're thinking, Columbus," he said. "And it's useless. Nothing will change what happened."

"But we at least have to try," I argued. "Do you plan on simply dying in here?"

"I have resigned myself to my fate. If my incarceration guarantees your safety and allows you to live another day, then I'm prepared to stay right where I am."

"But —"

"Don't argue with me, Columbus," my

father said. "I made up my mind a long time ago."

I knew I could spend an entire year trying in vain to get him to change his mind. That stubborn willingness to put my well-being before his erased all the hate I had felt toward him. Now, I loved my father even more.

"Can I at least visit you?" I said.

"I don't think that's a good idea. The guards might get suspicious."

"So?" I said. "You're the one behind bars. It's not like I can break you out."

"But one of them might be aligned with the Praediti. Don't you understand? They're *everywhere*, Columbus. Their ranks are far-reaching. You cannot trust anyone."

I gripped the door of his cell again. My father did the same, weaving his fingers between mine. It was the first time we had touched in fifteen years, and I wanted the sensation to last fifteen more.

"I'm going to visit you again," I told him. "Whether you like it or not. Damn my safety."

He smiled at my stubbornness. Like father, like son.

"You'd be putting yourself at risk," he said. "Still, I would enjoy that very much. But let some time pass first. And remember: continue to live life as you already do. Do not bring suspicion upon yourself."

"I won't," I said. "I swear it."

I released the door, letting my fingers slide

615

past my father's own before pulling away for good. Then, giving Magellan Holmes one last glance, I departed.

There was no sadness in my heart as I made the lengthy walk back to Callahan, waiting on the other end of the cell block. I knew I would see my father again soon enough. And if I had my way, it wouldn't be in that godforsaken prison but in the comfort and freedom of my home.

I had no intention of breaking my promise to him. I planned to live as I had been, going through life as Edward Clark. But also, I intended to learn all I could about the Praediti. I was going to find out who they were, where they were. And, when the time came, I would free my father and bring whoever killed my mother to justice.

Because even though I was Edward Clark on the outside, inside I was a new man.

I was once again Columbus Holmes.

POSTSCRIPT

There you have it — my full account of the murder of Lenora Grimes Pastor and how it came to be that I helped solve it. And while some parts may seem fantastical, I assure you that it's all true. I embellished nothing, for this particular tale needed no embellishment.

And yet there's still more to be told, for strange events continued to be a regular part of my life for quite some time thereafter. Much of it, however, can't fit into a single volume. It would be far too heavy to lift and very easily wear out a reader's welcome. This one is already too long as it is. So if you've made it this far, I thank and salute you.

But there are a few things I feel compelled to mention, mostly because Isabel, my dear granddaughter, demands it. She's been urging on — prodding might be more accurate — my progress all along, sometimes snatching pages from my hands before the ink has even dried on them. If she demands more, then more is what she shall get. She's spoiled, that one. Takes after her grandmother.

So, if you'll allow an old man to ramble on for just a few pages more, I'll tell you about what happened immediately after I left my father in that wretched prison cell. I returned home to Locust Street and found Stokely leaning against the stoop. Beneath his shirt, he later showed me, a bandage as wide as a pillowcase had been wrapped around his stomach. He also required a cane to help keep himself upright.

"Mister Clark," he said, mustering a smile even in his weakened state. "I've been waitin' for you."

"What are you doing out here?" I asked, surprised to see him out of the hospital so soon. "Come in, come in."

Even with the cane, he needed my assistance, which I was glad to give. Although his breathing was shallow and his steps weak — and although he constantly winced in pain — he was alive, which was frankly better than what both of us had expected.

"You should still be recuperating," I said as I eased him into the most comfortable chair in the parlor.

"I needed to thank you," Stokely replied. "You saved my life, Mister Clark. Just as sure as Missus Pastor did."

I sat across from him, undeserving of his thanks. "You're welcome, but there was no need to risk your health and come here. A

618

letter would have sufficed."

"It might have," Stokely said. "But I also came 'round for somethin' else. You see, I now find myself in need of a favor."

"Whatever it is, I'll do my best."

"Now that Missus Pastor can rest in peace, Mister Pastor plans on goin' back South to be with his people," Stokely said. "Can't say I blame him. He ain't got nothin' here anymore but bad memories. As for me, well, I don't ever want to go back there. That's where my bad memories are, see? I plan on stayin' right here. And, since I caught wind of the news that you might be needin' —"

I raised my hand to stop him. Stokely needed a job, and I refused to make him experience the indignity of having to ask for one. I would have gladly offered him enough money to live comfortably for a while if I hadn't known it would hurt his pride. Quite honestly, he had been injured enough.

"If you're wondering if I will let you come and work for me, the answer is yes," I said.

Stokely nodded his gratitude. "I'm a hard worker, Mister Clark. You won't regret it."

"I'm certain I won't. First, though, you need to get better. You'll be of no use if you don't give yourself time to heal."

"Thank you, Mister Clark."

"You're welcome. And from now on, I insist you call me Edward. I'm not one for formality."

Stokely winked. "Yes'sir . . . Edward."

The doorbell rang, prompting Stokely to try to stand and answer it. I stopped that nonsense at once, pushing him back into his chair and going to the door myself. Standing on the threshold, quite unexpectedly, was Lucy Collins. Dressed in a frock of yellow silk, she looked bright and lovely, like a spring daffodil blooming right on my doorstep.

"Oh, good," she said. "You're home."

"I am," I replied. "And thank you for ringing the bell this time."

Lucy's mouth drooped slightly, right on the edge of a frown. "I learned my lesson last time. By the way, how is Miss Willoughby?"

"She's fine. Is that why you're here? To talk about Violet?"

"I'm not," Lucy said. "This visit is solely about business."

Her green eyes, I noticed just then, glinted in a way that unnerved me. I had seen that mischievous gleam several times before, and I had the feeling I wasn't going to like whatever scheme she was currently plotting.

"I've been thinking about you quite a bit," she said.

"You have?"

"Yes. We make a good team, you and I."

I scratched my head. "Do we?"

"Of course. We solved a murder together."

"Two murders," I replied. "Three, if you count Laura Dutton's death."

"The exact number doesn't matter, Edward. What's important is that we work well together. And I'd like to continue that working relationship."

I must admit, I was intrigued. All of our other complications aside, I, too, had realized that we made a formidable team.

"What did you have in mind?"

"We can discuss that at length later," Lucy said. "But for now, I have a proposition for you. I have a client in need of a medium."

"Aren't *you* a medium?"

Lucy rolled her eyes. "A *true* medium. Someone who has the actual ability to communicate with the dead."

"I'm afraid you'll have to look elsewhere, because —"

"Don't you dare say you can't do it, Edward Clark," Lucy interjected. "I saw you with my own eyes. You were every bit as good as Lenora Grimes Pastor."

"No matter what you saw," I said, "I have no intention of becoming a medium."

"But this client is offering an obscene amount of money."

"I don't need any money."

"Well, I *do,*" Lucy said. "Because your article in the *Evening Bulletin* mentioned an elaborate fake séance at my home, the entire city now doubts my legitimacy."

While I should have considered that to be a good thing, I felt sorry about Lucy's plight.

She was on her own, doing everything she could to support a child. Then, of course, there was the fact that she had saved my life inside the Fairmount Water Works. I owed her something for that. So far, all I had given her was my thanks and a kiss, both of which had only served to complicate matters.

"Before I agree," I said, "what would this require me to do?"

"Exactly what you did the other day," Lucy replied. "Summon a spirit."

But I didn't know how I had summoned the spirit of Mrs. Pastor. I might have possessed the gift my mother had, but that didn't mean I knew how to use it.

"I doubt it's that easy."

"You accomplished it once," Lucy said. "Certainly you should be able to do it again."

"If I do this — and I still haven't made up my mind about it — you must promise me that it will only be this one time."

Lucy, impatient as ever, stomped her foot. "For heaven's sake, Edward. Just help me out in this instance. He's waiting."

"Your customer is with you *now*?" I asked.

"Of course."

She pointed to the street, where her battered coach was parked. Thomas, sitting up top in the driver's seat, spat a wad of tobacco juice in my direction. When the mismatched door to the coach opened, I was shocked to see none other than Jasper Willoughby

622

emerge. He ran up the steps and took my limp hand in his.

"Thank you for agreeing to do this, Edward," he said. "Please don't be angry at Mrs. Collins. This was all my idea."

"But why?" I asked.

"I was fascinated by what happened between you and Mrs. Pastor's spirit the other night. It was amazing to behold. I only hope that you can help me the same way you helped the others."

"Help you with what?"

"I need someone to help me speak with Joseph," he said.

"Joseph? Your dead brother?"

"I contacted him once before, when I attended a séance at Mrs. Pastor's house," Jasper explained. "Only something went wrong. Joseph, for reasons unknown, didn't depart after the séance."

"Where did he go?" I asked.

"He's stayed with me," Jasper said. "Haunting me. He's with me all the time now. Although I can't see him, I know here's there. I can feel it. And the things he's been doing! Tossing books around my room and moving chairs. It's a surprise I haven't gone mad. The only relief I have is when I drink. It dulls my mind enough to make his presence less frightening. But he's there. He's always there."

That explained the whiskey. And his presence in his old house. It even was the answer for the late-night noises in his bedroom that kept Violet awake.

"But what do you want me to do about it?" I asked.

"Talk to him," Jasper begged. "Please. Tell him to leave me alone. I can't bear it any longer."

Before the conversation could get any stranger, I pulled both Jasper and Lucy inside. Neither of them seemed surprised or bothered by the presence of Stokely, whom I was certain had heard every word. In fact, Lucy clapped her hands and said, "How nice! One more person for our séance."

Stokely tried to protest but Lucy helped him to his feet and led him and Jasper into the empty dining room. I had no choice but to follow, watching as she drew the curtains and placed a lit candle on the table. Then we all took our seats, me with Stokely to my left and Lucy to my right. Jasper sat across from me, keenly watching my every move.

"Before we do this," I told him, "you need to promise not to tell your sister. This must remain a secret. She can never know what I'm capable of."

"I promise. As your future brother-in-law, you have my word."

My gaze floated to Lucy, trying to see if the mention of Violet provoked any noticeable reaction. It didn't, for she merely said, "I suppose we should now form a circle."

I reached out to my left, feeling Stokely's massive, sandpapery hand wrap around mine.

To my right, I felt for Lucy's hand. We hesitated before joining them — an awkward dance of fingers — but when we connected, palm to palm, I felt a familiar pulse of excitement scurry up my arm. Was it unwelcome? Yes. Did I nonetheless enjoy it? Undoubtedly. And it made me question if continuing to associate with Lucy was the best idea.

By then, however, it was too late to back out. For Lucy nodded at me and said, "Edward, please begin."

"I-I don't know how," I sputtered.

I was still baffled by what was happening. It was as if I had been caught in a strong current and was being pulled, quickly and inexorably, under the waves.

"Just summon the spirits," Stokely told me. "That's what Missus Pastor did. If they're around, they'll appear."

I closed my eyes and, feeling like a fool, spoke to the air above the table. "Um, spirits from the Great Beyond. Are any of you there . . . ?"

"It needs to be more forceful," Lucy prodded.

"Yeah," Stokely said. "Say it like you mean it."

I cleared my throat and, as forcefully as I could, again said, "Spirits of the Great

Beyond, if you are present in this room, show yourselves!"

A breeze entered the dining room. Nothing like the gale we had experienced at Lucy's house, this was a light wind, soft and refreshing. It caressed my hair before swirling around the room. Opening my eyes, I saw a familiar black fog expanding just above the table's surface. Soon Lenora Grimes Pastor was there, those startling eyes of hers locking onto mine.

"Why, Mr. Clark, I wasn't expecting to see you again so soon."

"I'm surprised to see you myself," I said. "It wasn't my intention to summon you."

Mrs. Pastor gave me a bemused smile. *"That's easy to explain. I am what you might call your spirit guide, just as Philip was for me. Think of me as a bridge, connecting you to the spirit realm. Do you understand?"*

"I think so."

"Excellent. Are you ready to begin?"

I should have been terrified, considering what I was about to do, yet I felt no fear. I was more curious than anything else. Curious and eager to embark on the same journey my mother had started many years earlier.

Even though she wasn't visible to me, I felt my mother's presence, as if she could somehow see me. I imagined her smiling, just as gently as Mrs. Pastor was. I was about to continue her legacy and fulfill whatever destiny awaited me. It was, I imagined, exactly what she wanted.

"I think so," I said.

"Wonderful," Mrs. Pastor replied. *"Just try to relax and let it happen naturally."*

I did as I was told. I settled back in my chair and took a few deep breaths. Then, with Stokely holding one hand and Lucy grasping the other, I closed my eyes, at last ready to begin.

ACKNOWLEDGMENTS

As a newcomer to writing historical fiction, I was fortunate when it came to both subject matter and location. The rise and inevitable exploitation of Spiritualism proved to be endlessly fascinating, and all reading done on the subject ended up feeling more like fun than research. The same goes for Philadelphia, a city so proud of its past that digging into its history was an utter delight. Still, I am indebted to the many authors, past and present, whose own books were an invaluable help in the writing of this one. Any errors, intentional or not, are mine and mine alone.

On the topic of Spiritualism and mediums, I consulted *Ghost Hunters: William James and the Search for Scientific Proof of Life After Death* by Deborah Blum; *The History of Spiritualism* by Arthur Conan Doyle; *The Night Side of Nature Or Ghosts and Ghost Seers* by Catherine Crowe; *Behind The Scenes With The Mediums* by David Phelps Abbott; and

Spook: Science Tackles the Afterlife by Mary Roach.

For all matters Philadelphia and life in the nineteenth century, I was helped by *A Portraiture of Quakerism* by Thomas Clarkson; *Daily Life in the Industrial United States, 1870–1900* by Julie Husband and Jim O'Loughlin; *Wicked Philadelphia: Sin in the City of Brotherly Love* by Thomas H. Keels; *Everyday Life in the 1800s: A Guide for Writers, Students & Historians* by Marc McCutcheon; *Philadelphia: A 300-Year History,* edited by Russell F. Weigley; and *A Hand-Book for the Stranger in Philadelphia,* an 1849 guidebook written by Wellington Williams.

Special thanks go to the Fairmount Water Works, for its enlightening exhibit about that nineteenth-century marvel; the Greater Philadelphia GeoHistory Network, for its detailed maps of Old Philadelphia; and the folks at Eastern State Penitentiary who continue to keep the prison's history — and spirit — alive.

On a more personal note, I'd like to thank my agent, Michelle Brower, for her unwavering enthusiasm about this project; my editor, Ed Schlesinger, whose suggestions and advice improved the book tenfold; and everyone at Gallery Books and Simon & Schuster who welcomed me into their fold. Thanks must also be given to Sarah Dutton, the best first reader anyone could ask for, and to Richard and Robert Sherman for inspiring the title. No list of acknowledgments would be complete without me thanking both the Ritter and Livio families, my fellow writers in the trenches at Algonquin Redux, and all my former newspaper colleagues now scattered far and wide. Finally, I owe a ton of thanks and a long vacation to Mike Livio, who continues to walk with me — with patience and a level head — every day and every step of the way.

ABOUT THE AUTHOR

Alan Finn is the pen name of an acclaimed author of mysteries. He has worked as a writer, editor, journalist and ghost writer. He resides in Princeton, New Jersey, where he is hard at work on his next novel.